Praise for Cheryl Grey Bostrom

Fans of *Sugar Birds* will be delighted that the author has continued Celia and Burnaby's story in *Leaning on Air*. Bostrom is a fresh new voice in fiction, and I look forward to seeing what she does next.

T. I. LOWE, author of #1 international bestseller *Under the Magnolias*

In *Leaning on Air*, Bostrom has crafted the rarest of romances, one in which distance desired and space granted are meaningful elements of a deeply romantic relationship. It's a book about the power of unconditional love to heal us as people and partners, to plant the seed of faith in our hearts, and to resurrect hope within us. And it's as gorgeous as the landscape in which it is set.

KELLY FLANAGAN, award-winning author of *The Unhiding of Elijah Campbell* and *Loveable*

Leaning on Air has everything I love most in a story: depth, nuance, rich detail, authentic characterization, and heart. It's a beautiful and worthy follow-up to *Sugar Birds* and a work of art in its own right. Cheryl Grey Bostrom is a must-read for me, and I am impacted by her words every time. If you love literary fiction that's filled with humanity and hope, you absolutely cannot miss *Leaning on Air*.

KATIE POWNER, award-winning author of *The Wind Blows in Sleeping Grass*

Engaging, insightful, and original, *Leaning on Air* is a reader's dream of a book. With wonderful characters and unexpected story twists, Cheryl Grey Bostrom opens up a world that is both unique and familiar. Do not miss this beautiful tale of love and family and learning to live with both.

GAYLE ROPER, award-winning author of *Sea Change* and *Prayers for a Widow's Journey*

T0036149

Cheryl Grey Bostrom's latest book, *Leaning on Air*, is to be savored. Her penetrating prose and precise poetic language introduce beauty to the darkest of places and the most tattered losses in Celia and Burnaby Hayes's uniquely strained marriage. But through Bostrom's skillful pen, love looks unexpectedly courageous. With reverence for the land and its ability to turn our gaze upward, Bostrom aptly contrasts nature's beauty and power with life's hurts and betrayals, producing layers of suspense imbued with prayer and hope.

LINDA MacKILLOP, award-winning author of *The Forgotten Life of Eva Gordon* and *Hotel Oscar Mike Echo*

After reading and loving *Sugar Birds*, I wanted more of Celia and Burnaby's story. *Leaning on Air* delivered—in page-turning layers that don't shy away from difficult truths. Bostrom draws her characters with an artist's brush and exquisitely renders the natural world. Her writing is sheer poetry.

TARYN R. HUTCHISON, award-winning author of *One Degree of Freedom* and *Two Lights of Hope*

Leaning on Air reunites readers with beloved characters introduced in Bostrom's stunning debut novel, *Sugar Birds*. Like the birds she loves, Celia migrates home to Eastern Washington's rolling wheatland to sort through surprise, heartbreak, challenge, and joy. Masterful strokes of literary wordcraft paint us into the story, while pulse-pounding pacing keeps us there. Every golden hour spent within these pages is filled with grace. A complex, captivating read.

SANDRA BYRD, award-winning author of *Heirlooms: A Novel*

Cheryl Grey Bostrom has written another brilliant story in her newest, *Leaning on Air*. From Pacific Northwest forests and wheat country to Snake River canyons, characters live out brokenness and loss, romance and redemption that will echo in readers' own messes and hopes. This book is a multilayered, cross-generational masterpiece—and a fabulous read!

JANET HOLM McHENRY, award-winning author of twenty-six books, including the bestselling *Prayer Walk* and *Praying Personalities*

Of all the books I've read, only one or two moved me as much as Cheryl Grey Bostrom's *Leaning on Air*. Breathtaking scenes transported me, and I found myself copying lines that were simply too beautifully written to just read once. I'm predicting a tidal wave of readers' love for this book.

SY GARTE, PhD; biochemist and award-winning author of *The Works of His Hands* and *Science and Faith in Harmony*

Bostrom's *Leaning on Air* pulls you right in, then keeps you turning pages in this can't-put-it-down narrative. At characters' twists and turns, heartbreaks and sweet spots, you'll gasp, wipe tears, and cheer. The writing truly leaps off the page in the author's majestic poetries of the land. At one with the earth and heavens, she draws us into their soaring, stirring depths. Many times I pulled out my pen to underline wonder and beauty she captured in ways I'd never imagined. She gently allows the holy to find its way in, and therein is a gift that won't leave you.

BARBARA MAHANY, award-winning author of *The Book of Nature: The Astonishing Beauty of God's First Sacred Text*

Mystery. Tragedy. Romance. The magnificent natural world of the Palouse. With deft artistry, author Cheryl Grey Bostrom melds them all in this astonishing novel. Both unpredictable and plausible, *Leaning on Air* soars like the red-tailed hawk at its heart. Though I'm a huge fan, my accolades can't do justice to this stunning work. Prepare yourself for phenomenal writing.

MAGGIE WALLEM ROWE, national speaker, dramatist, and author of *This Life We Share*

Cheryl's beautifully woven romance delights the senses, cradles the heart, intrigues the mind, and even boosts the reader's desire to be a braver and better person!

PAM FARREL, bestselling author of fifty-nine books and co-director of Love-wise on *Leaning on Air*

Bostrom's prose is propulsive and detailed. Aggie is a wonderfully magnetic character: a scrappy, stubborn preteen whose father has taught her to survive off the land. The supporting characters are equally strong, including the teenager's bird biologist grandmother and Aggie's autistic brother, Burnaby. The story is a true page-turner all the way to the end. An engrossing tale of survival and redemption in the Pacific Northwest.

KIRKUS REVIEWS on *Sugar Birds*

Bostrom takes her readers gently by the hand and plunges them into an immersive tale straight from page one. *Sugar Birds* is a powerful coming-of-age story of betrayal and loss, rebellion and anger, friendship, forgiveness and redemption, all woven into a testament to the wondrous natural world . . . packed into one heart-pounding read. Highly recommended!

CHANTICLEER REVIEWS

Cheryl Bostrom's hard-to-put-down *Sugar Birds* reminds me of the classic, *My Side of the Mountain*—one of those rare books that appeal to every age; full of depth, pages that turn quickly, and most of all, ebullient truth.

KATHERINE JAMES, award-winning author of the memoir *A Prayer for Orion*

Leaning on Air

Leaning on Air

A NOVEL

CHERYL GREY BOSTROM

Tyndale House Publishers
Carol Stream, Illinois

Published in association with the literary agency of Books & Such Literary Management, 52 Mission Circle, Suite 122, PMB 170, Santa Rosa, CA 95409.

Leaning on Air is a work of fiction. Where real people, events, establishments, organizations, or locales appear, they are used fictitiously. All other elements of the novel are drawn from the author's imagination.

The URLs in this book were verified prior to publication. The publisher is not responsible for content in the links, links that have expired, or websites that have changed ownership after that time.

For information about special discounts for bulk purchases, please contact Tyndale House Publishers at csresponse@tyndale.com, or call 1-855-277-9400.

Library of Congress Cataloging-in-Publication Data

A catalog record for this book is available from the Library of Congress.

ISBN 978-1-4964-8152-8 (HC)
ISBN 978-1-4964-8153-5 (SC)

Printed in the United States of America

30	29	28	27	26	25	24
7	6	5	4	3	2	1

To Graham,
with more love
than all seeds
since the beginning.

Hope is a thing with a saddle
That gallops around in your mind
And carries you.

—GWYNETH ULLMAN, AGE 8

Pray continually.

—I THESSALONIANS 5:17, NIV

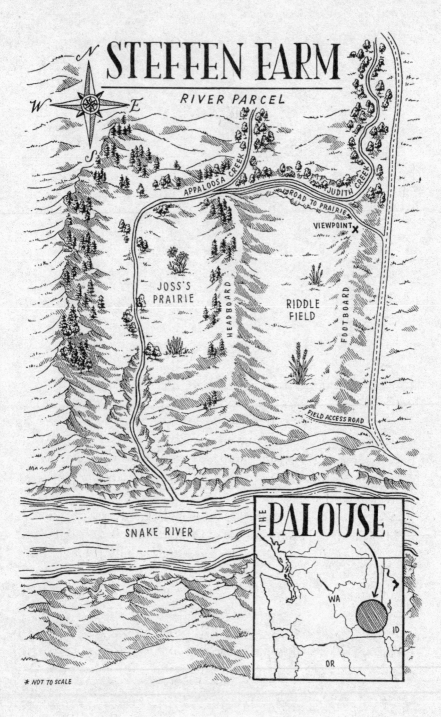

1

CELIA

SCRAPE

Above the pond, a cloud of gnats shimmered in the June morning as a Canadian goose rousted her brood through reeds of yellow iris toward a floating gander. On the opposite shore, Celia Burke leaned against a fat alder tree and watched the goose family cross the pond like a giant centipede.

Over them all, its white head a beacon in the green-black needles of a Douglas fir, an enormous bald eagle aimed its beak toward the paddling geese. Celia raised her binoculars slowly, anticipating the apex bird's strike, her eyes peeled for the twin metal leg bands her grandmother had spotted during repeated sightings of this aging raptor.

She didn't wait long. The eagle lifted its wings in feathered angles, flapped, swooped, and snatched a downy chick from the swimming spine of birds. The gosling's parents—their honks frantic, necks extended—launched their heavy bodies after the attacker. But the eagle rose nimbly out of range, the chick in its talons.

Celia dropped her field glasses and sprang from beneath her tree's leafy cover. The raptor passed overhead, swift and low and parallel to the narrow road beside the pond, the gosling a mere ladder's reach away.

She sprinted after it, her ridiculous urge to prevent the baby goose's demise as reflexive for her as breathing. For the next few seconds, she chased the eagle, propelled by the illusion that she could mob the raptor like a crow, that she could startle it into dropping the chick. She ran with abandon, watching the bird, not the ground, prepared to catch the baby when those wicked feet let go.

Instead, a rise in the country road caught her sneaker edge and sent her sprawling. Midair, she twisted, then hit the road's rough surface in a skid. From her outstretched right arm to her ankle— wherever her tee and jean shorts weren't covering skin—gravel, secure in its tarry substrate, scraped her raw. The spectacular tumble entered her memory in vivid, agonizing slow motion.

A goldfinch sang from a nearby field. Celia lay in the road, listening to it and a distant rumble. Numbed by endorphins from her sprint and the sweet relief of adrenaline, she felt oddly peaceful. Only her hip throbbed. Detached, she envisioned its purpling contusion as she ran her tongue over her teeth. Finding them intact, she inhaled a lungful of fresh rural air. On her exhale, a wave of pain arrived with a motorcycle's roar.

And with a motorcycle. Its tires crunched the shoulder's gravel as the engine's RPMs slowed and stopped. A kickstand scraped, and heavy footfalls hurried toward her. She pushed herself to an upright position with her good hand.

"No paralysis. That's favorable."

She twisted toward the deep, steady voice and craned her neck at the helmeted man in a brown leather jacket and goggles who shaded her like a tree. A smiling tree, with a two-day's growth of blond beard and a wide mouth of straight white teeth.

She rolled her shoulders. "I couldn't jump off a dime right now."

"Think you can stand?"

She nodded, reached, and the man pulled her upright with a leather-gloved hand.

"Oof. Hip pointer." Groaning, she cupped the bony protrusion at the top of her pelvis with her uninjured hand and winced at the condition of her other palm—and the arm attached to it. Blood dripped from her elbow.

"No doubt." He scanned her body-length abrasion. "I do not believe that hip is your immediate concern." Stripping gloves from huge hands, he pulled a thermos of water and a packet of gauze from a saddlebag on his bike, then held the supplies toward her. "May I?"

"Let me get this right. I trip, out here in the boonies, not a soul in sight. Fast as gossip you show up out of nowhere with road rash supplies."

"Ha." He crouched, inspecting her bloody leg. "I'm still awaiting permission."

"Fine. Have at it. I've got a mile hike home and I'm not going to carry half the road with me." She plucked a seed-sized stone from her forearm and flicked it away. "Dang. I'm sandpapered."

"An apt description." He turned from her to the bike, removed his helmet, and placed gloves and goggles inside it. His hands made one smoothing pass over corn-colored hair.

Celia eyed the backs of his ears, tight to his head, their lobes plump and flared. She'd know them anywhere, though nothing else about him matched the seventeen-year-old she hadn't seen for . . . what, almost twelve years? Well, apart from that hair. And his height, though this man seemed even taller.

"Burnaby?"

He answered with a grin, also unfamiliar. Back then, she'd spent a summer coaxing the corners of his mouth to rise.

"Hello, Celia."

She jigged with pain as he knelt on the road beside her.

"Here. Plant your heel here." He tapped the ground and pressed firm fingers inside her knee until she steadied, then he sluiced blood from her skinned leg. She looked away at the sting, then back to his hand, wielding gauze like an instrument to remove bits of gravel. "Superficial scrapes, but I'll need tweezers, unless you'd prefer an aggregate tattoo to commemorate this event."

His lips curved upward, wry, and he laughed again—a single-syllable marvel. Burnaby had cried back then, but laughed? Never.

"Which event? Skid of the Year? Running into you? Finding our eagle?"

"Our eagle? Millie?"

"Pretty sure she's the bird I was chasing. That wing you rebuilt has carried her into old age."

"The bald eagle population here is—is significant. What makes you think—?"

"How many bald eagles hereabouts have a red band on one leg and a chartreuse one on the other? I watched you attach them."

A new smile spilled into his cheeks. "A delightful find, Celia."

Delightful. He said *delightful*. Who was this remade man?

"Are you staying at Mender's?" He dabbed her congealing wounds.

"Yeah." She wanted to say more, but the hurting half of her body stung the talk right out of her.

"I'll take you back. Think you can hang on with that hand?" He inspected her palm's scuffed heel.

She wiggled unaffected fingers and nodded.

"Good. Climb on. Once we're underway, please don't lean."

"My binoculars. By the tree where I—"

"Right. I'll get them."

Celia boarded gingerly. With her cheek pressed to his spine and her good arm tight around him, her abraded limb's fingers hooked his belt. She was actually *clinging* to Burnaby Hayes, a fact that astounded her. Little more than a decade earlier, he'd flinched when she so much as touched his shoulder. Curiosity rattled her, competed with her pain.

The cruiser rumbled forward, first to the field glasses, then back up the empty, narrow road. A mile later, Burnaby turned the bike onto her grandmother Mender's treed lane, drove past the cavernous barn, and parked at the hilltop farmhouse.

Inside, Celia slipped off her shoes. Burnaby studied a framed photo on the entry wall of Celia, her father, and her grandmother, their identical eyes wide and dark, their cheekbones sharp. A blurry Ferris wheel filled the background and the three of them grinned over double-scoop ice cream cones.

"Our last pic together," she said. "Look at us. Not a care in the world. That fair was in August, and he was gone by December."

"I'm sorry, Celia." His index finger tapped the glass over her grandmother's gray braid, then outlined her father's face. "A good man."

Celia shrugged.

"Is Mender here?"

"Gone for a week. She took six flats of strawberries to her friend Imogene in Sequim. They'll make jam 'til they run out of jars."

He peered down the hallway, up the stairs, and into the kitchen before he crossed to the wide living room windows, where the blue Hawley River ribboned through mixed forests and fields below them. Past the farmland, the North Cascades rimmed the valley like a jagged fence. "Nothing's changed out there."

"Nothing, and everything." Celia parked herself at the kitchen table and picked another rock from her forearm. "We were kids then."

Burnaby unzipped his jacket, hung it over a chair, then sat beside her in jeans and a gray cotton tee, its sleeves and shoulder seams tight against bulging deltoids and biceps she'd never have guessed possible for the skinny boy she'd known. He looked good. Better than good.

He laid open hands on the table. "Let me see that arm."

She eased her forearm to him, and he lifted it, inspecting. "Does Mender still keep those sterile supplies beside the dryer?"

"Yeah. Doesn't rehab birds much anymore, though. I can't blame her. She turns eighty next year. Third drawer—"

"I remember." Water drummed in the laundry sink after he left the room, and he returned holding a small metal pan of surgical instruments. Sunlight poured through an east window and raised a sheen on his damp hands. He chose tweezers and set to work on her gravelly arm.

"So. Catch me up, Burnaby. I think the last time I heard from you, I was at Texas A&M, right? My sophomore year?"

"Yes. I last wrote you from MIT in—in January 1989. The fifth letter to which you didn't reply." His voice still lacked inflection and caught in those little stutters now and then, but sounded warmer than she remembered.

"Sorry about that. I met a guy that fall."

Burnaby tweezed another stone. "Are you still with him?"

"No," she said, scoffing. "Distant history."

"Others, then." A conclusion, not a question.

She cringed as he plucked. "Ow, Burn, you're hurting me."

"Hold on. Got it." He pulled a sharp-tipped sliver free of her palm. "I heard that after College Station, you left Texas."

"And you know this *how*?" *He kept tabs on me.* She watched his face but saw nothing to read. His eyes remained on her hand.

"Dad kept me apprised. He said you studied avian sciences at UC Davis."

"Yeah, first Aggieland then the Aggie Pack school. Funny, right? Reminders of your sister wherever I went." She laughed as an image of Burn's tiny, tree-climbing sibling, Aggie, came to mind. "I loved Texas, but I loved California more."

"I imagine so."

"Where's Aggie now?" Another friend, left by the wayside.

"Kenya, but when she's not on assignment, she calls Denver home. A freelance wildlife photographer she's been working with, and dating, broke his leg a—a week before he was slated to shoot a *National Geographic* piece on Grevy's zebras. The team was scrambling for a replacement, so he recommended Aggie. With her—her inoculations and passport already current, they spliced her in. Needless to say, she jumped at the opportunity." Burnaby pointed to his thigh. "You can stand, or place that leg right here."

"Well. I'm happy for her," she said, though guilt stained her long neglect. How many of Aggie's letters had she ignored? She slid her chair next to Burnaby's, stretched her calf across his lap, and rotated her foot laterally so the wide, stone-pocked scrape faced the ceiling. He rested the side of his hand on her heel and chose his next embedded target.

"Both your MS and PhD behind you now." He nodded thoughtfully. "What's next?"

His interest surprised her. *Buttered* her. "I thought I had a research grant at Davis, but the funding never came through. Hope to be here 'til August. I still have a couple of options in the hopper for next year, but if neither pans out, I'll stay here, submit a paper or two on West Nile virus antibodies in raptors. I can help Gram until I find a position. Ouch, Burn. Easy."

While the blond giant excavated her leg, Celia rewound more than a decade. Remembering the half-formed boy a year her senior, she hunted for evidence of him in this appealing man who was already, literally, under her skin.

"What about you, Burnaby? Four years at MIT? Sorry, but I lost track of you."

She wished she hadn't. Her intense study regimen and a string of demanding boyfriends for whom she fell too hard and fast had consumed her completely—and shelved relationships she now wished she'd nourished. She'd returned home to Houston, and her dad's hospital bedside, four days before he died of pancreatic cancer. And until this trip, she hadn't seen Mender since his funeral, two years earlier.

So much lost time.

"Yes. I studied physics at MIT until 1990, then attended Cornell for—for veterinary school. On May nineteenth I finished my residency in orthopedic surgery. I'll begin work as an—an associate professor at Washington State this fall."

Bones. Of course. He had reconstructed skeletons when she last knew him, had been *obsessed* with them since childhood. "Congratulations, Burn. That's a good gig."

He scooted his chair nearer and began swabbing her thigh, close enough for her to detect his fresh sweat, sweet breath. Did he smell this wonderful before? She couldn't remember.

A hank of straight hair fell past his forehead as he worked on her. "This summer's the first I've spent in—in the Northwest since I left for college. My parents are expanding Hayes Seeds, so Dad asked me to help him build a new equipment shed. He and Mama bought the former Hillman land, east of the home place."

"And in your off hours you patrol country roads on that Triumph like some sort of mobile medic. You tow that bike here from Ithaca?"

"I rode it. I shipped my belongings to my parents' place and gave myself two weeks to cross the country."

"Ah. Nice. You follow an itinerary or just wing it?"

"Celia. Can you imagine me without a plan?" He lifted his chin and looked sidelong at her from under thick blond brows. "I altered the schedule as I went, however, to deter my compulsivity. I slept outdoors whenever an inviting location presented itself."

"You camped on *whims*? Multiple nights? Burnaby, I'm having a little trouble with all this."

He shot her a worried look. "What kind of trouble?"

"Well, not trouble, exactly, but I really, *really* don't get it."

"Get what?"

"How did you . . . Unless I miss my guess, tests would have landed you on the autism spectrum when I first knew you. Or at least earned you an OCD diagnosis. But now? You're *better*." Her cheeks heated instantly. "Sorry. I mean—"

"Ha. Not cured, and I can't say I want to be. You—you are correct, however. I have mitigated some problematic behaviors." His smile held briefly. He finished swabbing, opened a tube, and dropped islands of ointment along her leg. In slow circles over her calf, knee, and thigh, he finger-painted the length of her leg.

"But *how*?"

He taped gauze loosely. Twice before he answered, he opened his mouth to speak but stopped himself. "Judah Kemp, mostly."

"Pretty cryptic there, mister."

He checked his watch. "Roof trusses arrive in an hour and Dad's counting on me. May I share the story over dinner? Pick you up at six?"

"On your bike?"

"Yes. Dress accordingly."

What on earth would "accordingly" mean to Burnaby Hayes?

2

CELIA

WATERFRONT

A LIGHT WESTERLY TEASED the flanges on patio umbrellas at Anthony's as the server led Celia and Burnaby to a glass-topped table overlooking Squalicum Harbor, a half-hour's ride from Mender's. Burnaby sat with his back to the water and sapphire sky, his face shaded. Across from him, Celia adjusted her baseball cap and tilted her face to the sun, now suspended between noon and the horizon. A sloop motored past, its pennants wagging from a halyard line.

She extracted a thick-crusted slice of sourdough from the basket between them, slathered it with a pat of thyme-garnished butter, and held it toward Burnaby. When he shook his head, she bit, chewed, and inhaled a gulp of briny air. "Smells good, doesn't it? Nothing like sea air in Washington."

He nodded and sipped ice water from a stemmed goblet, his eyes on her mouth as she took another bite. "What's good is seeing you again, Celia."

Burnaby, her long-ago friend, sounded like any of a dozen guys she'd dated, though none of them were on the autism spectrum. Through the glass table she noticed his leg jiggling. But even that modified stimming, and the way he twisted his spoon, were within the bounds of normalcy, if there were such a thing.

After all, guys were nervous around her sometimes. "Intimidated," she'd heard more than once, by what they called her "exotic" looks, or by the meaty IQ that felt like duck feet outside of her familiar academic arena. Not until she met Fitz had she renounced her chameleon tendency to dumb down or hold her tongue just to put a man at ease.

Fitz Coe. With his graying, bearded head superimposed over Burnaby's, she saw her academic mentor's eyes spark at graduation as he draped her with a PhD hood and pressed that ring into her hand, promising the life she thought she wanted. She blinked to clear his image and refused to picture Fitz finding that diamond on their bedside table. Shame heated her face as she recalled her note beside the ring: *I need time.* She was such a coward, running again—this time, to her grandmother's. But Fitz, like all the others, expected too much from her.

"Good to see me again?" She smiled. "Said like a regular guy, Burnaby."

"I mean it. When I saw you lying on—on the pavement today and realized it was you, I was as glad as I've ever been."

"I'm collapsed in the road, my leg and arm like raw burger, and you're glad."

"I didn't intend—"

Celia laughed, then reached across the table and squeezed his spoon-twisting hands. The utensil clattered onto the glass. "Just kidding, Burnaby." *Still literal.* At least she recognized that about him. She leaned back in her chair while the server set a glass of cabernet in front of her. "When I first knew you, you couldn't have said you were happy to see me to save your soul." She sipped the wine, then rested elbows on the table, her chin hammocked in long fingers Fitz called elegant.

Burnaby's eyes darted. His chest expanded with a deep inhale and he reclaimed the spoon. "Saving my soul's the—the fifth transformative thing that happened after I arrived in Massachusetts." He bobbed his head, his lips counting silently. "The first was meeting Judah Kemp, my—my roommate."

"The guy you mentioned this morning."

"Yes. Within an hour of my arrival in our dorm room, he adopted me. *As his project,* I recall thinking."

"Was your dad okay with that?" She tried to imagine Burn's father, Harris, leaving his brilliant, unusual son at MIT with a sticky roommate neither of them knew. Harris and Burn were tight. Saying goodbye would have been hard enough.

"He was relieved, I suspect, and, as usual, accurately so. He still jokes that Judah can walk through walls, though I—I question whether angelic beings have Kemp's capacity for German lager."

"You join him in his little hobby?" The thought of Burnaby drinking beer disappointed her somehow.

"I didn't. I figured I had enough issues without adding one more." A corner of his mouth rose. "Besides, I couldn't afford a—a loss of impulse control, considering my penchant for arson."

"Right, Burn. You're downright dangerous." She laughed again. "Seriously though, you'd never have made it through school if you'd kept lighting scraps of paper every time you got nervous." She paused and eyed him. "You don't still do that, do you?"

"Ha. I've found substitutes. My motorcycle, for example. The sound and vibration soothe both my brain and my overactive epidermal neurons. I used to—to wear the helmet for anxiety relief when I prepared for exams, though Judah insisted I remove it before I went to the library."

"Who *is* this Judah guy?"

"A description won't do him justice."

"Try."

Burnaby sat taller and looked past her shoulder, as if Judah himself were walking onto the restaurant patio behind her. "He's nearly as tall as I am. Six feet five. A 159-pound scarecrow, with an uncanny ability to—to look into people without judgment and extract the best from them. Before I met him, I didn't know such a thing was possible." He pulled out his wallet and showed Celia a snapshot of a grinning, sandy-haired man, his arms encircling a dark-haired, pensive woman. "Judah and Lizette, married last year. I was his best man."

"You *were?*" Burnaby showed no hint of wonder at being chosen for the honor. Friendship like that . . . She shook her head slowly. He'd have been incapable when she first knew him. "I'm trying to make the leap, Burn. Give me the skinny. What did this Judah *do* to you?"

The server arrived for their orders. She turned the menu toward him and tapped. "Medium rare, please." They looked at Burnaby.

"Sockeye, grilled, and roasted potatoes, thank you. Triple the—the broccoli, steamed."

The server scribbled and left.

"He changed my food, for one. I mean, for two, the second influential event. Judah's father is an internist-turned-naturopath. Baylor educated. He stumbled onto some anecdotal evidence of—of dietary influences on autism."

Celia tore another piece of bread in half. "Food."

"Broccoli convinced me." He spread a cloth napkin across his lap. "My experience corroborated Dr. Kemp's data. When cruciferous vegetables clearly lessened my repetitive impulses, I began my—my own research. I experimented with a variety of dietary changes and benefited."

"You can't give food all the credit."

"I don't. Detox played a role. Influence number three."

"Aha. You develop a little addiction since I last saw you?"

"Toxin elimination, Celia."

She arched a brow. "I get that. Toxins clobber some of the birds I study."

"Understandable. They kept me in a chrysalis of sorts."

One good-looking lepidoptera. While her eyes wandered over him, he explained until their meals arrived.

She sliced her steak. "Number four?"

His knife stirred broccoli. "Psychological flooding. Judah repeatedly exposed me to—to every sort of situation I found awkward. He did not intend to remake me, but to give me better access to the allistic—the non-autistic—world. To learn to speak the psychosocial language of those with no understanding of the neurodivergent."

"Interesting." She meant it. His transformation would have been unthinkable when they were teens.

"You know, conversation, crowds, handshakes—varied human interactions. Initially, we attended civilized scholastic functions. Farmers markets. Classical concerts. Then university athletic events. When I could navigate those with some success . . ." He twirled his empty fork like a baton. "When I could sit through a crowd's applause or roar without acting on an—an incendiary impulse, we began crashing frat events and sorority parties."

His voice rose and fell. Only by a note or two, but no longer robotic.

"How'd you do that?"

"Do what?"

"Dodge the gators." She suppressed a smile. "In the moats. Around those house functions."

Burnaby's lips tapped as if he were translating. She buttered more bread before he replied. "Ha. Everybody loved Judah. Besides, inebriated Greeks found my—my ineptness entertaining. We attended every feasible kegger, and every noisy, congested gathering within walking distance of—of campus. You ever been to a kegger, Celia?"

"A few." She swirled her wine. "More than a few."

"Judah considered keggers practice in chaos management. While others lost their senses, I pretended to sip from a Solo cup and developed mine. Judah coached me. When I talked with women, he would time the duration of my feigned eye contact with them. He'd eavesdrop and later critique my interactions. My first kiss was a sloppy one from an intoxicated girl I hardly knew. Kemp suggested I not disinfect until we returned to the dorm."

"Ah. Those germs." Of course a drunk girl would kiss him. So would a sober one.

His eyes went to her glass. "Everyone welcomed Kemp with open arms, which meant they welcomed me, since he refused to let me be sidelined. Fortunately, neither of—of us needed to study much, or we would have compromised our academic records."

She caught a glimpse of Burnaby at eighteen—intriguing, tender, exasperating, and socially blind—navigating college with his own human cane. *A rare one, this Judah.* Without him the college social scene would have eaten her friend alive.

"Well, the new you is a work of art. The man should be proud."

"Ha. He didn't try to change me, Celia. I like to think of Kemp as my trainer, who helped me expand my social vocabulary in a world both oblivious to my native language and uninterested in learning it. And he became a very good friend." He slid a fifty-dollar bill and two twenties under his plate. "Let's walk."

At the shoreline, Burnaby sank hands in his pockets, tensing as she looped her arm through his. A loping wolfhound towed a teen girl on Rollerblades past them on the asphalt path, toward the sun and the watery horizon. Across the marina, a stunt kite soared and dove above a close-cropped lawn, and they watched the kite's shirtless handler play the strings.

Burnaby pointed. "Zuanich Park. For years, my parents brought Aggie and me there for Fourth of July fireworks. Magnificent, soothing explosions, directly overhead."

At a curve in the walkway, a low hedge of wild roses lay between them, the breakwater, and the glistening, rippled bay. Celia caught the scent and drank it in. "The *colors* out here. The *air*. I'd forgotten." She fanned her face, then snapped her head toward him. "Say, do you still have that, uh . . . What did you call it? Synesthesia? If I remember correctly, your emotions affected your color perception?"

"I do."

"How are you seeing all this?" Her free hand swept toward the bay.

He smiled. "Shades of gold like you've never beheld." He pressed her arm into his side with his elbow. "We've talked enough about me, Celia. Your turn. I'd like to—to hear about you."

"Not so fast. I still have a couple of questions. What about number five?"

"Five?"

"Your MIT transformation. Your reference to number five started this whole discussion."

A gull cried overhead. He tracked its flight. "Five's the most significant of all."

"I'm all ears."

He surveyed her eyebrows. "I'd like you to understand this, Celia. It's the pivotal occurrence of my life."

"Oh-kay." She pulled Burnaby onto a bench off-trail. He watched the water; she, him. "You have my complete attention."

He cleared his throat. "Judah—who's now an experimental physicist with a PhD in molecular quantum mechanics—discovered physics and chemistry at twelve, while dabbling at home. By the time of the event I'm about to recount, those subjects were his singular focus and the key route through which his family connected with him relationally. He could take or leave his people. Science was his world."

His tone was flatter, more staccato, like she remembered. Under her fingers, his arm twitched. *Nervous. Why?* Where was he going with this? She squeezed him once, then pressed her hands together between her knees.

"The summer after his senior year in high school . . . the summer after you and I met . . ." Burnaby looked quickly at Celia, then back to the sea. "Judah's kayak flipped in the—the upper Elwha River. He spent more than two minutes inverted, pounded into a boulder by class four rapids."

"Oh, man. How'd he—?"

Burnaby pressed his lips together and raised his hand without looking at her. Celia nodded. "Sorry. Go ahead."

"Like I do when riding my Triumph, Judah calculates as he—he kayaks. Newton's laws, balance, fluid dynamics, buoyancy—he loves the sport as much for the exhilarating mental exercise as for the physical excitement of the drops and whitewater. But the day his boat flipped and he hung upside down and underwater, his capabilities failed him. His starving lungs, his panic . . . He couldn't think of anything but oxygen.

"He figured he'd been submerged ninety seconds or more when a voice quietly spoke a formula that directed him onto an elliptical trajectory of escape. He employed it, and approximately a minute later gulped air, slid past the boulder, and clung to a snag in an eddy until his dad and—and cousin hauled him out."

Burnaby got to his feet and swayed side to side. Celia rose, too, and followed his gaze to a slow-moving rowboat. Was Burn finished? If so, she'd sure missed whatever was pivotal. "Bet he sold his kayak after that."

"On the contrary, he felt safer than ever."

"Safer."

"Judah said the voice that filled his head was calming, specific, irresistibly loving. Imparting unfamiliar guidance he couldn't have manufactured in his own intellect. He called it a lit sound, like light, that came from outside himself, but was so near it inhabited him, *knew* him, and spoke truth in Judah's favored vocabulary of physics. He—he returned home rabid to know more, but not until his research led him to the book of John did he realize whom he'd met that day and how all of science pointed to him."

Him? Oxygen deprivation. Hallucination. Celia expected Burnaby to mention both.

"We'd been roommates for a week when he told me that story. At my dad's recommendation, I'd previously read John, though only as an analyst who dismissed the text as—as illogical. But after Judah showed me how the oneness in quantum entanglement both bloomed from and illustrated the oneness in the book of John, I met the Entangler—Judah's Rescuer—myself, and I have never been the same."

The rowboat cleared the breakwater and disappeared behind it. *Whoa. A real mouthful, Burn.* Her eyes locked on his cheek, its twitch familiar, and she shrugged. "To each his own. You're above my pay grade, mister. My knowledge of physics began with a single undergrad course and ends with some applications to birds in flight. I still love to read, though. Where'd you guys pick up that John book?" Mender had mentioned a book by that name—more than once.

His eyes dulled, but with what? She couldn't tell. Disappointment?

"It's in an anthology."

"You have it at your parents' place? Show me?"

"I do and I will." He squinted into the sun, its reflection a bright path on the water.

"One more question, Burnaby?"

"Of course."

"That kegger kiss. Any others? Any you initiated?"

"None."

"Why not?"

"None of those girls were you, Celia."

Surprise spread warmth she knew was a blush up her neck and into her cheeks. On impulse, she took his face in her hands and kissed him full on the mouth, then held her lips near his, waiting.

For a full two seconds he reminded her of a hovering rough-legged hawk, suspended in the breeze of her, considering the feast below him. His hesitation roused a familiar fear she would never, never let win again. Her mouth landed on his a second time, hungrily now, until he wrapped her in the shelter of his great, winglike arms and kissed her in return.

3

LAUNDRY

HAYES HEIRLOOM SEEDS. Celia squinted at the cedar sign, turned down the lane, and opened her window to the scent of honeysuckle twining the driveway fence. Ahead, Burnaby stood in the wide doorway of his parents' barn, frowning into the hot afternoon sun. He wiped a palm on his shirt and checked his watch when she pulled up, then opened the driver's door of her Jeep.

"Punctual," he said, and that smile returned, its allure linked to his kiss at the harbor the night before and to a longer, even more delicious one when he said good night at her grandmother's door.

"One of my strong suits." She'd have arrived at the crack of dawn if he'd asked her to.

Her attraction to him baffled and disturbed her. What was she doing, anyway? A day-old phone message from Fitz waited on Gram's recorder, unanswered. She'd gone to sleep after that dinner with Burnaby thinking only of this blond giant, whose kisses had reached her psyche as a gift, not as the taking to which she was so accustomed.

She glanced into the barn, then turned toward a tidy house framed by a riot of blooms. "Are your parents here?" Intuitive, kind, devoted Harris. Resilient, determined Bree. More friends she'd neglected for a decade.

"They're down at the Hillman property. At the new shed."

Playful, she spun back to him with one of her old tap-dance moves, grinning at the dust she roused with her shuffle ball change and fighting the absurd urge to kiss him again. His hands opened and closed, and he focused on something over her head, his face like stone.

"Hey, you. Kirk here. Beam me up?" Before last night ended, she had hounded him to see his paintings, and he'd seemed glad enough to invite her over. But now . . . his preoccupation. Or was it disapproval? Had she come on too strong? Had she changed his mind about her visit?

At her call, his expression lightened and he entered the barn. Celia crept after him, past rows of seed bins and shelves of agricultural supplies. From a stack of cardboard boxes on the far wall, he slid two poster-sized cases and carried them to a long table near the door.

Ah. His art. Her next breath came easier. "I remember so much about your work," she said. "Especially that diving peregrine. Oh, and that goose who mourned its mate. Still have those?"

"Mama framed the falcon for their new house. A female from my—my vet class hung the goose in her clinic." He riffled through one portfolio of watercolor paintings, then opened the second collection. "These are newer, completed between my sophomore undergrad year and the start of my surgical residency."

He laid four paintings along the table, beyond reach of direct sunlight from the yawning doorway. In the first, the only rendering of birds, a northern flicker probed soil for ants as its mate flew to a low perch, wings flashing orange. In the second work, the interior of a wolf's eye, images seen by the animal intersected across its amber iris—young pups at play, a deer carcass, the alpha leading the pack through snow. Horses filled the other two pages, one gaunt and mangy, the other foaling. Each told a story in layered watercolors, their hues unusual.

"Exceptional," she whispered. His earlier work paled next to these. From dates in the paintings' lower right corners, Celia tracked the chronology of Burnaby's artistic progress as she lingered over every scene, awestruck at his perception and talent. He leaned against a support post, his arms crossed. She could feel him watching her.

"Any more I can see?"

Instead of answering, he carried the first case of paintings back to his stored belongings, slid it between wall and boxes, and busied himself with a seed bin.

Oh well. At least he'd shown her a few. Subdued, she carefully gathered the exposed paintings and was stacking them at the table's end when she noticed more thick papers in the leaning, open carrier. She glanced sidelong at Burnaby, pulled one free, and gasped.

She quickly extracted another, then two more. Burnaby strolled toward her, thumbs hooked in his jeans.

"Of *me*, Burnaby? When?" Her eyes roved the paintings.

He dipped his chin toward the watercolors, now strewn across the table. "They're all dated."

"You knew I'd look, didn't you?"

"I suspected you might."

She straightened the paintings into a row and bent over a rendering of herself looking down, cutting her food at a holiday table. She pointed to the corner. "Nineteen eighty-nine. But the only time you sat across from me at Thanksgiving dinner was in eighty-six, I think. That sweater . . ."

"I wrote to you in January of eighty-nine. This was a—a proxy for your missing reply."

"Yeah. I'm sorry, Burn. Dropped the ball."

One at a time, she lifted the other three and examined them. In the nearest one, a remarkable likeness of herself sat on a rock in a

pine forest, her head thrown back in laughter. In another, she held a
goshawk on her gloved hand as she spoke to it. The third showed her
floating on her back in an aqua sea, her black hair swirling around her
close-up face with her eyes carrying every emotion she'd ever known.
How could he . . . ?

"These places. I don't recognize them." She stooped to decipher
the tiny dates. "Nineteen ninety-one. Ninety-six. Ninety-three." She
drew herself upright and stared at him, her lips puckering. By the
time he painted these, she hadn't seen him for years.

"Why?"

Burnaby looked at the floor. Stubbed his boot's toe on the post a
few times before his eyes caught hers.

"Look, Celia. I recognize the peculiarity of all this, but I really
did not expect to—to encounter you yesterday, much less have dinner with you. In fact, I never expected to see you again." A sigh blew
through that gorgeous mouth.

"I won a fair amount of money playing cards in college. My
expressive disconnect and emotional restraint lend themselves well
to a poker face, which has proven a—a useful device for more than
cards. Until yesterday. After last night I decided to lay every card on
the table with you. These paintings are my first hand and reveal the
fact that for twelve years you've dwelt here." He tapped his temple.
"And here." His fist thumped his chest twice.

"I do not know if you can reciprocate," he continued, "given what
I recall as your rather flighty nature—or if you'll want to, given the
eccentricities and limitations of mine. But if you're up for it, and can
forego any games, we have a—a window of time this summer to see
whether we have an actual affinity for one another, and not just my
imagined one."

Her tear lakes blurred Burnaby's features, and she thought of Fitz,
so different from the emotionally naked man in front of her. Fitz only
stripped himself of clothes.

She tiptoed to Burnaby. Her lips brushed his ear. "No games," she
whispered, before he caught her wrists, pulled her close, and kissed her.

The next morning a male was leaving a message on the answering machine when Celia entered the house from her grandmother's patio. She snagged the receiver before he hung up.

"I know that voice." She'd dodged him long enough.

"What's going on, Celia?"

"I wish I knew, Fitz."

"When are you coming home?"

"It's your home, not mine."

Fitz breathed into the mouthpiece, wordless. In the background, she heard a TV announcer and a distinct clunk as a golfer sank a putt. The crowd clapped.

"I'm not coming back." She had to say it. Now. "I'm sorry, Fitz, but I won't marry you."

More breathing, quicker. "Geez, Celia. I never saw that coming."

"Yeah. I didn't either. I—" Burnaby's name waited on her tongue but didn't make it past her teeth.

"Take your time, Celia. I shouldn't have sprung that ring on you. Just figured that you were . . . I thought we were—"

"You've 'figured' lots of things about me since we met. You think I'm something I'm not."

"But I—"

"I'd make you miserable, Fitz. I have a verifiable history of doing exactly that to your predecessors, if you recall."

"But I love you, Celia."

Did it matter to him how *she* felt? His claim on her felt like tentacles. "I don't think either of us knows what that means."

"But—"

"I'm going to hang up now. Goodbye, Professor." She eased the handset onto its cradle and returned to the lawn, where she lay face down on overlapped hands and breathed the calming scent of freshly watered earth.

Late June, a gold Lexus slowed at the gate, then turned onto the driveway. In the side yard, Celia climbed from the riding mower, where it teetered, high-centered on a tree root. Through bushy cedars, she spotted the sedan as Burnaby dropped his shovel into the posthole he was digging and muscled the mower free. Fragile, elderly Mender rose on her knees in a flower bed when the car stopped at the sidewalk. A man in sunglasses climbed out, tucking a polo shirt into wrinkled khakis.

Celia shaded her eyes with one hand and spoke low to Burnaby. "Remember when I told you I'd visited MIT?" Burnaby left the liberated mower and stood beside her, scowling toward the man. "I went with *him*."

"May I help you?" Mender braced a hand against the house as she eased to her feet.

"Mrs. Burke?"

Her grandmother smiled, removed her gloves, and swiped her forehead with the back of a hand. "Do I know you?"

The man smoothed his close-cropped beard. "We've never met, but I've heard a great deal about you from Celia. Is she here?"

Mender peeked at the side yard as Celia and Burnaby rounded the house. Burnaby spoke first. He wasn't smiling.

"Fitz Coe."

"You know each other." Celia's mouth gaped as she made the connection. Fitz—fifteen years Burnaby's senior, but with an overlapping stint at MIT.

Fitz stepped toward Burnaby, his hand extended. Burnaby's remained at his side. "Dr. Coe's reputation precedes him."

Mender gave Celia a questioning look and patted Burnaby's arm. "A pleasure to meet you, Dr. Coe. Now, if you'll excuse me . . ." She shook dirt from her gloves and plodded to the house as Fitz moved toward Celia, tentative and smiling, his arms an offered embrace.

Celia backed away, maintaining the distance between them as she edged toward Burnaby, whose jaw clenched, released, and clenched again. The nature of her relationship with Fitz was clearly dawning on him.

She touched his arm and whispered, "Give us a minute, Burn."

Without looking at either of them, he nodded once, retrieved his shovel, and strode to the barn.

"What part of 'we're done' don't you understand, Fitz?"

"You didn't call quits on our relationship, Celia. You only refused to marry me. Said you needed time. In good faith, I gave it to you." His eyes darted toward the barn. "Appears that good faith isn't as important to you as to me."

"I came here to think, not to replace you."

"Changed your mind awfully fast, didn't you?"

"I told you I wasn't returning."

"I'll give you that. You've said things you didn't mean before, though. I just assumed you'd change your mind. As usual." He shrugged. "You still may."

"Assuming. You're good at that, Fitz. What about asking? Listening? Getting the real skinny on what I think and feel, straight from the source?"

He licked chapped lips and nodded. "Your stuff's in the car. At least what would fit."

"Everything I left was dispensable."

"I'll carry it inside for you."

She sighed. "Right here will be fine." She pointed to the walkway pavers and peered through the windshield as he pulled boxes from the rear seat. "Are my books in the trunk?"

"Still in the garage. I figured you could get them next time you're in town."

"There you go again. Figuring." On the front seat, soiled clothes spilled from her laundry basket to the floor. *Dirty laundry. Imagine that.* She left them there.

He emptied the trunk and slammed it closed. "I'll miss you, Celia."

"Believe me, Fitz. I'm sorry." Her arms hugged her middle like a shield. "I misled both of us."

Hunched, she walked toward the house, then reversed direction and headed for the barn.

Fitz called to her. "What about your books?"

"Sell 'em. Give 'em away. Your choice. I'm starting over." *In every way.* This horrible pattern of hers had to stop.

※

Inside the barn, Burnaby sat at her deceased grandfather's grindstone with the shovel's blade pressed to the spinning, gritty wheel. His knee rose and fell above the treadle like a walking beam on an oil well's pumpjack, only triple the speed. His face was tight.

She stood apart from him until he lowered his foot to the ground. "He's gone, Burn."

Burnaby ran a thumb along the blade's edge. "My senior year at MIT, one of my professors—physicist Keith Dooley—invited me into a cohort of—of researchers on a high-profile project. Fitz Coe's concurrent research corroborated Keith's, so he—he asked Fitz to join us."

Where is he going with this? The disappointment in his tone raised her gooseflesh, and she rubbed her arms. She thought of running through the open barn door but forced her feet to stay planted.

"Coe was relatively unknown at that point, so one would think he'd have been grateful, cooperative. Instead, he stole data from Keith and—and claimed it as his own, then manipulated the team's findings. Surreptitiously, he raced to publication, naming himself as—as lead researcher. We read his abstract along with the rest of—of the scientific world, when it arrived in print."

Celia's hands flew to her mouth, then the top of her head. "Honestly, Burn, I had no idea."

She thought she knew the man. She'd been Fitz's student for a year before they hooked up. "A father figure," a colleague called him. *So be it,* she'd told herself. If Fitz's work ethic, intelligence, even his plodding, stick-in-the-mud style resembled her dad's? All the better. The fact that Fitz differed from the flashy sort she usually wound up with had only confirmed that the professor was the kind of man to build a life with, to have the children she wanted more with every passing year. Choosing Fitz, she'd made a rational decision this time, not the passion-fueled infatuations she ran from whenever her fear of genuine closeness reared its frizzled head.

Problem was, Fitz didn't understand her any better than her previous lovers had. Obviously, she didn't know him, either. Real intimacy, if she even understood the definition, hadn't come within a hundred miles of them. Rather than try to find it, she'd fled. Again.

"Any recourse?" she asked.

"Keith tried. For two years, he sought a retraction, but Coe had scrubbed the paper trail, and they landed in a stalemate. The controversy sank into the archives, enabling Coe to—to leverage his authorship, which got him the position at Davis."

Burnaby swiveled on the grindstone's metal seat to face her. Elbows on spread thighs, his hands dangled in the gap between his knees. "Look, Celia. We both know this is an experiment between us and that the most unpredictable variable determining its outcome is—is you. I explain this about Fitz not to enhance my self-interest, which is considerable, but to supply you with facts that will aid your decision making. Whether you and I end up together or—or go our separate ways, I care about you and want what's best for you. I can say with one hundred percent certainty that your best interests do not include Dr. Coe."

Celia scanned the floor as his comments registered. No question that other guys came across more complimentary and romantic than Burn. But their end game? *Their* wants and needs, every time. Fitz was right. Her "good faith" in him had gone the way it did with all those men, none of whom cared enough about her to climb the fence she erected to protect herself.

Now here was Burnaby, seeking her best, regardless. He wouldn't climb the fence. He'd tear it down, if she let him.

"'Unpredictable variable,' huh?" She wouldn't look at him.

"A man is unloading your belongings outside while you're spending time with me. I'd say *fickle* may be more accurate."

Fickle. Well, if that meant ending relationships when partners wanted more than either she or they could give, then yeah, the word described her. Obviously, Burn saw her debris. If she didn't want more wreckage, this time with *him*, she had to clean things up. Had to be brave and not default, again, to being fickle.

How frightening.

She thought of a boyfriend's dare during her sophomore year in Texas. He'd won, so the two of them jumped from a plane at ten thousand feet. Terrifying, exhilarating, that leap.

Would opening up to Burnaby feel like that?

By July, she knew. Every day now she came to him, or he to her, and instead of falling into bed with him to divert him from her heart, she free-fell into Burnaby's kindness, the depth of his thinking and beliefs, and his pure, unveiled self.

Truth was, he refused to get physical. The innocence she'd lost in college, he had somehow guarded in himself, though she knew girls like her would have thrown themselves at a brainy looker like him. Like she tried to do still. Without sex as her armor and her lure, she felt defenseless against him.

The clincher? Defense was unnecessary. With every, "I hear you, Celia," she actually *felt* heard. And, oddly, when he wouldn't let their kisses catch fire, *treasured*. Rather than fueling her insecurity, the tenderness and assurance in his restraint astonished rather than shamed her. She felt safe with him. Guarded. Before long she led him into private reaches of her mind and heart.

4

CELIA

RIDE

THE AFTERNOON OF AUGUST 2, Burnaby arrived at Mender's early, unexpected. Through a window, Celia caught her breath as he swung a long leg over the gleaming Triumph Bonneville motorcycle and removed his helmet. She met him on the lawn without a touch or a kiss, accustomed now to his lack of casual affection.

But oh, that smile.

"Dad has relieved me of my carpenter duties. The building inspector okayed us for occupancy."

"Joining the ranks of the unemployed, are you?" *Temporarily.* WSU wanted him on campus in two weeks. His departure lurked in the corners of their waning days together.

"I'm considering a road trip."

Celia's shoulders sagged. "A road trip?" Goodbye would come sooner than she'd expected.

"If you'll come with me." He showed her a single-burner camp stove, then stowed it in one of the bike's bulging saddlebags. "We'll travel light, like—like I did coming west." He unhooked a small, empty duffel from atop a bedroll and handed it to her. "For your things. We'll camp where ambient light won't compete with the constellations."

"I can't believe this." She shook her head and laughed. "Where?"

"Along Highway 20, then we'll drop into Idaho and Lake Coeur d'Alene. Eight days, total. We can adjust that plan, so long as I retrieve my belongings here and arrive at WSU by eight a.m. on August eighteenth."

Eastern Washington. Idaho. Open, unpopulated country, loaded with eastside raptors—and her, alone with Burnaby.

"Wouldn't miss it. When?"

He glanced at nimbus clouds creeping from the west, heavy with rain. "In thirty minutes, if we hope to stay dry."

One hundred miles later, they stretched their legs at a turnout high above the glacial aqua waters of Diablo Lake, ate apples and trail mix, then roared through the sawtooth peaks of the North Cascades' Washington Pass. The rumble of the bike's twin pipes bounced from rocky crags into dry, now-cloudless mountain skies. Roadside ravens scattered as they passed.

Celia hugged Burnaby's windbreak body, willing to bet he calculated gravity and centrifugal force as he rode, countersteering into the sweeping arcs that held their upright bodies in the breathtaking physics he loved. Did the wild air intoxicate him like it did her? Did he feel new colors with this astounding view? More questions for him, for later, when she could drink in his every word.

In the foothills near Mazama, he pulled over, reviewed a map from the saddlebag, and drove on. Two mile markers later, he slowed, turned the bike onto a dirt road at the edge of a meadow, and, a hundred yards in, parked in a cluster of tall pines. Hidden from the highway, he opened the saddlebags as a spring fawn and her mother bounded past them.

Celia pulled off her helmet and stretched. "Deer DNA in action. Headed straight for the road."

"They're my sole reason for riding only in—in daylight, when they're typically bedded," Burnaby said. "At dusk near Durango I missed a mule deer by inches."

"Did you skid?"

"I did."

"Fall?"

"No, remarkably. I took a day to recover my faculties, however. I rode the narrow-gauge railroad to Silverton while I calmed down. Nine hours round trip and I pressed my ear to—to the window casing for half of it. To feel wheels on rails, their vibration."

She visualized the deer and the split-second scene, invested in the story of Burnaby's rebound and recovery. Unusual, given her habit of avoiding others' traumas.

He didn't look away when she caught him watching her. "Make yourself comfortable," he said. "I have this down to a system."

She wandered into the woods to pee and returned to find the cookstove heating water. Hearty bread, dehydrated soup, and spoons waited in camp bowls, while Burnaby spread two sleeping bags onto a wide canvas bedroll he had laid on the thick mat of pine needles underfoot. An hour later, with a full belly and eyelids heavy from the ride, she opened the flannel-lined bag and crawled inside.

She awoke in the dark to the sound of Burnaby's bag zipping closed and a clear view of stars strewn on the night sky like salt on black ice.

"Alioth, in the bear's tail. The—the brightest one." His voice felt like brushed flannel.

"I see it. In the Big Dipper's handle, yes."

"You were my Alioth for twelve years, you know."

She sensed his arm as a perimeter above her head, felt him finger her hair.

"Eighty-two light years from me, but near as—as a thought. Like atomic particles separated after proximity. I always saw the two of us connected, despite the geography between us."

She propped herself on forearms, scanning his face in the dim light. "You're talking quantum entanglement, right?"

"Yes, exactly. Einstein's 'spooky action at a distance.'"

"Distance, with more of it to come. You'll leave for Pullman, and I'll end up who knows where."

"Unless you don't."

"Right, Burn. Easy as that. You have a better idea?"

He scanned the stars before he answered. "Marry me. Come to Pullman. Two universities within seven miles. One of—of them will want you. Not as much as I do, though."

She bolted upright. "Marry you."

"Yes, Celia. Maybe tomorrow?"

"Tomorrow." She flopped supine, eyes wide. "Tomorrow? Could we? Isn't there a waiting period? Blood tests?"

"Not in Idaho."

"Idaho. Where?"

"I know just the place."

Her laugh rolled toward the rising moon. "Talk about an ambush. You're good, Burnaby Hayes. How'd you come up with this?"

Beautiful teeth flashed in his shadowy face. "Ha. I considered comparable strategies in—in the event's design."

"Did you now. Such as?"

"Eagles' aerial courtship displays. The optical illusions of bower-birds. Fly-fishing."

This time her laugh echoed off the hillside behind them. "You've got to be kidding."

Burnaby raised the mountain of his shoulders onto one elbow. "Can you recall a time I kidded anyone, Celia?"

She squinted at him in the darkness as sparks raced her neural highways. The hard-won dampers on her passion crouched for liftoff like launching terns. "And now you want to elope. With me."

He tucked a strand of hair behind her ear. "Yes, if you will have me."

Her hand on his chest, she shifted to her side and laughed again. "You had me at particles in proximity, Burn. And fly-fishing." Her impulse to run had missed this ride.

He fumbled for the flashlight.

"Yep. Hooked me," she said. "No catch and release."

"Do you mean it?" He shined the beam on her. "Literal language from you will be excellent right now."

"So, Mr. Artist, you paint and dish out metaphors, but can't take 'em?" A warm giggle bubbled from her. "Okay then. For the record, Burnaby Hayes, yes, I will marry you. Maybe even tomorrow."

A surge of—what? disbelief? anticipation? happiness?—struck her like a sea wave and flipped her onto her back, though her eyes never left his face. Yes, she would marry him. And without having shared his bed once. Separate sleeping bags under the stars didn't count.

Burnaby's smile rose slowly. He held her gaze while his thumb found the switch and clicked off the light. His kiss was brief, withholding. "Only for now," he said, his lips two inches from hers. "When we marry, every bit of me will unite with you, even down to the atoms comprising our cells and the electrical impulses that enliven them."

Her extremities chilled. How often at weddings had the preacher's "the two will become one" terrified her? Was that why she ran when lovers wanted her mind and heart, too? It dawned on her that the sort of physical unions she'd dished out had been like a football cornerback's interception, halting touchdowns of emotional vulnerability and commitment that would absorb her, rob her of herself.

Burnaby, if she understood him at all, would take their intimacy further still. His science told him they would meld into the single identity of conjoined atomic particles, and his faith said they would become one in a spiritual world she knew nothing about, a world where he and she and this God of his would be indivisible, body and mind and spirit. Marriage would breach every boundary she'd worked so hard to fortify, every barrier she'd built against pain.

She shoved him, and he pushed himself away, his palms on either side of her, his arms posts for the roof of his body above hers.

"What?" he asked.

"I don't want to disappear."

His head tilted. A slice of moon at the ridge lit his eyebrows, folded with concern.

"I want us to love each other, Burn, but I don't want it to cost me everything." Her fear again, this time hurting her Burnaby. She had to voice it, though. What if she married him and he dissolved her? What if she couldn't find herself in all that oneness?

"Ha. Why would that worry you?"

She snagged the kite string of his small, strange laugh. The ease in it. And his question reassured her. Kept her from slipping.

"My daddy gutted himself for Mother. You know that? And when he did, she tossed his entrails and tanned his carcass. Used it for a throw rug, near as I could tell. Tell me, Burnaby. How did that happen? Early on, did he have a clue she'd devour him like that? Back when they were talking marriage?"

He found the sweatshirt he'd used for a pillow and pulled it on. "Of course marriage will cost us ourselves. Both of us, not just you."

"Then why—"

He touched a finger to her mouth, then ran it gently along her jaw. "The rewards have the potential to far exceed our investment and risk, and I believe they'll be—be well worth our individual sacrifices. Can you imagine the wonder and beauty of our entanglement—our marriage—if it resembles the Trinity's oneness?"

He'd shown her that John book in his Bible and had explained the concepts, but this was gibberish when it came to the two of them. How odd that with all his logic, he tossed marriage into physics and spirituality as if they belonged together.

He sighed, splayed both hands flat, then thumped knuckles against his thighs for emphasis. "I hope I have demonstrated my devotion to us together, as well as my conviction that unless you remain unique from me, there will be no 'us.' I will cherish your distinct personhood, Celia, and guard it with my—my life. *Us* is plural. Two *and* one."

That she understood. Those other men who said they loved her? They hadn't known her at all. What had they even meant, anyway? That they loved what she could do for them? Loved how she made them look or feel? Burn was showing her a new definition. And it already felt a lot like *cherish*.

She crawled to him. When she laid her head in his lap, he gently lowered it to the mat beside him and spun her hair into a rope.

"Neither of us are our mothers or our fathers, Celia. Though we certainly carry them with us, we—not they—will decide what parts of them we want to keep and what we'll discard."

When he eased her upright, she expected him to kiss her. Wanted him to. Instead, he held her sleeping bag open until she again burrowed into it, then he slid deeper into his own. Through slitted eyes she watched him turn to the dome of stars. His lips were moving, but not for her. She couldn't hear his whispered words.

And, in a thought she found peculiar, she felt glad he had looked up, instead of at her.

BURNABY

CAMP

RIMMED BY THE FOOTHILLS above Mazama, Burnaby awoke and stretched. A marmot's piercing whistle alerted more of the plump, hoary mammals, who ducked into a rockfall's crevices above him. Burnaby tracked them as a *Felidae* would—a bobcat, like the one he'd seen in the moonlit field catching voles while Celia slept. He had considered the cat's instinct as it hunted, had gauged its stealth before the pounce. Not unlike his own with Celia.

This woman he loved was a marmot too. Fearful. Dodgy. And now he'd captured her? Hooked her? Snared her? Such offensive terms. Though he hoped she had freely agreed to marry, doubt assaulted him. Had he misled her? Tricked her? He'd caught her affection with the fly line of this ethereal summer and secured her with this unexpected motorcycle trip and the condensed timeline between her yes and their nuptials later that day. He had convinced her with all the best of himself he could give, with no discussion of the winter he knew would come.

Apart from his too-lengthy illustrations from quantum physics—more like classroom lectures, really—he had said little about the faith they'd need to carry them through that winter, either. Did she trust his God? Believe at all? Early on, his parents prodded him to ask, but whenever he could have, and the opening slipped away, he felt only relief. He and Celia had time. Surely her faith would deepen, just as her trust in him had grown.

Besides, what if she said no?

He shifted to face her, there on her back, still sleeping as tendrils of the advancing light crossed her face. Her eyelids jumped from the watched dreams beneath them. He leaned close to inhale her scent, imagining the composition of pheromones that so attracted him.

The night before, minutes after she said yes, he'd explained himself to her, of course, in more detail this time, so she understood, theoretically, how his skin reacted to another's touch. How he pretended otherwise. Without that disclosure, his conscience would forbid him to marry her. Still, he knew how anticipation, lived experience, and hindsight weren't always friends. His aversion to being touched would eventually hurt her. He'd told her that, as well.

"Nobody's perfect, Burn," she'd said. "Pretty sure I'll hurt you, too, though I won't mean to or want to. People do that, you know, autistic or not." She'd laughed and kissed him. "Too late to backpedal, my mister."

She rose to his spoon stirring oatmeal on the cookstove and smiled. They ate without talking, while the sun climbed pines like an athlete and Burnaby memorized her there, cross-legged in the trees' duff, hunched over her dripping spoon, her hair a mess he could drink. As he packed their gear, he thought of how he would paint her, with the light washing her shins below black capris wrinkled from sleep.

"So, Burn." She stretched a bungee cord across her sleeping bag and hooked it to the bar behind her seat on the Triumph. "Let me see if I've got this right. First stop: Kootenai County Recorder's Office for the license. Next, Clark's for a pair of rings, then some mysterious location on Lake Coeur d'Alene." A shudder of delight left her shoulders and shimmied her hips. "Best surprise of my life, this wedding trip." She reminded him of a spring leaf unfurling as she rolled upright from the bike, until concern drew her face into a pucker. "What'll I wear, Burnaby? It's our *wedding*." She had changed into jeans, a light fleece, and her leather jacket. She ran hands down her body. "Not this."

Burnaby stowed the camp stove, then dug deeper in a saddlebag, extracting a flexible, tissue-wrapped package tied with a strand of hemp. She took it from him as if it would singe her.

"Go ahead. Open it."

She pulled strings and paper and the dress unwound like a cloud: white, gauzy.

"You *brought* this for me? For *today*?" She held it to her shoulders, her eyes shining. "What if I'd said no?" She unbuttoned her jeans, then looked up at him and ran behind a tree. She emerged minutes later grinning, her arms spread. "Be my mirror, Burnaby."

He absorbed her slowly. The tops of her bike boots—black, unlaced, and sturdy—grazed the hem of the flowing fabric that nipped her waist, skimmed her hips. The V-necked, sleeveless bodice defined her upper torso as if it understood her—elegant, unpretentious, stunning. As he knew it would, when he saw the gown in that window and compared it to the shape of her stored in his brain.

His emotions wheeled, colorful, before they landed on Celia like snowflakes, melting into the skin on her face and neckline and arms. "As if it were made for you."

She pinched the skirt and spun, slowly. "I would choose this myself, Burn. How did you . . . ?" Her face lifted to his. "When?"

"I spotted it on the way to the lumberyard last week. In the window of that clothing store for women on Front Street."

"The boutique? The Dresser Drawer?"

"Yes. I noticed it as I passed, so after my purchase of roofing nails,

I returned by the same route and asked the proprietor to remove it from the mannequin so—so I could inspect it."

Celia giggled. "Wilma helped you?"

"If you mean the owner, then yes. I was about to measure it with the retractable tape I had on my—my belt, but she kindly provided a tailor's tape. Unnecessary, since I knew it would fit you, but confirmation never hurts."

"So you saw the dress and just bought it? On the spur of the moment like that?"

"No. I asked her to keep it for me, so I could consider the purchase. I returned the next day and—and viewed it again, then left a deposit for her to hold it for one more day. When the store opened the following morning, I inspected the—the integrity of the seams, and paid her. I asked for portable wrapping." He watched her finger the stitching tenderly. "A box wouldn't fit in the saddlebag."

Then the river that was Celia spilled toward him, nearly drowning him in an embrace into which he dared not swim. He returned her kiss, arms at his sides, before he took her shoulders and pushed her to arm's length. He was sweating, though not from exertion or temperature. "Not yet, Celia."

"Still a little shy, I see?" She twirled again, and he steeled himself against rising panic. Celia saw his lack of physical expression as naivete, and as self-discipline fueled by his convictions. Both true, of course, and though she teased him, both made her feel safe and loved, she'd said. How then, after they married, would she trust his love when he shrank from her touch? She hadn't believed him about the physical hurdles they would face. Hadn't taken him seriously.

How could she, given his inconceivable condition? He knew that the sensitivity of his skin would compromise his everyday—and maybe his intimate—physical reactions to his affectionate Celia, who moved like a hummingbird, constantly surprising him with nerve-jarring touch.

With this woman he treasured more than his own life, his neurons could ruin everything.

When camp was an hour behind them, they stopped at a cafe in Pateros, where Celia pilfered Burnaby's blueberries and sipped coffee until her cinnamon roll arrived. "Well, Burn. Look at this doughy spiral, will ya?" He watched her mouth ease over the fork as a section of polar curve disappeared between her lips. "That man back there?" she said, pointing to a hefty, mitted baker, moving pans. "Our *pi*-baking brother."

Ha. He smiled, encouraged. Their shared, yeasty fondness for math? Uninhibited.

Another sixty miles east, they reached the ramparts of Grand Coulee Dam, where they stretched, rehydrated, and stood over spillways. With their faces to the cooling mist, he compared the open floodgates and the converging waters below them to double-slit physics and atomic streams and explained how the entangled currents described their forthcoming marriage.

"It always comes back to that for you, doesn't it, my love?" Side by side at the dam's overlook, she pressed her shoulder into him, her forearms on the rail.

"Always," he said. He almost elaborated, then remembered Kemp. *Keep it brief, bud. You'll lose 'em with those marathon explanations.* He considered the reservoir behind him and stored his proof for later, when they discussed the subject again.

They rode through the open, horizon-kissing sweep of eastern Washington then, until the freeway funneled them into Spokane and an exit spit them toward Riverfront Park, where they lay in shade under maples, shared a burrito the size of a man's shoe, and added salsa to their accumulated road grime and sweat.

The petri dish of Burnaby's skin squirmed, his need to wash grown to an itchy contortion. "On the way home from Ithaca, I—I slept not too far from here. We have time to shower at the camp-ground before we secure our license and shop at Clark's. The jeweler is expecting us at two."

Glances her way told him she was smiling, even amazed.

"I love this, Burn. All of it. Every mile, every thought you put into it all. And I love you, my mister, you know that?"

He fumbled to reply.

6

CELIA

CAUGHT

TEN YEARS LATER
SOUTHEAST WASHINGTON STATE, 2008

The call arrived seconds before Celia Burke-Hayes drove her Jeep between two dunes of Palouse soil. The steep hills on either side would gut her phone's reception.

"Hold on, Tara. I'm coming into the draw by that hogback on Kittleson's farm." Celia slid her phone into the console trough and cranked the wheel, bumping through low ground, then up the dirt road's rise until hillsides on both sides of her fell away into a May sea of young wheat. A white pigeon shrugged in its cage on the seat beside her, adjusting its balance with every jolt of the rig. The bird crouched for stability, its red feet wide.

Celia braked on the ridge and retrieved the phone. Three bars now showed in the screen's corner. She shifted the SUV to park. "I'm topside. What's up?"

"Say again which hogback you're driving? You cut out."

Celia squinted, as if to dim the brightness in her colleague's inflection. Tara Soto's twentysomething voice pushed on her with eagerness Celia remembered but had lost somewhere in the nearly eleven years between her marriage to Burnaby and her thirty-ninth birthday.

"Kittleson's. Just drew blood from RT-27." Celia's eyes roved the distant peak of Steptoe Butte, protruding like a time-softened pyramid from the surrounding hills, its slopes interrupted by an archipelago of shadows from the pillowy clouds overhead.

"Nice hawk, Twenty-seven. Any trouble trapping him?"

"He considered his alternatives. Still caught him in three minutes. Snowflake here looked too delicious." She smiled at the caged pigeon.

"Ready for another one? We've located RT-5."

"You're kidding." Celia's gaze jumped south toward Moscow, Idaho, thirty-five miles away. She pictured fourth-year PhD candidate Tara working in their University of Idaho lab, poring over tagged redtail sightings on short- and long-range flyways. Tara would be as ecstatic about this raptor's reappearance as Celia was.

No wonder. West Nile antibody data from this bird had initiated Celia's research and had driven the hunt for corroborating statistics from the forty-seven redtails she and Tara now monitored. Her hawks, all previously infected, had survived a mosquito-borne virus that killed thousands of birds—and that posed a serious risk to other animals. Though small, her study was providing crucial insights for development of a single-dose, cross-species vaccine.

For four years she had tracked and sampled this raptor—until his readouts stopped moving and they presumed him dead. Then a UC Davis research team found his detached satellite transmitter on a boulder in the San Jacinto Wildlife Area, where he must have spent his winter. No one had seen the bird.

"You sure it's him?" Celia scrambled for the notepad on the console.

"A geocacher called in his tag number—*and* his nest coordinates. It's our boy, all right."

"So where is he?" News of the bird's survival countered the fatigue Celia had fought for months. She pressed a palm against her stomach and left it there, imagining the bird in Pocatello, Idaho—or Baker City, Oregon. "Know anyone in the vicinity who can catch him?"

"You're it, Celia. He made it home. His nest's out near Penawawa, three miles from the Snake. Two routes of access. I contacted both landowners for permission, but only one replied. She said it's a bit of a hike. Got something to write with?"

Celia recorded the location, roughly an hour away. "I'm on it. Heading there now."

"Keep me posted?"

"Of course, but . . . uh . . ." Celia palpated her belly, the unfinished sentence hanging between them. "I don't know how long I can do this, Tara. I felt the baby move last night."

"Your worry's talking again, Celia."

"Twenty weeks doesn't mean we're home free." She leaned her head against the Jeep's window and sighed.

"You lost the others in your first trimesters. Everything about this pregnancy's been textbook. Has your doc changed her tune? She suspect any problems?"

"No, but I'm still high risk. At my age—"

"Forget your age, Celia. You saw the ultrasound. She's healthy. Perfect. After you bring me that runaway bird's blood sample, we'll catch a late lunch. Celebrate your baby girl."

"Okay. Okay. I'm buying." Celia released the brake and eased forward, along the familiar network of back roads that led into the Penawawa drainage and the breaks of the Snake River. At a trio of corrugated steel grain bins, she parked and confirmed her GPS route before she extracted her pack from the back seat and bound the pigeon cage under the pack's cover flap.

Already warm for early May, the temperature was rising. Clouds had all but disappeared. Two miles of steep, mostly shadeless hiking lay between her, a couple of landmarks the treasure hunter mentioned, and the nest. Not far by her usual standards, but to dodge the teeth of the day's heat, she'd have to hurry. She wound her hair into a knot and shouldered her pack, impatient for a diamond-patterned snake twenty feet from her car—and the stack of rattles on its tail—to disappear into rocks so she could set out.

A mile uphill, she reached a weathered, split-rail corral sandwiched into a ledge on the slope: her first landmark. The enclosure's wire-wrapped rock jacks supported posts the igneous bedrock refused, making possible a simple catch pen for the beef cattle that terraced the hillsides.

Damp with sweat, she lowered her pack to the ground, climbed the fence, and filled her baseball cap from the spring-fed trough at the corral's far end. Twice she poured the fresh liquid over her head, her shoulders, her chest—and plunged her face into the clear water. Ignoring the tepid drink clipped to her pack, she bent to the iron pipe jammed into the stone above the trough and sucked its trickling outflow until her thirst was slaked. She traced her fingers across her swelling abdomen, remembering the ultrasound, the strong heartbeat, the normal growth. The doctor's reassurance.

"Your typical activities are fine for now," the obstetrician had said. Surely this hike qualified. She'd trained on hills like these before she ran the Seattle Half Marathon six months earlier. *A month before I conceived.*

She arched backwards, her shirt tightening against her belly as she massaged the small of her back. "No worries, little girl."

Her little girl, whom she would love—*already* loved—with all the treasuring Celia had missed from her own mother. She hoisted her pack and sang to her baby, the tune distorted as she climbed the grade. Ahead of her, the sparsely treed ravine led to a tight bowl of the Palouse region's legendary loam, now greening with the tips of sprouting wheat.

There, at the exact location sent by the geocacher, a single ponderosa pine grew from a patch of untilled land wrapped in groomed farmland. The size of a pair of dump trucks, the wild island stood a full five feet higher than the plowed earth surrounding it—five feet above the deep topsoil that had curled away from the native sod with each of 130 years of passing plow. Two small, weathered headstones poked from the native grasses near the tree, each etched with eroded lettering and a lamb.

Someone's babies, she thought as a sharp pain radiated across her lumbar region. She dropped her pack at the draw's grassy peak. *Just my hips, loosening with the hormone flood.* She was a mother now, after all.

Closeting her fear, she scanned the island's pine until she spotted the redtails' twiggy nest, where the mother hawk's tail jutted from the rim as she tended her nestlings. From the air, the male buteo *screed* a warning to his mate, then landed on a branch ten feet below his family. He tipped his head toward the researcher, his white ID tag vivid on one wing.

Celia removed the pigeon's cage and pulled her gear from the pack. She sweated profusely now, hot and unnerved. Five minutes were all she needed. Five minutes to catch the hawk and extract a blood sample. Then she'd rest, finish her water, and head back down the trail without pushing her pace—a gentle stroll with her baby before she drove back to Pullman. She'd take a rain check on lunch with Tara and check in with the doctor instead. Five more minutes here wouldn't change the cause or course of whatever her body would do next.

A dozen nylon filament loops sprouted from the pigeon's cage like strands on a balding head. Celia adjusted the snares as the bird huddled inside the shoebox-sized enclosure, blinking and irresistible to a hungry male redtail responsible for feeding a nest of eyases *and* their mother. This wouldn't take long.

The hawk remained on his perch as she carried the cage to the edge of the unplowed island, settled it in the wild grass, and returned to crouch near her equipment. Noting her watch's second hand, she whispered, "Go," and started The Game, the timing competition into which she entered every raptor she captured. Nothing to do with her research, this game, but she usually enjoyed it and had become as obsessive about it as she was about the accuracy of her data. Besides, each bird's dive for prey added another piece of information to her stockpile of raptor minutia. The quickest hawk she'd caught had pounced on its prey in nine seconds.

Concentrating hard, she tried to let The Game—and this crucial bird, the one her team had lost track of months ago—deflect her from the fear that had haunted her since she learned she was pregnant. Pregnant again. She forced her eyes to lock on the scene in front of her and engaged long-practiced denial.

The pigeon pecked the mesh. The hawk inclined his football-shaped torso toward the ground, raised his wings, and plunged toward the captive bird, talons leading. Simple as that, the raptor landed on the cage.

Celia marked the time: eighteen seconds. Not quite a record, but quick.

Gripping the wire cage now, the redtail spread his wings over the pigeon, instinctively mantling the captive bird to hide it from competitors. Smiling at the familiar behavior, Celia kept binoculars on him until the hawk's foot slipped through a waiting noose, which tightened when the bird stepped across the cage. Startled, the raptor flapped—his nape erect, mouth agape, tail flared as he tumbled sideways, caught by the translucent line.

A pinching ache spread across Celia's belly as she rose to retrieve him. Tense with pain, she moved stiffly to the cage and spread a light-weight towel over the hawk's head before she righted him, carefully folded his wings, and snipped the noose free.

"We'll be done in a flash, gorgeous." Not only for the bird's sake, but for hers. A fresh cramp bit the heels of the first, advancing like a wave through her midsection, curling her toward her core.

She stumbled with the hawk to a small, towel-draped field table she'd unfolded from her pack. Laying the bird on his back, she snugged a leather hood over his eyes, then extended one wing and swabbed the basilic vein.

Sightless, the hawk lay immobile. Her hands shook, so she waited one minute. Two. Until the pain subsided enough for her to hold the syringe steady, insert the tiny needle, and draw the bird's blood. Until she could stabilize the vein with pressure, then transfer the sample to waiting tubes.

"Look at you, RT-5. My anchor bird, caught on the lam." Through clenched teeth, she confirmed his leg band number with her records. "And with a family, no less." She quickly examined him for injury or illness and checked the attachment site of the large wing tag. She jotted notes, exhaling gratitude with quick, shallow breaths as she staved off a new spasm, a stronger one. If that hiker hadn't spotted the tag, hadn't reported the nest's satellite coordinates, she'd never have found the redtail here, only an hour from her lab—and even closer to her and Burnaby's home in Pullman. Hunched, she willed her uterus to calm, and momentarily, it did.

Her hand rested lightly on the supine hawk's chest while the wave of pain withdrew. Then she straightened, lifted the bird to a toweled hand, and removed his hood.

"Off you go, mister." The hawk flew before the words left her mouth.

But Celia didn't track his trajectory. The next contraction slammed her, dropped her to her knees below the babies' graves. The raptor, the only diversion from her greatest dread, sailed down the draw.

On elbows and knees, her face in her open palms on the ground, Celia exhaled as warm liquid oozed between her thighs. That last fierce contraction had obviously conquered her bladder. *Or amniotic fluid.* She rejected the latter thought. At least she'd packed shorts.

Only when she stood to retrieve them did she notice the red stain soaking denim and the blood on her hiking boots, its brilliance a stark contrast to a lone cumulus cloud, and to the caged white pigeon.

She fumbled for the phone in her chest pocket. Punched speed dial for Burnaby. No signal. A howl rose in her then, as she stumbled past the graves and up through the dirt field striped with rows of young wheatgrass. At the hilltop, she again tried her husband. But the ringing phone dropped from her hands when pressure and an oceanic pain forced her to shove her new maternity jeans to her ankles and squat.

In the next contraction's siege, she pushed a tiny, squirming baby girl into her waiting hands.

7

BURNABY

ORBIT

GOWNED AND GLOVED, Burnaby watched the sorrel gelding sway. As the sedating injection took effect, four WSU veterinary interns leaned the horse into the cushioned wall until the animal folded to the floor and settled onto his side. A second-year resident inserted an endotracheal tube, then gripped the halter's cheek straps like handles, supporting the animal's head as cables drew his hobbled feet toward the ceiling. Suspended like a cinched drawstring bag, the thousand-pound thoroughbred rolled into the WSU Veterinary Hospital's equine surgery room, guided by fourth-year vet students and the hoist that tracked an I-beam overhead.

The team lowered the horse left side down onto the padded surgical table, positioning the animal's right legs in elevated stirrups that would relieve muscles when the horse's bulk compressed them. An anesthesiologist hovered, connecting tubes and wires. Techs swabbed and prepped the shaved backbone, positioned surgical instruments and electronic readouts.

A handful of students, gathered to watch Burnaby's "kissing spine" surgery on the horse's thoracic vertebrae, kept their distance. He liked it that way, grateful that both his reputation as a brilliant surgeon and his atypical, aloof mannerisms kept them on tenterhooks. Here in the teaching hospital, absorbed in his work, he had no time to modify his eccentric tics or the availability of his eyes. His awed students gave him wide berth.

Resident Mac Winthrop approached Burnaby from the scrub room with latex-clad hands upheld. "Confirming, Doc: dorsal spinous process subtotal ostectomy. No changes since our review, correct? I'll open for you at T-10?"

Burnaby nodded at his assisting surgeon, distracted. His phone was buzzing again, in its fourth series of silenced rings since he'd begun his surgical prep. Four incoming calls on a bacteria-laden phone immediately before surgery. He'd ignored the first three and expected no more, given the statistical infrequency of calls to his cell. Hadn't he extinguished regular voice calls by never answering? Friends, colleagues, the emergency dispatcher . . . even his wife—they all knew to text, knew he'd reply on his schedule, not at others' arbitrary prompts.

The buzzing quit, then began again within seconds. Burnaby grimaced. Jerked an elbow toward his hip in a spasm that caught Mac's eye.

"You okay, Doc?"

"Neglected to remove my phone. Back pocket. The buzzing's—"

"Got it." Mac waved a gloved hand. "Sarah?"

A coverall-clad student left her post at the closed-circuit camera and hurried toward them. Mac cocked his head toward Burnaby. "Dr. Hayes's phone. Pull it from his pocket, please."

Shoulders bent, Sarah reached under Burnaby's surgical gown and pulled.

"Who's calling?" Burnaby hoped his monotone eclipsed his annoyance. The horse's cardiac waves blipped on the suspended screen, and he dipped his chin with every beat. The surgical team stood ready.

"Nobody now, Dr. Hayes." She flashed the screen toward him, then looked again as another call arrived. "It's Celia," she said.

Celia. His wife. His other sphere. Calling him here? She registered dimly. Here in the operating room, her face and body were distant concepts, her mind an idea. Here, surgeries stripped him of her, reduced him from man to electron, generating a charged field of healing bones where his fingers and brain participated in regeneration that came from beyond himself. He clenched and unclenched his hands. His cheek twitched.

Mac, his brow furrowed, studied his mentor's profile. "Answer it, Sarah."

Her thumb ticked the screen. Before the phone reached her ear, the pull of his wife's heartrending cry found its way to Burnaby three feet away and spun him into that other orbit—where Celia was his nucleus.

"Oh, oh oh oh, Burnaby, Burnaby. Our *baby*."

He lunged toward Sarah. Seized the germy phone as Celia's words disintegrated into gut-wrenching sobs.

"Go, Hayes. I've got this." Mac gestured toward the door.

All eyes in the silent surgery clung to Burnaby as he ran from the room, his course tilting as he assembled the fragmented data pouring from his phone.

"Come get us, Burn. Hurry. She's still alive. She's trying so hard . . ."

"Where are you?" His thoughts whirled. He tore away his surgical mask and cap. Phone between his ear and shoulder, he stripped off his gloves.

"Climbed to the pine to test the hawk."

"What pine, Celia? *Where?*"

On speakerphone now, Celia's voice came from far away, high and small and loving as she sang to their baby. "She's struggling, Burn. I'm bleeding."

"*Where*, Celia?" He summoned solutions. "Does Tara know?"

"Yes, Tara. Yes. She sent me here." Her voice wobbled between hiccoughs.

"Keep the phone near you, Celia. I'm hanging up to call Tara. I'll return shortly." She was singing again as he disconnected.

Tara picked up immediately. "Good morning! To what do I owe the pleasure of talking with the illustrious Dr. Hayes? Celia tell you we found Hawk Five? Want to join us for lunch?"

"Where is she, Tara?"

"Probably on the road headed here. Or she will be shortly. Why?"

"She's not. Where's the hawk? You have specifics? Coordinates?"

"Why? What's up?"

"No time, Tara. Just tell me where."

"Aren't you a bucket of laughs today. Just a sec."

Two minutes later, with farmer Glenn Culbert's address and a GPS route in hand, he summoned paramedics. Two calls to Celia went to voicemail. Burnaby shrugged off his medical gown as he accelerated out of Pullman and sped toward the pinpoint on the screen.

Gravel flew when Burnaby's truck skidded right, then left into Culbert's farmyard. He straightened the wheel and resumed his speed past the machine sheds and barn, where the rutted farm road bottomed the old truck's shocks. Powdery dirt billowed behind him as he followed the road deep into Culbert's fields and toward the river, until the tip of a pine appeared beyond the next ridge.

A second vehicle appeared in his mirror, gaining, its horn blaring. A pickup, not the ambulance. Boiling clouds of topsoil enveloped both trucks as Burnaby braked to a stop and the second rig pulled up behind him. Burnaby drummed his fingers on the wheel. He was losing seconds. Minutes. He rocked with impatience as a graying, plaid-shirted man jumped from the pickup, his face red with sunburn and anger. A paper napkin fluttered from his neckline as he shouted a curse at Burnaby, who focused on a dab of mayonnaise at a corner of the man's mouth.

Burnaby lowered the window. Airborne dirt swirled into the cab. "I presume you're Mr. Culbert." He spoke without inflection.

"You *presume*," the farmer sputtered. "Presume you can drive out here without permission, like all those hunters and photographers and nutsos hiding little doodads for treasure hunts. I suggest you turn that sorry truck of yours around right here and get outta my fields."

Burnaby opened the door slowly and stood, the sun at his back as he towered over Culbert. The farmer retreated a step.

"Mr. Culbert. My wife just bore an infant over near that tree." The man's sneer faded as Burnaby pointed to the pine. "An ambulance will turn onto your yard any moment now. I'd be grateful if you'd lead them to us."

Culbert, slack-mouthed, nodded once and jogged to his rig. His tires spun, returning him down the road, as Burnaby aimed his truck straight through a sprouting field toward the pine jutting above the ridge ahead.

He braked when he touched the ridgeline and checked his GPS. A solitary ponderosa, set apart from scrubby brush in the draw below it, stood a dozen yards downhill, directly in the crosshairs of his screen's coordinates. It grew from an elevated hillock and shaded two overgrown graves—the markers he sought, exactly as the geocacher described them to Tara. *Two routes of access,* Tara said. Celia must have climbed here from below.

But his wife was nowhere in sight.

His heels cratered the soil every four feet as he descended, until he reached the raised patch of ground. "Celia?"

A squeak preceded the sound of wing flap, as a hawk launched from an overhead branch, its cry a steam-whistle rasp.

But that squeak was no hawk's. Ears tuned, Burnaby rounded the island to the foot of the small graves. There, hunched against the bank, her tank top bloody, her saturated jeans at half-mast, Celia hugged a tiny, naked baby, the child's skin bluish against his wife's tanned upper chest. A pale umbilical cord trailed from the infant to the clotted mass by Celia's hips.

He dropped to his knees and pressed a hand to her cheek. "Celia. Can you hear me?"

Eyes glassy, lips parted, she lifted her head and squeaked again. Burnaby laid two fingers to her neck and found her pulse. A map of her vascular system rose complete behind his eyes, its vessels constricting in shock at the loss of the blood that soaked the ground beneath her.

"I'll hold her, Celia." He reached for the child, prying at his wife's fingers. "Let go. I've got her." But Celia's clutch was like iron, her pupils dilated. Burnaby checked his pockets for the Leatherman he carried everywhere. Weeping, he unfolded the blade and sliced vessels and sinew until knife and cord dropped onto the placenta below. Then he reached beneath his limp wife and dead baby daughter and lifted, cradling them as he charged uphill to his truck.

Halfway to the farm, Culbert's pickup, trailed by the aid car, veered toward them. The farmer pulled off to let the ambulance pass. Doors swung open and two medics hurried to stabilize Celia as they extracted her from the crew cab's bench and strapped her and the baby she held to a gurney.

"I'd like to ride with you," Burnaby said to an athletic, blonde medic.

The woman looked askance at him as she connected an IV line to a vein on Celia's hand. She touched the baby's head. "I don't think . . ."

"But I can assist."

The EMT pursed her lips. "No. She's critical. Best if you follow us to Pullman Regional, sir." She climbed into the aid car behind the gurney, and the driver slammed the doors.

In Burnaby's mind, a monochromatic curtain dropped. Blank-faced, he stood under charcoal skies as the gray ambulance barreled down the black earth road. He lurched into his silvered truck, where shock set his teeth chattering and shook his ashen hands as he buckled in and shifted the rig into drive. His mind grasped for his Celia and their little girl, hidden in a leaden mental cloud that wouldn't clear. When the vehicles reached the paved county road, the ambulance lights flashed like shiny, spinning dimes. The siren wailed. Burnaby, in close pursuit, did too.

The ICU nurse replaced an empty blood bag with a full one and checked Celia's monitors. Burnaby sat near her head, intent upon her respiration and heart rate, reading obsessively the oxygen saturation levels that convinced him she had lived through her blood loss and plunging vascular pressure. That she had survived the ruptured uterine artery.

His Celia, even as he was hers. He mentally traced her jaw and ocular sockets and calculated their perfect curvatures. He imagined painting them on canvas—along with that mouth of hers—in watercolors he'd have to blend with sunlight to capture. The prior afternoon's memory came to him—how her lips had lingered on his. Outside in the warm grass beside the river, they had again confirmed their entanglement, sure as the quantum principles that drove the subatomic world between them. At the tactile echo of her hair spilling over him, so black he could hear every strand, his tears welled again, and he smoothed the ebony tangle now strewn across her pillow.

Even after ten years, he could scarcely believe she'd promised her life to him. From beyond his cognition, the wonder of their union flew at him, rousing him, as it always did, with astonishment and joy that defied description. Words she asked for but that he could no longer find, none being substantial enough vessels to hold the heft and volume of his affection. He had yet to discover a linguistic conduit with the capability to transmit how much he treasured her. Now, before he deciphered how to give her all that in a language she recognized, he had almost lost her.

Or maybe he *had* lost her. He knew well enough that successful surgery could restore an animal's body without reviving its will. Physically, Celia would make it. But would her essence survive? He had watched her attachment to their child deepen with every passing day. This morning, without him, she delivered their baby, then held and kissed and sang to the little girl until death tore the artery of their profound symbiosis. No surgery, no tourniquet, no words could stop that hemorrhage.

At the hospital's shift change, he scooted his chair back from Celia's bed as a new attending nurse checked her chart and vitals. Through the observation window, another nurse assessed the patient from across her desk, then returned to her paperwork. The clock above her told Burnaby he had contacted no one for seven hours. Missed calls littered his phone. Mac, Tara. Texts. Voicemails.

He tapped Tara's number, and she answered immediately. "Where *are* you guys? Celia hasn't checked in since before I talked to you. The vet school said you took off like a greyhound."

"We're at the ICU in Pullman. Celia lost the baby. She almost bled out."

"*What?* Lost the baby? How? Why? She okay? I'll be right there. I—"

"She's stable and sleeping. No point in—in coming. Preferably you'll retrieve her equipment before it gets dark. The location coordinates are accurate. You'll find the designated tree more accessible from the top field than from below."

"The top. Okay. On my way."

"Stop at Culbert's farmhouse first. He'll let you pass."

"Got it, Dr. Hayes. And hey, Burnaby."

"Yes."

"I'm so sorry. When she wakes up, tell her I love her. If you guys need anything. Anything at all . . ."

Her voice was dusky. He heard her swallow.

"Thank you, Tara. Please text me to confirm the retrieval of her supplies."

"Will do, Doc. I'm—"

He slipped the phone into his pocket and again turned to Celia. Her eyes were open, studying him.

"Tara's collecting your things."

"Did you see her, Burnaby?"

"No, just talked to her on the phone."

Celia's eyes brimmed. "Burnaby. Did you see our baby girl?"

He nodded. Inspected his hands.

"Her little face, Burn. Her ears and feet."

"I know, Celia."

"I tried to keep her warm, Burn. Held her over my heart so she could hear it." She lifted a pinky. "She gripped my finger." Her tears spilled.

Burnaby petted Celia's hair where it sprawled on the pillow slip. He couldn't look at her. He knew if he touched her, his fingers would scorch her skin with his sorrow. Sobs wracked her strong, lanky frame until she looked bone-loose fragile, unfamiliar to him.

"She couldn't breathe. She wanted to. I know she did. She knew my voice. Moved when I sang to her . . ." Celia's lips turned white as she pressed them together. Her chest heaved.

Burnaby leaned toward his wife. His tears dripped onto her hand, which lay open on the sheet between them. He bent and kissed her palm, then turned his cheek onto it, imbibing her grief.

"Where is she, Burn?"

"Kimball's came for her two hours ago. She was—"

"The funeral home? Nooooooo!" A bellow erupted from her as she tugged her hand free and bolted upright. Nurses came running.

Burnaby reeled. Her heartbroken cry invaded his lymphatics, his lungs, his neurons with what, he imagined, was the raw, collective agony of bereaved mothers that had broken the heart of God since time began.

"You let them *take her*? YOU. You let them TAKE HER!" She roared the words. Beat the mattress with her fists.

Burnaby knew he should have reached for her then. Should have let her pound his shoulders and chest so he could absorb her anguish as if he were gauze. Should have swabbed her with compassion and tenderness grown and harvested from his own suffering and his love for her.

But he didn't. Instead, as her query turned to accusation, a neural explosion somewhere in his prefrontal cortex dismembered his ability to field his own grief, and he could no longer soothe her.

"She's dead, Celia," he said. And walked out.

8

CELIA

FLIGHT

A DOUBLE TAP ON the back door's pane roused Celia from the sofa she had scarcely left in the three days since her return from the hospital. She kicked off the blanket Burnaby had spread over her during the night. He'd brought her that cereal on the coffee table, too, after he *again* opened the blinds on his way to work, ignoring her repeated plea for darkness. More proof that he wasn't listening to her any more than she was to him.

He'd upped the ante on his ridiculous rituals, too—scrubbing the bathroom within an inch of its life, folding and refolding laundry until their corners could injure the unsuspecting, wiping fly specks from every window in the house. She swigged the milky dregs from the bowl and trudged to the kitchen, where she set it in the stainless sink he'd polished to newness.

Tara stood on the porch, shading her eyes as she peered through the window. Celia waved her inside, squinting against the sun's assault while her friend sailed into the kitchen, set a grocery bag on the counter, and fanned the air.

"Hoo-ee. No mincing words here, Dr. Burke-Hayes. You're ripe." Tara's nostrils flared. "Turning feral on us?"

Celia smoothed her wrinkled tee, its fabric stained from the milk that dripped from her braless chest. She considered the condition of the pad between her legs. "Maybe."

"C'mon. You need a shower."

Celia scratched her head through knots of tangled hair as her protests flagged. Of the six qualified candidates who'd applied to work with Celia, she had chosen Tara Soto for the same formidable resolve that now swept Celia to the bathroom. Buck Tara? *Right.* Celia couldn't muster anything, much less resistance.

Tara pointed to two toothbrushes in separate cups by the sink and handed Celia the toothpaste. "Use it."

Like a chastised child, Celia brushed. Tara disappeared into her closet, rummaged, and returned with an armful of clean clothes. She plucked a fresh towel from a drawer and tossed it to Celia.

"You good, or do I need to strip you?"

Celia smiled for the first time in days. "I've been better, but a shower will help."

"Meet you at the table," Tara said. "I've got food."

Half an hour later, Celia shuffled downstairs, her wet hair trailing loose and smooth over a black cotton tee, her lean, tanned legs shiny with lotion below the hems of her jean shorts. She slid into a kitchen chair and rolled her shoulders into a patch of noon sun at her back. Tara delivered two green smoothies and placed a tray of deli sandwich quarters, napkins, and sliced apples on the table. She set a plate and spoon in front of Celia.

"Good. You still look like you've been swallowing rocks, but at least I recognize you now. Load up." Tara nodded toward the platter.

Celia sighed and ran a finger through condensation on her smoothie cup, then chose a sandwich quarter and one slice of apple.

"Forgive me if I'm overstepping, Celia, but talk to me."

Celia shrugged, her eyes welling. "About what?"

"That." Her friend touched the corner of her eye, then pointed at Celia's.

A quick inhale broke Celia's dam of tears. Her gaze roved Tara's face, then dropped to her sandwich. She pulled a pickle loose.

"She was exquisite, Tara. My tiny love. My dream." The room retreated as she remembered. "I don't know when they took her from me. When I finally came to, I only wanted to hold her a little longer, to memorize her before I said goodbye. To tell her again I was sorry."

Tara nodded, her food untouched, hands folded beneath her chin.

Celia frowned, and her eyes swung to her friend's. Her tone shifted, sharper. "But the same Dr. Hayes you *idolize* had already sent her to the *furnace*."

Tara's tongue poked through tight lips. She twisted a copper ring on her index finger.

"And then . . ." Celia's adrenaline surged with the memory. She leaned on her elbows toward Tara. "While I'm lying there half dead, with somebody else's blood dripping into me, shredded by our baby's death, and I ask him where she is?" Her spoon pinged as she slapped the table. "He walks out. *Walks out.* What kind of man does that, Tara?"

"He was hurting too, Celia," Tara whispered.

Celia stiffened and sat back. She lifted a corner of sandwich bread like a wing. Lowered it. "I should've figured you'd take his side. Of course you would."

"There aren't any 'sides' here. Just—"

"Hey." Celia lifted her hand, its palm toward Tara. "I appreciate your help. I really do. You're a stellar colleague. But let's stick to hawks, okay?" She pushed her plate aside and stood.

"I'm sorry, Celia. I only—"

"I know. I'll be fine." She walked to the door and held it open.

Tara retrieved her bag and touched Celia's shoulder as she passed. "I'm sorry."

Celia nodded once, then stood at the open door, her hand on the knob, until her assistant climbed into a green Subaru and backed onto the street.

Two weeks into June, Celia checked the window for Burnaby, home any minute. She washed a jalapeño and laid it on a cutting board, but instead of slicing into it, she reseated her knife in its wooden block. Sounds and smells were coming to her in taunting, detailed memories-turned-enemies.

She rested her hands on the counter and saw ghosts. Of Burnaby—on their magical wedding day, when she lost, then found, herself in him. Of him holding her when Gram Mender died. Of his tenderness each time her womb emptied too early and tears ran down their cheeks, their dreams for each child flushed with blood and tissue. Of his great hope and faith, willing them to try again for the family he wanted, too.

And of Burnaby in the years since, here in their kitchen after work, his magnificent hands adjusting the volume on the playlist to which each of them kept adding. His songs. Hers. Songs as different from each other and as surprising and wonderful together as Burnaby and she had been. The music. The food. How together they blended and stirred and chopped and broiled. Hummus and lentils, infused sockeye and ginger-laced slaw, all from recipes each chose for the other, each with flavors that explained Burnaby to Celia, and her to him. Their choices of ingredients read each other's minds, in culinary pursuits so unitive that Burnaby had called their cooking *holy*.

Overkill, the way he connected the temporal to the spiritual, though sharing cutting boards and recipes had—like their hiking and music and gardening and lovemaking—led them past the snares of their profound differences.

Until this terrible spring, on the terrible day they'd lost their daughter because Celia didn't protect her. The awful day Celia had hiked and put a hawk above the safety of their baby. The day her little girl drew breath, then died because Celia failed her as a mother.

What gall to have believed she *wouldn't* fail her.

Her eyes burned. No, she would never cook in this kitchen again. Preparing a meal here, now, would feel like she was undressing for a stranger. Cooking was too intimate to undertake with or for Burnaby, with this distance between them. He wouldn't admit and even adamantly denied that he held her responsible for their child's death, but she knew better. Hadn't his response to her in the hospital clinched that fact?

Oh, he'd stay faithful to her. She knew that. They'd go through the motions of being husband and wife, but he'd never love her like he did before. How could he? A loss like this? Where could they go from here?

She didn't dare go to him. Hadn't he clearly told her before they married that he felt crawling, biting ants whenever she surprised him with a touch? "A sensory aberration," he'd called his screwed-up epidermis. "Common to many of us on the spectrum. I need to prepare mentally for you." Apart from planned, anticipated contact, or when she held his waist on the soothing back of a motorcycle, Burnaby was *hands off*.

Angrily, she swept the pepper and cutting board into the sink, then wagged her head in contempt. How had she missed *that* red flag? How had she thought she could contend—for a *lifetime*—with his awkwardness, his detachment, and his awful, awful flinching when she contacted his skin unexpectedly? She felt like a tool. A pariah. And a fool.

Burnaby could make his own dinner. She untied her apron, threw it on the floor, and tore her keys from the hook by the fridge. His truck passed her at Dissmore's market, but of course he didn't see her, didn't stop. Fuming, she slipped inside the grocery, bought sushi, and ate it in her Jeep, unable to remember how she'd ever loved him so mightily.

As the summer solstice approached, crops on the rolling Palouse hills shouldered toward the sun. Celia traveled through them and over the state line into Idaho on the rote, seven-mile drive from home to her university office. While evasion grew in her like the burgeoning wheatgrass, she scarcely noticed the push and brilliance of the season she usually loved.

She returned home each night steeled against her husband, whom she passed on their porch like a sylph. In their narrow hallway and laundry room, she answered him in monosyllables. While daylight stretched like taffy into ribboned sunsets, she declined his offers of evening hikes into the hills outside their windows, the contours of her emotions gone flat.

Instead, she worked, head down, until night chased off the colors with the dust of stars she could no longer see. She doubled down on her research. Fed mountains of hawk data to Tara with the detachment of a statistician. Taught a fresh cohort of students without her usual fervor. Take-out boxes littered her Jeep.

She slept on the single bed in the baby's room, where she raised the sides of the adjacent crib around her fury, sadness, and longings. Sometimes she rocked a small pink urn—with contents she dared not name. And while Burnaby shopped and cooked, her untouched plate remained on their table, and she toyed with the thought of living alone.

The third Saturday in June, Burnaby zipped his suitcase, set it by the front door, and cornered her in her study. "My itinerary's on your desk and in—in your email, should you need it. I'll be in New York tonight, London tomorrow afternoon. The symposium there ends June twenty-seventh, after which I'll spend two days with Kemp at—at Oxford. I'll be home late on June thirtieth."

She looked at him dull-eyed and closed her book.

"I'll be back, Celia. We'll decipher this." He waited, studying her.

She shrugged, pulled an owl's wing feather from a jar of pens, and ran her finger along its length.

"Death's contagion kills more than bodies, Celia. I love you. Let me help you." He stepped toward her, but she rolled her chair out of reach.

"Pretty good at that, are ya?" she said. "Love's overrated. Tell Kemp I said that."

9

CELIA

MESSAGE

CELIA'S PHONE RANG from her pocket as she folded laundry.
Burnaby? His absence lowered her defenses, and a fleck of hope
jumped in her. He'd be in the Spokane airport by now, checking his
bag, she figured. Expectantly, she lifted the screen. But instead of her
husband's ID, the number of a Chicago law office appeared.

Mother.

A quick tap declined the call, which would surely suck from her
whatever emotional reserves she had left. She hadn't received more
than a text from Judith Burke in the preceding six months. Total
contacts in the years since her dad died? She could count them on
her fingers and have digits left over. So why now? She pinched the
hem of her shirt and sniffed it. Almost two thousand miles away, and
she swore Mother could still smell her vulnerability. No doubt the
woman had called to kick when Celia was down.

Oh, she missed her dad—and Gram Mender. Wished she could talk with them.

Thirty seconds later, her voicemail pinged. Her thumb opened a recording from an unfamiliar woman.

"Hello, this is Marian Gibbs, from the law office of Swift, Burke, and Markworth, calling for Celia Burke-Hayes. This time-sensitive message will be better delivered in person. Please return my call at your earliest convenience."

Her mother had all but unstitched herself from Celia, snipping their already tenuous connection to a few flimsy threads. What urgency could possibly prompt a call from her office? Celia would get this over with so icy Judith could flit away for another eon. She held her breath and dialed back.

"Marian Gibbs."

"Hello, Marian. Celia Burke here. I got your message."

"Yes. Celia. Thanks for getting back to me. I'm a paralegal, working primarily with Doug Swift and assisting your mother on occasion. Doug asked me to call. He understands that you have had infrequent contact with your mother, but he believed you'd want to know she died in a head-on collision two days ago, while returning from an extended case. Her car crossed a centerline near Darien. I'm so sorry. He'd have called himself, but as her husband, he's understandably too distressed."

Celia swayed against the dryer, spilling a load of folded clothes. *Dead?* Her mother? Her *remarried* mother? When had she . . . ? And now she was *dead*?

The news settled on her like cat-foot snow—quiet, numbing. She jotted details for the Chicago funeral four days away, jolted by the realization that she wanted to attend. For closure. That's what this ceremony would allow her. Closure on the thousand—*million?*—tiny deaths Celia had endured each time her mother didn't bother to greet her in the morning or say good night or share in Celia's joys or frustrations . . . or any emotion, really. Closure on all the belittling and accusations.

Omission. Commission. Heart crimes against a child.

All those teary times Mother found fault with . . . her entire childhood? Not completely true, she knew that, but when she hunted for any memory of her mother smiling directly at her, Celia could only envision her mother's profile, or the woman's eyes averted, distracted, loveless. Celia had carried those deaths in her since her earliest recollections.

She thought of her children, gone now. Had she passed death to them? Were they casualties, too? She shivered.

Yes. Time to end this sad story . . . and maybe, while she was at it, hers and Burnaby's.

Fitting, a funeral. Not what she'd ever dreamed, but it would do.

10

CELIA

DOPPELGANGER

THE JET BANKED TOWARD O'Hare in a slow curl over Chicago. Aft of the left wing, a bright ricochet of sunlight bounced through Celia's tiny window and bathed her. Below, skyscrapers grabbed at the plane's shadow before it escaped onto the sparkling, sunlit surface of Lake Michigan, where a pair of sailboats heeled against a stiff breeze, distancing themselves from shore, their sails like wings she wished she could ride.

When the plane banked again, a hatch thumped and landing gear lowered. The jet aimed for one of the runways now strewn below her like pick-up sticks. Flaps raised, the craft eased toward the ground. The descent countered her rising dismay at leaving the Palouse for this place that swallowed girls' mothers—*her* mother. In the twenty-three years since Judith abandoned her and her daddy and moved here, the hungry city had never spit the woman out.

Tires hit the asphalt, bounced once, and the jet slowed, joining the procession of planes rolling to their gates. The funeral procession, begun *now*. An attendant near the cockpit announced connecting flights beyond Chicago. *If only.* Celia's seatbelt clacked as she released it, and she steeled herself for what lay ahead.

The plane emptied, and still she sat, thinking, unable to move forward or back to when her hopes meant something and she believed in them. The cleaning crew reached her row and stood aside until Celia slid her carry-on from the overhead bin and slowly left the plane.

She sighed. So many hoops to jump through in the next twenty-four hours, and she had no jump left. Ten hours of sleep and she'd still dragged herself from bed to catch this flight, unable to out-rest the constant weariness that dogged her now. *Hard work, breathing.* She shifted her thoughts to her stride, then to her feet, as they pressed into her shoes' footbeds and carried her toward the rental car counter.

If Burnaby were here, he'd describe the rolling of her feet, heels to toes, as if he were stroking them, in steady talk about her bones and how they connected in the synergy of forward motion. Soothing, sensual, his timbre. His connection to her a strange skeletal thing, but nothing more than a memory now. How long since her brain or body had lit in his presence? She couldn't remember. No point in answering his calls. So many of them. Too many to answer. *So much work, talking. Walking.*

Ahead of Celia in the rental car queue, a black-bobbed woman in a flowing skirt and beret tossed keys to a goateed companion guarding a suitcase as tall as his hip. The woman gathered paperwork and sashayed toward him, her smile spreading, her kohl-lined lids at half-mast as he reached around her waist and kissed her lightly on the lips.

The heat in Celia's chest as she watched them confused her. Was it envy? Warmth spilled up her neck as she redirected her attention to a doughy man behind the counter.

"Upgrade, ma'am?" The agent slid her a laminated selection of vehicles. "A top-down kind of day." He tapped a Mustang convertible as his mouth curled upward. "Only thirty dollars more."

For a sweet instant, Celia remembered being happy. "What a deal," she said, and handed him her credit card.

The morning of the funeral, room-service oatmeal cooled as Celia pored over a city map, deciding her route to Hinsdale Memorial Chapel and reconstructing paralegal Marian's call.

"The mortuary is two miles from Doug and Judith's," Marian had said, before she tossed Celia a bone from her mother's life. "Their wedding was so lovely. Doug regretted you couldn't join them. A small affair. Under the arbor in their backyard."

Couldn't join them? An invitation would have helped. She wondered what "small" meant, curious about who mattered enough to her mother to be included.

Last she knew, Judith Burke had lived alone here in Chicago, in a condo on South State Street. Celia had tried to visit once, during a five-hour layover at O'Hare. She was nineteen, on her way to a semester on the Strait of Gibraltar and full of dreams about the migrating birds she'd study. In those days, Mother still sent birthday cards, so Celia sent Judith her flight plan. "Call when you're in the terminal," Mother replied. "I'll be home."

Within minutes of landing, Celia found a pay phone and dropped a coin inside. She trembled at the recording of her mother's voice, then left a message. "I'm at the airport, Mother. Pay phone. Call you again in fifteen." She did, every quarter hour until her boarding call. With every unanswered ring, rejection settled into her joints like arthritis, and she ached the entire span of the Atlantic.

A light flashed on her silenced phone and she clicked Burnaby to voicemail. *Now* who was ignoring calls? She refused the comparison and returned to her oatmeal.

Cars jockeyed for parking in the funeral home's lot by the time Celia pulled her rented convertible, its roof up, to the curb. Attendees, most in pairs and groups of three, strolled into the building. Her mother's business associates, she guessed, or clients, in suits, smiles. Celia examined their faces for any sign of pain over her mother's dramatic, unexpected exit from their lives, but saw none. What would they notice if they examined hers? What would a mirror tell *her* about her own reaction to her mother's death?

Nothing, most likely. The paralegal's call four days earlier only deepened the detachment that had lodged in her soon after her baby died. She was glad for the insulation of numbness. Thankful that she couldn't feel, at least for now.

She heaved her leaden body from the car and followed three young women about Tara's age inside, where she waited her turn at the guest ledger. A basket of jumbled envelopes rested on the table beside the book. Condolences, of course—but for whom? Who would read them besides her mother's new husband? His family?

The three women deposited their cards and passed from the foyer into a long receiving room, its coffered ceiling lined with heavy moldings. They filed toward the room's far end and disappeared behind a folding velvet screen. Celia followed, rounding the screen to the open-lid casket and a view of her mother's unmarred face—now waxy and off-color. With Judith's nervous, perpetual motion stilled, she looked relaxed. *Almost likable,* Celia thought, then chastened herself for the sarcasm. She scanned her mother's exposed skin for a sign of the traumatic injuries that took her life, curious about the magnitude of concussion or tear or fracture that could conquer this woman when no human being could.

Celia lingered, inspecting the carcass that had been her mother, uncertain of when to move on, wondering just how long it would take for her to complete this closure and lay to rest a lifetime of heartache. Where was all the sorrow and anger and confusion that plagued Celia's half of their relationship? She pinched the skin at the base of her palm until she winced. At least she felt *that.*

A chinless man rounding the screen coughed, jarring Celia back to her position there at the coffin. She reawakened to the others in line behind him, waiting their turn to view the corpse. All were strangers to her, and none were crying. But then neither was she.

Parallel to the coffin, a short row of chairs stood empty, save for a deeply tanned, elderly woman, whose lined, sharp features, loosely banded silver hair, and large, weathered hands contradicted her pearl choker and the classic black sheath that draped her lanky frame. The woman dabbed a wet cheek and studied Celia.

Familiar, though Celia couldn't place her. Celia took a seat two chairs down the row, her bag in the empty space between them. Her attention landed on the parade before her, where mourners paused at the open lid and perused her mother as if choosing groceries. She silenced her vibrating phone again and slid it into her jacket pocket.

The old woman's startled eyes remained on Celia. She now mapped Celia's hair and face, throat and torso. Her thin lips parted in concentration.

Celia looked away. Shifted. Crossed and uncrossed her legs. Finally, she returned the woman's gaze and was about to speak when the woman reached across the seat between them and laid a wrinkled, age-spotted hand on Celia's knee.

"Forgive me, dear. My husband called me his audacious girl more times than I can count, and I'm sorry to subject you to that problematic little trait of mine. Still, you look incredibly familiar. May I ask your name?" A steady voice belied the woman's advanced age. Celia sensed her kindness.

And she knew this woman. But from where?

"I'm Celia. Celia Burke-Hayes. And you are?"

"Doesn't ring a bell. Oh well. Not the first time I've been mistaken." She sat back and splayed work-thickened fingers across her chest. "Hazel Steffen."

Celia nodded. "Mrs.—"

"Hazel. Please."

"Okay. Hazel." Celia spoke slowly, mirroring the woman's close inspection with her own. "No, I don't believe we've met."

Hazel cocked her head. "Uncanny, the resemblance."

Resemblance? Celia scowled.

Hazel again leaned over the empty chair. "How did you know Judith?"

Celia hesitated. Her mind flew from the only answer available but found nowhere to perch. "Judith was my mother."

Hazel sat back and blinked as her jaw unhinged, exposing gold crowns on her lower molars. "Your . . . mother."

"Uh. Yes. Only child."

"Your mother."

"You look surprised. How did *you* know her?"

"Judith was my daughter. *My* only child."

11

CELIA

BURIAL

IT WAS CELIA'S TURN TO GAPE. This woman? Her *grandmother*? Her thoughts whirred. Mender, gone for years now, was the only grandmother she'd ever known. Celia had loved her so intensely that she'd never missed a *second* grandmother.

But what had her mother ever told her about Hazel? What had she said about the maternal side of her family *at all*?

Not much, Celia realized.

Then she recalled a rare window of friendliness with her mother when Celia was nine or ten. She remembered asking, "What about your sisters, Mother? Any brothers?"

Her mother had exaggerated a shrug. "None."

"Your parents?"

She had dismissed Celia with a wave. "Long gone." Her voice was singsong, as casual as a breeze—the tone Mother used to end every discussion that bored her. Celia had sensed nothing behind the words, either. Nothing loaded into them that lingered in the room after the sentences themselves were spoken.

"When did they die? How?"

"Before your father and I married," Judith said. "Both were sick a long time. Not a story worth telling."

Her dad had been no help at all. "She told me the same thing shortly after I met her," he said. "Curiosity got the better of me. I scoured twenty years of obituaries from her hometown but came up empty. Without a peep from her about them after that, I bagged it. You know your mother."

Did she? The mother Celia had known was originally Judith *Stevens* from New Hampshire, not this old woman's child. Mother must have changed her identity before she met Daddy, effectively disconnecting him and Celia from her family line, with neither of them the wiser.

And now this grandmother, Hazel, here beside her and very much alive. Celia's buried ire at her mother stirred. Another theft.

"Whoa, Hazel. Whoa."

"When you turned from that casket, I couldn't have been more astonished. You there, my reflection in a glass, only fifty years younger. Please don't let that gobsmack you, Celia. I doubt you'll see the resemblance. Time translates us in ways the young can't decipher. Give me some new suspensory ligaments and a little ironin' and you might see the likeness."

"I thought you looked familiar."

Hazel took Celia's hand and held it awkwardly on the purse between them. Celia almost withdrew, but warmth from the woman's fingers seeped into her cold ones, wrapping them with full-belly comfort. Questions tripped on her tongue, unasked.

The funeral director popped through a side door, then stepped briskly into the space between them and the coffin. Hands clasped behind his back, he tipped his head, acknowledging each.

"Family?" he asked.

Hazel jutted her chin toward the man. Her clasp of Celia's hand turned fierce. "Darn tootin' we are."

He closed the coffin lid. "This way, please."

Minutes later, they filed back into the room behind a somber Doug Swift, four couples, and an assortment of preschool children. Hazel's arm looped Celia's as they settled into a row behind a cadre of her mother's new in-laws. A small pamphlet on her chair named Doug's four sons, daughters-in-law, and seven grandchildren as her mother's survivors. Below their names, she read Hazel's and her own, their relationship recorded right there in the leaflet.

"A loved one's passing prompts us to consider our legacies," the chaplain began. "Our futures."

Legacy? Celia's mind wandered, clobbered by her mother's long betrayal. Judith had erased a *grandmother* from Celia's childhood with the same calculation that she undertook one of her corporate take-overs. Celia would bet her right arm that Mother's reason had nothing to do with protecting her child from this old woman.

Or did it? Was this a case of "like mother, like daughter"? Celia had written papers on genetics—and the dynamics between nature and nurture—and had run from, or fought, the implications her entire adult life. What role had this woman played in who her mother had become?

In the next row, a wispy-haired baby girl lifted her head from her mother's shoulder and laid a tiny hand on the woman's cheek. Celia's heart clenched. She glanced sidelong at Hazel, whose tears erupted as she, too, watched the child. How would life be different if Hazel could have held Celia's baby—and baby Celia herself? If this grandmother could have sung to them, a generation apart? Did Hazel sing?

The chaplain raised his voice. ". . . restore to you the years that the locust hath eaten . . ."

Celia huffed, and a few noses down-row pointed her way. *Yeah. Right.* No getting her childhood back any more than she could revive her babies. Or her marriage.

As if on cue, her phone vibrated against her hip. She eased it out and silenced another call from Burnaby just as a frumpy clerk trudged to the front and mumbled Judith's praises. Stodgy, serious Doug, a stepfather who wasn't one, replaced her, gripped the microphone by its throat and droned. Two others spoke before the chaplain reclaimed the podium, his words a smear. The organist played.

Oppressive, this room. She itched to escape and ask her new grandmother more. She tugged Hazel's hand, and they slipped outside while the others sang.

"Why, Hazel? What happened?" Celia asked. She and her grandmother stood nose to nose. Tall women, both wearing flats, their height identical.

Hazel licked her withered lips and watched a robin fly past. "Here, darlin'. Let's sit." She strode like a younger woman to a courtyard bench surrounded by peonies and patted the wood beside her. "Where to start?" Her thumbs skimmed eight close-clipped fingernails before she pressed her hands to her lap and angled toward Celia. Her eyes brimmed.

"The real story isn't one you're gonna like, honey. Ugly enough to curdle soup. Want me to make up a good one instead?"

"That bad, huh?" Celia mustered a wan smile. "I can take it. I doubt you'll surprise me."

"Okay, then. The short version." Hazel paused and rubbed the crease between her brows. "I'm no blamer, but years and miles of thought and prayer have led me to believe that there were weevils in Judith's flour sack early on. I refused to admit that until a good ten years after she disappeared. Blamed myself for the lion's share of her infestation. Then I spent ten more years sifting out the bugs I actually sowed."

She sniffed, wiped her nose with a tissue from her purse, and continued matter-of-factly. "Until my friend Leona gave me the what for. She accused me of playing God by thinkin' I was the sole arbiter of whether Judith went this way or that. Her words packed a punch, honey. She smacked me, I tell ya."

"Smacked you." Hazel's linguistic flair reminded Celia of her own, in her livelier Texas days. Nothing like Mother's.

"That Leona was a barn of a woman, with an even bigger voice, so when she stood in our yard with her hands on her hips and said, 'Lissen here, Hazel,' I shut my whiny trap and paid attention. I remember it like yesterday. She said, 'Who's to say your daughter wouldn't have turned out *worse* if you'd treated her differently? I watched you and Joss raise that little wildcat. Heard you pray for her. Cared for her in my home the time you two went to Florida, remember?'"

Mother was a little girl once. Had Celia seen even one childhood photo of her?

Hazel squeezed Celia's hand. "Leona told me that girl could have skinned a wolverine alive and emerged without a scratch on her body or her conscience, if she had one. 'That girl has free will,' she said. Then she pinched my cheeks and told me in no uncertain terms that no matter how hard I tried, I couldn't make Judith love me. She said I could bury that hope right next to our car-struck dog.

"After that she took me by the shoulders, looked me square in the face, and said it was time for me to release Judith back into the hands of the Father who made her. Said that while I was at it, I'd better quit berating myself, quit trying to wash the blood of the Lamb off of my dirty old self and instead let that plasma of grace for my failings soak into my soul.

"By golly, she was right. Took me a time to own what she was saying, but when I did, I sat right down at that big old table of forgiveness and ate the feast the good Lord kept warm for me."

"So what *happened*?" The old woman's narrative was taking the turtle road, and Celia was rabbit wild to hear it. "You said she disappeared."

"I'm getting to that, honey. You first have to know that early on we knew our Judith was scary smart, and headstrong. A debater from the age of five. Your grandfather Joss and she bucked heads over, well, everything. Joss was stubborn too, so when the stakes ramped up as Judith got older, so did their conflict. Both set their jaws. He, to keep her in line for her own good, and she, to prove him wrong. Neither softened, ever.

"I tried to make peace between them, Celia, and I truly thought I was helping. But Joss rebuked me, and Judith raged at both of us." Tears wet the creases in her weathered cheeks. "I'm sorry, honey. I've let this go, I really have, but talking about it? Scars still have nerve endings."

Some legacy, Mother. Celia pulled a peony petal from an enormous bloom and flicked it toward roses and lilies across the walk. If she could, she'd infuse her grandmother with the flowers' fragrance, balm for her decades of grief.

Hazel collected herself. "I figured it would pass. Teens act out sometimes. I knew that. On the plus side, Judith excelled in everything. Teachers loved her, and she thrived in every academic forum. She worked two jobs every summer, and every Saturday during the school year. Saved like a squirrel.

"But by her senior year, I knew that hers was no typical teen behavior. Not a young person's normal eagerness to venture off to college. In retrospect I should have recognized that Judith had already cut her ties to us and was merely biding time until she could fly. She strategically planned her exit—from us, from our church, from everything that connected her to our community. As if she had already erased us."

Erased. Yes. Celia knew the feeling.

"Then the University of North Carolina offered her a free ride with that Morehead Scholarship. I figured we'd still have the summer, and a chance to make our peace before she left, but unbeknownst to us, she secured a job at the university, finagled permission to rent a room in a Chapel Hill dorm open for summer students, and bought her own plane ticket. The Tuesday after her high school graduation, she left for work as usual. I was expecting her home for dinner until she called from Raleigh to tell me where to find her car at the airport."

A bubble of breath caught in Celia's throat. "She didn't even say goodbye."

"No, she didn't." Hazel tracked Celia's sight line to the flowers. "Her storm calmed after that, though. At least toward me. I wrote to her every Sunday, and she replied a time or two. I even flew out for a weekend that fall. Two amiable days, when she seemed to receive my kindness. I hoped things were mending. Then she came home for Christmas, had another blowout with her father, and left in a fury."

Hazel sighed. "I couldn't stand in Joss's gale, Celia. Or in hers. Those two were converging storm fronts, and I'm afraid that all my attempts to explain them to each other only stirred up lightning between them. And between her and me. She never came home after that. She quit writing, too."

Celia bent over her knees, studying her shoes.

Hazel folded her hands. "My, I'm overwhelming you, aren't I?"

"I'm okay. Go on, Hazel. You're answering questions I didn't know I had."

"If you're sure, darlin'."

Celia nodded, her own eyes filling. She rested a hand on Hazel's knee and leaned into the story.

"Not that we were ever close. We weren't. But years have taught me that even if I'd known how to love her better, I still couldn't control her choices, much less what was happening in her heart. I couldn't control anything. I'd been trying to manage things only her Maker could."

Like something Burnaby would say.

"February of her freshman year, she wrote once more. No return address, but the Carrboro postmark led me to believe she had moved off campus. How she got permission when the school makes freshmen live in dorms is beyond me, but . . . well, what Judith wanted, Judith usually got. Anyway, she wrote us a two-sentence letter. In the first she said she was disowning us, and in the second she insisted that we stop all contact with her."

A thin breath escaped Hazel's lips. "You can imagine how my heart broke. I couldn't believe her finality. I gave her a month to cool her heels then tried to call, but she'd swapped her number for an unlisted one. I wrote her via the university, but the letter came back to me, unopened, with *return to sender* scrawled across the envelope.

"The last photo I saw of her showed up, oddly enough, in *Sports Illustrated* the following year. Joss stumbled across it one Sunday—a close-up of her and a handsome, dark-haired boy in the bleachers at some college playoff game. Their mouths were open like they were screaming, their arms up like goalposts. I clipped it out. Still have it somewhere."

"My daddy's that boy," Celia said. That pic hung in her dad's study for years—above his diplomas, below a photo of her two-year-old self on his shoulders. "He and Mother met at Chapel Hill as sophomores. Eloped at the start of their junior year, in time to beat my arrival."

Hazel nodded thoughtfully. "She'd dropped out of sight by then."

"Couldn't the school help you find her?"

"We weren't paying for her schooling. She was a legal adult."

"That's awful."

"You have no idea."

Celia weighed the comment. No idea? She had lost three babies, not one. But Hazel was right. How could she understand that kind of bereavement? To lose a young adult child—and from the poison of rejection? Such dirty grief. No, she couldn't imagine.

"That last letter from her . . . My Joss refused to accept that Judith could simply remove us from her life, so two days after he finished the spring seeding . . ." Hazel tapped her chin. "Uh, that would've been mid-April, before the end of Judith's freshman year, he climbed in his pickup and drove off. To town for tractor parts, I thought. Until he didn't come home. Not like him to miss lunch. I called shops, but nobody had seen him. When he didn't show for dinner, I called the State Patrol. Drove farm roads looking for him. Ten o'clock that night he called me from a motel two states away and told me he was driving to Chapel Hill."

"Did he find her?"

"It took him three days, but yes. He intercepted her on the top floor of the New West building after one of her debate team meetings." Hazel shivered. "He couldn't talk about their encounter for weeks after he returned home. I swear the man had PTSD."

"Ouch."

"Maybe if he had tried a different tactic? Like waving a white flag? Asking forgiveness for his role in all those battles? But that wouldn't have been Joss's style. Though their rift made him sick, he still would have tried to set her straight." Hazel loosened her hair and gathered wisps. Reclipped it. "The restraining order—against us both—beat him to our door."

Celia knew her mother's wrath but had never considered that anyone besides her and her daddy endured it. Mother stabbed and skewered white flags for sport. "Maybe nothing he could have said would have made any difference at all. Never did for me."

Hazel's brow rose, questioning.

Celia wasn't ready to answer. "Did he ever hit her?"

"Oh, heavens, no. Joss wasn't a violent man. He never lifted a hand against her—or anyone, to my knowledge."

"What do you think he said to her?"

"Nothing cruel, though I've come to understand that inflexibility does its own wounding. Control stunts love's growth, that's for darn sure. How can connection thrive without surrender—on both sides? Joss didn't believe that, though. Everything had to be his way, Celia. Everything."

The lines on Hazel's face seemed to deepen. "Judith, ever the student, learned those ways. But instead of becoming a complementary, balancing force, she imitated him and became equally ... no ... *more* deaf. More controlling. And unlike Joss, she showed no compassion, no empathy, except as a charade, when it served her interests. As you'd suspect, that dynamic made their collisions inevitable."

Celia traced a filigree in the bench's metal arm. "And we're the collateral damage." More than bloodlines connected Celia to this grandmother. *Judith's legacy of pain.*

"Hurt, yes, but victims, no, unless we choose to be." The old woman straightened. "Not a word from her, all those years, until her office called about her death. And then I only learned where she lived and that she was an attorney. I never knew she married, or that you even *existed*." She touched Celia's shoulder. "And now isn't this grand? Here you are."

Two young men wandered into the courtyard, laughing. Hazel's voice flattened at their approach. "So much to talk about, honey, but I've bent your ear with more than my share. May I hear about you?"

Twin doors banged open, interrupting Celia's reply and releasing mourners to gather near the waiting hearse. Pallbearers emerged with the casket and crawled like a human-legged prosoma down the sidewalk and through the crowd.

"Want to ride with me, Hazel? Cemetery's only a few miles north of here."

"Well . . . I hadn't planned to attend graveside. I won't intrude on a private family gathering. Thought I'd call a cab and head for my gate. I fly out tonight."

Celia sighed. "Ironic, right? Judith's only blood relatives, and they don't know us from Adam. The airport sure sounds better than watching Mother collect more dirt." She shook her arms, relieved. "Sorry. No offense intended."

"None taken, honey. Puns can win wars, you know."

Celia smiled. "What time's your flight? I can drive you."

Car doors slammed behind them. More drivers joined the procession behind the departing hearse. Celia retrieved Hazel's carry-on from the chapel's cloakroom and loaded it into her convertible, alone now on the empty street.

"You mentioned seeding," Celia said. "And tractors? You're from farm country?" An irrational panic bubbled from somewhere deep as she merged onto the freeway toward the airport. Would this new grandmother simply fly away?

"Oh yes. We're wheat farmers in Washington State. Outside the little town of Colfax. Near Pullman. Ever heard of the Palouse?"

12

UFFINGTON

A VINYL BANNER ANNOUNCING the International Veterinary Orthopedics Symposium flapped from the awning of London's Grosvenor House Marriott, pelted by driving rain. Inside, 250 surgeons from four continents spilled from the convention's concluding banquet. Burnaby wheeled his suitcase outside, dodging the crush of questions he had encountered all week. A *Keynote Speaker* ribbon fluttered from his ID badge as he raised the collar of his sport coat against the storm.

A tub-chested veterinarian hurried after him into the light pooling below the entry's awning. "Before you go, Dr. Hayes . . ." The man thrust his open palm toward Burnaby, who inhaled sharply and speared his hand into his fifty-seventh handshake that week. "Thank you. I expect your plating techniques to transform my surgeries."

An animated second man in a green bow tie joined them, his accent thick. *Fifty-eight.* When a woman in the lobby pointed at him through the glass and pushed through the door, Burnaby stepped away. "If you'll excuse me." He walked toward the street and peered at the stream of headlights brightening the twilight. Where was Kemp?

Seven minutes passed before an ancient blue Peugeot left the parade of vehicles and swerved into the hotel turnout. The driver's door opened, and Judah Kemp, Burnaby's first and only college room-mate, leapt to the curb, as gangly at forty as he'd been at eighteen. Like outgrown clothes, Judah's lips seam-popped over huge teeth into an enormous smile.

"Kemp." Burnaby reached for his suitcase, but Judah snatched the bag and tossed it in the trunk.

"Keynote, huh?" Judah pointed at the bustling lobby. "And in your happy place, a human anthill. Cat's out of the bag about you, Doc, now that they've heard you speak. Bet you didn't use any notes either. Am I right?"

A corner of Burnaby's mouth curved upward, and he tapped his temple. "They're up here. You know that."

Kemp's laugh followed them into the car, warm and generous and disproportionate to the skinny man from whom it came. The sound glazed their long-overdue reunion with the connection Burnaby had all but forgotten. Cocooned with Celia in the life they'd known, he hadn't made time for anyone else. Hadn't felt the need.

Absorbed in his work and his hobbies and his wife, he'd relegated everyone else, even Judah, to his life's margins. A phone call with his friend each Christmas? A hurried airport dinner during a layover four years earlier? The Kemps' baby announcement, to which he'd let Celia reply? Insufficient contact, all of it. He cringed, remembering how he hadn't replied to Judah's text when his friend got the Oxford assignment. He and Judah had been brothers once. Close. *I should have tried harder,* he thought.

Even their correspondence about his trip had been skeletal. Burnaby had attached his itinerary and a link to the symposium details, and they'd exchanged three more short emails, arranging. Burnaby hadn't mentioned that Celia had carried, and lost, their baby. Nor did he tell Judah that he was coming to London anyway because, even living in the same house, he felt transoceanic from her.

Now here was Kemp, promptly cinching the gap between them. For the first time since the baby's death, Burnaby took a long, cleansing breath and stole a piece of his friend's high humor. "Ha," he said. "Ha."

Judah slapped the steering wheel and shifted into gear. "That's a start, old man."

Burnaby relaxed as his friend pulled the Peugeot into the stream of cars. Was there a better friend than Kemp, who knew to spank that wheel rather than sideswipe him with a slap to his knee? His first and, apart from Celia, his *only* age-mate friend, his appearance little changed from the day they met.

That day, Burnaby and his dad had located the assigned dorm and barged through door number 323 to the roommate Burnaby only knew through two letters—one from Residential Services confirming their shared assignment, and another from Judah himself. Kemp, his sandy hair parted and glued like a TV preacher's, had tossed a box of books onto a single bed, its plaid quilt tucked and tidy. He met Burnaby mid-room, those ropy arms lifted straight as a crossbeam on his fence-post body, his expression serious. *Like someone crucified,* Burnaby thought.

But not for one minute did his new roommate treat their dorm pairing as a sacrifice. Judah extended his hand, read Burnaby's discomfort, and let it fall. His grin burst as he sidestepped Burnaby and flung closet doors wide. "Taj Mahal storage!" he said, then crossed the room to the narrow window framing another dorm's brick wall. "And views!" He laughed, and his eyes jumped from Burnaby's laced leather boots to the top of his head, a few inches above his own. "Extra-length mattresses, too. Welcome to Geekland, Burnaby Hayes," he said. "We'll knock 'em dead."

The memory retreated as the hotel shrank behind them. Burnaby pressed his skull into the headrest and allowed tension from a week of handshakes to release. Judah peppered him with questions Burnaby deflected with a wave. "Later, Kemp," he said and closed his eyes as the car joined the stream of traffic on the M40 motorway. They had passed from the city into the sleeping countryside before he roused and mumbled to Judah, "How are Lizette and Marcus getting along without you?"

Lizette—lithe, black-haired, and dark-complected like Celia—had spent endless hours with him and Kemp in physics labs. Burnaby had often tagged along during their two-year courtship.

"Unshakable, but she's getting tired. Eight weeks is a long time to solo parent a baby T-Rex. Seven weeks down, one to go."

"Ha. A strategic sacrifice on her part. Considering you've raved about Oxford since you two met, she likely hoped a visiting scholar stint would get England out of your system."

Judah guffawed and wobbled the gearshift. "You may be on to something there. She'd love it here, though. So will you."

Ever the optimist. Burnaby's eyelids drooped again as his friend launched into the next day's itinerary. How like Judah to tailor their limited time together to Burnaby's interests, though right now, with the symposium behind him, his primary interest was sleep.

An hour later, Kemp whistled him awake and pointed at a steep-gabled brick building, tree-shadowed in the darkness. Random windows on three of the floors glowed warm.

Burnaby read the sign out front. "Wycliffe Hall? The theological college?"

"A bit of a twist, right?"

"You're lecturing *here*? Teaching what, biblical physics?" He turned to his friend as they parked. "Even if—if I were serious, would you have any takers?"

Kemp's laugh erupted again. "You aren't so far off, brother. How about an eight-week course called *The Science of Oneness*? In prayer? Marriage?"

"Rather misleading, Kemp. Smacks of a sex education class." Burnaby massaged his tired eyes. "Eight weeks? With theologians? That must have been some proposal."

Judah's hands left the wheel, and he rubbed them vigorously. "Oh yeah. I've been counting the days until I could tell you about it. Stay awake now, man." He whapped the dashboard. "You're gonna love this. It'll take you back. You ready?"

Burnaby yawned. "Ready." *Barely.*

Judah set the brake. "MIT, freshman year. How many times did we hear that prayer has no scientific corollary?"

"In our circle? Every time you argued that the natural world illustrates the spiritual one." Burnaby's eyes closed.

"Right? So the first day of this class, I led with that 'no corollary' premise, like a skeptic, suggesting that science couldn't substantiate the instantaneous interaction with God we call prayer. We rattled around there for an hour or so. Then I took a U-turn. 'But what if the opposite is true?' I said. 'If the natural world reveals and explains its Creator's MO, then science will *confirm* prayer's plausibility.'" He laughed. "I gave them a formatted hypothesis, but that's the gist of it."

Judah's fervor resembled a puppy's. Pouncing, nipping. *Irresistible.* Burnaby had missed him.

"After that, we dug in. I gave them a crash course on quantum mechanics. Zeroed in on how subatomic particles attached through close proximity remain entangled—even when they're separated. I explained how, even at vast distances from one another, entangled particles can communicate instantly."

"Which you have frequently substantiated in the lab." Burnaby yawned again.

"Yeah. I showed them. Said, 'If dinky particles can do all that, who can say God's immediate reception and response to prayer is far-fetched?'" Judah's fingers ran piano scales on the steering wheel. "I demonstrated for hours. Proof right there in front of them. *Instant* communication between those particles across varying distances."

Burnaby smiled. "Faster than light in a vacuum."

"Yeah. Yeah. You see where this is going, man. Next, I applied entanglement's principles to the Trinity, and the students were all over it. 'Imagine the three Persons in the one Godhead,' I told them. 'Distinct, but so connected they actually *are* one being.'"

Burnaby's brain lit, remembering his dad's fiddle singing the Trinity into his understanding. He had been nine, lying on the grass, finding constellations in the July darkness. His father sat on a stump, violin under his chin, explaining—and playing the concept on individual strings before he combined them in a single harmonic tone. *The triune God, entangled. Three in One.* Burnaby's grasp had been only a seed back then.

Judah swayed above the steering wheel like a weaving horse. His words were galloping now. "I told them, 'Imagine the Godhead splitting up. The Spirit leaves to hover over the earth at creation and to quicken beings with the spark of life. Later, that same Spirit enters believers' hearts. Meanwhile, the Son leaves the Father to travel to earth, where he dies and descends into hell, a considerable mileage from the Father.

"'Each of these actions puts distance between Son and Spirit and Father,' I said, 'yet no matter how far apart they are, they remain one God, their connection complete, their conversations instantaneous. And when the Spirit helps a human reach for God? *Boom.* An immediate conduit is created. Instant communication through prayer.'"

Judah's gum snapped frenetically. *Enthusiasm. Wonder.* He practically lotioned himself in them.

"Total entanglement, Burn. Total holy entanglement, illustrated and explained in quantum physics. Never gets old. An indwelt believer prays and the Father gets the message instantly. Not at the speed of light. *Instantly.*"

Unabated, Judah followed Burnaby to the curb. "You should see my students' zing when they connect this stuff, Hayes. And when we use it to talk about oneness in marriage? More dazzle."

Marriage. At its mention Burnaby bent an ankle on root-broken asphalt and tilted, smacking a knee into the car's grille. He had banked on entanglement with Celia to carry them through.

Judah didn't notice. "You'd be all in, man. I get to synthesize everything you and I have talked about since we were freshmen. Quantum mechanics and Scripture, hand-in-hand compatible. *Elegant.*" He hefted Burnaby's bag. "C'mon. They left the lights on for us."

He led Burnaby upstairs to a narrow gray room, sparsely furnished with a desk, dresser, and twin beds in low metal frames. From a small closet he tossed a sleeping bag and pillow onto the unmade mattress opposite his own, then grinned and pointed two fingers back and forth from his eyes into his reflection in the dresser-top mirror. "Bring back memories?"

"Ha." How often had Kemp insisted Burnaby stare at himself in their dorm room mirror until he could simulate eye contact? And until he could gaze at a girl's eyebrow for fifteen seconds while he conversed with her? Eventually, thanks to Judah, Burnaby learned to translate himself enough to marry Celia.

He hoped Judah could help him keep her.

"Bath's down the hall. Get some sleep, brother." Judah grabbed a toothbrush and towel, and his footfalls retreated. A distant door squeaked.

Burnaby was texting Celia again when Judah returned. "C'mon, Doc. You've got five minutes to kill that light. And if you aren't on your feet by a quarter past four, I'll douse that yellow head of yours with the coldest water I can find."

"Early, even for you, Kemp."

"Golden hour doesn't wait. One view of those downs at sunrise and you'll pull that Palouse off its pedestal."

At four fifteen a.m., Burnaby's eyes popped open to his phone's alarm. Judah, dressed and eating an apple, sat on his bed, staring at Burnaby.

Burnaby groaned. "Don't do it, Kemp."

"You're on countdown, man. We leave in ten for the oldest road in Britain. We'll catch the light and miss the crowds." He tossed the apple core in a three-point arc to a basket by the desk.

A thirty-minute drive later, Kemp hung his Nikon from his neck, locked the car, and the two set off on a path into the tumbling hills of Wessex Downs. Judah crouched and aimed his camera at hedged fields, wildflowers, and the open, rolling landscape, gilded and shadowed by the rising sun.

At the trail's intersection with the Ridgeway, Judah lowered his lens. "This track's been here three millennia. It used to run clear to the Dorset coast." He jutted a thumb. "Up that slope's the castle, what's left of it, and the Uffington White Horse, which is why we're here, bone man."

He ushered Burnaby through a gate at the hilltop and snapped more pictures, this time of grazing sheep. Green ridges swelled like gums behind them. Kemp stood on a tooth of rock. "Uffington Castle ramparts. Iron Age."

Frankly, Burnaby didn't care. Before him, a dew-embroidered ocean of grass swam in the energy of early summer's growth. He needed the life in this scene, not the relics of the dead. He also needed to talk to Judah, but the photographer roved the fields, chasing light while the morning magic lasted.

The sun hung like a peach when Kemp called to him across a short-cropped slope. "Dragon Hill," he said. "Legend says this is the place where St. George slew the beast that devoured villagers' children. Fourth century." With a flourish, he removed his cap and held it over his heart above a white patch of ground. "The dragon died in a pool of blood, on this very spot. No grass has grown here since." He punched his side with an imaginary dagger and collapsed sideways in fitful jerks.

Burnaby sank to his knees in the barren circle, his lungs tight. "You're not funny, Kemp."

Judah sobered and righted himself, scowling. "Sorry. A little too full of myself over here. What am I missing? Used to be I could smell something bothering you."

Burnaby stared at the ground. "In May we lost a baby. And Celia . . . I'm losing her, too." His muscles twitched and he bowed over forearms pressed to his waist. Judah hurried near, then sat cross-legged as Burnaby rocked side-to-side and told of his wife and daughter beneath the hawk's nest. The hospital. The decline of their marriage in the nearly two months since. The story unwound in a reel of detail, in a monotone pocked with dates, times, and minutiae of his pain.

Light bounced from Judah's wet cheeks. "I wish I could carry that heartache for you, man. I am so sorry for both of you." Finally, he stood when Burnaby did—and unfolded a photocopy he pulled from a pocket. "Even more reason for you to see the horse," he said. "Here. Taken from across the valley."

He handed Burnaby an image of a stately equine stick figure, its ears forward, arched neck extended low, long tail floating as if in speed, or wind. Graceful legs appeared to carry the beast at a gallop across the crest of a ridge.

"It's up there," Kemp said, pointing. "A Bronze Age geoglyph, three thousand years old. The length of a football field."

They climbed the rise, where wide white strips stretched across the slope. Shorter lines formed a rectangle around a solid circle as large as a car's wheel.

Judah tapped the photo Burnaby held. "We're standing at the horse's head. That circle is the eye; I'm at its ear." He pointed along the diagonal. "Those slanted lines? Muzzle."

Burnaby walked the grassy fringe of the horse's head and knelt at the jawline. He ran his hands across the surface, rubbing fragments of the unusual earth between his fingers.

"Chalk," Judah said. "A pictogram three feet deep, pummeled by prehistoric Brits. Thirty centuries later, people are still wondering why."

"Knowing you, I suspect you've convinced yourself that this—this animal somehow illustrates entangled states. Am I correct?"

Judah punched a thumb into the air. "Guess how."

They hiked a chalky stroke of backbone until, mid-spine, Burnaby stopped walking. "How, Kemp? You explain it. What's this horse have to do with Celia and me and entanglement, right now?"

"Not the animal, Doc. The *call*. Picture all those primitive, breathing people, an entire community of them—calling out to the Breath who gave them theirs for help with their families' survival. They needed their Creator for everything, and they knew it."

Burnaby dusted chalk from his hands.

"Fast forward to you and me—scientists, at the tops of our fields. Who needs humility, or God, when we know everything, or at least believe we can discover it? When have you or I said a prayer as big as this horse?"

Burnaby circled under the horse's flank and sat on his haunches, taking in the swells of turf on the downs, the grid of agricultural fields in the flats. He sieved the chalk of ancient petitions through his fingers. Kemp was right. Since their baby died, Burnaby had asked no one for help. Until now.

And he hadn't prayed once.

13

CELIA

HAZEL

"COLFAX. PULLMAN. The Palouse," Celia repeated slowly, her head bobbing at each name. All those years she and Burnaby had lived in Pullman, Hazel and Joss had been farming the nearby hills. While Burnaby pieced together shattered scapulae in his operating room, her grandfather had seeded and harvested, his combine chewing wheat from forty- and fifty-degree slopes—and Celia had trapped hawks in the shrubby draws between them. Likely as not, she and Hazel had passed one another filling grocery carts at Dissmore's and swallowed dust from each other's tires on country roads.

"You've been there?"

"Hazel. I live in Pullman."

"No. You don't." Incredulous, the old woman twisted against her seatbelt and leaned across the Mustang's console. She planted fingertips on Celia's thigh. "Where? How long?" Breathing fast, she sank back into her seat. "Celia, our farm's on Old Hollow Road. Out the Penawawa drainage. Half an hour from you."

"Penawawa. I know that area." The name left Celia's tongue with reverence. And her mind reeled. Was Hawk Five's nest on Steffen land? Celia navigated by coordinates and paid little attention to owner names, but Tara kept track. Her colleague contacted land-owners and secured access permissions before Celia stepped foot on anyone's property. If she had hiked the Steffen farm, Tara would have spoken to one of Celia's grandparents and written their name on the map Celia kept in her Jeep.

"Well. I'm surprised you do, far as we are off the beaten path. We're one of the last farms before the river," Hazel said. "Smack in the heart of the best loess around. All that rich topsoil, dropped from the sky since time began. When Joss first brought me out there, he called our ground the wind's final destination."

Celia smiled at the description, read the airport exit sign, changed lanes.

"Spring of '46, he invited me to meet his parents. Bus and train all the way from Dalhart, Texas, to Spokane, where he picked me up. All that country, thousands and thousands of miles, and I'll tell you what, Celia, I never saw the likes of our Palouse hills. When we reached his parents' land—our farm—I made him stop. I took off my shoes at a plowed field and waded ankle deep into that fertile womb of earth. Joss held his sides, he laughed so hard."

Fertile womb. Unlike Celia's empty one. She declined the reminder and instead pictured her grandmother as a teen, riding some high-spirited buckskin bareback. Apparently, she and Hazel even had Texas in common.

"You're from Dalhart? How'd a Palouse boy connect with you, way down there?"

"FFA. Future Farmers of America, though I considered myself a future rancher. Met him at the national convention my senior year. I—"

"Hazel," Celia interrupted. "What shall I call you, anyway?" She needed an endearment to link them before the old woman told this or any more of her stories.

Hazel clenched the hair at her nape and drew it over a shoulder. The question dangled between them. "Call me?"

"A name. To make this a family story. Something like Oma, Amma, Nana." Celia ran through tags that friends called their grand-mothers. "Gram's taken already." Mender laid claim to that title in Celia's childhood and held sole rights to it still.

Hazel laughed, then pressed a finger to her lips. "How about Nolly? My childhood name for my grandmother. For that name to leapfrog to you? Oh, that would delight me no end." She rubbed her hands together as if warming them.

"Nolly." The name landed in a sweet spot as Celia pulled the car into the terminal. "Yes. Nolly." That they could call each other *at all* staggered her.

Hazel took her bag from Celia and pressed a kiss into her cheek. "Come visit when you get home? Maybe Sunday?" Her warm gaze caught Celia's and held it like an anchor.

"Sure. Sunday." She watched Hazel disappear into the terminal as a diesel shuttle passed, belching. *Enough dirty air.* She fanned herself, waving away the bus's exhaust and the black cloud she'd carried to Chicago, concentrating instead on her grandmother: a blue patch of sky. Maybe Celia would visit her Monday, too, when Burnaby returned. No point in welcoming him to a home that was ending.

14

CELIA

FARM

SUNDAY, ON OLD HOLLOW ROAD, a stiff breeze caught soil and spun it into a child-sized tornado. Behind it, Celia slowed, matched a mailbox number to the one in her hand, and turned toward a two-story folk Victorian house in a grove of shade trees. At her Jeep's approach, two boys raced the length of a spindled porch, threw a screen door wide, and vanished into the house. Hazel met Celia at the door and waved her into the foyer.

"Now?" A child's voice, from behind Celia's grandmother.

"Now," Hazel said.

A small fist thrust a bouquet of wilted dandelions toward Celia. The shorter boy peered around Hazel with eyes the color of plowed earth. "For you," he said.

Celia reached, but a taller blur of dark-haired boy slapped the gift and sped outside.

"Excuse me, honey." Hazel followed the offender into the yard.

Celia rubbed the gift-giver's sand-colored head and bent for the strewn flowers.

The boy scowled. "He wrecks my stuff."

She knelt beside him. "Your brother?"

The boy nodded. "Willie's younger but he's taller and we're fraternal. That means we have the same birthday but comed from different eggs. I'm five. So is Willie."

"And who are you, if I may ask?" She tapped the bunched flowers on his nose.

"I'm Cobb."

"So good to meet you, Cobb. You know, I always wished I had a twin," Celia said.

"You gots a brother?"

"Nope."

"A sister?"

"No sister either. Just me."

"I gots two sisters. Ruthie and Candy. Ruthie's sixteen, and Candy's in heaven but she went there when she was just a baby so I didn't cry because I wasn't borned yet. Ruthie said she cried, though."

Celia's heart skipped.

Hazel came through the door, a stocky boy in tow, his chin to his chest. He walked straight to his brother, his voice gruff. "I'm sorry, Cobby."

Hazel tapped his crown. "Try again, darlin'. Like you mean it."

Willie raised a fistful of fresh dandelion blooms to Cobb. "Sorry."

His brother sized up the offering. "They don't got stems, Willie."

Willie rolled his eyes and made for the door, but Hazel snagged him by the collar.

"Celia, I'd like you to meet Willie."

Willie glared at his brother, then took Celia's hand in his empty one and shook it like a pump handle. She suppressed a smile. "Hmm. Cobb. Willie. Ruth. Candy. Somebody in your family like baseball?"

"Daddy!" the boys yelled, and Willie pitched a fastball of stemless flowers at Cobb.

"Long tradition," Hazel said. "Before he met Flory, their father, Satchel—he's our farm manager—played for the Tacoma Rainiers. Triple-A."

"His name's Satchel? Seriously?"

Hazel grinned. "*His* dad was a Mariner." She shooed the boys outside. "Run and tell your parents we'll eat at four."

On the hour, Celia tossed a salad. As Hazel pulled a roast from the oven, a clean-shaven man with a salt-and-pepper buzz cut knocked on the open door's jamb.

"C'mon in." Hazel took a dish from a fair, pear-shaped woman diverted by the twins and a yellow lab roughhousing on the porch.

"Thanks, Hazel. Nanaimo bars," she said, shooing the boys inside. "Willie. Cobb. Hang a Larry to that washroom and get that dog off your hands." The twins sobered under their mother's glare, then disappeared around the corner, screeching like race cars. Celia heard water blast the sink.

Hazel looked past the woman and through the screen. "No Ruthie and Ivan?"

"They'll be here." The man eyed the wall clock and frowned. "Want me to slice that meat?"

"Be my guest." Hazel set the dessert on the counter and handed him the carving knife. "Though you're hardly a guest anymore, honey." She perched hands on the woman's shoulders. "After Joss died, Celia, these two filled his shoes as well as their own. I'd be lost without them. Satchel and Flory Milk, here she is. The granddaughter I met in Chicago."

Satchel touched an invisible cap. Flory clasped Celia's hands, her expression warm. "If you knew how welcome you are, we'd have to buy you a tiara, eh?" Her eyes twinkled playfully.

Celia liked her immediately. "Canadian, right?"

Flory's laugh rang. "Fifth-generation Canuck. How'd you guess?"

She hooked an arm through Celia's, led her to the table, and sat beside her.

The twins reappeared, wiping wet hands on their pants. Satchel settled them between him and Flory. Hazel asked a blessing, Flory spooned vegetables, Willie spilled his water, the dog barked at the patio door, Hazel passed bread, Satchel explained a dad joke to Cobb, and Celia allowed herself to be swept into family. And while twins and parents and grandmother served and mopped and chewed and shared and asked and answered and included her in all of it, she caught herself laughing.

Plates were half empty when a slight, sunburned teen burst in the door, shoeless, her long blonde hair damp. A wet swimsuit showed its floral pattern through the fabric of her shirt. A muscular young man followed close behind, his eyebrows raised, sheepish. Both avoided Satchel's sight line.

The girl's full-bodied voice outsized her. "Oh, Hazel, I'm sorry I'm late. I made Hugh take me for another loop and I fell twice. Took us longer to get back to the marina."

"That's what time buffers are for, Ruth. I've discussed this with both of you." Satchel's hands remained in his lap. His voice was level.

Ruth's locution sped, defensive. "Daddy, this isn't Ivan's fault. I *made* Hugh pull me downriver again. I skied *slalom*, Dad! Crossed the wake!"

"Regardless, you—"

Flory interrupted. "Ruthie. We'd love a recap later, but unless you two slide right into those seats, you'll miss the number-one astonishment of Mrs. Steffen's life."

Ruth went silent. She and Ivan looked from Flory to Hazel like cats at a mousehole. The twins giggled, squirmed in their chairs, and pointed.

Flory stretched freckled hands toward Celia. "This, kids, is Hazel's long-lost granddaughter."

After dinner, Celia started the dishwasher and went outside to join Hazel, who waved from the porch at Ivan's retreating Blazer. To her left, the Milk family walked a dirt lane toward a blue gabled house a hundred yards distant. Satchel and Ruth trailed behind Flory and the boys. Ruth watched the ground, not her father's animated mouth and hands.

Celia considered the pair. "No last word for Ruthie."

"Wilder than an acre of snakes, that one. Satchel's as wise and loving as they come, but he's got his hands full with Ruth."

A white-bellied hawk ascended silently from behind the barn and dipped low over the wheat. Celia sat in a wicker rocker. "What I wouldn't give for a daughter like Ruth."

"It isn't too late, honey," Hazel said.

"On the contrary, Nolly, that ship has sailed."

Her grandmother lowered herself to a settee. "There's so much to learn about you yet."

The rocker creaked as Celia shaped a reply. "Well, for starters, I've had two miscarriages and a preemie, who didn't make it either. The doctor advised against any more."

Hazel leaned, squeezed her arm. "That's a hard row to hoe. The preemie. How long ago?"

"Not quite two months. The baby was born on your land, below Culbert's farm. I checked my map."

Hazel stared at her. "Satchel heard about that. He thought it happened on Glenn's property, not this gone-yonder place. Oh, to think that was *you*, honey. And my own great-grandbaby."

"I had her by those graves and that old pine."

"Oh my. The graves. Joss's sisters. Two other little ones lost at birth, a year apart. Their sorrowin' mother planted that tree to shade them. She went down there every week to water it until she died." Her chest expanded and she exhaled slowly. "I'm so sorry, honey."

Celia closed her eyes. More children, gone too soon. Her great-aunties. She rocked the chair faster, swaying those babies and her own. "I should never have gone on that hike."

"Oh, darlin'."

"Her perfect face, Nolly. Her fingers and feet. Those squeaks. I hear her, see her right now. All the time." Her eyes pleaded with Hazel. "Sadness is eating me alive."

"No doubt, honey." She patted Celia's hands. "Your husband. Burnaby. He's gone, you say?"

"Yes, he's been in England for more than a week, but he's been gone *from me* since she died. I'm sure he blames me. And when I look at him, I think of her. I can't imagine him touching me again. Before Mother died, I started looking for an apartment."

"You're leaving him? You're sure?"

"Yes, I'm moving out, but no, I'm not sure about anything."

"Come here instead, sweetheart. Plenty of room to think."

⚶

At home by dusk, Celia filled her largest suitcase and carried it to the front hall. In her study, she slung a valise over a shoulder and was retrieving her purse when the garage door's chain gear activated. Frozen in place, she heard the door rise and a vehicle enter.

Burnaby? He wasn't due for another twenty-four hours. She scrambled for her phone, and checked the string of texts she'd ignored. There it was, sure enough. **Caught an earlier flight. Home Sunday night.**

She was staring at the phone's screen when her husband ducked through the kitchen door and set his bag by the table. When he spotted her luggage, he strode toward it, turned, raised eyes to her.

"Thirty texts, Celia. Eighteen calls. You replied to none of them."

"I need time, Burn. I don't know what I want anymore."

"Where are you going?"

"To my grandmother's."

Burnaby studied her, confused. "She's dead, Celia."

Those words. Still sizzling in her memory. Loud and clear in the hospital, right before he walked out. Her brain triggered.

"No! She's not!" she shrieked. Pushing past him, she snatched her suitcase and hurried to her Jeep at the curb.

15

COBB

TUNE

MIZ STEFFEN TELLED me her little girl's baby was a growned-up girl now and was coming for dinner, and then I knowed Miz Steffen's oldness was a grandma oldness. She singed when she fixed dinner and I feeled Miz Steffen's singing inside me and so when Miz Celia comed, I gived her flowers with the singing in them.

16

CELIA

GOATS

WHEN FRENETIC BARKING woke her, the shiplap ceiling above the twin bed gave Celia no clue to her whereabouts. Nor did the vintage quilt pulled to her chin or the fresh bouquet of lilies on the antique dresser.

"Rocket! Stop!" Hazel's reproof sailed through the open gable window. The dog quieted, and Celia's last conversation with Burnaby—and her move into this bedroom here at Hazel's—returned to her in a flood. She rolled toward the wall and yanked the quilt over her head until checklists prodded her and her phone buzzed. *After eight already.* She cleared her throat and returned Tara's call.

"Yep. Yep. Got it." Her colleague's efficiency relieved her. And left her feeling useless. Her students wouldn't miss a step with Tara at the podium in her place.

"I'm going to be gone for a while," Celia said. "I'll call the dean and ask him to slot you into my position, if you're willing."

"In a heartbeat. Take all the time you need."

"Our hawks. I'm still in, but I'll add you as the study's co-author. You call me anytime, okay?"

"Will do. Uh . . . Celia?"

"Yes?"

"Thanks. I'm sure sorry for what you're going through, but I hope you know I'm grateful for your trust."

"You're as good as they come, Tara. I'm the one who's grateful."

She hung up. Her pillow lured her, but so did coffee, so she dressed and plodded to the stairs. At their foot, Willie hung from a newel post with a frosted brownie. A scrawny man in his late forties stood in the foyer, briefcase in hand. Frosting streaked his slacks.

Hazel held the door open. "Thanks for stopping by, Karl. I'll look over those papers. Sorry you didn't get to meet—"

"We gots brownies, Celia!" Willie held the treat toward her.

The man brushed past Hazel toward the stairs. "Well, well!"

She wished she'd stayed in bed.

"Oh, Celia, honey. Good morning." Hazel caught the man's arm. "Say hello to our accountant, Karl Lydiard. Took over our financials when his dear father passed. What's it been now, Karl? Twenty years?"

"Twenty-two." Karl rubbed his nose. "Makes me one of the family."

Not my family. Celia waved feebly and sent a pleading look to Hazel.

Hazel tugged Karl toward the door. "Here, honey. Show me that new car of yours." The screen banged behind them.

Willie dogged Celia to the coffee pot. "Our goats gots ribbons. At the fair. Mommy said you could come. Mine's a Boer, but we won't eat him."

"The fair, huh?" She filled a cup and joined Flory and Cobb at the table.

The smaller boy pushed a paper across to her with two hands. "I drawed this for you," he said.

A pencil sketch of a floppy-eared Nubian looked at her from the page. Hyphen pupils, two teats on a bulging udder—the goat's features were accurate, drawn to scale.

"Thank you, Cobb. It's wonderful."

"That's Posie. I had to 'member her in my mind 'cause she gots twin babies just like Willie and me and she won't stand still. And she's not here anyways. She's at the fair. You wanna see her?"

Adorable, these children, but all Celia wanted was to sleep. To forget. To be alone, where she could beat back the thoughts and feelings that ravaged her. Talking to Tara and getting dressed had already emptied her of whatever still kept her afloat.

"Palouse Empire Youth Fair," Flory said. "If you don't join us, I'll have a revolt on my hands."

Hazel reappeared behind her. "The fair may do you good, honey."

Too tired to say no, Celia pushed her chair away from the table. "I'll get my shoes."

A medley of the best days in a hundred childhoods met Celia as she and Flory followed the twins onto the fairgrounds. Festooned with flags for the upcoming July Fourth weekend, the vitality of the place didn't exactly energize her, but it squelched her doldrums, for now. She isolated high notes: A lanky boy leading his steer from a Quonset barn, blue ribbon in hand. A pen of spring-shorn sheep. A teen girl, braids flying, cane waving at her runaway ewe.

Flory leapt at the sheep as it steamrolled her way. "Cobb! Willie! Help me here, eh?" Arms wide, the trio shooed the flop-eared animal back to the red-faced girl—and the waiting judge in the show ring. Flory snagged a pocket on Willie's jeans and whispered to him, then rubbed Cobb's head. Both boys raced away.

At the goat barn, Ruth and a freckled age-mate, their show tags pinned to their shirts, converged on Flory, who waved Celia toward a far row of animals. "Join you in a sec," Flory said and pulled the girls aside. Even across the interior alley, Celia could hear Ruth's voice over her friend's rising one, both shrill with concern.

Celia found Willie inside a stall, gripping the curved horns of a tawny, muscular goat. Feet braced, the animal aimed its horns at Willie's chest and lunged. Another Boer reared and butted at them both.

Celia rested her elbows on the pen's short wall. "Who have we here?"

Willie released his hold and bent both fists toward his head, flexing. "I'm stronger than Biff, and Cliff is Ruthie's and he's scared a me."

"So this is Biff? And he's yours?" She scratched the withers of the goat nearest the pen's slats.

"Yep. He's a wether, but not like rain and snow."

Celia's laugh sounded foreign to her, but she liked its feel. This castrated ram? Definitely not rain or snow.

"Mommy said to help Ruthie." Willie climbed the pen's slats and leaned over the half-wall for a halter and lead rope on an outside hook. When Ruth appeared at the stall, he buckled Cliff's cheek strap and handed his sister the rope.

"Thanks, bud. You comin'?" Ruth led the goat though the gate. Willie frog-hopped down the alleyway after them as Flory hurried toward Celia with the freckled girl. "Do you mind keeping an eye on Cobby? Stall twelve? Ruthie's 4-H leader's delayed, so the girls are a little frantic for help at the show ring."

"Happy to," Celia said.

Five stalls away, Cobb stuffed alfalfa into a feed net and hung it from a post within reach of a glossy brown Nubian doe. He brightened when Celia approached, gazed up at her with night-deep eyes, and slid fingers around hers. "Show you somethin'?" He slid the gate latch open, towed Celia into the goats' stall, then sat in the shavings, where two tiny kids the color of their mother slept in a heap. Celia knelt beside him.

"They came right outta Posie. Like poop, only magic." Cobb

stroked the sleeping babies with his fingertips. "When they was borned I tickled their noses with a wheat straw like Daddy showed me and they sneezed and right then they breathed with their nostrils. Daddy said they breathed through a hose in their 'bilicals before." He frowned. "A hose in their belly buttons? How do they do *that*?" He lifted his shirt and poked his navel. "You know every goat gots a belly button?"

Oh, this little boy. His words rolled to Celia like the scent of warm bread. She inhaled, sniffing for his sweet, leavened heart.

Late afternoon, Flory wound the car through the hills toward home. In the back seat, the twins' cotton-candied faces went slack with sleep. "Thanks for your help today."

"Thank *you*," Celia said. "I needed this day more than you know."

"Maybe I do know, eh? Hazel told me about your baby. Probably not her place to do so, but she means well." Flory tapped the steering wheel with her thumbs and looked sidelong at Celia. "She's match-making our sorrow, I guess. I lost a babe too."

"Candy? Cobb told me." *The woman had survived.*

"Yeah. Ten years ago. I wanted to crawl in that grave right along with her."

This was pain Celia understood. "My baby doesn't have a grave yet. Or a name. My whole life's on hold." The gloom that had lifted at the fair circled and landed. Celia leaned against the window. Lightning forked in the distance.

Flory reached across the console and patted her thigh. "Don't let anyone tell you to get on with it, either," she said. "Grief has its own gestation."

Celia drew her knees to her chin. Hugged them.

"But if you ever want to talk—"

"Thanks," Celia said. Inches from her nose, her wedding ring glinted in another flash of lightning. Celia twisted the band, pressed her thumb over the inset stone, and pulled the ring from her finger.

17

MISSING

UNTIL THE NIGHT HE RETURNED from England, Burnaby had never considered that Celia was as socially isolated as he was. But when she didn't come home, and he had no idea where to look for her or whom to call, he had to acknowledge reality: she had no close friends at all. Family she trusted—her father, Wyatt, and grandmother Mender—had been dead for years. His parents, though supportive and loving, lived nearly four hundred miles away. With the possible exception of Tara, Celia's university colleagues were merely professional acquaintances.

Unsettled, he drove past Tara's place after midnight but saw no sign of Celia's Jeep. Nor was her vehicle in the U of I lot when he parked there the next morning. He was waiting outside Celia's office when Tara arrived at eight.

"Well, lookee here. You by yourself? This has to be a first." Tara unlocked the door and Burnaby followed her inside. She rounded her desk and set her bag beneath it. "What's up?"

"Have you seen her yet today?" He crossed the room to a larger desk behind Tara's cluttered one, empty but for a mesh bird cage and the tooth-lined jawbone of a deer that Celia used as a paperweight. He'd found it trailside on one of their hikes.

Tara's lips pursed. "Why? Should I have?"

"She's teaching today, isn't she?"

"Man, Dr. Hayes. You need to get out of that surgery molehill more often. She hasn't been in since her mother died."

Burnaby lifted the jawbone and ran thumbs over the molars. A muscle in his cheek jumped. "What do you mean?"

"I mean I've been covering her class. She's working from home, in case you haven't noticed." Her brows bent. "Isn't she? She said she was extending her leave."

"Her mother died?"

Tara wheeled her chair, tracking him as he paced. "You didn't know? What's going on, Doc?"

"I—I've been in England." He returned the bone to the desk and spun it like a propeller. "When I arrived home last night, she said she was leaving for her grandmother's."

Tara shrugged. "So?"

"Her grandmother's been dead for eight years."

She stared at him, open-mouthed.

"I'm worried about her, Tara. Since our child died, she's been remote and occasionally irrational." Fidgety, he cleared his throat. "She refuses to talk with me in person, by phone, or by—by text. A friend at Oxford suggested I investigate postpartum depression. Several of her symptoms meet the criteria for that diagnosis. Do you know where she might be?"

"Wow. I'm sorry, Doc. She called in this morning, but I figured she was home." Her forehead creased and she shook her head slowly. "I couldn't tell you where she is."

"This morning? How did she sound?"

"Fine. Normal. All business, which is all we ever talk about now. Did she tell you I tried to help her after she came home from the hospital? I overstepped, and she shut the door on our friendship. She's been quieter and a little cranky toward me ever since, but I figured I had it coming. Just glad I still have a job."

"I see. At least we know she's—"

"Yeah." She looked thoughtful, then stuck a finger in the air. "I have an idea." Her hands flew to her computer's keyboard. "Before I booked her flight to the funeral, I took a call from her mother's law office. They wanted details about Dr. Burke-Hayes for the obituary." She typed fast. "Let's see . . . Chicago *Tribune* . . . nothing yet. *Sun-Times* . . . Ah! Here it is." Tara scrolled and squinted, inches from the screen. "Bingo. Grandmother number two." She turned the screen to Burnaby.

"Hazel Steffen." He glanced at Tara and returned to the obituary. "Colfax, Washington?"

"Hold on. I know that name." She reclaimed the screen and tapped the keyboard. "I thought so. Burnaby, I have *spoken* with that woman. She gave us access to Hawk Five. Your baby was born on her land! Oh, Dr. Hayes! That's her grandmother? Is that what she meant? If it is, and if Celia really is visiting her grandmother, you'll find her forty-five minutes from here, on Old Hollow Road."

He was already at the door. "Thank you, Tara. Please stay in touch with her."

Within the hour, Burnaby's truck juddered over Old Hollow's washboard, chased by heavy clouds, low and fast. Ahead, sunlight bent, warm, onto Hazel Steffen's house, the crouching barns, and a patch of wheat bathed in unusual colors.

Even after his sleepless night, the scene arrested him. Long ago, he'd learned not to resist his synesthesia but to observe it, learn from it. He pulled over, and hues modified by his paintbrush brain glazed the landscape with gradients of relief. An overlay of greens, mostly, saturated the house that he hoped held his Celia and a grandmother he'd never met.

Then other colors rose, warlike. Black threats to his wife and marriage advanced behind gunmetal buckler clouds, clashing with a full-spectrum flank of light that seemed to hold the farm and guard it. He forced himself to breathe, then drove down the lane.

An aged woman answered his knock.

"Mrs. Steffen?" Burnaby ran the zipper on his sweatshirt like a schoolboy. She was tall, like Celia.

"Yes?"

"I am Burnaby Hayes. I have reason to believe that my wife, Celia, may be here. Is she?"

"Oh, you just missed her, honey. She left with Flory and the boys about ten minutes ago. I don't expect them home until late afternoon, though they may cut the day short if this storm sets in."

Burnaby peered back down the road. Had he passed them?

"To Pullman?" he said.

"No, no. To the fairgrounds. Other direction." She cocked her head and measured him. "You're as jumpy as spit on a skillet, young man. Would you like to come in? Have some nice herb tea?"

"Such fickle weather today." Hazel set two steaming cups on the table, then pulled a cardigan from the back of a chair and draped it over her shoulders. "Rain, we can use, but I don't like this drop in temperature."

Burnaby knew he should inquire about the crop and the farm—should say something civil and sociable—but his colors were changing as quickly as the storm outside. He didn't answer. His leg bounced wildly.

"I must say it's a pleasure to meet a previously unknown grandson-in-law."

Burnaby understood that Hazel was observing him, and though he wished it were otherwise, he also knew he wouldn't pass any evaluations right now, this day.

"Were you as astonished as I that Celia and I are related?" Her words hit him like rubber bullets.

"Mrs. Steffen—"

"Hazel, please. I know you two have been . . . are going through a difficult time."

Burnaby looked out the window to trees bent sideways in the wind. "She told you about the baby."

"Yes. To think that the child was born on this property. I don't believe in coincidences, though. Do you?" Hazel pulled the tea bag from her cup and watched it twirl.

The memory overwhelmed his ability to answer. "Did she say if she'll be—be staying with you for long?"

"She hasn't said, and I don't know her well enough yet to ask. I hope so, though. Your daughter's death has—well, I suspect it's best if she's not alone."

He looked out the window, gathering thoughts. "I'd like you to know that I adore Celia, and that before the baby died, she reciprocated that devotion. After the trauma, she forgot who we—we were together. An emotional, relational amnesia of sorts."

Hazel locked her eyes on him. "Death. Like that cloud out there. Must have blocked her view of the two of you."

"I believe so." Burnaby sipped. Sipped again.

Hazel blew on her tea. "The woman she left here with? Flory? She lost a baby to stillbirth ten years ago. Her baby blues and heartbreak turned south—and near killed her."

"Do you see a parallel to Celia's emotional state?"

"As I said, Burnaby, I don't know her well enough yet, and she's a hard nut to crack. I don't see debilitating depression like Flory's, but loss affects us all differently. I can't say how she'll choose to respond."

"Do you know this woman well—this Flory?"

"Oh my, yes. She and her husband have lived next door since

their eldest was a toddler, so for over fifteen years. Too early to say for certain, but it could be that Celia's arrival here will be providential for them both. Suffering has instructed Flory, made her wise beyond her years, so if Celia will let her in, she could be a marvelous friend."

Burnaby stared into his mug. Celia met his every need for human companionship. Before their great loss, she might have said the same about him. Now, however, how could he ever be enough for her?

"It's up to Celia, though. Depending upon how flighty or guarded she is, this could go either way." She lifted the tablecloth and peered at his knees. "If you're so inclined, I suggest you activate those prayer bones of yours."

"A friend in England made a similar suggestion."

A curtain of rain billowed their direction, doused the lawn, whapped the windows like a flyswatter.

"I'll leave now," Burnaby said.

"I welcome you anytime, new grandson, though I can't say your wife will do the same. I *will* tell her that you and I met."

He couldn't say if she would, either. His colors swirled to mud.

18

CELIA

NEIGHBOR

CELIA RETURNED FROM THE FAIR, emailed the university to extend her leave, and fell into bed. Ensconced at Hazel's without Burnaby to raise window blinds to a new day, and with no scheduled university classes or research deadlines, a fog far darker than her previous malaise enveloped her, and she surrendered to it. Twelve, then fourteen hours a day, she slept—or lay in her narrow bed in a mental mire, her waking hours distorted, at first by grief and anger and confusion, and then by nothing but gloom. She picked at the oatmeal and fruits and soups on her bedside table, ignored the bathwater Hazel drew, and played mindless games on her phone, avoiding texts and voicemails from Burnaby.

"C'mon now, honey. Talk to your husband. Or at least to me," Hazel said, a dozen different ways.

"Leave me alone. I'm tired," she said in as many replies, every one resistant.

As days passed, Flory's animated, muffled conversations with Hazel seeped upstairs and fed Celia's disturbing dreams. Men's voices reached her, too: Burnaby's, Satchel's. Once she heard children. *Whose?* Living people, floating on the surface of a murky sea in which she was sinking, paralyzed, detached. Except for Hazel, she declined them all.

On the eleventh morning since Celia first refused to come downstairs, Hazel yanked the covers from her clenched hands and stripped them from the bed.

Bleary-eyed and startled, her legs and arms cramped fetal, Celia squinted into streaming morning sunlight. The curtain rod and curtains lay on the floor beside the bedding.

Hazel stood over her with Celia's running shoes suspended from one hand. "Rise and shine, sugar bean, before you grow roots in this bed—or the sheets rot."

Celia groaned and rolled over.

Hazel reappeared on the opposite side of the mattress. "You may prove to need medical or psychological intervention and a fistful of drugs, but it's been my experience that fresh air, some meaningful nourishment, and putting that piranha phone away can jump-start most stalled engines," she said. "Where would you like to begin, Celia? With a country walk and some proper food, or with a trip to the clinic?"

"Neither," Celia groaned. "Leave me—"

"Not anymore, sweet pea. You choose or you're evicted. Burnaby will come get you in a heartbeat, if I call him."

"You wouldn't."

Hazel leveled a stink eye at her.

"You would."

"Darn tootin', I would. I'm not willing to aid and abet your demise. I know you've got gumption in there. Now use it. I'll wait downstairs while you decide." She set Celia's sneakers on the exposed sheet, then swiped the bedding from the floor and pitched it into the hallway. "Either way, unless you're going to contact your husband, a phone amputation is in order."

Celia snatched her iPhone from the bedside table and clutched it to her chest, as angsty as a sixteen-year-old. What gave this bossy old woman the right to treat her, at thirty-nine, like a teenager? She balked and shook her head rapid-fire.

But when Hazel thrust her hand toward the device, Celia meekly let it go.

"That's better. I want you downstairs within the hour with an answer for me, so I can plan my day."

Forty-five minutes later, Celia descended the stairs in the leggings and ratty green tee she'd worn since she entombed herself upstairs. At the landing she pulled on clean socks and tied her running shoes.

"Looks like I won't need the car today after all." Hazel smiled, opened the front door, and handed Celia her sunglasses. "You want someone besides Rocket to come with you?"

Celia shook her head, aware that her face reddened when Hazel whistled for the yellow dog. *A babysitter,* she thought, but almost smiled when the retriever approached, his thick tail wagging.

"Now get outside. I don't care where you go, just work those skinny legs of yours for a while. Walk and breathe, girl. Fill those lungs. You keep moving under that big blue ceiling for at least an hour, you hear me?" She strapped an old Timex to Celia's wrist and handed her a water bottle. "And drink."

An hour and ten minutes elapsed before Rocket lapped from a bucket under a spigot and collapsed in the barn's shade. Flory, giggling, met Celia as she crossed the barnyard. "She must have threatened you, too."

Celia pinched her shirt at her sternum and pumped the fabric, fanning. Sweat dripped from her chin as Flory sidled up to her and hugged her waist.

Celia lifted an arm and sniffed. "I'm stinky."

"Good to sweat it out. Your shower will feel nothing short of amazing, eh?"

Flory emptied Celia's water bottle and refilled it in the faucet's cool flow. "When I lost Candy, it took a month before Hazel could drag me out of bed. I didn't know I could smell that bad. I think the grief seeped out through my pores, and it was rank, I tell ya."

"Yeah. I guess," Celia said. She had no doubt that Flory understood the pain of losing a child. But Flory didn't jeopardize her baby, didn't *cause* the death, like Celia did. And Flory had borne three live children—two after her baby died. She was still a *mother*, which Celia would never be. Flory had emerged from a tunnel that Celia, given her marriage and her family baggage, would likely travel for the rest of her life.

"Things will get better," Flory said. "I know you don't trust that yet, so let us believe it on your behalf. Hazel and Satch did that for me. We'll be here for you. Pray you through it. You're going to be okay."

The next morning, drill sergeant Hazel appeared at the bedroom door at eight. Celia moaned but sat up, grateful for this alter ego of her previously funny, flexible grandmother. After all, intellectual and athletic training had filled the bulk of Celia's educational years, and she'd thrived under the discipline. Flory had promised that Celia's optimism—her *hope*—could return with similar self-care.

Fair enough. She'd place her mind on a shelf and go through the motions Hazel and Flory prescribed. They could bust their guts trying to rescript her feelings as long as she didn't have to pretend they were succeeding. Anything was better than lying in that bed, hating everything.

"Go now, while it's cooler, and you can step up the pace. I'll have breakfast when you get back and I expect you to clean the plate, missy."

On day six of her new walking regimen, Celia awoke at 7:30 a.m. from a rapturous dream about running, in which her feet lifted her into treetops and clouds. Fresh from the flying, she beelined for her dresser and dug for the only running gear she'd brought from Pullman. She answered Hazel's knock dressed in a fluorescent green tank and neon orange shorts.

"Stars! You're brighter'n a lighthouse," Hazel said.

"So you can find me in the ditch when my legs give out—if I even remember how to run."

"Oh, with your history, I 'spect it'll be like ridin' a bike, honey. Burnaby said you ran marathons a few years back? Twenty-six miles?"

"Only two. Halves were more my style. Thirteen miles and change."

"Well. If that bug bites you, I probably should know where to look in case you twist an ankle. You have a route planned?"

"East on Old Hollow, then south, if I get that far. Don't worry, Nolly. If I make it a couple of miles today, I'll be happy." *Happy?* When did she last use that word?

Gravel crunched with every footfall as her first sweet dream in months propelled her onto Old Hollow. Scattered cumulus clouds and the trees in roadside draws—locusts, willows, hawthorns—matched the fleeting images she'd dreamt about and the feelings they evoked: buoyancy, anticipation. Her breath quickened until she linked its rhythm to her pace—a nine-minute mile, she figured.

Though slow by her usual standard, moving her body and pushing herself faster than the previous days' strolls got her blood flowing and her lungs working harder. She responded mentally. Her brain fog, which had been thinning since Hazel got her outside, dissolved into the green-gold wheat that rode the hills around her. She gulped lungfuls of the morning air, each inhale plump with the scents of ripening grain, creek-side cottonwoods and willows, and wild roses on the steep, unfarmable strips of land Hazel called eyebrows.

The scratched face of Joss's old Timex said she'd been running for twenty minutes when the road forked, and she turned south on

Earmark Road. Beyond it, the gravel climbed abruptly through a notch in a fallow hillside.

Celia puffed as she jogged uphill, slowed to a walk, then urged herself back into a trot. Long dormant, the competitive nature that had impelled her over far higher hurdles than this brief climb barked orders. *C'mon, girl. Step on the shovel. Dig for gold.* She welcomed the old friend, who sounded a lot like her daddy.

And she caught sight of the steely resolve her childhood peers called spunk.

More like *independence*, she thought—and she wanted it back, wanted to shed the desolation and the conflict and the grim memories of the past few months and move forward into something new and better, in a life without all that heartache.

If that meant shedding Burnaby, too, so be it.

At the next turn, she danced sideways as a pair of adult quail burst from the grassy shoulder, leaning into black feather topknots that bobbed like commas over stubby beaks. Their crowd of chicks scurried across the road behind them and vanished into a stand of tansy.

All those kids, she thought. *Ten, at least. I can't even keep one alive.* "No!" she cried aloud. *No more self-pity.* If she couldn't carry a child, well . . . life would be a lot easier.

Sprinting, she left the birds behind her, then slowed and jogged another five minutes. Seven. Until the roofs of farm sheds and galvanized silos showed above the topline of a hill. *I'll turn around there,* she thought, and checked her watch again. She'd run outbound over three miles, give or take—farther than she'd expected. Sweat flowed at her hairline and formed glossy islands on her exposed skin. The sun hung like a yellow coal, hot and thriving. She'd forgotten water.

When the farmhouse and outbuildings came into view, she dropped into a walk and wiped her face with her shirt. She raised arms overhead as if at a finish line and ogled the manicured spread to her right. On both sides of an asphalt driveway, wide white plank fences enclosed two spacious fields. She appraised the one closest to her. *Horse hay. Timothy, second crop, most likely.* In the other, two tall, stocky horses—one white, the other, bay—grazed in a close-cropped, weedless pasture.

The fence stretched around the yard too, separating large, tidy farm buildings from the verdant lawn. A dozen trees—mostly tough-leafed sycamores—shaded a beefy picnic table and an impeccable brick ranch house, hip-roofed and landscaped with junipers and sheared boxwoods. Mounding and drooping from a slatted pergola, a robust, thick-limbed wisteria sheltered wooden lawn chairs. Behind the house, under a lone maple, a white cabin crouched shabby, its neglected state a sharp contrast to the meticulous home and grounds.

She smacked her sticky tongue against the roof of her mouth and returned her gaze to the horse pasture, eyeing the animals' water trough at the field's far end. Only then did she spot the man standing at the mailbox fifty yards away, his back to her, his head tipped toward an open newspaper.

Hazel's neighbor? She bet their land touched somewhere out there. She also bet he would share a spigot before she headed back.

The man folded the pages, raised his head, and noticed her. Twisting the paper into a tube, he tapped it absently against his thigh while she closed the distance between them. She caught the hand-painted inscription on the mailbox—*ZENDER, 995 Earmark*—and eyed him more intently. No denying the likeness. A seasoned version of Ivan was smiling at her. A dead ringer for the younger man.

"You're a glutton for punishment," he said. "Last I checked, the mercury read eighty-two, and that was an hour ago." A dimple edged his smile. Disarming.

Celia smiled back, then swung her gaze when a horse squealed and the animals bolted, tails high. She watched until they resumed grazing. "Flies?" she asked.

"I expect so."

When she turned back to the farmer, *he* was studying *her*. He quickly dropped his gaze to the ground, then returned kind eyes to hers. "My apologies. Not every day a beautiful woman shows up at my mailbox."

When had any man last called her beautiful? "Compliment accepted," she said. "If I can trouble you for some water, I'll be on my way."

"You bet," he said. "I wouldn't recommend that trough, though. Pond water." He raised an elbow toward the house. "I've got ice up there." He wore a loose-fitting shirt and jeans, but his muscled forearms and neck told what those clothes hid. Appreciation rushed her.

She folded hands over her hot scalp. If only she'd worn a cap. "Thanks, but it's the liquid I'm after. Its temp is irrelevant."

He tugged an ear. "Fair enough. But I don't carry a canteen to the mailbox."

She gauged the distance to his house, knowing she'd follow this stranger to his door. Her California colleagues would gawk at the risk, call her reckless. But out here? Neighbors waved from pickups and tractors. Farmsteads and families seemed to *belong*, anchored to the land and with an unspoken—even nosy—accountability to each other.

Besides, strong as he looked, he had a good ten years on her. She was pretty sure she could outrun him. "Zender?"

"Yes. Sorry. Out of practice. Been alone too long." He laid his hand over his heart as if pledging the flag. "Oren Zender."

"You've *got* to be related to Ivan. Ruth Milk's boyfriend?"

His gray eyes sharpened. *Yes, fifty-ish.* And undeniably attractive.

"I'm his father." His brow squatted, then rose with recognition. "Hazel's granddaughter?"

Celia laughed. "Yessir. I'm Celia. I met Ivan at Sunday dinner."

"Ivan mentioned you, but he didn't tell me you were so . . ." Still facing her, he walked backwards toward the house. "Let's get you some water."

I'm so . . . what? she wondered. She followed, willing him to continue talking, unable to see herself anymore. "Ivan lives here, right? Doesn't sound like you're alone to me." She was fishing—and knew it. Knew she shouldn't be. *Wouldn't.* She'd stop at the yard, drink her water, and head home.

Oren turned and fell into step beside her. "But his mother doesn't. She preferred greener pastures."

Celia scanned the expansive, shady lawn, fertilized to a deep emerald. "Hard to picture anywhere greener than this. What a park." A masculine park. Not a feminine touch in sight.

He tipped his head toward the door. "It's air-conditioned in there. You look like you could use it."

"Right here's fine, thanks." She tapped the ground with her toe, imagining ice and resisting his attraction. *Best to gulp that water and skedaddle.* But when his canted eyebrows asked, and his open hand offered, she slipped into the pergola's shade and sank into a cushioned teak lawn chair.

"Be right back," he said. He returned with two glasses of ice water, handed her one, and lowered himself into the chair beside her. He sipped, lowered his glass, and watched her gulp, catch her breath, and drink more. His eyes flicked over her left hand, void of rings.

The attention fueled her.

"Ivan, the neighbors, myself—we're all glad you're here," he said. "Not good for Hazel to be alone, running that big place by herself. After Joss got that ALS diagnosis, I told him I'd look after her, help her keep the farm going when he was gone. Gotta say, she's not making it easy. I've been a friend of the family for decades, but since Joss passed, she's been reluctant to accept any help." He took a long drink of water this time, the apple in his throat rising with each swallow. "It'll be good to have you there with her, Celia. You planning to stick around?"

"I'm not sure. She's asked me to stay, but I have a few things to work out first."

"It's no picnic running a farm that size. Or any farm in this economy. Even if you know what you're doing."

"Yeah. I won't be much use to her, though. I don't know the first thing about farming."

"Doesn't hurt to pay attention. Satchel can't do everything." Oren swirled his water and drank, then crunched the ice cube distending his cheek.

"I want to get to know her. We only just met."

"So I heard." He shifted into a slat of shade, closer to Celia. "If I can help by adding a little history, or by showing you around, I'm happy to. I try to stop by her farm once a week at least." He raised his glass. "Speak of the devil."

A trail of dust meandered after her grandmother's green Crown Victoria, crawling up Earmark.

Celia tapped the face of her watch. "Oh man. I've been gone too long." She drained her glass and jumped up. "Thanks, Oren. I may take you up on that." Fingers to teeth, she whistled, waved, and ran toward the road. The car jerked to a stop at the mailbox and she leapt inside.

"I'm mighty thankful for that beacon fabric you're wearin'." Hazel patted Celia's knee and backed into Oren's driveway to turn around. "Easier to check ditches, knowing you were in that get-up."

"Sorry, Hazel. I worried you. Met your neighbor, though."

"I figured as much." Hazel swerved past a pothole, tight-lipped.

"He sure looks like Ivan."

"Sure does."

Celia smiled inwardly. Understandable, Hazel's coolness toward the man. Her grandmother's resolve to stay independent probably required it. *More power to her.* No need to bother her when Oren stopped by. Celia would be more than happy to intercept him.

19

CELIA

RIVER

PALOUSE GRAIN RIPENED as summer progressed, in a bumper tribute to the region's friable soil, water from heaven, and farmers who trusted enough to plant. As wheat heads swelled, the crew at Steffen Farms emptied and cleaned grain from galvanized storage bins, serviced machinery, and filled water and fuel tanks. Satchel and hired man Hugh checked and rechecked combines and headers, tractors and wagons and trucks.

True to his word, Oren swung by the farm almost daily, helping Satch and Hugh where he could. Celia watched for him, caving to her legs' volition when they carried her to the porch or barnyard or machine shed. To where their paths would intersect, and she'd go schoolgirl tongue-tied, her wit gone AWOL.

He showed up until the languid last days of July, when readiness left the Steffen crew little to do and his own farm's harvest preparations demanded his attention. Instead, while Satch and Hugh tested moisture in wheat samples, jabbed thumbnails into hardening kernels, analyzed weather forecasts, and waited to harvest Hazel's 3,500 acres, Oren and Celia bumped into each other elsewhere.

This day, Celia knew which lonely road to run. Breathing to the rhythm of her strides, she inhaled the scent of ripe grain and raised a wrist to check her pace. Dirt puffed around her running shoes like bath powder. The dawn air promised heat.

From behind the next hill, a cloud of tire-stirred silt rose and tumbled toward her like fog. *Where there's smoke . . .* she thought, smiling, and followed the road's curve toward the dust.

A memory interfered: A glimpse of a winter fire—maple and locust. Their woodstove. Hers and Burnaby's. She snapped her head, dismissive, as a white Chevy pickup towed banners of dust around the hill. Oren pulled over, lowered his window, and leaned on an elbow. A half-smile tipped his mouth.

She stood in the shade of his cab, awkward again. "Got a harvest forecast?" she asked, aware that she cocked a hip. "Moisture reading?"

He squinted at a far field. Ticked his head. "This time tomorrow I'll be in a combine, right out there."

Telling me not to expect him. She studied his profile until he turned to her, caught her gaze and held it, searching her eyes until she looked away, rationing him. Boulder-colored eyes. Mica-flecked. More than she could bear. Thirsty, she caught her breath and returned for another sip. She'd begged Burnaby to look at her like this.

Oren shifted his gaze back to the field and to the propriety of their early hellos. Finally, he tapped his hat with a forefinger and drove on. She watched him go, braiding the thread of their conversation about, oh, nothing, really, into a belt she'd wear. They'd talked for twenty minutes this time.

That afternoon, Celia watched from the porch as Burnaby's blue pickup left the house and turned onto Old Hollow, just as it had every day for weeks. Since Burn's first visit to her grandmother, he'd arrived precisely at noon to ring the bell and sit in the kitchen with Hazel—or on the porch for thirty minutes alone—before he left sprays of cinquefoil or daisies or asters for Celia inside the screen door.

Now that she felt better, she sometimes, dutifully, joined him, though at first they seldom spoke. Lately, talk of farming or birds punctuated their silences. And she described Willie, Cobb, Ruth. Today, he'd talked about horses, and his surgeries—repairs of pastern, olecranon, and cannon bones. "I planted your garden," he told her. "For when you come home." Neither mentioned the stones lodged in their hearts since May, whether they wanted to excavate them, or how.

I'm done with all that, she told herself as he drove away. *Done with this impossible man.* She chastened herself for sitting on that porch with him, for leading him on. Blurring the replay loop of their conversation, she refused to consider him. Planned her goodbye. Fell asleep certain. Welcomed Oren to invade her thoughts.

At midnight she awoke weeping, drenched in sweat. And doubt.

The next day Celia dropped her feet from the coffee table to the floor and turned an open photo album to her grandmother. "So you've never farmed that prairie, Nolly?"

Hazel looked up from a newspaper and squinted at the snapshots. "No Steffen would dare put that ground to the plow. They kept cattle off of it, too. Plenty of years Joss was tempted to break it out, but his granddad set it aside. Went to his grave insisting the family leave it that way."

Celia turned a page. "It's like a beautiful mirage."

"Darn tootin', sweet pea. Only it's real as rhubarb. Folks from the local tribes sure liked it. That prairie was a rest stop on one of their ancestral routes down to the Snake. Some years their great-grandkids still camp along the creek."

"How big is it?"

"Three hundred eighty-seven acres. Virgin meadow, mostly. Plus that piney ground on the slopes."

"Whoa."

"I'll say. Finer land than frog hair split twice. Plants and animals you'll never see on our cultivated ground. Ever hear of Piper's milkvetch?"

Celia shook her head.

"You'll see it. And the *birds*. Like returning to Eden." Hazel tapped an old photo. "Joss's granddad watched most of the Palouse Prairie get plowed under—ninety percent of it by 1900. Just a smidgen's left now, most in small parcels here and there and on land too steep or rocky to plow. Fortunately, he had the foresight—and the heart—to set that ground apart."

"Some people would kill for land like that."

"There's been lots of interest through the years, for a variety of reasons. University people have wanted to study the area for some time, but Joss even denied them. Didn't trust anybody when it came to that property. He was downright fierce about it—and our privacy. If he'd answered the phone when your Tara called, you'd never have seen your Hawk Five." Her lips flattened. "Another arena in which Joss's and my opinions differed. For the sake of preservation, I've been chewing on WSU's interest."

"When can we go?"

Hazel folded the newspaper and stared at her. "I believe that's the first request you've made since you've been here, honey. Good to see you resuscitating." She rolled her lip, thinking. "After harvest will be soon enough. No time right now. If this heat holds, the crew's looking at mighty long days. We'll be feeding those workers."

"We?" Celia fought the urge to retreat upstairs.

Hazel stood—and considered her for a solid three seconds. "Flory, Ruth, me . . . and you, if you're willing. We could use the help."

Celia spotted Burnaby through the window, arrived for his daily visit. She closed the photo album, set it on the stairs, and met Hazel exiting the kitchen with a platter of sandwiches.

"Those aren't all for Burn."

"I bet the boys at the shop are hungry, too."

Celia smiled. "As if those *boys* don't bring their own lunches? Here. Give me those. I'll pass them out."

Burnaby raised his hands when she nearly collided with him at the door. The closest she'd been to him since May. He held wild roses. Her favorite, from a happier time.

"Oh, Burn." Her sleepless night—and those roses—cracked her. She leaned over the sandwich tray, smelled the flowers, and cast a quick glance at him. But why bother? Long experience told her any connection in those moss-green eyes came rarely or not at all. She'd known that when she married him, back when she thought their differences wouldn't matter.

Unlike Oren's eyes. She brushed past him. "C'mon. Let's go see Hugh."

At the machine shed doorway, Hazel's retriever sniffed the air and wagged.

"Rocket, move!" An overnourished young man snapped fingers black with grease and pointed to a straw-lined box at the end of the workbench. The dog trotted to his bed, circled once, and plopped.

"Hey, Hugh."

"Hellooooo, Celia!" The mechanic raised his dirty hands, palms out. Laughter shook his double chin as he zeroed in on Burnaby. "I'm Hugh Eldon, jack-of-all-trades, including the twins' T-ball coach. Be glad I'm not shaking your hand."

Burnaby smiled. "I am."

"Meet Burnaby . . . my . . . husband," Celia said. "And Hazel sent *food*. Satch around?"

"He drove the twins to town." Hugh set folding chairs in the building's shade and they passed the platter. Hugh raised a sandwich. "Cheers. After this, I'm outta here for the day." A quarter section of tuna on rye disappeared in one bite, and Celia watched bread roll in his open mouth. "I'm meeting Ivan and Ruth at the river. Our last afternoon on the water for a while. Satch says we'll start tomorrow. Cut the north fields first."

"You driving a combine?" Celia asked.

"Yeah. Satch, too. Ivan's in the bankout wagon. Neighbors drive the trucks. High school and college kids, usually."

"Bankout wagon?"

Hugh pointed to a tractor-like vehicle with rubber tracks instead of wheels. Behind the cab, an auger protruded from a slope-sided hopper like a milkshake straw. "Grain hauler. Follows the combine."

"Does Satch take passengers in that combine?" she surprised herself by asking.

"Absolutely. When Ivan and I were in high school, we rode with him for days while he taught us the ropes."

See the prairie. Ride the wheat mower. And yes, she would cook. Her *want to* was expanding.

"You two oughta come with us today. To the river, I mean. If you don't wanna ski, we have a skiff you can putz around in." He looked back and forth between them. "Ever been to Boyer Park? My parents run the marina there."

"Skiing," Celia whispered. Burnaby scanned the hills between them and the Snake, their geography hazy in the heat. Burn didn't swim and didn't like small boats, but if the invitation worried him, his face didn't say so. *As if it would.*

Rocket wandered outside, wolfed a chunk of sandwich from Hugh, then lapped water under the spigot. *That sound.* Celia thought of water slapping the underside of a boat and of the scent of lakes in her childhood. She hadn't stepped foot on a boat since she and Burn married and hadn't skied since college. A sweat bead dripped between her breasts and another *want to* squeezed through her resistance.

"We'd love that, Hugh," Celia said. "Can we hitch a ride?" The river might do Burn some good, too, poor guy.

The two-lane highway to Almota whipped into the Snake River breaks like a tail of the serpent river itself. The three of them leaned into hairpin turns as Hugh drove his pickup like a centrifuge, spinning them down the steep grade to a stop sign at the water's brink. To their right, the Almota elevator stood ready for the new season's crop, its massive grain bins dwarfed both behind it and cross-river by slopes that defied perception of scale. Angus cattle grazed the massive north-facing breaks like fleas, oblivious to the dizzying plunge to the blue river below them. Ravines and canyons stretched and forked like gold antlers, their velvet rubbed by towers of basalt.

Hugh turned left and followed the road to Boyer Park, where Ruth and Ivan waited on the lawn in a sycamore's shade, surrounded by water ski equipment and catching mist from a nearby sprinkler. Beyond them, tents and RVs hunkered in the treed oasis, sheltered from the wiggly waves of parking lot heat.

"Must be twenty degrees hotter down here," Ruth said.

"You say that every time," Hugh laughed. "You're right, though. Ninety-eight on my truck thermo." He eyed Burnaby's jeans. "You're gonna cook down here, man. I've got extra shorts in my truck, but . . ." He gripped his ample belly through his tank top. "They'll fall offa you."

"Not your concern, Hugh. I don't plan to swim." Burnaby pulled his shirt off the body Celia had forgotten she loved. Off his *pale* body. Without sunscreen he'd fry. For a decade, she'd cared for his skin as if it were her own. She hesitated, then reached in her bag. She couldn't abandon it now.

"Here, Burn." She dug out a tube and waved him toward her, then slathered cream down the tense arms and back she'd long ago memorized. She braced her jelly legs as she smeared the lotion over chest muscles she knew by heart. Hands at his sides with his lids closed, he flinched when she spread sunscreen on his back and arms, the ridges of his lean stomach. His nose and cheeks, forehead and ears. His lips.

"There you go." She capped the container and walked toward the river before anyone could see her eyes well. If only he had reached for her.

At the dock, Ruth handed skis, life jackets, and the tow rope to Ivan, untied lines from cleats, then held the boat's bumper. Ivan cranked the motor into a rumbly idle.

"Best if we take turns," Hugh said. "The engine will bog if all of us go."

"I'll stay," Burnaby said. Celia followed his sight line to a pair of ospreys soaring midriver. She wished she knew what he was thinking. Before, when they were together, she would have asked, then wound his answer into the braid of their unusual life together.

For a moment she absorbed the image of him there on the dock. While sunlit air glistened with threads of airborne spider silk and swallows darted overhead to their own music, she remembered him as he was before their baby died. Her beautiful Burnaby, with his sparkling mind and his own foreign language of love. How could he speak anything but duty to her now? She knew he would honor their marriage, but would he ever love her again? How could he?

Gurgle from the boat's exhaust pipes drew her back. Ivan coiled the tow line beside a glossy O'Brien slalom ski.

"You comin', Celia?" Ruth asked.

Celia almost stayed behind with Burnaby. Almost. After all, her swimsuit was still in Pullman, in that drawer she hadn't returned to since her hurried departure. She hadn't worn it since her pregnancy, since before her hike to Hawk Five.

In an instant, the memory shanghaied her. Slammed her. Her yearning for reconciliation with Burn lurched and reversed direction.

She turned away from him, climbed into the boat, and zipped a life jacket over her tank top and shorts. She rubbed the skin where her ring should be, then shook her head against despair. "Care if I ski first?" Either that or collapse in a heap on the deck.

Gentle, funny Hugh seemed to read her. "That glassy river is begging you to crack it," he said. "You don't need us big boys worrying that engine." He threw an arm up and over Burnaby, who practically ossified at contact. "Ever fished for sturgeon, bro?" He pushed the boat from the dock and waved the skiers out toward smooth water.

The wake curled behind the ski boat like a lace ribbon as Celia's water skills returned to her. Though she didn't try any of the fancy stunts she'd perfected as a teen, she thumbed Ivan for more speed and found a rhythm of jumps and leans that shredded her gloom—for now, at least. Sunlight and hot wind kissed her, made her hungry. She considered a third loop, until she thought of Ruth, eager for her turn. Reluctantly, Celia tossed the line in the air, sank to her neck, and treaded until the boat circled back to her. Her foot found a transom rung, and she hoisted herself aboard.

"I wanna jump like that," Ruth said, and she leapt into the water, grabbed the floating ski, and fumbled to adjust it. She crouched, her ski tip upright, the line stretching with the boat's advance. Three attempts later, the girl rose wobbling into the wake, then caught an edge and veered sideways in a clumsy collapse.

"Skier down," Celia called to Ivan and thrust a flag into the air. Without looking back, he sped up and cranked the wheel hard right, unaware that instead of a free towline, its handles bobbling across the water's surface, he dragged open-mouthed Ruth by an arm entangled in the rope.

Celia yelled over the engine. "She's caught!"

Ivan jerked the throttle to neutral. Ruth screamed from the water.

"Take it," he barked to Celia, before he leapt to the gunwale and dove.

"Ow ow ow ow, Ivan!" Ruth cried. Ivan fumbled to free her hand as they drifted downriver. Celia steered the boat near.

She raised her sunglasses and squinted at the pair, both swimming now. She snagged the ski Ivan shot her way and imported the rope, fast.

"Caught her ring," Ivan shouted. Grim, he helped Ruth aboard. The girl shook her hand, prancing with pain. "Settle down now, Ruth," he said. "I know it hurts, but if you want to keep that finger, we've got to get to shore and get that thing off of you."

Ruth wailed louder but dropped to a seat.

"Let me see, Ruthie." The girl winced as Celia grasped her wrist and inspected a discolored index finger, already swelling around a crushed gold ring.

20

FISHERMAN

"I DON'T SWIM," Burnaby said.

Hugh settled a pole into a rod holder and grinned. "No sweat, bro. That's what we got these for." He tossed Burnaby a life vest and zipped himself into one before he seated the second pole and opened a tackle box in the boat's stern. "I bet you tie knots, though, Doc."

"I do. Snell, blood, Palomar, clinch, uni. Cushing, square, strangle, Miller's. I believe I—I can tie every recognized configuration." Superfluous information, but the knots kept Burnaby's mind off the water depth out there in the river, where only principles of buoyancy stood between him and the bottom.

"Then we're in business," Hugh said. He thumped Burnaby's knee, his smile warm. "I like the Palomar knot for braided Dacron on eight-aught circle hooks." He pinched a large fishhook and twisted the shaft between two fingers. "Barbless. Don't want to hurt 'em."

Burnaby pressed a hand to the spasm in his cheek. Hugh cut

leaders and chose weights and beads from the tackle box for himself and Burnaby, who walled off his anxiety by tying Palomar and uni knots. Lots of them.

His twitches had calmed by the time Hugh flipped the choke on the nine-horse outboard and jerked the pull cord. When the engine putted to life, Hugh twisted the tiller handle's throttle and steered them cross-river to the cliffs. "A nice deep trench under us," he said. "Sturgeons dig it."

Their rods still stood in pole holders when a scream erupted from the water and bounced off the rock face behind them. Hugh rose to a wide-legged crouch as they tracked a man's dive, a dark-haired woman's leap to the driver's seat in a bobbing boat midriver.

"Celia," Burnaby said. "I don't see Ruth."

"Ivan's got her." Hugh flipped the tackle box closed, cranked the throttle, and steered toward the skiers. They were within fifty yards when Ivan helped Ruth up the ladder. He and Celia bent over Ruth's hand.

Celia spotted the fishing boat and scrambled to the gunwale. Her hands cupped like a megaphone. "Pliers! You got any pliers?"

"Yeah! Comin' right up!" Hugh motored parallel to the ski boat, disengaged the engine, and dug through tools. He lifted pliers in each hand. "Needle-nose. Flat-nose."

Ruth whimpered from her seat. Held her hand like a pup with an injured paw.

"Her ring's smashed, Burn," Celia said. "Cutting off her circulation. Swelling fast."

From the skiff, Burnaby squinted at Ruth's plummy finger. "I see that. Hugh, get me closer."

Ivan dropped two bumpers between the boats, tossed Hugh a line, and pulled. When the bumpers squeaked, Burnaby stared into the gap between the crafts, filled his lungs, and swung one then the other leg into the ski boat. The boats rolled with the shifting weight, then leveled in the current's flat, slow twist.

"Here," Burnaby said. Ruth, her face screwed with pain, eased her hand into his. He assessed the finger. "Flat-nose pliers." Celia snatched them from Hugh and planted the instrument in Burnaby's other hand. As soon as she did, the deck of that twenty-foot ski boat morphed into his surgery, Ruth's purple finger became the digit he would save with a simple procedure, and the dark water beneath him blurred into nothing. Nothing at all.

Hugh tied the boats together and joined the huddle watching Burnaby, who bent the crushed ring from a tight ellipse to the semblance of a circle—without evoking so much as a squeak from Ruth.

"I'd never a guessed *that* from those garden-hose fingers a yours," Hugh said. "'Cept for how you tie hooks. You could handle humming-birds for a living, ya know? Tiniest—"

Burnaby interrupted Hugh's irrelevant chatter. "Two feet of that braid leader. And a large fishhook. Stat." He heard his voice revert—as it always did when he entered this realm. Clipped, robotic. He'd worked hard to temper his tone for social interactions, but doing so took time and concentration inappropriate for emergent medical procedures.

Hugh clambered to the tackle box and hefted it to Celia, then snipped the requested fishing line and dangled it in Burnaby's periph-eral vision. Celia held the fishhook.

"That thing's sharp," Ruth whined and pulled back.

Burnaby held firm. "Skin's intact and I see no evidence of a break, so I'll suppress the edema and remove the ring. If we wait, and swell-ing buries the metal in her tissue, she will require more significant intervention. Ivan: Window cleaner. Or sunscreen. Oil. Some kind of lubricant."

Burnaby held the fishhook's shank, ran the leader through the eye, and eased the threaded metal between the damaged ring and Ruth's finger. He pulled the hook free, passed it to Celia, and pressed the line—now stretched under the ring—against Ruth's palm with his thumb.

Beginning at the ring, Burnaby coiled the leader in tight loops over her ballooning knuckle. The tissue compressed. Ivan dug Windex from a cubby and sprayed the finger's length.

"Easy now, Ruth. This may hurt." Burnaby pinched the Dacron tail crossing her palm and slowly unwound it toward the tip of her finger. Without a hitch, the spiraling line caught and carried the band over her knuckle. When the ring rolled into Burnaby's hand, applause erupted from Celia and Hugh. Ivan puffed his cheeks and exhaled.

"Good as new?" Ruth spread her fingers as Burnaby palpated tendons and bones.

"I expect so, once the trauma dissipates." Burnaby's eyes roved to the cooler. "Any ice in there?"

Ivan pulled a half-thawed gel pack from the Igloo chest and hucked it on the lid, harder than necessary.

Ruth laid her hand on the pack. "Somebody's tail's in a knot," she said.

At the fringe of his vision, Burnaby caught Celia observing him— her head tilted, lips parted. Above her, the sky dripped a persimmon color of their better days.

21

CELIA

COUPLES

"IF YOU'D STILL like to ski, Ivan, I can drive. Ruthie, do you feel well enough to spot?" Celia's attempts to salvage the afternoon fell on deaf ears.

"Are you kidding? I'm done." Ivan's brow furrowed. He jerked lines from their cleats, disconnecting the tethered boats, and flipped the bumpers to the deck.

Watching Ivan, Ruth slid toward the gunwale and wagged her head slowly. Hugh went quiet and held the skiff for Burnaby, then climbed in after him. Engines revved, and both boats motored toward the marina. Minutes later, they all trickled from the dock to the sweltering parking lot, their arms burdened with gear.

A scowling Ivan started his Blazer and cranked the air conditioner, then loaded duffel and cooler, life vests and the skis into the cargo hatch. He stomped back to his door and slammed himself inside.

Ruth sidled up to Celia. "Ride with us?"

Was Ruth frightened? Sure, Celia had sat near Ivan at Sunday dinners, had seen him come and go from the Milks' home, and now had ridden alongside him in a noisy ski boat. In every interaction Celia had witnessed, taciturn Ivan deferred to Ruth, gave her the stage in her lively family interactions. But with no memory of a one-on-one conversation with the man, Celia realized she'd been too foggy, too self-absorbed to get to know him. She had no inkling of how this conflict would land on Ruth inside that rig of his.

She knocked on the truck window, and Burnaby lowered the glass. Cool air poured from the interior where he and Hugh waited for her. "I'm riding with Ruth," she said. At Hugh's thumbs-up, Burnaby stared through the windshield, unblinking.

"See you in a few?" She searched Burnaby's profile, but when he didn't turn to her, she slapped the truck's door panel, returned to Ivan's SUV, and crawled into the back seat.

The Blazer was climbing the grade behind Hugh's pickup before Ivan squeezed the wheel, then thumped it. Celia tensed, ready to intervene—until Ivan's voice swelled, not with anger, but with concern.

"What were you thinking, Ruth? You forget what happened to Lamar? You could have torn that finger right off. Ropes and jewelry . . ." He shook his head—disgusted, Celia thought. "How many times have we . . . You *know* better."

Ruth looked out the window and into her lap, then at red-faced Ivan.

"When you screamed . . . Oh, Ruth. If something more serious had happened to you . . ." He palmed her head gently. Ran his thumb on her temple.

"I'm sorry," she whispered.

"If Burnaby hadn't been there . . . don't you *realize*?"

Ruth stretched her seat belt and leaned to kiss Ivan's ear. "I better thank him."

So much for running interference. Sixteen and nineteen years old, this couple, and they could teach her and Burn a thing or two.

Ruth twisted toward her. "I wanted to ask you, Celia . . ." She looked at Ivan. "Well, *we* wanted to ask you . . . Mom and Dad's twentieth anniversary's on September seventeenth. Want to help us plan a party?" She giggled. "A *surprise?*"

Celia laughed. Ruth had wanted her with them in the Blazer as a co-conspirator—not a referee. Anticipation buoyed her but surrendered within seconds to her Eeyore side. *Twenty years?* What would it take for her and Burn to reach that milestone? Even if they did, who would plan their party? *Without kids . . .* No. She wouldn't go there. Self-pity would land her back in bed.

"Nothing would please me more," she said.

Dust from the departing vehicles hung in the air as Celia and Burnaby walked to the house. Celia's arms folded over her bag, its canvas damp with used towels.

"You're making me crazy, you know that?" Celia said.

He stuffed hands in his pockets.

"There. Like that. We're actually doing something together for the first time in forever and you don't look at me or answer me . . ." She stopped in the lane and turned to him. "You know what, Burn? On their next anniversary, Satch and Flory will have been married twenty years. *Twenty.* If we could be like them, I'd want to celebrate twenty years too."

"We've only been married for ten. Next week, eleven."

She dropped her bag in the gravel, grabbed her hair with both hands, and pulled. "Argh! Exactly. Pretty big 'if.' You act as if I'm a fishing buddy, or a tech in your surgery. Some old-fashioned affection would go a long way right now, Burnaby. I hoped Kemp would give you a little pep talk in those Oxford hills. Bring you up to speed." She was ranting now but couldn't stop. "Maybe even renew your husband license."

Burnaby's shoulders hunched, as if against rain. She looked at him, waiting.

"I'm listening," he said. "I'll speak when you're finished."

"Finished? *Finished?* I'll never be finished." She scooped her things from the ground and marched off, but Burnaby snagged her arm.

"This is progress, Celia. Good progress."

"So, more data for your Celia study, huh?" She knew she was being petty, picking this fight, off-sourcing her blame and frustration and guilt.

"What study?"

"C'mon, Burn. All your brainpower, and you play the dense card?"

"Let's summarize events since you arrived at the hospital."

"I don't want to—"

Burnaby raised his palm, and something in his demeanor stilled her. He wasn't forcing her to listen. He didn't seem angry. This was Burnaby, who, even when she rarely had energy to string two sentences together, even when she spewed vitriol at him, had brought her flowers every day for weeks. Had refused to retaliate. His patience alone had earned him the right to speak.

"You were unconscious when the ambulance delivered you to the emergency room. You required multiple units of blood, surgery, and bed rest consequent to your ruptured artery. Once you regained consciousness, the trauma of our—our child's death exacerbated your response to hormone fluctuations."

"Burn. You're not *Spock*. Why must you reduce *everything* to a *diagnosis?*" Maddening, his calm rationality. In their earlier years, she'd have gone for a ten-mile run . . . or thrown something. Why didn't he just say how angry he was at her?

He raised his hand again. "I, too, had a physical response, Celia— both to your precarious condition and to our daughter's death. An overwhelming one. I dealt with it poorly by—by walking out of the hospital when you needed me. Again, I'm sorry."

"After I came home? You wouldn't talk to me." Not like Ivan and Ruth talked. She wanted that kind of talk.

He brushed dust from her bag. "May I ask you to reevaluate? As I recall, you have played a significant role in our limited interactions."

Oh, to outsource this nightmare. To make it his fault. But Burnaby was simply too reasonable. Too kind.

"Maybe. Some," she said.

"Good progress," he said again, and his mouth drew up at the corners. "And rapid, considering. Kemp showed me a—a prayer pounded into the earth for centuries." Her eyes closed when he touched her cheek, her every nerve alive to his fingers. "But no hurry. This is a long healing for you, Celia. For us. I can wait."

A tide of yearning arose in her, a desire to melt into him, to give herself to all the ways she missed him, all the ways she had loved him and he had loved her. But then what? Another baby she couldn't take care of? Another unburied urn? Easier to resist her longings . . . or redirect them . . . than fight with them. Or with him.

Besides, her want for his affection was futile. She'd known in their best days that unless his switch flipped, he rarely thought of physical contact with her, and her casual touch repelled him.

At first, she thought he could learn and insisted they exchange affection anyway. She'd directed his lips to her ear or neck, had asked for a caress or kiss when they passed in the kitchen, and had reached for his hand on a date. She had coaxed, then welcomed him to slide his arms around her waist. So much practice, early in their marriage, when he'd asked what she needed.

She also knew that if he had to, he could temporarily override his aversion to her fingers or lips when she touched or kissed him unexpectedly—and that he could remind himself to touch and kiss her. For her sake, for a while, he did. But his disconnect was clear. His hand didn't clasp hers in return. His back rubs mimicked his equine palpations. She had finally refused to be a duty and quit asking, resigned to the fact that they only touched when making love.

Now, compounded by what she'd done to their baby? What chance did they have?

A sigh rolled from deep in her lungs. "I can't come home, Burn. Or return to the university." The empty nursery. Her research lab.

Her detached Burnaby. All reminded her every day that she'd chosen a hawk over their child. "They're killing *me*."

He looked at his hands. "Where would you go instead?"

"I dunno. Stay here? Hazel said I'm welcome."

"What about our proximity?"

Not this again. She wanted to scream.

He cocked his head at her. "Seriously, Celia, wouldn't you rather be—be together?"

"No, Burn. I just can't." The psychic pain lodged in her muscles, her bones.

A white pickup truck pulled in. Oren stepped from the cab, his smile fresh, unencumbered. Inviting. Aimed at her. She brightened as he walked toward them. So much easier to let this man distract her. She'd known men like him in her earlier life—men who took her mind off her complicated history and her heart. Few had left her as disarmed as Oren did, though.

"Celia." He touched his brim. "I hoped you'd be here." He noticed Burnaby like an afterthought, thrust his hand Burn's direction. "Oren Zender."

Had he heard they were married?

She sensed her husband's reluctance before their handshake, expected his silence. As usual, introductions were up to her. They stood in a triangle, equidistant.

"Oren, Burnaby." Still holding towels and bag, she opened her palms like flippers, aiming as she named the men. First names only. Burn had never come up in her and Oren's conversations. Nor had her marriage, or its changing status. If Oren didn't know about Burnaby, she wasn't going to muddy things now.

Oren's chin lifted and his cheek rose, crowding an eye. *He's reading all this,* she thought. *Reading Burn.* She saw Burnaby as Oren would: sweat-stained from the river's heat, his jeans and work boots dusty—another strong worker, like the others who'd showed up in recent days seeking harvest jobs. When he clapped Burn's shoulder, her husband's jaw clenched.

"You drive semi?"

Burnaby frowned, his confusion evident. "I know how."

"You've come to the wrong farm," Oren said. "I talked to Satch this morning. His crew's full up. I'm still short a driver, though. College kid cancelled on me this morning. Chicken pox. Imagine that, twenty years old with chicken pox. You free in an hour?"

"Yes," Burnaby said.

"Meet me at the shop and I'll show you around. We start tomorrow. Take Old Hollow to Earmark. First farm on the right. You need a place to stay, nobody's claimed the cabin yet this year." He checked his watch. "If I'm to get there on time, I'd better go. Got another stop yet." He smiled at Celia, touched his cap, and was gone. Burnaby gave no hint of a reply.

Lost in translation, she thought. Straightforward Burn answered questions with facts, rarely corrected others, cared little about others' assumptions or where his answers might lead them. Solid traits, usually, but prone to misunderstandings for which she'd run interference their entire marriage. When he didn't show at the farm and left Oren short one driver . . .

"This one's on you, mister," she said as they walked to Burn's truck. For the hundredth time, she decided she'd start fresh. The only step left was to do it.

22

CELIA

WIRE

HARVEST OFFICIALLY BEGAN the following morning, when Satchel climbed a ladder to the wheelhouse of a combine the size of a small cabin. Thankful for the diversion, Celia followed him and took a seat. On the computer screen, Satch pointed to a satellite's elevation map of the surrounding hills.

"Forty-two to fifty percent slope on most of this parcel." His voice competed with the machine, now whining like a Boeing 737. "With a crop this heavy, we won't set any speed records. Two and a half miles per hour, give or take, so we'll relax and enjoy the ride."

Celia narrowed her eyes at the incline. "Relax?"

"Steep, but this cab self-levels. You won't even notice the slope. The header'll ride the ground, and our speed will adjust with the yield, as calculated by my friend here." He tapped the electronic screen.

Behind them, Hugh waited in a second combine. His voice

crackled over the radio, Satchel answered, and the massive machines crept onto the hillside in a parallel, staggered course. Engaged now, a reel at the front of the machine slapped bats of sharp-toothed tines into the wheat and drew stalks to the sickle bar. The dense crop fell and rolled into the thirty-foot header, where an auger screwed the crop into the body of the combine.

"Then what happens?" Celia leaned into the window above the header.

Satch changed screens to new readouts, this time showing grain intake and tank capacity. "An interior drum threshes the wheat, which falls into a collecting tank. Chaff and straw shoot out the rear for reintegration into the soil. An elevator empties the tank into the bankout wagon or a semi." He pointed at the grain cart fifty yards distant, its auger poised behind its bed like an alert brontosaurus. Ivan's silhouette showed in the cab.

Two loops of the hill later, the bankout pulled alongside, matching the combine's speed. Grain poured from the harvester's auger into the moving wagon until the rattling stream of kernels slowed and stopped. The bankout crossed the slope to a waiting semi, and the combines turned south, off the stubbled hillside to more ripe wheat.

Satchel's gaze swept the new field. "Look at that crop. Hazel's poised for her best year ever. The gift of rain at perfect intervals all season. Now this good heat, low humidity, great weather forecast. And the machinery's in A-plus condition. We needed this. Last year was tough."

At the pace of a rowboat, the combines passed through rolling hills of standing grain. Celia's mind roved the wheat sea to squat hawthorn trees in eyebrows of land too steep to farm and to the dry ravines and magnificent, stream-carved canyons that branched like tree limbs. Dollops of clouds drowsed overhead, their shadows sparse and lazy on golden grain that stretched to a tiered horizon of uplands.

At noon they sat in stubble, eating sandwiches in a combine's shade. Hugh closed his lunchbox, rinsed his mouth with a swig from a thermos, and played a single, bluesy riff on his harmonica. At the final note, he hoisted his portly body and spanked dirt from his jeans. His sparse goatee bobbed. "Time to go, boss. Night's coming."

"Already?" Celia said. "I could stay here forever." Overhead, a golden eagle caught an updraft in the dreamy heat. More lullaby.

"You've never worked harvest before," Satch said. "If we dally, we'll never get done." He adjusted his cap. Within minutes, both machines crawled into another amphitheater of ripe wheat. Barbed wire hung in swags from weathered fence posts at the hill's crest.

"Whose land's over there?" Celia tracked the fence until it sank past the bowl's rim.

"Belongs to Oren," Satchel said. "On two sides, his ground borders Hazel's."

She added the fence line to her spotty mental map of Hazel's property, floored by her eagerness to make sense of the terrain. How long would it take her to know the entire topography—and all those shared boundaries? And what could Satch tell her about Oren? He never talked about himself much—and she'd fought the urge to ask.

"Could there be a better neighbor?" A rhetorical question, she figured. She'd watched Oren help Satch with the most mundane tasks, day after day.

But Satch mulled his answer. "He promised Joss he'd watch over Hazel and has kept his word on that. I appreciate the extra hands around here. I truly do. And I respect how he keeps that home place of his spotless."

He hesitated. Rubbed his nose. "His farming practices leave a lot to be desired, though, and when they cause problems here, he doesn't seem to care." A sideways pucker momentarily skewed Satchel's mouth. "You'll see for yourself, Celia. He pulverizes his dirt, and it flies in dusters that bring the 1930s to mind. Whenever we get our fast thaws or big rains, his land sends rivers of mud that block Hazel's drainage and bury roads."

Celia's eyes roved as she absorbed the new information. For the first time, she noticed the deep cuts in a wheaty hillside past the fence. *Runoff. Erosion.*

"Joss was a pioneer of no-till. He proved a dozen ways and backwards that when he seeded straight into the stubble instead of plowing first, the land held more water. Oren wanted none of it, though. The two of them battled about land management for decades. Oren's stubborn. But then, so was Joss."

"Why's he so averse to no-till? Transition too expensive?"

"Who knows? Set in his ways, I guess. No-till takes some initial equipment setup, but it's worth it. We don't irrigate, so in a dry year, the improved water retention means the difference between a good harvest and a lousy one. With undisturbed wheat roots holding the soil, wind and water don't move the ground much, either. Why Oren doesn't buy the concept, or at least try it, is beyond me."

Celia wondered too, annoyed that a disregard for the land—for nature—could interrupt her interest in the appealing man. But it did. *What else would that say about him?*

And what would Burnaby think of Oren? The unexpected question shocked her. And so did the answer. Though miles away in Pullman, her husband was here, wading her thoughts, pulling rocks from the river of her mind and comparing this sandstone trait of Oren's to the jasper of her and Burn's marriage. What their marriage used to be. Could never be again. Even so, here he was, guarding her with integrity and wisdom she couldn't drum up on her own.

Satchel drove the combine high on the bowl now. Uncut wheat rose like a wall to Celia's left. On her right, stubbled ground sloped away from the machine's underbelly in a steep descent. She shifted in her seat, hoping Satch had lubed the combine's self-levelers and tightened all the screws.

"This earth's a golden goose," he said. "And Oren seems set on killing it. Either he thinks there's an endless supply of his dirt or he doesn't care if the land outlives him—though for his boys' sakes, I'd think he would."

"So Ivan has brothers?"

Satchel slowed and opened the auger to the bankout wagon at the top of the hill. "Just one. Name's Mike. A few years older than Ivan.

Moved to Arizona for college and hasn't been home for more than a week since. Wants nothing to do with the farm. He's young yet, though. May change his mind."

"How big's their farm?"

"Bigger than this one. Five thousand acres. Except that all of it—farmland, house, buildings—belongs to his ex-wife, Ingrid."

"Where did she—?"

"From her parents, God rest their souls."

"Divorced, huh?" She had figured as much.

"Legal separation. That was the only lawful structure that gave Ingrid any peace about leaving him. She's lived in town going on three years. I guess they're still officially married, but they divided assets. Now Oren leases from her."

Oren, still married? And the land he farmed was his wife's? If Celia dodged those attentive gray eyes, what other red flags would she see? She pictured Oren on Hazel's porch, leaning on the jamb, his knock-her-over smile doing exactly that, his foot and the chemistry he exuded blocking her mental door from closing on him. But why? Why didn't she slam that door and bolt it? She again thought of Burnaby, and her cheeks filled with heat.

"Must have been some drama in that house. Is that why his son's working with you, instead of his dad?"

"I asked Ivan that same question. He said we paid better and left it at that. You may have noticed that Ivan's a man of few words, but he's careful, efficient, reliable. I'm happy to employ him."

His emphasis on *employ* gave Celia pause. "None of *my* business, but are you as happy about him spending time with Ruth?" *Dogs*, she was nosy, but glad to be. Her curiosity was another old friend, back from a far country.

He raised his eyebrows. Rolled his lower lip over his upper one before he answered. "I question—"

Kck kck kck kck. The rapid clatter of metal on metal interrupted him. His hand shot to a switch and the humming machine whined to a stop. "Uh-oh. What was *that*?" He leapt from the cab and swung down the ladder. Celia's foot hit the ground just as the same sound rattled from Hugh's machine, approaching in the next swath.

"Wire!" Hugh yelled when he reached his header, and both men leaned over their respective combines' reels. Sweat circles grew at Hugh's underarms and neck as he climbed to the cab, descended with leather gloves and a toolkit, and lumbered toward them. Grim-faced, he jerked a snarled piece of barbed wire from the sickle bar and held it toward Satchel. "We're outta commission until we can replace these sections, Boss." In unison, their heads turned to the ancient fence above them.

"Deer or moose snagged that line, most likely. Dragged it into the field," Hugh said.

Satchel grunted. "More of Oren's slop. Joss was after him to get rid of those downed wires for years." He scowled and spat toward a tire. "But . . . you know . . . I checked this boundary before we planted. All lines were intact."

The men climbed to the fence and backtracked fifty feet. Seventy-five. Three strands, obscured by the uncut wheat, ran the length—all loose, but attached.

Celia caught their intent and scouted the wire in the other direction. Within twenty feet, three strands became two.

"Here!" she called.

"And here!" A hundred feet away, Hugh pointed to a whip of wire running from a crooked post into the wheat. Satchel hurried to Celia, who crouched near a foot-long spur of the rusty bottom line, still attached to the wood.

"A clean cut," she said.

The wire's shiny silver core, its edges fresh and sharp, caught the light like an accusing eye. Satchel studied the ground at the next two-strand post and pinched something from the soil. "Staple. Pulled." Three posts later, he found another, half buried at its base.

Hugh peered at the sharp, U-shaped wires in Satchel's hand. "No bull moose I've ever met carries staple pullers."

They returned to the machines. Jerked and chewed by the

combines' blades, scraps of barbed wire lay in nearby tangles. More wire snarled reel bats and sickle bars.

"That line was stretched straight, to blade height, and flattened out of sight. No animal drags wire like that. And the wind sure didn't blow it there." Satchel scanned the ground. "I don't see any tracks."

Celia waded the stalks, found the wire's far end, and dragged a length into the fence line. "No fur on this thing. Must have been a bald moose."

Neither man laughed. Hugh grunted as he yanked another rusty snag from the sickle. "We've got ourselves a real shambles here, Satch. I'm gonna hafta change out all these blades. Think they'll have full sets in town? We don't have enough for both machines at the shop."

"Hard to say. Regardless, we're down." Satch scanned the horizon. "This was no accident."

Celia pulled a barbed scrap from the sole of her boot. "Why would anyone want to hurt your machines?"

"You tell me, young lady." Satchel lifted his hat and rubbed his scalp. "Hugh, get Ivan on the radio. Have him dump that last load, send the semi to the river, and meet us at the machine shed. Drivers can haul for Zender for the rest of the day, if he still needs them, but I want those trucks back here tomorrow morning at seven thirty. Celia, you want a job?"

"What kind of job?" No office. No research. No decisions about men. She squirmed with anticipation.

"If you're willing to scout, I'll put you on the four-wheeler. Whoever did this may have other obstacles waiting for us. You can ride fence lines and check for more wires. Drive the stubble edge ahead of us and check for debris in our path. Until we know what we're dealing with here, we can't be too careful."

"Absolutely."

Worry creased Satchel's face. "Long hours for you on that little quad, but we don't have a choice. Under optimal conditions, it takes three weeks to harvest this farm, but only if we have three trucks, the bankout, and two combines running. We can't afford breakdowns. Or accidents. Sabotage changes everything."

"I'll help, Satch. Wherever you need me." She could push through fatigue. She'd done it before.

"Thanks." He tossed chunks of wire into a pile and began winding a longer strand. "Let's get this booby trap out of here."

The first day Celia rode watch, she turned left at the property corner where Zender's three neglected strands of wire met Glenn Culbert's three tight ones. Along the Culbert boundary, a bevy of pheasant hens flushed downhill through milkweed, mullein, and cheatgrass before they flew, their dowdy wings whirring. Past them, a lone pine's crown rose like a shrub from behind a far hill. *That tree.* She had marked the pine and the field wrapping it on her map, had drawn a third tiny gravestone beside her young aunties' graves. Lost in the memory, she almost missed the fourth strand of wire, buried in hawthorn and teasel, and a stub cut clean at the post.

Frantic, she snapped the walkie-talkie from her waist, flung an arm at the combines approaching the corner, and screamed into the radio. "Satch! Hugh! Another one!"

Both machines stopped abruptly. The men hurried to the ground. Celia spun the four-wheeler in a tight arc and sped back uphill to the corner, where she killed the engine. A wire snaked down a post and into thick, standing wheat.

Hugh reached the far end of the wire first. "Fresh cut," he said.

Satchel assessed the distance, hands on his hips. "Twenty posts' worth."

"What's going on?" Celia snipped the trap wire free and coiled it. Barbs bit her gloves.

"Not a clue," Satchel said. "I called around, but nobody's seen or heard anything. This farm appears to be the target, but I can't guess who stands to benefit by hurting Hazel. She couldn't have an enemy in the world. I don't believe Flory or I do, either. That leaves Hugh."

"Hugh?" Celia looked at him in disbelief. *"Hugh?"*

"Exactly. Who doesn't love *him*?"

23

INTERLOPERS

WHETHER ON THE ATV or in the wheelhouse with Satchel, Celia vowed to read that golden ocean for any sign of a threat. Hunting even the slightest disturbance in the standing crop, she raised binoculars and scanned the combines' paths as if she were a sailor shouting out waterlogged trees, half-submerged and dangerous. Tedious, yes, but a welcome relief. The required concentration deported her marriage and growing reservations about her job to an island in her mind.

Still, the long days and too many false alarms from wildlife trails through the grain added up. By the end of her first week, the yellow waves were drowning her. Saturday evening, she parked the quad at the shop, exhausted. "I'm going cross-eyed, Satch."

Hugh's feet and an air hose protruded from the rear of the combine, where he blasted dirt from the machine's underbelly.

Satch waved Celia past the noisy compressor. "What'd you say?"

"Three weeks nonstop of this? I'm willing, Satch, but I might croak in the process."

Dirt mired every wrinkle in her work boots, jeans, and shirt—and her sunburned, weary face. Satchel appraised her and laughed. "Three weeks start to finish, not three weeks *nonstop*. Tomorrow's Sunday."

"So?"

"Sunday we rest."

"What?" Glad as she was to hear that, taking a day off seemed starkly irresponsible to her. The farm's livelihood depended on getting their wheat into silos, and they were up against all kinds of odds. "What if it rains?"

Satchel raised eyebrows and a shoulder. "What if it does?"

"What if *whoever* does something awful when you're not out there?"

"What-ifs are rats in your wheelhouse, Celia."

"Seriously, Satchel. You've worked a year for this harvest. It's ready and waiting out there, someone's trying to wreck it, and you're going to put your feet up?"

"Seriously, *Celia*. Crop won't come in at all if we keel over. I ignored life's rhythm when I was younger. Learned the hard way that if our Maker wants me in a hammock for a day while he looks after a crop he grew in the first place, I'll take it."

🌿

Sunday morning, when Celia padded downstairs before the sun warmed her window ledge, she figured Satch was still snoring. Hazel, however, was not. She sat at the table, dressed and reading.

The old woman closed her book. "Well. Bright-eyed and bushy-tailed." She glanced at the clock. "And at the break of dawn, no less. You do know it's your day off."

Celia poured coffee for herself, then topped off Hazel's. "Crazy, right, being up this early? Even crazier, I was actually glad to get out of bed."

"Another sign you're on the mend." Hazel patted an adjacent chair. "And just in time for the show. All these years and I still hate to miss it." In the east window, a brilliant seam opened along the ridge and lit Hazel's profile. Her grandmother lifted her chin and bathed. "A mercy, every morning." Her hand flew to the glass. "Look there, a honey biscuit." Like baking dough, the moon bronzed with the sun's arrival. Below it, shadows soaked into the lee of hills. A hawk kited the breeze, sunrise on its red tail.

"Think that's your number five?"

"Could be." Suddenly she wanted to catch Hawk Five again, remove his tag and leg band, and release him forever.

"So many more species on the prairie," Hazel said. "I'm eager to show you the place—and see it again myself. I haven't been out there since before my Joss died."

"Do we have to wait until after harvest? What if we go right now, before the temperature ramps up?" Oh, this sunrise, her mood— Celia would preserve both as long as she could. Before she mounted that four-wheeler again and drove into the threat of more vandalism.

Hazel stood, pondering. "Well, if we leave by six, and you drop me off at the church on our way back, we'll have time. I promised friends I'd meet them at nine to pray before the service." She carried her cup to the sink. "Wildlife will be more active before the heat, too." Her fingers swept the air, broom-like. "You shoo now. Get dressed. I'll pack us some muffins and fruit."

Celia drove. Hazel directed her onto gravel roads that led into new territory through crumpled blankets of hills, all striped and swirled by stubble, fallow, and swaying grain. A roadside creek dogged them. When it curved into a shallow canyon, Hazel pointed Celia up a low ridge and they climbed from the Jeep at the top. Hands on her hips, Hazel surveyed the land below, where a wheat field sagged toward the canyon and creek. Directly across the field, a higher hill defined the field's far border. An eyebrow of nearly vertical untilled ground stretched beneath the taller hill's crest.

Celia stood beside her. "Parallel hills—like a headboard and footboard, with that grain for a quilt. Looks like a big old bed, doesn't it?"

Hazel chuckled. "Formerly a sloppy, unmade one. After pioneers named Riddle first plowed that land, the creek sucked its mud every wet season and spit it into the Snake. Turned the big river brown at the stream's mouth. Dry months, topsoil up and flew away.

"No different after Joss bought it. Then he met a group of farmers who seeded into stubble and tried it himself. This ground practically sent him a thank-you note. Wasn't long before organic matter composted, microbes went to work, and the pH changed. Land held water deep again. Yields increased and roots held the soil. It's still drier out here, though, so we plant and harvest this acreage last."

The Riddle Breaks, dubbed for the rocky canyons between the field and the Snake River to the south. Celia added the five hundred acres to her mental map.

"How does big equipment get in there?" Celia said. Below them, the field road they'd climbed dropped sharply to the edge of the wheat, then veered right into the narrow canyon. Terrain like this was the reason she'd kept her Jeep.

"Satchel brings it in over there, toward the river, at the footboard's south end. Nice gentle access before the breaks. We only came this way to get to the prairie."

"So where—?"

"Behind the headboard." Hazel pointed toward the canyon. "Thataway. We'll follow the creek."

Celia scanned the rugged terrain and geared down. "Buckle up, Nolly. We're going in." As if sitting a mule, Hazel rolled with every lurch. Branches scraped the rig as they crawled into the shade of cliffs pocked by basalt and hawthorn.

At the bottom, Celia eyed her placid grandmother. "Have you driven this?"

Hazel looked at her, aghast. "Heavens, no. Joss did, but when I came alone, I always parked on the footboard and hiked in."

Celia sighed. "How far to the prairie?" Ahead, the road shrank to an easy footpath between the creek and the headboard hill.

"Past the headboard, this creek merges with another stream coming from the north. The prairie begins at their confluence." Hazel opened her door and hung a foot from the slow-moving vehicle for another twenty yards. "Park here. We'll walk the rest of the way."

Hazel led, talking over her shoulder on the footpath, her arm raised toward the merging streams. "Over there's the trail I told you about— the one the tribes traveled. Runs along that creek clear through the prairie and down the breaks to the Snake. In Joss's granddad's day, a bunch of them—Palouse, Coeur d'Alene, Nez Perce, most likely— grazed horses and dug camas in the meadow you're about to see. I used to stand on the hill and imagine Chief Joseph's clan out there."

On a mud bank, Hazel toed a boulder the size and shape of a wooly ewe. "At five, your mother straddled this rock, struck the water with a stick, and dubbed it 'Judith Creek' as if she were Moses. I can picture it like yesterday." She plucked a sprig of watercress from a pool and nibbled it, then led Celia around the headboard hill's last outcrop and into the buttermilk prairie.

Celia gasped. Like generous hands, the surrounding hills held a bowl of beauty no photo could do justice. The talkative creek— a tributary of the Penawawa, Hazel said—ran off-center through a spacious grassland before it exited through a precipitous canyon. Pines, unheard of so close to the Snake, dotted the steep slopes framing the meadow.

Fifty feet away, her spry grandmother plunged into clumps of bluebunch wheatgrass and Woods' rose, calling out names of each flowering plant her fingers brushed. "Spalding's catchfly! Little sunflowers! Goldenweed! Yampah!" Where the old woman passed, small clouds of monarch butterflies lifted, then relit to drink from flowers Celia recognized: asters and thistle and pleated gentian. Unseasonably late-blooming Indian paintbrush. Milkweed.

Celia spotted more plant species she knew as bird forage and others she couldn't name, all thriving in the hill-guarded, stream-fed ecosystem. Flowers punctuated hundreds of acres of prairie, their seasons extended to heavy-handed August in the unique microclimate.

And in every direction, birds. Passerines—mostly songbirds—flitted and hid. A falcon roved overhead, hunting breakfast. Quail called from chokecherry and hawthorn in the willows and cottonwoods, their whoops and chatter like the nearby creek that ruffled, then pooled clear. In the distance, more hawks circled the valley's humps and angles. Blackbirds gurgled.

Wonder. Variety. Vitality that Celia would drink if she could. All of it canted toward the creek and its downhill chase to the mighty Snake in an uninterrupted chain of life that entered her mind and swept her clean.

Nearly girlish, Hazel zigzagged from one clump of flowers to another, adding to her bouquet. When Celia caught up, her grandmother pointed to tracks on the creek shore, a guest book of hooves and pads and twiggy feet. "I used to visit mornings earlier than this. I'd hide in the woods and watch." Over Hazel's shoulder, a bobcat slipped past willows into the creek bottom.

"And nobody bothers them," Celia said.

"All the land's posted, and the only ones Joss allowed access were descendants of the Natives that passed through in the old days. Joss held this land as a remnant, so none of us—whatever our culture or heritage—would forget the Palouse's original condition. The gifts in it. So we'd know how to restore the areas we tore up, if we ever decided to."

"I love this place, Nolly. I can help you make sure it lasts, if you want me to." At that moment, nothing seemed more crucial to her.

Hazel straightened, her eyes soft. Her head tilted toward Celia. "You're serious? I'd love nothing more. I thought all this would end when I do. But to think of you carrying on after me . . . ?" She raised her arms and let them fall. The bouquet bumped her thigh.

Their attention jumped to the slope above them as the heads

of half a dozen grazing deer erupted from the grass. The animals spun and bounded, white tails upright and wagging as two bear-sized forms descended from pines on the headboard and entered the meadow. Butterflies lifted in flicks of color behind them.

"Riders." Celia pressed hands to her forehead, squinting toward a lean man on a white horse and a thicker man on a bay, trotting their direction.

Hazel pulled her into the creekbank grass.

"Guess they can't read, Nolly." Celia caught her breath when the smaller rider raised a rifle. A shot cracked and echoed. While the bigger man waited, the man on the white horse trotted a hundred yards out, then dismounted and dropped the reins in wildflowers. When he bent and lifted an animal, Celia raised her field glasses to him.

"It's Ivan."

The horse circled the dangling reins, exposing another dead coyote hanging from the saddle horn. Ivan lashed the fresh kill atop it, remounted, and trotted to the waiting man, now turned away from them.

Frowning, Hazel brushed her knees and stood. "Who's on the bay?"

"Oren."

"He knows better. Both of them do. Zenders! Hey!" Hazel shouted. The men turned toward her as she stomped their way, her arms pumping, hands tight. Celia followed at her heels, subdued by Hazel's ire.

The men sheathed their rifles. Oren leaned back in his saddle, relaxed. The bay danced sideways at Hazel's furious approach, but Oren's smile rose easy, guileless. Behind him, Ivan's face clouded. Three coyotes, not two, hung from his saddle by their ankles.

"Well, Hazel." Oren touched his hat and grinned at Celia. "Good to see you again, Professor. You doing well?"

Celia felt heat crawl up her neck.

"My granddaughter is not the subject at hand, Oren Zender." Hazel planted a flower-filled fist on her hip. "Explain yourself before I throw a rock that will convince that horse of yours to throw *you*."

Ivan suppressed a smirk. Celia stared at her flushed grandmother. The old woman's eyes blazed.

"Too many of them, Hazel. They killed two lambs at Culbert's place last night. Time for a little thinning."

"You can thin them on his land, or yours, not mine. The second they cross into this valley, they can live as God intended. You have known that fact since you married Ingrid."

"Aw, Hazel. They—"

"Don't 'aw, Hazel' me. Joss's death doesn't change a lifetime of understanding between our families." She spun to Ivan. "Young man, you're of age now. No need to do your father's nasty bidding."

Celia studied the older man, his handsome features repeated in his son. Wild grasses brushed Oren's stirrups as he shifted in his saddle. He caught her looking at him and winked.

Hazel stomped her foot. "You're not taking me seriously, Oren. If I have to camp out here and supervise this prairie, I will. Wouldn't be the first time."

"They're coyotes, Hazel. Coyotes. Roaming your land, killing animals you've protected since you married that man of yours. I promised Joss to look after you and that's exactly what I'm doing." He cast a glance at Celia. "You know anyone better equipped to do that than me?"

Hazel didn't budge. "Don't you let my birth date confuse you, Oren Zender. I'm of sound mind, and I'm well able to decide the definition of 'lookin' after.'" She thrust an arm toward Celia like a circus ringmaster, announcing. "And I now have plenty of help."

She snagged the reins of Oren's horse below the bit and glared at the man. "Your—or anyone's—degree and specifics of involvement in my life are my decision, not yours. I am not your charge, nor are you my guardian, and noble as you sound, I happen to recall pelts you sold for your college spending money. How many of *those* did you shoot on this land?" She released the horse, started for the Jeep, then turned back to him. "I also happen to know that you have sixty skins curing in your machine shed at this very moment."

Oren's head jerked toward Ivan, who reined his horse clockwise, pillowing his father's glare with the animal's rump.

"How many of the animals hanging on that saddle died on my land, Ivan?"

"Dunno."

"Young man, you do know, and I expect you to tell me."

"Couple." Ivan spoke low, his eyes averted.

"I'll take them off your hands. Right now." She stood beside the dangling bodies, her arms crossed, until Ivan pulled a knife and cut two free. The carcasses dropped to the ground.

"Now *get*. Both of you."

Oren pinched the crown of his Bozeman hat and reseated it. A monarch landed on the brim. "Calm down, Hazel. You know I value your farm every bit as much as you do. Maybe more."

"More? *More?* I hear you clucking, Oren Zender, but this is *not* your nest." Hazel threw her hands in the air. Flowers flew. Oren's horse shied, and he bumped the animal into a lope. Ivan fell in behind him. A lift of butterflies marked their route as they retreated.

Celia rubbed Hazel's shoulders and twined the elderly woman's banded silver hair in a long loop.

Still Hazel fumed. "That man has always treated me like a child. Like an accessory—to Joss, to the farm. Dismisses me as if I'm brainless. A brainless *woman*."

"You two have a long history." Celia had experienced only a slice of it.

"I thought I'd be free of his condescension once Joss died and I took over operations here. Unfortunately, I think he's now added age to my list of perceived incompetencies. He seems to think he's my new parent—and the only silo of farming wisdom around here. He shows up uninvited, challenges my decisions, rebuts my rationale, and pressures Satchel. I've put up with him because he was a steady friend to my cantankerous Joss, and for a year after Joss died, I was too heartsick to resist him." She shook her fists. "I'm telling you,

Celia, killing wildlife on this prairie is the last straw. And to see that boy following in his father's footsteps?"

"You think he is?"

"You saw the kills on his saddle. Ivan does his father's bidding."

With a hind leg in each hand, eighty-one-year-old Hazel dragged a dead coyote over a knee-high rock, then bent for the other.

"I've got it." Celia intercepted her grandmother, flopped the second animal alongside the first, and huffed. "Forty-five pounds, if it's an ounce."

"See those mammaries? She's pregnant." Hazel's wrinkled mouth sagged. "Raven food, now. C'mon. I've got to get to church."

White doors to the clapboard, steepled building closed behind Hazel, but Celia remained in the parking lot, hands on the wheel, grateful that her Nolly hadn't invited her along this time. Mother would scoff from her grave if Celia went inside.

Turmoil she'd been ignoring ripened as the dead woman came to mind. Was Mother's scorn why Celia refused Hazel's invitations? Why she kept her distance from the God both her grandmothers and Burnaby loved?

Or was it simply because life's lessons weren't lost on her? Especially the truth that if she relinquished control of her heart to someone, she could expect to be chewed up and swallowed.

God sure hadn't disproven that fact. Didn't Burnaby look to him for guidance? Burnaby—who walled off her touch and wouldn't look in her eyes? And when had God cared about her babies, dead no matter how much she'd loved them?

Surrender? *Right.* Dangerous to survival.

How timely, Oren's arrival in her life. A good distraction from all this, without strings or commitment or baggage. She'd be careful this time. No snarls. None of that entanglement stuff.

No reason she couldn't enjoy the man's company and stay friendly with Burnaby. She'd keep her boundaries. Stand her ground like Hazel did in the meadow.

But oh, Oren's eyes. That smile. The swell of his shoulders under those shirts. She couldn't imagine *how*.

24

BURNABY

SKETCH

LASERS READ THE STEADY oscillations in his atomic clock and prompted Burnaby with a jangle. He depended upon the precision timekeeping for his appointments, classes, surgeries. And for his daily seven a.m. call to Celia, now that she left for the fields by seven thirty.

Despite the odd encounter with that Oren fellow, he'd caught a softening in her since their day at the river, a yellow thread between them that persisted despite her double-digit work hours. He would hold his end like a bowline. For her, he would be as constant as the vibrations in his clock, with steadiness she subconsciously cried for but still refused to trust.

At seven o'clock sharp, he dialed. Three rings.

"Hey, Burn. How'd you sleep?"

It was the same question she'd asked every morning at first light, when he awakened next to her, the air in the gap between them warm, the scent of her skin like indigo.

"Well enough, considering the unusually capacious mattress. Ten degrees cooler than customary."

"Aw, tall as you are, you have to lie down in shifts, anyway. Don't need me taking up space."

He could hear her smile. Wished she could see his. And as usual, he wished for a quip that never came.

"Hazel invited the twins and me for the noon meal," he said. "Lentil stew and cruciferous vegetables. Did you suggest my preferences to her?"

"Good guess, Mr. Broccoli, but you don't have the market cornered on plant-based food. Wait 'til you watch those little boys eat. Flory's seen Cobb respond to that diet like you do. And get ready. Lately Willie's talking twelve words a second, with gusts to forty."

"I'll take notes. I hope your day is incident-free."

"Thanks. Eight days now with nothing unusual in those fields. Redundant, but I'll take it."

"Yes. Definitely." Words heaped in his throat. If he overwhelmed her with them now, the two of them could lose ground. "I'm due in the surgery at eight—a fetlock arthrodesis. I'll call again tomorrow."

At lunchtime, when Hazel answered the door, Burnaby held out a cluster of blooms as big as a basketball. "Today, they're for you," he said.

"Aw, zinnias. 'Nough petals here to make an acre happy. Beautiful, darlin.' Thank you." She touched the flowers to his chin, and he followed her inside, where a small, sturdy boy sped past the stairs, tripped on a braid rug, and sprawled at Burnaby's feet.

"I am. O-kay." He scrambled upright. Turned a circle, straight-legged and stiff-armed. "I. Am. A. Ro-bot. I. Was. Fly-ing. My. Feets. Crash-ed." His head wagged with every mechanical word.

Hazel rested palms on the boy's shoulders until his legs and arms stopped moving. "Dr. Hayes, this is Willie." Her hands stilled his head. "What do you say, dear?"

"Hell-o. Doc-tor. Hayes. Good. To. Meet. You." He raised his hand like a cantilever gate at a railroad crossing and giggled.

"Robots laugh?" Burnaby said.

"Sometimes they do." The robot had disassembled. "Wanna meet Cobby?" He hooked a finger through Burnaby's belt loop and jerked him toward the kitchen table, where a slight boy hunched over paper, his pencil gripped tight. The child brushed shaggy hair from his forehead and kept drawing.

Willie speared a finger toward his brother. "This is Cobby and he's my twin even though he's littler. He was borned first and he's my bestest friend and he knows how to draw stuff and Cobby . . . Cobby!"

The young artist raised mild eyes to his brother.

"Cobby, this is Doc Hayes. 'Member Miz Steffen told us he's a vet for aminals and he saws horse bones and sews up owies?"

Cobb craned his neck at Burnaby. "Hello, mister. Can you draw a horse?"

Hazel pulled bowls from the cupboard and handed one to Burnaby. "You'll work up an appetite with this pair. Cobb . . ." She paused until the boy looked up. "Lunch first, then art. Please move your stuff and I'll set the table. How long can you stay, Burnaby?"

"One thirty at the latest. I'm teaching at two."

Half an hour later, the dishwasher hummed. While Burnaby wiped counters, a giggling Willie sneaked in the back door and released a banty hen under the table. Rocket nosed through the screen and cornered the bird near the pantry. The dog's barking roused Hazel, who stowed leftover stew in the fridge, shooed animals and Willie outside, and followed them with a basket of wet clothes. She paused at the door. "Table's all yours, boys. I told Cobb you were an artist, Burnaby, so he's hopin' for a bushel of instruction."

Burnaby returned to a kitchen chair and watched Hazel clip a red shirt he recognized as Celia's to the clothesline. Hazel's posture and mannerisms echoed his wife's. He saw Celia at eighty, right there, and loved her all over again. Loved her still, and wished she believed that.

Near a raft of loose papers, Cobb set a tin and a spiral pad. Burnaby opened the lid, pulled out a blue pencil, read its stamp. "Watercolor pencils. And real watercolor paper. Are these yours?"

"Mommy buyed them for me because you were coming for lunch. I only drawed before but she said you paint and these pencils turn into paints if I put water on 'em with a brush." His eyes widened. "Just a sec. Miz Steffen gots a brush for me."

He raced to the counter and found a thin, pointed brush against the backsplash.

Burnaby pulled a shield from the bristles. "This is fine equipment, Cobb. Your parents must believe you'll put it to—to good use."

"I like to draw aminals." He riffled through his stack of papers and handed Burnaby sketches of Rocket, the chicken, a toad—all lifelike, detailed.

Burnaby's eyebrows rose. "Did someone teach you to draw these?" The boy's proportions were excellent, his understanding of scale and perspective good even for a talented teen. But for a five-year-old? Remarkable.

"Willie likes coloring books and crayons and markers, but they're too fat for me and somebody else makes the pictures and I like to make my own from what I see and like and touch. My hands and my head know how to draw already."

"I see. How may I help you?" Clearly the boy already spoke and intuited through his sketches—with superb perception. Further instruction on technique should come later, not when his interpretive eye was finding such a foothold. What could Burnaby possibly teach him now that wouldn't hamper or squelch him?

"Horses. I see 'em in books, but only in real at the fair. Or when we drive by 'em. Sometimes Mommy stops so I can look, but Willie starts to yell, so never very long. I only sawed them running one time."

"What horses have you drawn so far?"

Cobb hurried to Hazel's kitchen desk and located a tape dispenser. Again, the boy dug through the pile of artwork. "Don't peek."

Burnaby focused on a window and waited.

"Okay. Ready."

Three horses hung from the table's edge—one muscled, one gaunt, one ewe-necked. A dish-faced Arabian, a Roman-nosed Standardbred, and a drafty, leopard Appaloosa stood in static positions, all looking out from the page, their details as accurate as an overexposed photograph. The year Celia convinced him to judge the local Pullman arts competition, he'd awarded ribbons to work far less accomplished.

"Well done, Cobb. What would you like to improve about these?"

"These are already real. How do I paint them?" The child stood the brush on end and flicked the bristles.

"I'll get some water," Burnaby said, then immersed himself in the wonder of a small boy learning. When he resurfaced, it was after one o'clock.

"I drawed another horse I sawed in a book, but it's only pretend and I want to draw it real. If I show it to you, will you teach me how to draw it real even if I haven't seed it or touched it for real? It's not like these other ones. It's moving, with bigness making it move. I like it a lot."

"I'll try." Burnaby checked his watch again, then folded his hands on the table while Cobb pulled two sketches from the bottom of his pile. Of the same subject, they differed only in perspective. Though they were drawn in graphite pencil, Burnaby's mind turned the lines a chalky white as he reconstructed them. In his brain, the page's background morphed into the green of a grassy, sunlit hillside.

He knew this horse: a stylized, cantering animal—its neck arched, tail flowing, hocks tucked. "The Uffington White Horse," Burnaby said. He raised his eyes to Cobb. "From a book, you say."

"I found my mommy's book about horses from the olden days and this picture was in it but I think it's a mystery because it's only a idea and not real."

"Yes, Cobb. This horse is a mystery. Did you know a—a mystery can still be real?"

"Nuh-uh."

"This horse is a mystery, an idea, *and* it's real. I saw this horse earlier this summer, in a place called England. Have you ever heard of England?"

His tongue waggled left to right, which Burnaby took for *no*. "You sawed it? For real? It looks like this, not like a real live horse?" He held the paper upright, inches from Burnaby's face.

"Yes, I saw it. And no, the horse is not alive. It's composed of lines shaped just like yours. People didn't *draw* the lines. Instead, they cut and—and pounded the design into a hill made of chalk. The horse is as big as a—a football field and grass grows all around it."

Cobb's eyes grew wide. "What people made it?"

"Can you count to one hundred?"

The boy nodded.

"People who—who lived three thousand years ago. That's one hundred birthdays, thirty times."

"Way older than Miz Steffen."

"Way older."

"Why did they make that horse?"

"Nobody knows for sure. That's part of the mystery. I have a theory, however. Would you like to hear it?"

Cobb nodded again.

"I think the people who made that horse needed help that only their Maker could give. But since they didn't know this Maker's name, or where he lived, I believe they sent a message into the sky—a prayer, asking for help. A prayer that looked like a—a horse."

"They didn't pray like we pray at bedtime?"

"They didn't know how." Or perhaps, Burnaby thought, they knew an alternative language. Ancients, their children, and their children's children had pounded prayers into that chalk horse over their entire lives.

"Why would a horse be a prayer?"

Burnaby weighed his answer. "Another mystery. Maybe they thought a—a fast horse would carry their cries to their Maker. Or maybe they thought the horse could bring God to them."

"Hugh told me a man named John made a book about a white horse that brings the Saver. Did they know about that horse?"

"Perhaps, but not from John. They made this horse a long, long time before John wrote about it."

The boy's face was tight as he concentrated, listening. "I talk to God. And I draw."

"I understand. Sometimes I pray by painting."

"Does God talk to you when you paint?"

"He does."

Cobb stared at Burnaby with intensity that forced him to turn away. Then the boy climbed from his chair. He hugged Burnaby's arm, slipped outside and disappeared around the house.

The beauty of their talk lingered, and longing wrapped Burnaby like fragrance. Would he ever talk like this with a child of his own?

He walked to the back door and called to Hazel. "Thank you for lunch."

"Oh! You're leaving already?"

"It's one twenty-three. Yes."

"Burnaby?" When he heard her, he stepped outside. She crossed the lawn and met him on the patio, empty basket on her hip.

"Yes."

"Forgive my meddling, but I'm a pretty good meteorologist, and sometimes a man needs a little help reading the weather."

"Innuendo takes me a while to translate, Hazel."

"That's why you need to hear this. You're burning daylight, you know."

"Same with idioms."

"Okay. Okay. No offense now, honey, but I can see your Celia's comin' out of her dungeon, and if you ever expect to move past bringing flowers and sitting on my porch or calling her while dawn's still in its pajamas, it's time to make a move."

The basket left her hands and thunked the patio table like punctuation. Fists went to her hips. "You're acting yellow as mustard, and I don't believe a single squirt is true of you."

She clutched his forearm, and though her words and contact struck him like rocks, he stayed put. Hazel had invested many summer lunch hours with him before his wife began her intermittent noon appearances. Though never this personal, those conversations with the elderly woman had been multilayered, topically far-reaching, respectful. He recognized her compassion. Forced himself to hear her out.

"I haven't seen you touch that woman since she's been here. Have you shown her even the slightest bit of physical affection?"

Physical affection. He flushed, frustrated and ashamed. Hadn't Celia begged him for it? Cried at his pathetic efforts?

As long as his prefrontal cortex prevailed, his brain fed on data and logic, formulae and systems for everything from science to cooking to art to half a dozen outdoor hobbies. He liberally shared them all with his wife, and he felt a tender closeness to her through their intellectual and communal experiences.

But her touch? Unless he prepared for her and could see her coming, touch from Celia made his skin crawl. He'd learned adaptations, of course, but when she had felt well, Celia moved fast and touched him constantly, often without warning. He couldn't sustain acceptable reactions to her incessant demands on his sensory neurons. And so he kept his distance.

Except in the bedroom.

Only when his subcortical brain fired, when passion overrode his autistic sensitivities, was he able to receive her gift of physical affection and respond in kind, with the other-focused *oneness* he imagined—and read about in John and the Song of Songs. A connection he had described to her on their way to Idaho, and after their wedding, when they first tasted it themselves.

Hazel waved a magpie off Rocket's food bowl and watched the bird fly. "Now don't get me wrong here. I'm mighty happy Celia moved into that room upstairs when she left you. Your third baby and her mother dyin'? Her heart took some sucker punches, that's for sure. All those weeks she spent flat out on that bed upstairs and slouching around here, I wondered if she was down for the count."

A hum rose in Burnaby's brain that shrank Hazel, relegating her to his mind's screen, volume off. Despair drilled him. For years now, he'd been unable to pretend with Celia. She knew his artifice, and it hurt her. His inability to let her touch him without a sexual outcome had gradually changed how she experienced him. *A taker,* she occasionally called him. *All that talk about oneness? Yeah, right,* she'd said on a terrible day and had accused him of using her. Worst of all, since their baby died, they hadn't shared a bed—which was where he could speak her language best.

He tried to control his reactive cheek. His fingers fidgeted with his car keys as he refocused on Hazel.

"Trauma like that? You just never know who'll get back up, and once they do, what exactly they'll do next. Some return to the life they knew and spread that new hurt around in their marriages. Some pour heart and soul into making their relationships better. But others ditch the circumstances that held all that pain and vamoose to greener pastures."

Hazel was not leaving space for his words, but Burnaby had none to offer, anyway.

"Appears to me that Celia's a greener-pastures kind of gal. The fact that she stuck around for all those years speaks buckets about you, but it's going to take more than phone calls and flowers to keep her from jumping the fence. If you love that woman as much as I think you do—if you want to save your marriage—it's time for a little exploratory surgery, Doctor. On yourself."

Her words rang metallic but shiny. "I'm open to advice, Hazel."

She returned to the basket and clipped a clothespin to its edge. Pinched another one open and closed as if it were talking. "You're a barn cat, Burnaby, believing that beautiful wife of yours will devour the dead mice you bring her. Ditch the rodents, young man. Bring her what'll nourish her, not just what's easy for you to catch and leave at her door. You ever ask her what she needs most?"

He knew what Celia needed, and it wasn't that stilted anniversary card he'd left for her. He nodded, checked his watch again. "I'd better go."

Hazel picked up the basket. "It takes two, Burnaby. I realize Celia will have to read her own vitals. Let's just hope she's willing."

25

COBB

ALIKE

MIZ STEFFEN TELLED ME that Doc Hayes has a heart like my heart and that he has pictures that go from his head to his fingers like my pictures do, so before he comed over for lunch I thinked he would be little like me, but he was a great big giant. I didn't see his heart because it's inside him but I seed how his hands know the pictures, and he said things that were in my head too and I feeled like he knowed me, and so now I think he is a knower.

26

MEMORY

BURNABY SMELLED ROCKET before he saw the skunk-sprayed dog slink from Hazel's flowerbed, tail between his legs. The animal and the odor followed him to his truck. *Apropos,* Burnaby thought. Hazel's admonition weighted him with the stink of his incapabilities.

But by the time he turned from Old Hollow onto the highway, sweeter air sent his mind to a morning eleven years earlier—to the motorcycle trip with Celia, on the day he married her. They'd awakened in the Mazama foothills and had ridden that old Triumph Bonneville of his to Idaho.

They had parked the bike outside Clark's to shop for a ring when Celia said something new. "You let me know how I can best love you, okay? I'll learn this language of yours."

Asking her for anything more had never entered his mind.

Nor had wearing his own wedding ring, though its certain effect on him registered when a slight, bespectacled jeweler pulled a size seven from a hoop of graduated metal bands, slipped it over Celia's ring finger, and tested it against her knuckle.

"Just right," the man said. "Breathing room, but it won't slip off. I have quite a selection in your size." He dangled the ring sizer above Burnaby's huge hands, folded on the glass counter between them. "Now you, sir?" He scrunched a cheek, evaluating. "At least size fifteen, I think."

"No need," Burnaby said. "In my profession, working with unpredictable livestock, rings heighten risk of injury." Besides, any metal band encircling his finger would drive him through the roof. Surgical gloves had warranted the long, tedious desensitization, but a ring was optional. "I trust you'll have one Celia likes."

Celia's mouth, poised to speak, snapped closed with an equally quick nod. She flipped her braid off a shoulder. "Alrighty then. I get that. Let's look."

The jeweler unlocked a case at the far display counter, removed a tray, and chose an exquisite diamond solitaire from its midst. "This one's especially nice." The store's lighting caught facets, threw brilliance seductively.

Celia waved him off. "No offense at all, sir, but in *my* profession, a ring like that is a blue egg at a crow convention. I'd snag that rock on a bird cage and come home with nothing but prongs."

"Ah, an inset stone then. A channel design, perhaps." The jeweler stowed the solitaires, then stepped to another case and returned with a tray of bands. Celia bent close.

The store's confines squeezed Burnaby. He calculated the number of steps to his bike and yearned for its comforting vibrations. Celia's selection was irrelevant to him. He would buy her a planet if she asked.

He refocused when she addressed him. "Burnaby, I'm swooning. Look at this one. Already sized."

Her limp wrist aimed unpainted nails at the floor. On her ring finger, a single, centered gemstone nested in a silver band the width of a fat birthday candle. Purple-red, blue-green, orange—the stone's color shifted with every wag of her finger. *A stone with opinions. Ha.*

Burnaby checked angles on the overhead lights before he returned to the stone. "Light-dependent. An internal palette. Chrysoberyl?"

The jeweler nodded. "Yes. Lovely, isn't it? Alexandrite, emerald cut, set in white gold. I'll check the weight, but I believe it's just over a half carat. An in-house creation."

Celia pressed her sparkling hand to her chest and claimed the ring with her right. "I love it, Burn."

He smiled and pulled out his wallet. Five minutes later, the bike rumbled beneath them, this time with a velvet box zipped into the breast pocket that held their marriage license.

Their ride's last leg reminded Burnaby of photographs, faded by years. Between the cities of Spokane and Coeur d'Alene, brushland, farmland, and neighborhoods zipped past, flattened and featureless in the high light and heat. Even the trees seemed two-dimensional.

Then, in the distance, a bath of blue, with inlets and coves and depths like the stone he carried in his pocket. All of Lake Coeur d'Alene for his Celia. Soon they rode into pines on a shoreline road, the glass lake wavy beside them, refracting sky. *Yes.* He reviewed his mental checklist. He thought of her dress and hair. The proprietor said they'd have flowers.

Past a small cafe, Burnaby pulled the bike to the shoulder and raised a thumb. A weathered *Heyday* sign and an arrow made of driftwood pointed them down a lane heady with the scent of warm pines and wild roses. Trees thinned into a sweep of lawn, and he caught a splashy scent of the lake beyond it.

He recognized the two white houses from the brochure the owners had sent. A thickset woman waved from the porch of the larger home—a tidy Craftsman, shingled, beamed, and porch-wrapped. Down a trail to the lake, two pines framed a cottage of like vintage, overlooking the water. Flowers grew everywhere.

That cottage . . . the guest house. His and Celia's. He felt himself blush.

"What *is* this place, Burn? Who lives here?" Celia stood beside him now, helmet under her arm. Sunlight glinted off her black braid, and he reached for it, the weave like music in his fingers.

Her enthusiasm was palpable. And the eyes he tried to watch reassured him. "The property has been in—in one family since they built both homes in 1904," he said. "A great-grandson owns it now, a former Army chaplain. Weddings are their specialty."

The woman walked a flagstone path toward them, a basket of flowers on her arm. Her broad smile hung from ruddy cheeks. "Welcome to Heyday," she said. "I'm Rose."

Cheeks like her name, Burnaby thought. His mind was racing now, hunting similes. Searching for colors to calm himself.

"Congratulations, you two. Arthur and I hope these next hours are the start of a heyday that lasts for your lifetime." She checked her watch and the sky. "But if we want to catch that sunset, we'd better get a move on. I'll give you a quick tour, you'll meet with Arthur, and I'll get you settled. Prewedding, it's girls in the cottage and boys in the groom's quarters at the main house." She lifted her basket. "Celia, your young man thought you might like flowers for your hair, so I tucked a packet of bobby pins in here. And if you need anything ironed . . ." She eyed the bike's panniers, patted her chest. "Rosie, at your service."

The sun leaked butter across the lake when Burnaby planted himself, per Arthur's instructions, on a flagstone marker in the lawn. The mélange of colors in the lake and sky melted into those his mind created and joined scents from the rose pinned to his pocket and those twining the arbor behind him. He smelled his sweat, too, and sensed the weight of his jeans, the seams of his socks aligned between his toes and the interior of his boots, and the slick texture of his blue oxford, freshly ironed. The shirt Celia liked.

A tune arrived like a horse plowing earth. Then a melodic lilt. *Like swallows,* he thought, and recognized Pachelbel's Canon in D. He turned to see Rose, flute to her lips, and Arthur on cello, under a tree. Gold light, everywhere.

And Celia, walking toward him in that gown, barefoot, her hands buried in flowers, her hair wavy and loose but for a few blooms, pinned. He felt her watching him as he scanned the lake to quiet himself, then gauged the temperature of her hand on his arm. To quiet his skin, he imagined her fingers as a graft.

With Rose as witness, Arthur opened his Book of Common Prayer and they—he and his beautiful, beautiful Celia—promised their love and their lives to each other. Yes, and yes, and yes. All of himself, everything he was or ever would be. The vows skinned him, gutted him, refilled him.

Afterward, a candlelit table waited on the dock, which was lined with luminarias that glowed when dusk settled. Arthur brought a grainy bread and poured wine. "To oneness," he said, while Rose delivered dinner, then sorbet, then left them alone.

Celia and he talked then, reliving hours together and years apart and imagining the unknown ahead of them, while the Milky Way draped like a loose-weave scarf above the lake, its starry spangles shaken and strewn. Water shimmered and lapped the dock, and night scents rose in the charged air between them.

The main house had gone dark when Burnaby opened her hand and kissed her palm. He spun her changeable new ring with a thumb and ticked his head in the direction of the cottage. "I've never done this before, Celia."

She considered him. Ran a finger up his cheek. "This, Burn? Us? Neither have I."

All he remembered about carrying her across the lawn was the feel of her hands behind his neck and how he liked them there. How, at the threshold, his lips found hers with permission from his resistant neurons and mind. And how, as the rising moon chased a path of light across the water and into their cottage, when she reached for him, his skin welcomed her touch—and he could at last respond with joy equal to hers. And in the ensuing hours, while his brain melted into an otherworldly array of colors, their dance bloomed with auroras and meteors and lightning and atomic proximity that explained to him the beauty of the Trinity and the Song of Songs. A holy, wild, wondrous dance that entangled him and his breathtaking Celia as one.

Eyes closed, forehead on his truck's steering wheel, Burnaby inhaled the memory. Then he stepped into the veterinary hospital, carrying Heyday, and their years of nights like it, into the surgery. Those times had mostly sustained Celia and him, had usually carried them around the days his rebellious skin shed her, rejected her. Mostly. Usually. Until their little girl died, and she wouldn't let him undo the distance and pain. Wouldn't let him touch her at all.

But she needed him to. Hazel was right. Their survival depended upon it.

27

CELIA

RIDDLE

THE TWENTIETH MORNING of harvest, Celia faced into a rising breeze and shoved a gas nozzle into the ATV.

Satchel drove past the shop toward her and lowered his pickup window. "You're early," he said. "Glad I caught you before you headed out." Fatigue leaned him into the vehicle's frame.

"Hey, Satch. Yeah. I'd like to see the prairie sometime today. Meet you at the south end of Riddle's? Seven thirty? Cooler today, at least." Long hours and ninety-degree heat had wearied them all. She'd been counting the days until they cut those last, farthest fields. Only a hill separated the Riddle property from the wild preserve.

She pinched the phone in her pocket, then released it. With no reception here at the pump, Burnaby's 7:00 a.m. call would go to voicemail. He'd wonder why she didn't pick up. From a hilltop, later, she'd text him.

Tomorrow she'd paint fresh verbal pictures of the prairie for him, adding to all she'd told him already. Since her visit to the wild land with Hazel, that untouched ground had taken up residence in her yearnings, her desire to tend and nurture the habitat nothing short of motherly. Her grandmother had all but handed her the adoption papers. Now she thought about the meadow and its surrounding hillsides and trees before she left her bed each morning and wished the place into her dreams before sleep. She couldn't wait to see it again.

"I've been thinking," Satch said. "Two weeks with no incidents. No wire fences anywhere near the Riddle place. It may be best if you stay here today. She puts up a good front, but Hazel's wearing down. Flory says that even with three of them cooking, prepping all those meals for the crew is getting to her. If you're around to help, maybe she'll lay off."

"Yeah. She's up early again." *No prairie.* Disappointment streamed over her, but Celia waved it past. Her grandmother needed her. At least the kitchen wouldn't be so warm today. "If you're sure."

"Crop's thinner at Riddle's. Debris will be easier to spot, if there is any. I think we'll be okay." He shuffled some papers on his dash. "You should probably know that we had an incident with Ruth last night. None of us got to bed until late, so Flory's dragging. I doubt my daughter will be much help at all today."

Celia waited, but he didn't say more. "Sorry to hear that, Satch. And yeah, I'll get over to the house to see what I can do." She checked the time on her phone. "Late start for you this morning, then."

"I called Hugh. I'm meeting him at the field in twenty to fuel the combines. We lubed both of them last night, so that'll save time. We should be up and running by eight." He looked toward a larger fuel tank behind her. "Ivan went to the field early to get the service truck. He should've picked up another load of diesel here already. You see him?"

She shook her head. "You took all the equipment out there last night then?"

He smiled. "We did. Sorry you missed our caravan."

"Aw, you had plenty of help. I'd have been in the way and you know it. Even your flagger was a pro."

Satchel's laugh evaded his eyes. He shrugged, swayed his raised hand, and steered toward the road.

At the house, Hazel was peeling potatoes and looking wilty.

"Satch canned me, Nolly. Promoted you to supervisor." Celia untied Hazel's apron, claimed the peeler, and patted a kitchen chair. "Here. Sit. Breakfast first, spuds later."

Rocket was eating a leftover pancake when a tap sounded and Flory stuck her head in the door. "Ready for me, Hazel?"

"Better ask this one here. I think she benched me."

"About time." Flory hoisted an oversized slow cooker to the counter. "Your blinkers are at half-mast, Hazel. Why don't you go back to bed? Celia and I can handle this."

"Oh, honey. I really—"

"Celia, except on Sundays, the woman never rests. There, Hazel, I said it. Now go make a liar out of me, eh?" Flory moved a paperback from the coffee table to Hazel's lap. "If you can't sleep, read. Make yourself useless. You've earned it."

Hazel rubbed her face and stood wearily. "Well, I won't fight you. *Useless* sounds mighty good." She took two steps toward the couch.

"Unh-unh. If we're going to work our tails off in this kitchen, you'd better make it worth our while." Flory pointed upstairs. "Your chamber awaits, m'lady." She stood at the counter, listening for Hazel's door to close, then removed her sunglasses. Her eyes were bloodshot and swollen from crying. "Satch tell you what happened?"

"Just that you were up pretty late with Ruth."

Flory flopped into the chair Hazel had vacated. "They've been sneaking out, Celia. Midnight last night, Satch heard scraping against the house. He hurried outside and spotted Ruth's behind draped over the sash of her bedroom window, her feet shoving off that yellow pine's trunk as she crawled back inside. Almost made it, he said.

Another few seconds and he'd have missed her. She didn't see him, so he circled behind the trees, spotted Ivan's Blazer parked on the road, and waited.

"Sure enough, there came Ivan, sneaking straight through those cottonwoods. To his credit, he didn't resist when Satch jumped him, though when Satch marched him to the house, he probably wished he had."

Celia poured coffee into two mugs. "Deep weeds for good old Ivan."

Flory sighed and blew on the steaming drink. "Too old for our daughter."

"Did Ruth know Satch was out there?"

"Not until he came back with Ivan. Then she tore downstairs, yelling like a banshee. By the time I wrapped my sleep-muddled self in a robe, she was glued to Ivan's arm like pitch."

"You say anything?"

"No, no, no. Satch was already quizzing them. Ivan wore that hangdog look of his and was doing a lot of shrugging. Ruth was the one who spilled the beans."

"Beans."

"As in, *yes*, they snuck out and *no*, it wasn't the first time, eh? At least three late-night rendezvous in the last month. Ruth swore they weren't doing anything except watching the stars and talking. I tell ya, Celia, I get so scared for her I'm no good to her at all, and I can't tell if she's telling me the truth or not. At sixteen, she doesn't understand how many ways she could ruin her life with that boy. And I'm not sure Ivan even cares."

Celia thought of the river. Of Ivan and Ruth in the truck on the way home. Now was not the time to say that Ivan cared. "So what'd Satch say?"

"Not much. He said they'd given him a lot to think about, and since it was late, he wouldn't deal with it then. I think they believed they were off the hook, as reasonable as he sounded. Then he told them that without trust, things would be different now, and that until he decided what 'different' meant, he didn't want them to contact each other. *At all.* And he told Ruth to go get her phone.

"I held my breath. Until she started for the stairs, I doubted she'd comply. She looked like a woodpile rat, slinking up there.

"That's when Satch told Ivan to go home and get some sleep. Said he wanted him waiting at Riddle's with a full tank of diesel on the bed of the service truck first thing in the morning. Celia, if that boy's looks could kill . . . All that lightning toward the river last night? I swear it came from those daggers he was shooting."

Celia could picture him. "At least your husband didn't fire him."

"Nah, Satch doesn't act on impulse. He tried to usher the boy out while Ruth went for her phone, but Ivan dragged his feet. When Ruth saw him leaving, she almost slid the banister to get to him. She would have followed him to his rig, if Satch hadn't blocked her at the door.

"Then things really got crazy. I'd never have suspected words like that inside of her, much less coming out of her mouth. She upended my blue chair, knocked books from shelves, threw her phone. The racket woke the twins, and when she fell in a heap, they wailed right along with her."

Poor Flory. And Satch! Celia's palms sweated.

"My Satch took those ugly words like a knife to the heart, but he stayed calm. Stuck with her. They talked for an hour before she crawled in bed. Then we waited up 'til after two. Made sure she was sleeping."

So much for Ivan and Ruth hosting that anniversary party. "Ouch, Flory. Ouch. Where is she now?"

"Still in bed. The boys are outside with their goats, so they won't wake her. I want to be home for her when she gets up, eh? Try for the eleven hundredth time to show her that love may change its clothes, but it never quits."

Never? Celia thought. *In the Milk family, maybe.*

Flory splashed her face at the kitchen sink. Eyes closed, she felt for a towel in a nearby drawer. "That girl's default is to bury a problem and move on. Leave a trail of unresolved messes. Getting her to work through an issue with someone she hurt or tricked or misunderstood is next to impossible." She wagged her head. "Ruth's got to realize that love asks us to wear a miner's headlamp sometimes, or work boots. Or a surgeon's getup. Not just party dresses."

Celia watched Flory punch garlic cloves into the roast. Her friend settled the lid and turned the cooker's thermostat to low before she spoke again. "I got lost for a couple of years after her sister died, eh? Ruth was six, and with me out of commission and her dad dealing with all that, she moved into self-preservation mode. Unfortunately, the only tools she had at that age were to run from problems and try to conjure happiness. I must say, she heads toward bright and shiny distractions like a June bug to flame, and woe to anyone who tries to stop her. And if we attempt to talk about an issue? She flips out. Good gravy, you'd think we were trying to kill her, eh?"

"Must feel like that to her," Celia said. Flory's words returned Celia to her own childhood, when her imaginary friend Doozy found her crying under her bed, pulled her out by her toes, and taught her to fly—up the chimney, over trees, out of Mother's reach—so Celia could breathe and laugh again. Magical days. Flying had saved her.

But it didn't work at sixteen. Or, she realized, at thirty-nine.

"Yeah. I guess." Flory shifted the fridge's contents, assessing, then pulled a cucumber from the crisper drawer and laid it on the counter beside an onion and carrots. "I'll be back in a bit. Can you keep Hazel out of the kitchen?"

Flory's wheat-colored hair tossed in the wind as she trotted home. Watching from the window, Celia heard echoes of Ruth and their foul night, and her own emotional boil swelled somewhere deep. No, Flory wouldn't quit when life got hard. Twenty years of marriage and her own dead child proved that. But how on earth did Flory summon that sort of love when life dealt such wretched hands?

The landline jangled. She lifted the receiver as Hazel answered her bedside phone, their hellos simultaneous.

"Hazel. Elaine here. At the fire station. You hear me okay? Got somebody with you?"

"Yes, honey. My granddaughter." The bed creaked. Hazel, sitting up, Celia guessed. "From the station, you say. Can't be good news."

"'Fraid not. Dispatcher got a 911 on a blaze at Riddle's, spreading fast. Onecho District is sending two trucks and a tanker. Crews from the Wilcox and Dusty stations are on their way. Soon's I hang up I'll group-text everyone in a ten-mile radius and get water trucks and disc harrows out there. We're worried about this wind. Where's Satch? He didn't answer his cell."

Hazel stretched her exhale. "Somewhere between here and there. You won't reach him unless he's up a hill. He didn't report the fire?"

"No. Ivan called 911."

"Ivan. God bless that boy," Hazel said.

Ivan? Celia's mind leapt. *Ivan, sleep-deprived and angry at Satch.* Was he vengeful, too? Impetuous? The conclusion formed before she could arrest it.

"Yes, Ivan. He figured twenty acres were already gone but said wind was pushing it through the field next to Joss's prairie. Could be fifty acres by now. A hundred."

"Oh my, honey. We're on our way."

"No, no, no, Hazel. You stay put. I'm gonna need you to make more calls if this thing gets away from us. Keep your line open. Gotta go."

The connection broke. "Nolly. This as bad as it sounds?"

"I'm coming down, honey." Hazel's receiver hit the cradle as Celia's cell rang. Flory.

"Fire at Riddle's!"

"We heard. Any word from Satch?"

"Not yet. We've got to get out there, Celia."

Hazel appeared on the stairs. "Is that Flory?" Celia nodded. "Tell her I'll watch the boys."

Celia heard Flory's voice through the line, distant. Calling to Ruth. "I'm back. Just woke Ruth."

"Hazel said she'd take the boys. I can drive. What do we need?" Celia pulled boots from a box by the patio slider.

Her grandmother dug in a drawer. "Shovels. Gunnysacks from the shed. Buckets. Long sleeves and pants. Heavy boots. Ah, here they are. Bandannas. Hurry. Flory's worked fires before. But don't let her get in front of that wind."

"I heard that." Flory's voice again, through the phone line. "I'll grab supplies. Just get over here. The quicker we leave, the better."

28

CHASE

"HURRY, CELIA!" Ruth drummed her mother's headrest from the back seat. The farm dissolved in dust behind them, and Celia raced toward the Riddle field through hills, valleys, and more hills. Swerves on the roller-coaster roads felt like slow motion—a disorienting warp of emergency and fear—and she pushed the Jeep faster. Flory punched Satch's speed dial at every hilltop and eyed the growing wall of smoke. Powdery dirt from vehicles ahead of them penetrated the Jeep's cab until they passed a tractor hauling a disc harrow, then a truck, laboring uphill, its flatbed tank heavy with water sloshing from the curves and the rush.

At last the footboard hill came into view, and Celia eased off the gas. Smoke billowed from behind the ridge. Flory pointed to the field road. "Turn here." Acrid air bit their sinuses and throats. A cloud of smoke swallowed the vehicle's headlamp beams like spoons in soup.

Celia slowed. "The road to the prairie? You sure? Isn't that down-wind?"

As if it had ears, the wind shifted and the field road opened, dim. No flames in sight.

"Wind's all over the place." Flory peered through the windshield toward the footboard and raised her voice over Ruth, coughing behind them. "We're not going to the prairie. Just to the top of the ridge. We can see the whole Riddle place from there and decide our approach. That smoke wall's still a ways off. We'll be okay."

"You sure?"

"Sure as I can be without seeing it."

Celia cast her a dubious glance, then drove up the field road to a view of the unfolding scene. Before she could set the brake, Ruth and Flory jumped from the Jeep. Celia joined them at the crest, where they held cloths to noses and squinted into the smoke.

Below them, a snaking wall of flames chewed into Hazel's ripe wheat and belched devouring, off-gassing black clouds that turned to charcoal, then putty as they rose from the burned crop. Celia's first thought was of gangrene—with its fast-moving red edge and black destruction in its wake.

And like an eighteenth-century battle line, she thought. A brazen mow-down, only of bearded wheatgrass, not men, with flames not much taller than the combine and semi exiting the field. Farther away, the bankout wagon and diesel-toting service truck also rolled to safety. Behind them, the wall of smoke from the quick-burning crop had grown monstrous, menacing.

"One rig left." A rogue gust swayed Ruth as she pointed at the lone combine still in jeopardy. "Whoever's in there sure is taking his sweet time."

Suddenly, fed by the fire's heat, the wind again shifted—and routed the flames in new directions. Flory pointed at a miniature tornado. "Fire devil," she shouted, and the three watched in dismay as an arm of the blaze high-stepped toward the stationary combine, the only obstacle between the fire and Joss's prairie beyond the headboard hill.

"Uh-oh," Flory said. "That wind's turned uphill. Those flames will really run now."

Ruth cupped hands around her mouth, screaming, *"Go, combine, go!"* A man's silhouette showed in the cab window, left their sight, then reappeared, but still the machine didn't roll.

Flory, pacing, pressed her palms together and touched them to her lips as if in prayer. "He can't get it moving."

At the field's far end, a green tractor surged through the blowing wheat, its disc harrow cutting a twenty-foot swath of the ripe crop into the soil. Within seconds, one line of flames bumped the fire-break, shrank, and died.

Too far away. Celia estimated the tractor's speed against the fire's faster onslaught elsewhere and tensed at the obvious. *Too slow. Too late to save the combine.* Flames neared the machine now, incinerating wheat stalks, torching heavy heads of grain in their path.

They saw the operator again in the combine's window, moving fast. Then the door opened and Satchel flung himself down the ladder and into the field.

"It's Dad! *Dad! Run!*"

Satchel sprinted as flames wrapped the combine, met beneath it, and continued in his direction—a scant twenty yards behind him, and gaining.

Then a black Blazer roared in a tight arc around the fire's leading edge. A door swung wide, and Satch leapt in. Tires careened on the slippery stalks as the SUV sped laterally across the steep, golden side-hill, above but in the fire's path until it crossed the firebreak, slowed, and circled behind the flames to safety.

Satch and Ivan climbed from the Blazer and watched the engulfed combine tip and sink with the pop of each burning tire. Paint buckled and charred as yellow fingers reached into gearbox and engine, bins and fuel lines. Fast smoke rose from each point of engagement.

The water truck arrived on the blackened field and sprayed the ruined machine. Hugh and the semi drivers spilled from a pickup seconds later, as the fire continued to race uphill, chewing through and around the headboard's eyebrow, on ground too steep for anyone to follow. In the distance, sirens sounded, their promise moot.

At their footboard vantage point, Flory sank to the ground, her face as ashen as the cinders suspended in the swirling air. "Thank God they're okay."

Ruth plopped beside her. "Ivan saved him, Mom."

"Yes, sweetheart."

Celia turned to hide her scowl.

Ruth pressed her face into her mother's shoulder. "Will they let that whole hill go? Can't they get behind it?"

"No road up there, sweetie. Only trees and prairie on the other side. Too steep for trucks. They'll monitor the periphery and let it burn itself out." Flory was on her feet, walking toward the Jeep. "C'mon. Those firemen will need us to kill hot spots."

"That's it? They'll let the whole prairie burn?" *That exquisite meadow, destroyed.* Intellectually, Celia knew the land would regenerate, but her heart could hardly bear it. And if Ivan had anything to do with it . . .

While she watched, pheasants launched from behind the headboard in flocks of ten, twenty, then what had to be a hundred multi-colored males and earth-toned hens fleeing the fire. *Evacuees,* she thought. If not for the gush and crackle of the wind and fire, she would have heard the collective thrum of their wings hoisting them past danger. Were the land-bound creatures escaping? How fast did butterflies fly?

The Jeep's rearview mirror framed Ruth and Flory after Celia deposited them on the scorched field. They raced to Satchel, who draped an arm around his wife and kissed her neck before he rubbed his daughter's head. When both leaned into him, Celia turned away and let her tears stream with relief and loss. Not the loss of wheat or equipment. Farmers anticipated fires and insured their crops and machinery against the lightning or engine sparks that ignited blazes like these. It was the destruction of the prairie that lay on her in yet another blanket of grief. She had promised Hazel she would protect the land—the grassland and pines and wildlife she already secretly claimed. Instead, its sooty ash filled her nostrils and burned her eyes and transformed the noon sun into a feeble, ghastly moon. Wild land, her land—destroyed before she even got to know it.

Farther along the firebreak she drove, past the assembled neighbors dunking burlap bags in buckets, dousing embers and sparks the hoses missed. Smoke rose with renewed vigor from behind the headboard. Below the eyebrow, she parked the Jeep midfield and trudged up the steep, black slope. The cloud above the prairie deepened, spread, and rose higher still.

A man shouted behind her, close enough that she could hear his labored breathing, the whump of his boots in the soft earth. "Celia. Wait."

She turned and faced Ivan. *You.* Her suspicion simmered. She let her glower speak as she pulled off her bandanna and wiped her sweaty face. "What."

His hands hung at his sides. "Ruth told me how you feel about that valley."

You should have thought of that. She retied the bandanna over her nose and mouth, her lips a tight weld beneath it. She gave him a quick nod and continued uphill. When he caught her by the arm, she shook him off but slowed and hung her gaze on the smoky ridge.

"You'll only feel worse if you go up there right now."

She bent, hands on her thighs, and stared at him. "You a mind reader?"

"Sometimes things happen you can't stop or change."

"Can't they call planes? Extinguish it from the air?"

He aimed a finger at high ground. "I've been on that hill, trying to call somebody. Anybody. The prairie's on private property with no threat to government land, so the federal agencies aren't interested. State said it's a natural burn, necessary to the ecosystem. Even if we could find someone from the private sector with a plane, available air tankers, scoops, and smaller, local aircraft are all working that Nine Mile Falls fire up north."

He inclined his head toward the workers below. Grasped her arm again and tugged it. "C'mon. It'll be hard enough without that picture in your head." He looked square at her with eyes so limpid and sad they confused her, compelled her, and she followed him downhill. He was hurting too. What did she know for sure about anything?

Though she stopped at her Jeep, Ivan didn't turn. Heat liquified the air around him into waves as Celia called to him. "You or Satch—take Ruth and Flory with you? Tell them I'm leaving?"

Ivan raised a hand and kept walking, his form blurred by smoke and tears.

29

BURNABY

BREACH

AT JUNE'S END—after England, after the night Celia left him for Hazel's—Burnaby had found the diagram in her study, pinned to the bulletin board behind her desk. Celia had drawn it to scale at their kitchen table back in January, during the third heavy snow in as many weeks. While temperatures dipped into the low twenties and downy powder buried their in-ground garden, they'd thrown split rounds of maple into their woodstove and sketched raised beds of cedar two-by-twelves, named the plants that would grow in them, and labeled precisely where. Celia had described a remembered heirloom tomato, hot from the vine in an earlier, dilating August, then smacked her lips and laughed.

Planning complete, they'd ordered seed packets from catalogs. He found those pinned to the board too. A dozen envelopes full of seeds, none planted because, before that same January snowstorm, they'd begun growing their baby girl. By April, instead of building planting beds, they'd constructed a nursery.

Burnaby had prayed over nails and screws and slats as he built a crib for the child. His and Celia's child, for whom he'd be a father, Lord willing, like his own had been for him. As he sanded the dresser and painted it white, he had imagined the baby's cells specializing in Celia's womb—heart, lungs, eyes, bones—and love for their little girl had grown in him as if in its own pregnancy. He had anticipated his delivery of that love as boundless and vast.

On July first, he'd run his fingers over Celia's careful garden map as if it were braille, or Scripture. Read and reread variety names of cucumber and broccoli and leafy greens, peppers and onions, nasturtiums and cornflowers and her heirloom tomato. He pulled the pins and arranged the packets on their kitchen table. Then he built the beds, hauled the soil, and, though late in the season, planted.

This August morning, the routine he'd followed since planting didn't waver. At five fifty a.m. he pulled on jeans and flip-flops, walked directly to the garden, and bent over kale or onions or whichever vegetable his rotation dictated, pinching weeds.

At six fifteen, he checked the tiny holes on his watering can's rose head, removed a debris clog from one of them with a stainless surgical probe, and irrigated the beds—the volume for each plant calculated according to height and species.

At six thirty, he returned to his kitchen and ate equal portions of hot oatmeal and blueberries. He chased them with twelve ounces of water, consumed in uniform, mouth-rinsing swallows.

He turned on the shower at six forty-five sharp and stepped inside, washed his hair with a nontoxic Liggett's Shampoo Bar, and shaved at the mirror hung from the streaming head. Then, after he scrubbed—left to right, top to bottom—he stepped onto a bath towel, dried himself in the same order, and donned the clothes he'd laid out the night before.

At six fifty-nine, he picked up his phone and waited to call Celia. Today he'd tell her about the zinnias.

When his atomic clock clicked to seven o'clock, he pushed speed dial, anticipating the color of her voice. Four rings, but no answer. He hung up, entered the number by individual digits, and tried again. This time, five rings, and voicemail.

Already pacing, he closed the connection, recalling the weeks she'd gone silent and all those days he'd texted and called her without a single reply. He remembered the agony of missing her, the concern that he'd pushed her too far, the fear that she'd fled.

Prudence suggests delay, he told himself. And so, determined to hold the ground he believed they'd gained, he slid the phone into his pocket. Not until the day's second surgery wrapped up would he try again.

Four hours later, while resident Mac Winthrop closed Burnaby's incision over a thoroughbred's plated femur, he left the operating room, removed his gloves, and dialed again. In another half hour, when Celia still hadn't replied, he wandered past stalls of recovering patients and called Celia's grandmother. She picked up on the first ring.

"Hazel."

"Oh, hello, honey. I guessed you might call. I'm not one to eavesdrop, but I didn't hear Celia's voice through the wall this morning like I usually do."

"No. We didn't talk."

"I wondered. She was out the door by six forty-five."

That meant he was entering the shower as Celia left Hazel's. Atypical. Their routines were out of sync.

"And after that, there wasn't time. Soon as Satchel sent her back here, the station called that our wheat was on fire and she left with Flory and Ruth for the Riddle place faster than a toupee in a hurricane."

"A fire at Riddle's? Near that unfarmed land she talks about?" His brain raced through wind directions and the fire's likely fuel load from the region's typical crop density, then projected the fire's potential speed and size. Celia took risks. She'd likely get too close to the flames. Anxiety rushed him.

"That's the place. They—"

"You've heard from them?"

Too loud. Too pushy. He instantly regretted the steamroll in his voice, as if he could squeeze news of Celia's safety from Hazel and slather it on himself. He inhaled sharply, then counted during the exhale to slow his reactivity.

"Easy there, Grandson. Satchel's called twice already. Celia's fine. Everybody's fine. Can't say the same for my brand-new Case combine or a hundred ninety acres of ripe wheat or that beautiful prairie that wife of yours has caught the bug for, but all the humans involved will come home, shower up, and sleep in their own beds tonight, none the worse for wear."

Limp with relief, Burnaby dropped onto a hay bale outside a horse stall and forced the kindness he felt toward Hazel into his voice. "I'm sorry. I imagine your concern has been every bit as substantial as mine."

"I doubt that, honey. The unknown grows longer teeth with every passing minute. You've been in the dark since this morning, while I've been tracking this thing from the get-go. Besides, as fast and deep as my love for Celia's growing, I can't possibly love her like you do. Now don't get me wrong. If she got blistered by that fire, my own heart would ache something fierce, but it wouldn't bubble—like it would if I were one with her. Like yours would."

Her words sparked in his brain. "You've no need to clarify, Hazel."

"Well. Good then, honey. Please don't worry. I've lived through four of these blazes, and thanks in part to the bundle I pay for insurance, I've gained more than I've lost in every one—once I quit being pigheaded and accepted the lessons."

"Relevant to the nature of all suffering, most likely. My head remains porcine, I'm afraid."

"Good one, Dr. Grandson. I thought you were the straight man in our discussions."

"Ha." Burnaby shifted on the bale, the hay stems concussive through his jeans. "Celia has spoken of little else since she saw that prairie. She'll grieve its demise."

"She will, young man. I'll need to talk her through it. You will, too, so be ready. So far, she's taken her losses like bullets instead of surgeries. I'm hopin' this fire is her turning point."

Highly unlikely. Turning Celia would take more than blazing grass.

"That land needs fires for its best life. Wait 'til you see that valley next spring," Hazel said.

"Next spring's a distance away. Celia tends to—to live in the immediate."

He nodded at a veterinary student leading a mare down the surgery's alley, pointed her toward a padded sedation stall, then read the time on the alley's clock. "I have to go."

"Okay then, honey. Thanks for calling. Best if you know, though, that Satch's second call was to tell me that Celia's quite upset. Ivan stopped her from hiking right into that burning meadow, and she drove off alone after that."

"And you haven't seen her yet?"

"Oh, I expect she'll be here any minute. Want me to give you a ring when she pulls in? Unh-uh, Willie. No squirt guns in the house."

"I'd appreciate that."

A cadre of veterinary students assembled in the concrete passageway as Mac scanned the clipboard at the wide door to the surgery. Burnaby signaled his surgical colleague with an upraised finger, then returned his attention to Hazel.

"On second thought, I'll get this next procedure underway, then—then join you. I'd like to—to be there when she arrives, or shortly thereafter."

Hazel was feeding the twins their lunch and fielding calls from Satch and Flory, still on clean-up in the Riddle field, when Burnaby arrived at the Steffen house. No one had seen Celia or her Jeep.

"Only one place she could be," Hazel said. "Now stop that fretting, Burnaby. Upset as she may be, she's not foolhardy enough to catch herself on fire. Flory would have my hide if I took the boys into that valley, but I can show you how to get there. Follow me?"

She shooed the jam-faced twins from the house into her sedan and aimed toward the deepening haze. Burnaby tailed her to the prairie turnoff and parked behind her.

Her face filled the side mirror as he approached her car. "Park at the top of that hill. You can drive farther, but it may be faster to jog the rest of the way. Down the other side, the road drops and follows the creek to a confluence. The prairie's to the left. She'll be by the creek, I expect, upwind of whatever's left of that fire." Hazel dug a clean bandanna from her purse and passed it to him through her window. "Here. Wear it. There's cell reception on rocks farther up-canyon, if you need to call. And don't you worry, honey. This will all turn out just fine." The boys hooted from the back seat. Hazel shifted into reverse, waved her arm out the window, and swerved around the bend in a cloud of dirt and smoke.

So easy, her exit. Offhanded. Her certainty of a favorable outcome contradicted the smoke still rising from behind the hill. Surely she knew fires tricked people, caught them. He swabbed runnels of sweat with the kerchief and, after he parked at the crest, jogged fast over the uneven trail, praying aloud.

He reached the confluence as a pair of raccoons rounded the hill from the prairie, panting, frantic. *Footpads blistered,* he thought, and spotted two more descending green-topped pines where flames had crawled beneath them, and moved on. His sinuses burned, and he envisioned the animals' throats seared. How many more had escaped ahead of the fire? How many hadn't?

The land bore no resemblance to the enchanting valley Celia had described. Fire had marched from a tall ridge down through the sparse hillside woods into the meadow. A mosaic of unburned islands pocked the fire's black, smoldering wake. Flames had caught the parched leaves of cottonwoods and jumped the creek to new fuel on the stream's opposite shore. Hurried by the wind, fire now advanced the last hundred yards uphill, exiting the valley with a convective plume that heaped mashed potatoes of smoke on the gray plate of sky.

On a charred cutbank, Celia sat in her bra and jeans, her booted feet dangling over the water. Oblivious to his approach, she curled over something shaped like an artisan bread loaf and wrapped in her red tee.

When his shadow crossed her, she looked up, then spread her fingers wider over the object in her lap. Without speaking, Burnaby sat on his haunches, his senses keen to the rattle of water over stones and the snap of embers and the pungent scent of burned grass and leaves.

Then Celia's hands jostled, and a curved beak rotated toward him.

30

WRONG

THE RAPTOR'S BEAK OPENED and snapped closed. Burnaby looked from the bird to his breathing, uninjured wife and heaved a sigh.

"A redtail. Unbanded." Celia bumped the creek bank with her heels, then quietly pulled the cloth more snugly over the bird's head. She uncovered its feet. "I bet a vole lured her too near the flames." Stroking the hawk through the cloth, she surveyed the ridge, where a dozen raptors circled. "See those birds? Heat's flushing rodents ahead of the fire line. The picnic's moved uphill."

She lightly pinched a tarsus and inspected the bottom of the bird's foot. "I caught her on a hop, trying to fly. Doesn't look like her skin's burned, and her wings seem fine. Just these tail feathers. All twelve of them." Celia uncovered the bare, straw-like shafts protruding from the bird's rump, then retucked the cloth. Her eyes roved, haunted but resolute.

How he wished he could lift her ache, carry it for her. Hear her laugh. Fortified by her presence, he again reviewed his plan—the one spurred by Hazel's warning about rodents, about giving her what she needed. Eleven years and he'd never thought of it. Neither had Celia. She'd look like the cold one, but who was looking?

"You'll cage her until they grow back?"

"Not a chance. She'd be confined way too long. Her next molt won't be 'til spring."

Celia found a sooty twig the diameter of a cigar and pressed it into the hawk's footpads until the talons clenched. "I'm done with caging birds that can survive in the wild. Done with trapping them, tagging them, drawing their blood. If I hadn't been so wrapped up in catching Hawk Five, our baby—"

"I understand, Celia."

Three lines of thought from her. One regarding the bird; the second, her future, her life, and her professional identity; the third, her self-condemnation. He had to address the easiest and most immediate before she could hear him on the others. If Celia wouldn't euthanize the hawk, or keep it captive until it could fly again, she only had one good option.

"You'll imp her, then."

"Yes."

"With that many feathers to implant, wouldn't your colleagues recommend a recovery stint in the aviary? At least two months?"

"No way I'll keep her cooped up all that time, Burn."

"What if she pulls the replacements? She'll die if she's not supervised."

"She won't pull them and she won't die. She's got to return to the wild. Fast as I can get her there."

Disputing her seemed unwise. Her fierce resolve smacked of desperation, and her strong attachment to the redtail seemed irrational, as if the bird were a life ring and she were clinging to it.

"I see. Would you like me to anesthetize her for the procedure?"

She hesitated. "I don't think so. She's already stressed. Even working fast, she'd have to be knocked out for two hours, at least. If I cast her so she can't move, she won't need any sedation. It'll be like getting a haircut and extensions while wearing a straitjacket. I'll give her a break or two. Still risky, but at least she'll be conscious."

She stood and rocked the bird as if it were a baby. "Will you hold her while I work on her?"

Her hesitant, cautious request, her doubt that he'd support her shocked him. "Certainly I will."

"You can keep her comfy rather than monitor anesthesia. And we can imp her at the house, so I can stay with her if she needs me."

At *their* house? She hadn't even visited in nearly two months.

"I presume you have replacements?" He thought of the dozens of molted flight feathers they'd found on their hikes or runs and how they'd identified, tagged, and stored them in her office. How, when he suggested they'd collected enough, she'd protested.

They've got to match, Burn. We need all kinds, she'd said. For previous impings, she'd fitted feathers according to their species, gender, age—even correlating the same follicle locations on both donor and recipient, when she could. The more closely old and new feathers aligned, the better chance the restoration would succeed, and the more likely the hawk would fly again.

"A drawer of redtails in my office. Multiple sets. She's young, so will need longer ones. I've got at least two full juvenile tails. Adults in the lab freezer, but they're shorter."

He knew that freezer, had helped her catalog its contents. Lining the shelves were whole wings and tails of raptors hit by cars, killed by planes, and shot or shocked by hunters or power lines. He knew when she added to the collection, too, when her distress over a bird's death cast a temporary pall over their home.

Falconers, rehabbers, and universities tapped her impressive feather bank. But rarely did anyone imp an entire tail. Even Celia, to his knowledge, had never imped more than four flight feathers at once.

"Very well then. I can drive so you can tend her. Do you have a way to transport her to Hazel's, so we can return a vehicle to the farm?"

"That mesh pigeon cage clipped to my pack will work. It's behind the seat, under some of Flory's fire gear."

When they arrived at Celia's University of Idaho office, the door stood open. Celia, her face and clothes sooty, lowered the hawk's cramped cage onto Tara's desk and adjusted its bandanna covering.

"You two are a sight for sore eyes," Tara said. "And with stories to tell, from the look and smell of you." She peeked at the hawk, then scrambled for chairs.

"Later, Tara. We can't stay. This girl needs better digs and a new wardrobe, and her stress clock's ticking. Bringing her in here doesn't help. Too hot to leave her in the car."

"Got it, Celia. That cage you like is under your desk."

Burnaby retrieved the portable crate as Celia scuttled to a filing cabinet, flipped through manila envelopes of varying dimensions, and waved two jumbo ones at Burnaby. "The kit's in my desk, top right."

Burnaby opened a drawer and recognized the hinged box Celia had outfitted for feather repair. A quick inspection confirmed the contents.

"Thanks, Tara." Celia was already in the hall. "You've got chicken at the house, Burn, right? I want this girl to eat after we put her in that straitjacket for two hours."

Had she forgotten he didn't eat poultry? "I believe there's still a package of thighs you purchased in—in the freezer."

Burnaby watched her closely when she entered the house, but nothing in Celia's demeanor hinted at her long absence. While he parked the crate in a corner of the kitchen and the repair kit on the table, she dropped her shoulder bag, as she always did, in the chair by the door. He pulled chicken from the freezer and plated it to thaw. She transferred the hawk into the larger crate and hooked a bowl of fresh water to its gridded door.

Then she spread a dish towel on the island countertop and transferred bamboo splints there from her repair kit. From barbeque skewers, Burnaby remembered, their diameter right for the shafts of a midsized raptor's flight feathers. Alongside the splints she set sandpaper, jackknife, rasp probe, needle-nose tweezers, curved clippers for cutting feathers, and a syringe of five-minute Araldite epoxy.

Good, Burnaby thought. *Not superglue.* They'd have four minutes to reposition the cant of the feathers, if need be, time to align them perfectly before the glue set. He pictured the bird's wings as oars, that tail as a rudder. For them to function, feather angle mattered.

Finally, Celia laid out the twelve tail feathers she called rectrices in the order they'd splint them.

Only then did she stretch her arms over her head and survey the spotless surroundings.

"Looks better than when I lived here."

He could have been made of feather, and she, fire, for the way her use of the past tense singed him.

"When did you last eat?" He set a glass of water for her on the counter beside the supplies.

"Oh, a while ago."

Before his first call to the farm that morning, most likely. How often had he fed her when excitement or stress distracted her from meals? "Breakfast?"

"Yeah, about six, I guess."

The clock now read four. The work ahead of them would be lengthy, with a need for accuracy. She had to eat.

"I made some chili last night. I'm having some before we—we begin, while we wait for the hawk to drink. She'll fare better during the procedure if she's hydrated. Will you join me?" He felt like he was baiting a rabbit. Or a feral cat, gone ribby from hunting.

"Sounds good. Thanks." She eased onto a barstool, tested the clipper's spring, and snipped the first donor feather's hollow calamus—the unfeathered part of its shaft. The quill opened clean, round as a coffee straw. She repeated the procedure with each of the loose feathers, then rasped keratin debris from inside the shafts with her probe.

Burnaby pulled food from the refrigerator to the side counter. He set the saucepan on the stove and stirred. The chili warmed while he cleared the table and set utensils and napkins and salad plates on two woven mats opposite each other. Between them, he placed watermelon and green salad, corn bread and honey.

She didn't notice that he stood behind her, growing his resolve so that when he took the next step in his plan, when he laid both hands on her shoulders and said, "Here now, let's eat," he could follow through.

This time, it was Celia who flinched. *Because I surprised her,* he thought. *Nothing to take personally.* Still, her involuntary response evoked in him a sense of rejection that shamed him. Was that how she felt when he, preoccupied, froze her out? Or when his skin rebelled, and he brushed her off?

"Wasn't expecting *that*." She sat across from him, dressed her salad, and settled corn bread into her bowl of chili. They ate half of their meal silently, the air between them electric, though Burnaby couldn't discern with what.

"That valley, Celia. I can envision it unscathed." Only now did Burnaby dare mention the fire. "You must be heartsick."

She cut her melon into cubes with her fork, then halved them into triangular prisms before she answered. "When Hazel first took me out there, I was so into it, so *awestruck*, I forgot to take pictures. Soon as I got home to the farm, I pulled some of her best pics from an album. Hung them above my bed." One side of her mouth curled. "With her okay, of course. I loved that place. No, I *love* it."

Frowning, she stretched her neck toward him. "But then this morning I watched fire wreck that crop and march over the hill to obliterate Hazel's family's paradise. *My* family's paradise."

She snapped her fingers. "Quick as that, the fire was about more than the land. It was an embodiment of all the destruction in my whole life—a flashback reel of the trauma with Mother, the losses of people I loved, the hopes that never materialized. A grand finale of carbon fibers, up in fumes. Though I was in no physical danger, I felt like my days were over, right then and there, and I was as close to giving up on living as I have ever been."

She continued before he could shape a reply.

"Then guess what. That little redtail started hopping down the creekbank in my direction, off-balance from a tail of kebab sticks in her pincushion rump. Her entire world, and her ability to navigate it, had just been destroyed, but she was still trying to fly with everything in her. She didn't seem frightened at all. Just . . . *determined*."

Celia's hands went to her head, her fingers a skullcap. "Right then I felt a surge in me of something from beyond myself—nothing I had manufactured or talked myself into. I was confused for a minute. I couldn't understand why I felt happy while this ruined, stub-tailed little buzzard was stumbling around in a charcoal dust bath. Then I realized it wasn't happiness I was feeling. It was *hope*, imparted from beyond me, as tangible as that scrawny little hawk who carried it."

Her palm pressed the table. "And right there, in the culmination of all the miserable hands life had dealt me, I realized I had been wrong about everything, Burn. Dead wrong."

A chill ran down Burnaby's spine, as if ushering a verdict on her epiphany. He stared at his plate. Hope, for Celia, could mean anything, including divorce. "Dead wrong." Burnaby poked a thumb through his napkin. "May I ask how?"

Celia tilted sideways and peered at the hawk. Even without its tail, body feathers plumped by their home's cool interior made the bird appear larger. "I can't answer that just yet." She speared a chunk of watermelon. "Still sorting it out. I do know I want to see everything through the eyes of that little bird, who behaves as if rotten fires are a given in life, but who acts as if all will be well anyway."

"Then let's fulfill her expectation."

She smiled at him then. "You got it."

31

IMPING

WHILE BURNABY STOWED FOOD and dishes, Celia whittled a bamboo splint for the first donor feather and tested its fit in the shaft. Satisfied, she rolled one end of the wood in glue and inserted it halfway into the feather. Burnaby transferred thawed chicken from the microwave to the counter, washed his hands, and straddled a stool beside her—where they worked until a full set of wood-tipped tail feathers lay on the towel in front of them, ready for implantation.

"Ready for the main act, mister? I know it's going to kill you to watch, but I'm doing this myself. All I need you to do is hold her. You good with that?"

"However I can help." As glad and grateful as he was to be with her, talking and working, he'd have agreed to anything, even if the flight feathers she attached were her own and flew her away from him.

"We're in business, then. Hold this while I get her."

Burnaby nodded, and she spread a chamois-lined canvas the

dimensions of an open *Smithsonian* magazine across his chest. Velcro straps dangled from one side. The hawk *screed* and then quieted as Celia seated a leather hood and pressed the bird's shoulders into the chamois.

Burnaby knew the drill. He secured the bird's legs and grippy talons before he and Celia tucked wings into the hawk's body as if closing fans. Celia folded the chamois wrap and pressed the straps across the bird's torso.

"Like diapering a baby," she said.

Innuendo? A jab at their circumstances? He couldn't tell.

Subdued, the hawk rested, completely still. "Lay her face up, on this." Celia folded another towel in half and spread it beside the supplies.

Burnaby eased the bird down and aimed the tail at Celia.

"Keep those feet out of my way, and we'll be good," she said. Already she'd run a strip of paper under the first burned tail feather, isolating it from the others. She snipped the stub a generous thumb's width from the bird's body, checked the fit of the correlating feather's splint, then glued it in place, her adjustments precise. She repeated the process five times more without a hitch, while the hawk lay as immobile as if Burn had anesthetized her.

As he watched, nothing in Celia's procedure distressed him. In fact, everything pleased him, even delighted him. "Beautiful work," he said. "That hawk will claim those feathers as her own."

"Why, thank you, Dr. Hayes. That's the goal." Celia shoved her stool back from the counter and stood. "Let's give her a break."

Freed from the wrap and returned to her cage, the bird fluffed feathers and shook her partially installed new tail. *Claim them, buteo.* He wanted Celia to be right.

An hour and another six feathers later, they left the hawk to rip chicken from bones and swallow chunks of meat, not a singed feather in sight. Celia gathered her supplies. "I may as well pick up a few of my things, while I'm here."

Burnaby followed her upstairs to their bedroom. She riffled through a dresser drawer, set a few shirts on the bed, and raised her chin to him. Tears rose onto her corneas.

"In the kitchen, Burnaby. You touched me. And unless you're nuts, which I highly doubt, you had no expectation of making love. What gives?"

He settled his eyes on hers, determined to connect without the forced, blinkless stare she so disliked. "Whenever I have touched you in—in the past, what has typically occurred?"

She blew through pursed lips, lifted a porcelain osprey from the dresser and stroked its beak. He'd bought it for her on a work trip to Bozeman. When she opened it on her thirty-fifth birthday, she'd called it a perfect gift.

"You know what happens. You touch me, either with your 'I'm in surgeon mode' or your 'It's my duty' hands. Then I either ignore you, and we proceed under relational anesthesia, or I touch you back, and you wince as if I'm contagious with something nasty. Unless . . ."

"What?"

"Unless we're in here, with the door closed—or on a hill or river somewhere, a mile from anybody. It's like we have two lives, and by the time I get in here, I'm so beat up from your rejection in the first one that I take a while to come around, if you get my drift."

She'd forgotten the other ways he loved her. Formerly, she'd recognized them. Before the baby.

"What hurts you most, the detached contact you describe or my reaction to your touch when we aren't conjugally engaged?" He'd watched affectionate couples communicate nonverbally, but imitating them was useless.

"What do you think? Honestly, Burn. Sometimes you're as dense as a post."

"I didn't want to presume again. But I'd like to—to propose a solution."

"This oughta be good."

"I'm serious."

"You're always serious."

"What if you were to know that the only time I touch you, I will truly intend to connect with fond affection, even if my style is stilted or awkward. Could you receive that differently? Not perceive me as simply being dutiful?"

"Like *that's* going to happen. You'll still jump out of your skin when I touch you back."

"Likely so. Therein lies my proposal: Don't touch me unless we're in this room, or in some similarly purposed location. Ever. Instead, accumulate your responses inwardly. Save them until my body allows me to reply in kind. A new protocol."

"You're a lot of work, you know?" She shuffled to the closet, found a duffel, and stuffed an armload of clothes inside. He expected her to leave the room, but she dropped the bag, slumped over it, and held her head again in that skullcap way. "No, Burn. *I'm* a lot of work. I'm sorry."

For fifteen seconds, he didn't breathe. Then he whispered, "Don't leave. Stay here tonight, Celia. Give us another try."

"After what I did? I was *careless*, Burn. She needed me to protect her, and I didn't."

"Sometimes we don't have that much power," he said. She backed up when he reached for her. "You could have lost the child while sitting in a chair."

"But I didn't."

"Oh, Celia. Like yours, my thoughts of her arrive unbidden, and they wrench me to my core. I don't understand why her time here ended when it did, but I don't have to know. I trust that the span of her life wasn't up to us."

"Who was it up to, then? That arbitrary God of yours? Why would you trust anyone who takes your *baby*?"

He ran his hands into his pockets and rested his eyes on the osprey. "Because he loves her, just as he loves us. He *is* Love and does everything from that essence. He is *for* us, Celia. For *her*."

"How can you say that, Burn? She's dead." She could hardly speak. Again he reached for her, but she shrank back.

He shrugged. "I don't know. I can't comprehend how her demise fits into that love right now. But I do believe—with everything in me—that our Maker only allows that which will result in a beautiful outcome."

"Beautiful for him, maybe. What about for us? For her?" She picked at a loose thread on her bag.

He ached at the sight of her cheeks, awash with tears. "This death's not final for her, Celia. Do you think God would have allowed his own boy to die if it were? He knows what it's like to lose a child." He dropped to his knees beside her. "Come back to me, Celia."

"Then what? Lose another baby—or die delivering one?"

"We can take—"

"Take *precautions* that make me bleed or throw up or worry myself sick because latex failed?" Her spittle caught sunlight and colored her words.

"We didn't worry last time."

"Well, we should have." She stood and slung the bag over her shoulder. Lowered it.

"There are permanent solutions." He'd balked previously, but now? What *wouldn't* he do for her? "I'll have a—"

"No, Burn. There's no point in you doing that for me. And I absolutely won't. What if they figure out how I can carry a child to term—before my ovaries hang it up for good?"

"At least consider my proposal?"

"I dunno." She raised a finger and disappeared into the bathroom. A drawer's contents rattled before she returned. "C'mon. Let's turn that remodeled bird loose while there's still daylight for her to roost."

Bird, duffel, and repair kit cluttered the rear seat of Burnaby's crew cab before she spoke again, fingering the porcelain osprey in her lap. "If that little hawk can plow through smoldering charcoal without a tail and still think about flying, so can I, I guess."

His hope glinted all the way to the prairie.

At the confluence, Burnaby took the hawk from Celia, and they hiked to the piney hillside, where fire had claimed the understory and sprinted on. Though the sun dipped behind the far ridge, trees' crowns would hold gold long after the valley surrendered to dusk. Plenty of time for the bird to get her bearings.

Celia lifted the hooded hawk onto a gloved hand and stroked the speckled breast tenderly. "When you're ready for breakfast tomorrow, little bird, all your voley meals will be above that burned ground without cover, looking for theirs." As if in reply, the bird shook like a dog. Her feathers ruffled, then went flat and slick when Celia removed and pocketed the leather hood. Immediately, the redtail stretched her neck low and raised her wings in an easy lift toward a tree, into sunlight that hung in her fresh russet tail. The new rudder worked perfectly.

The shadow line pushed uphill in the dimming valley, the demarcation crisp against the blackened slope. Tendrils of smoke rose from embers that glowed like evening windows. When Burnaby climbed a boulder and sat, Celia slumped with exhaustion beside him.

Oh, to carry her home, to care for her. He remembered Heyday and laid his hand on her head. She reached hers to top his, but retracted it and let her arm fall. The feel of her hair imprinted on his palm. "Meadows are created to heal," he said. "So are we."

Her inhale was long; her exhale, longer. "I'll try," she said.

He wished he had shown her their garden.

32

CELIA

SUSPICION

WINCHED ONTO A FLATBED TRAILER, the burned combine crawled down Old Hollow behind a Steffen semi—the last vehicle in the caravan of machinery making the post-harvest trek home. Hugh parked the destroyed chassis beside the machine shed and joined Celia and Satchel on the shop's gravel yard, while two men pulled away in a red short-bed Ford pickup.

Hugh tracked the retreating vehicle. "Fire marshal, right? They find anything?"

Satchel shook his head. "Nothing. No apparent lightning strike, no evident accelerants. The inspector said they covered the ground from the location Ivan called in and expanded the search in all directions—quite a ways. He said that finding anything was unlikely, though, what with the way all those responders beat up the ground."

Hugh squinted into the distance. "A truck could have sparked it, dry as it is."

"Or a match," Celia said.

The men's heads snapped her way. They spoke in unison. "Whose match?"

"I don't know, but Ivan might. According to Flory, he was spitting mad at Satch the night before the fire. No offense, Hugh, but teen boys can be impulsive. As in missing-bricks impulsive. As in strike-a-retaliatory-match-and-throw-it-in-the-wheat impulsive. Do you think—"

"Not a chance!" The shake of Hugh's head wagged his fleshy cheeks. "Not Ivan. I know him better than my right foot. Even if he was bent out of shape at Satch, he'd never jeopardize his relationship with Ruth, or his integrity, or anyone's safety by doing something like that. You saw the risk he took to rescue Satch. The only one who can get him to do anything remotely dicey is his old man, when he puts the screws to him on their little horseback hunts, and Ivan hates it every time."

Hmm. Celia remembered the sadness in Ivan's eyes at the fire, but she'd let her stubborn assumptions rule. *You'll only feel worse,* he had said when she wanted to climb the burned hill. How did he know? Did Oren teach him that lesson?

"That fire was an act of God, then—or our mystery vandal," Satchel said. "Unless somebody squeals, we won't find out."

They'd gone quiet when two small boys burst around the shed. "You bringed the burnt-up combine! Is it still hot? Can me and Cobby climb on it?" Willie jumped from Satchel to Hugh, bumping Cobb, who walked a circle around first one man, then the other, his arm extended like a spoke rotating at their belt lines.

"If it's okay with your dad." When Hugh caught his eye, Satchel nodded. "Then we'll practice those T-ball swings I taught you. I'll pitch." Hugh opened both hands. The boys grabbed them like fish on bait, towed him to the flatbed, and they all climbed aboard.

"I love that guy," Celia said.

"There's nobody like him," Satch said. "About Ivan—"

"Sorry, Satch. I shouldn't have said that."

"Easy to point fingers, and I've been tempted, but there's something bigger going on around here. I only wish I had a glimpse of who's behind it. With harvest over, hopefully we won't have any more incidents, but keep your wits. Pay attention, will you—if you're still around? How long you planning to stay with Hazel, anyway? If I may ask."

"Good question." She picked up the end of a tangled extension cord at the shop door and began coiling it—looping wire over thumb and elbow, like Hazel wound yarn. "Maybe for a long time, depending."

"Now I'm really curious."

She hung the cord over her shoulder. "Before he died, Grandpa Joss formed a trust to preserve native flora and fauna on his prairie. Hazel and I have talked about expanding it to include soil research and education. She wants me to manage it after she's gone, if I'm willing. She's adding me as a trustee, so I can direct maintenance, development, programs. But why wait? More fun to get started while she's still around. Lots of birds out there, too—and no hooks from research grants."

The boys leapt from the trailer, ran ahead of Hugh to the shop, and returned with baseball gloves, a plastic bat, and a Wiffle ball.

"Daddy. You wanna field?" Willie cocked a leg in his windup, then planted it when he threw to his father. Satchel caught the ball in an exaggerated leap and tossed it underhand to Hugh.

Satch laughed. "Only if you'll run bases, Willie Mays Milk. I'll be with you in a few minutes."

Willie saluted, sprinted into the shop, and emerged to stomp a plywood home plate onto the gravel.

Cobb, gloved and serious, tugged Celia's arm. "You wanna play?"

She bent and cupped his cheeks in her hands. "Thanks, sweetie. I'd love to, but Burnaby's coming over."

"Doc Hayes? He can play too."

"You go ahead, Cobby. We'll join you another time."

Satchel took the electrical cord from Celia. "Early August, the year I started working for the Steffens, I saw that meadow burn. For almost nine months after that, it was bleak, I tell you, top to bottom. But you should have seen the place come May. That land gave birth every way it knew how. Paradise."

"Doesn't matter what I understand about regeneration, Satchel. Seeing that field burned almost took me down again."

"You'll be a lot better at trusting the long view come spring. Glad to hear you want to hang out around here."

"Yeah. This place suits me."

"How about that man of yours? You including him?"

Dang, Satch was as nosy as she was. "Too soon to tell, but I'm giving us a shot."

"Make it your best shot, Celia. In my experience, you won't regret it."

In the past, she'd have blown him off. But this wasn't the past, and the advice was coming from Satchel, who had paid his marriage dues. "I'll think about that, Mr. Milk. You better go play ball or those boys will put you on waivers."

After Celia showered, the twins were still shouting, swinging, and running bases in the barnyard. Burnaby sat on Hazel's porch, a backpack at his feet. He'd come after work the last three days instead of at noon, with vegetables from their garden instead of flowers. He held the screen open for her, ran an index finger down her cheek, and smiled. "Let's walk."

Her cheek retained the sensation as if he'd painted her. Yesterday he had run a fingertip across her neck, and she'd felt it as wind. The day before that, when he laid a hand on her knee, she'd held as still as if it were a finch she dared not startle, absorbing the warmth from his touch.

And without her reciprocation, he didn't recoil.

Her thoughts were already changing with their new plan, too.

In light of his insistence that she *not* respond, his contact, though straightforward and as unnuanced as chalk on a blackboard, arrived as gift, not barter. Doing her part, she overlaid his intent of "fond affection" on the gestures and was pleased to find that, instead of cataloguing what his touch lacked, she felt a whisper of that fondness in return.

Today, the fourth day since the imping, whenever he had come to mind, she'd lingered, glad to have him there in her thoughts. She'd changed her running route and avoided Oren since then, too. Decisively. That little hawk didn't waffle. Neither would she.

"Where to this time?"

Burnaby pointed. "Sunset, due west."

From Hazel's backyard they left the lawn and walked into the soft, stubbled field behind it. Celia's boots sank into the soil and she tilted into the steep incline, counting steps until her thighs burned and Hazel's house and barns shrank below.

Burnaby reached the crest before her. Silhouetted against the cloud-pocked sky, he waited until she neared, then set out again along a new ridge, climbing the more gradual rise until the ground fell away on either side and deer in swales below shrank smaller than cats.

A dip, another rise, and the Steffen farmstead left their view. In every direction, hills tumbled like wicker baskets, flung and upended in spills of waning light. Burnaby opened his pack and spread a faded, checkered tablecloth over the slanting dirt. Celia sat, her legs stretched downhill. He handed her a grocery sack and parked himself on the cloth beside her.

"Look at that big old egg." Celia leaned back onto her elbows as the sun flattened and filled the horizon like a yolk.

"That reminds me." Burnaby pulled a ripe tomato the size of a baseball from the sack and passed it to her, then took a second for himself. "Your heirloom variety," he said. "From a start I found at the nursery. I planted too late to grow it from seed." He raised the tomato like a toast and bit it as an apple. Juice and seeds erupted.

"I know you've got napkins in there." Celia dug in the sack, set a pile of paper towel squares between them, and almost dabbed his chin before she remembered. "Nope. This mess is all yours." Laughing, she sank her teeth into the fresh-picked fruit. "Mmmm. Ambrosia, right?"

"The plant's brimming with them. I had to—to reinforce the cage."

"I should have looked when I was there."

"You can come home. See it then."

"Yeah. That. I've kept you hanging long enough." She took another bite of tomato but made no move to intercept the dripping juice. "I figured out why that hawk affected me so much. Why I wanted to be like her."

A killdeer flew past, its cry piercing the path of air ahead of it as Celia waited for her husband to reply. But true to form, Burnaby showed no sign he'd heard her. She chafed. No comment from him? No question or encouragement for her to say more?

Whoa. No more accusations. No more blame, given or received. Of course Burnaby was listening, with that "fond affection" of his that, if she were honest, she knew never wavered.

"You know, Burn, for my whole life, I've believed that life happens *to* me. And if I don't like its hammer, I have three options: run away, fight back, or lie down and let it pound me. When great stuff happens? I haven't trusted it. I've viewed life as an adversary, out to get me."

Tomato seeds dotted her shirt. She brushed them off and tamped the red gel. Wiped her face.

"But that little hawk? She lives through the worst thing ever and comes out hopping as if life happens *for* her, and she's going to fly, with or without a tail. As if there's nothing that can happen to her that can't be worked into something amazing. Like life is her *friend*."

Her words hung in the air. As if in affirmation, flimsy clouds at the horizon deepened from crimson to beet.

"I want life to be my friend, too, Burn. That's why I want out."

The skin on his face melted. "Out. So you're leaving me after all."

"What? Oh, Burnaby, Burnaby, no!" Oh, her clumsy explanation. She had hurt him. "I'm *sorry*! No, I'm not leaving you. I'm leaving *part* of my old life behind—not you, but work that holds me and my birds captive and a house where I hear our dead baby cry."

Burnaby stiffened and stared at the horizon. His distance was palpable.

Was he pulling away from her? Just when things were finally turning between them? "Oh, Burn, listen. This is a good thing." Panicked, she almost grabbed him before she remembered and pushed her hands into her lap. "You listening?" she whispered.

Still scanning the hills, he nodded.

"Okay. Okay." Her heart still thundered. "Soon as I decided for sure to leave the job and house, you know what happened? Over the breakfast table Hazel tells me the entire farm will be mine after she's gone. All these acres. The prairie. The house and barns. She said it was a done deal. Apparently she changed her will before harvest started."

"On the condition that you live here? Even if it—it divides us?"

"Not at all! Her only condition was that I protect the prairie in whatever way I think best. Joss's trust is a good start, but I'll need to arrange for it into perpetuity. Put it in some other format. A conservation easement, maybe. She said I can keep the rest of the land or sell it. Doesn't matter to her. But it matters to me. I want to stay here, Burn. Live here. Farm."

"While I live in Pullman."

"No, no, no. We could rent out the house or even leave it vacant while we figure this out. You could move out here with me, and we can give this marriage of ours our best efforts. Hazel's told me a hundred times that you're welcome."

"She has?"

"Well, yeah. She's a matchmaker, in case you haven't noticed. And she has plenty of bedrooms upstairs, so there's one for you."

"I see."

"For now. Until we figure out how we'll . . . um . . . get along."

"You already know where I stand, Celia. I'll join you tomorrow."

Her insides roiled. She was still so afraid. But there was more to oneness than just her.

33

CELIA

SLEEP

THE AFTERNOON OF September 17, 2008, Burnaby, coated in zinc oxide, yanked a rotted fascia board from Hazel's porch. Celia poked her head through a window. "You want something to drink?" He raised a gloved hand, nodded, and swiped neck and face with a bent wrist. When Celia tossed him a T-shirt and pointed, he turned.

A powder-blue Volkswagen Rabbit churned a stream of road dust along Old Hollow. Dirt followed the car, then swirled around the slight blonde woman who emerged and walked toward Burnaby, her step as flowy as her voice.

"There he is!" The woman scrunched her tousled pixie cut with hands on their way to the sky. "Oh, my sweet Burn." She stopped short at his lotioned, sweaty skin and emitted a tinkling laugh. "Aren't you a sight, big brother. Glad you're not a hugger." She reached, and her knuckles bumped his.

"We didn't expect you until tomorrow."

226

"How about a 'good to see you, favorite sister,' or at least a 'so glad you're here'?" She patted his shoulder. When he shied, a belly laugh spilled from her like water. "Sorry, love. Couldn't resist."

Celia backed through the door carrying a jug of ice water and two glasses. She set them on the porch table and wrapped her sister-in-law in a tight, swaying hug. Then she gripped the pixie's elbows and surveyed her as if she'd discovered gold. "Aggie. At last."

Burnaby pulled a small suitcase and a backpack from his sister's car and walked toward them. "Not much stuff for six weeks," Celia said.

"I've learned to travel light. Mostly." Aggie took the pack from Burnaby and lowered it to the porch. She pulled a parcel from the top and set it on the table. "Zucchini bread from Mama and a book for Burn from Dad."

Celia hoisted the backpack. "Oof, baby sister."

"Yeah. I need one of those pack mules, but they don't fit inside hides so well."

"Hides?"

"Photography blinds. Like duck blinds, only without the dogs and shotguns. I brought one for that Potholes wildlife refuge but decided not to stop. Cancelled my room and came straight here." She arched her back, stretching. "I do mean *straight*. Seven hours from Mom and Dad's with one five-minute potty break in Ellensburg. Sorry. I should have texted."

"Aggie, you could walk in here at midnight with the measles and we'd call it a party," Celia said. "But no need. You're just in time for one. Twentieth-anniversary shindig for our farm manager and his wife. Here, tonight." Ice clinked as she poured water. "They'll walk up those steps in five hours."

Celia's upright hand screened her grin as Burnaby carried the bags inside, and she whispered to her sister-in-law, "Eighty-three degrees, but Burn thought he should replace and paint that board before guests arrive." Celia rolled her eyes. "I'm choosing to love every nail. Every stroke of that brush. You lived with him, so you get that.

I know you do." She held the door open for Aggie. "Here. I'll show you to your room."

At seven, Celia opened the front door to Satch and Flory and led them to the patio, where a crowd of well-wishers burst into view and surrounded them. Aggie, rested and showered, caught the moment on camera—just as Hazel glommed onto her. "You know, Aggie, I have every single issue of *National Geographic* since 1950. Stacks and stacks of them in our storage room." As if shooing a chicken, she paddled the air underhanded, directing Aggie toward the house. "Here, honey, I'll show you."

Aggie twisted a button on her linen tunic and eyed her brother wielding tongs at the barbecue. Celia hurried to them. "Nolly. Aggie's earning her keep tonight. We've asked her to take pictures of the party. How about starting with us, Ags?" Celia pressed a cheek against her grandmother's and grinned. Aggie raised her lens and clicked.

A few feet away, Ruth, a straight pin between her lips, positioned a rosebud on her father's collar.

"You have to meet her, Aggie. Ruthie's the composer of this event." Celia plucked a stuffed mushroom from a nearby tray and led Aggie to Ruth and her parents. "Since she took over the kitchen two days ago, we've been living off her hors d'oeuvres."

By twilight, neighbors were congregating at a dessert table under fiesta lights strung between an old oak and the house. When Celia appeared with ice cream, Cobb and Hugh conceded their cornhole game to Willie and a repatriated Ivan and made their way to the pies. Ivan lowered the volume on a playlist of eighties love songs and joined them at one of nine makeshift tables.

Other than Hugh, Oren, the Milk family, and Ivan, Celia recognized few in the crowd of three dozen. "Farmers," Hazel said. "Friends from church. I've known most of them their whole lives. And there's Ivan's mother, Ingrid—the blonde wearing lilac, under the tree."

Celia assessed the beautiful woman appreciatively and noticed Oren watching her too. She elbowed Hazel. "He still has a thing for her."

"I suppose." Hazel sank into her chair. "She's a lovely woman. I'll introduce you, after I sit a bit." Celia sat beside her as their table filled.

Aggie crept around the group's edges, snapping candids. Her lens lingered on Satch and Flory, laughing, on the twins, and on Ruth, as she stood and waited for the group to quiet.

"Thank you all for coming . . ."

For the next half hour, stories, tributes, and love poured from the little crowd.

Hazel reached for Celia's hand and squeezed it between both of hers. "This night. These people. You. I believe it's the happiest of my life."

Celia kissed her cheek. "It's a keeper, all right."

Hazel panned the group once more before she gripped the table and got to her feet. "I think I'll hit the hay, though. Long day. You'll give these folks my warmest send-off, honey?"

Celia shifted, but Hazel pressed her shoulder. "Now, honey, you stay put. Lots more goodness to come, I'm sure. I need you here so you can tell me all about it in the morning. Try that cobbler for me, will you?"

Celia smiled up at her. "Will do, Nolly."

Hazel took two steps before Cobb collided with her on his shortcut to the cookies. Heads turned when he yelped, "Sorry, Miz Steffen!"

Hazel touched her own lips, then the boy's. "Hush now, honey. I'm fine." She waved at the onlookers and made her way inside.

Heavy overcast moved in during the night, but with a scant quarter inch of rain since June, no one complained when they awoke to dark skies. Clouds spat intermittently and promised more. Celia and Aggie were stowing clean dishes and folding linens when Ruth and Flory arrived at eight to help. Outside, Burnaby folded card tables and directed the twins to stack chairs.

"Great party, Ruth. A beautiful gift for your parents," Celia said.

"Fun, wasn't it?" Ruth said. Flory smiled and swirled fingers on her daughter's back.

"Hard to get up, though." Celia yawned, replenished her coffee. "Those clouds are like permission to sleep in. Hazel's not even up yet."

"No kidding. Good for her. About time she let us do the heavy lifting." Ruth worked as efficiently as her mother did. Celia could glimpse her as a woman.

Flory checked the kitchen clock, thoughtful. "Did you check on her? Unless she doesn't feel well, Hazel *never* sleeps past six."

"Aw, I don't want to disturb her," Celia said. "I'll look in on her in a bit."

A half hour later, Flory packed leftovers and platters into Burnaby's truck. When she returned, she paused at the stairs. "I still don't hear her."

Celia pulled her head from a cupboard of seldom-used trays. Aggie returned a crumpled towel to a laundry basket.

Ruth dried her hands. "I'll see how she's doing." She skipped steps going up. Her feet thunked down the hallway to Hazel's room. Celia and Aggie returned to work, but Flory stood with a foot on the bottom stair, her hand on a post. And when Ruthie cried out, she ran to join her.

Aggie and Celia raced after her and reached the bedroom as Ruth flung herself at her mother, shriveled into her arms and keened.

Celia's breath hitched. She circled the bed and touched her grandmother's bluing skin, absorbing Hazel's smile, stilled and permanent. "Call for help," she said.

Aggie slipped outside.

Ruth tucked into her mother's throat, her cheeks flooding. Flory stifled a sob and pressed lips to Ruth's hair. She raised crimped eyes to Celia's.

Briefly, Celia held her gaze. But when Flory looked away, she crumpled over her grandmother's quiet chest. *Oh, Nolly. We only just started.* Inside her, sorrow and love stirred their familiar watery concoction of grief.

Another black field. Her feathers were stubs.

WASHED

THE SCREEN BURST OPEN as Burnaby rounded Hazel's house from the patio, a folded table under each arm.

Aggie leapt off the porch, missing the stairs entirely. "Burnaby!"

She sprinted to him, her eyes wild and wide. Rocket sprang to her from the shade of Burnaby's truck, hackles raised. The dog ran his nose like a vacuum over Aggie's legs before he raced to the house, nosed the screen open, and charged inside.

"It's Hazel! She's . . ." The twins, dragging chairs across the lawn, snapped their heads toward her. Gasping, she turned her back to the boys. Lowered her voice. "She's dead, Burn. In her room . . . her bed. We need to call somebody."

"Where's Celia?" He turned toward the porch as Ruth and Flory curled onto a wicker settee. At Ruth's wail, the boys dropped their chairs and ran to them.

"She's with her." Aggie squeezed her upper arms.

Burnaby dropped the tables onto his tailgate. "Call 911." In four strides he reached the porch, where Flory huddled her children. He took the inside stairs three at a time.

Celia's whisper stopped him at the door, her words unclear. Rocket, stretched on the bed beside the corpse, raised his head when Burnaby entered, then resettled a furry chin on Hazel's ribs. Celia sat opposite the dog at Hazel's hip, stroking her grandmother's forehead.

Burnaby crossed to his wife, laid hands on her shoulders. She looked up; her sorrow bludgeoned him.

He crouched beside her grandmother, checking. No pulse at wrist or throat. Black pupils—unresponsive, dilated. The loose-hinged jaw. Lowering his ear to her open mouth and nose, he listened for breath that didn't come.

"If we'd only gotten here earlier. Flory wanted to check her. I didn't listen. I—"

"No, Celia. Don't." He touched her cheek, settled her. "I'll be right back."

Shortly, he brought a fresh washcloth and bowl of warm water to the bedside table and knelt. He moved slowly, wanting Celia to watch, knowing this was important for her. He dunked the cloth and wrung it, then washed the right side of Hazel's forehead, face, and chin. Her right ear. As if tending a petal, he moved to her eyes, closed as if in sleep, and wiped her right eyebrow and lid. He rinsed and wrung the cloth again and moistened the right side of her neck, where pallor competed with her tan from the year's garden hours and from time at the line with freshly laundered clothes.

Crepey brown arms poked from her sleeveless nightgown and crossed the quilt folded at her waist—the fabric turned, he speculated, in the too-warm September night or in the heat of dying.

He rinsed the cloth again and washed her right shoulder, but when he pulled her arm toward him, Rocket stretched his neck, growling low. He petted the dog until the animal's rhythmic panting returned, then continued bathing to the back of Hazel's hand. When he wiped her palm and fingers and the valleys between them, he knew he was painting her into his memory. This woman who saved his wife when he couldn't. This woman who knew how to love.

He dropped the cloth into the bowl and offered it to Celia. She shook her head, but he held it toward her, above Hazel's body, like a baptismal font.

"A washing for heaven," he said. "Part of the healing."

She took the cloth, then looked from Burnaby to her grand-mother and back to him before she wrung it and dabbed her grand-mother's ear.

He sat quietly, watching the holy unfold. The pinch in Celia's countenance softened as she moved to Hazel's face, inclining her head as if tending an infant. Burnaby felt each swipe of the cloth as if Celia were webbing the three of them together, then wiping away Hazel's tethers to earth in a release for which he had no words.

Rocket licked Hazel's left hand as Celia reached for it. She gave the dog time, then wiped Hazel's wrist and the sunspots that riddled her tissue-paper skin.

"Look at her knuckles, Burn. No arthritis. She didn't hurt." She raised Hazel's hand and aligned their fingers, alike but for their years—Hazel's left to Celia's right—as if in prayer.

Burnaby touched Hazel's wedding band, its edges worn sixty-years thin. "We can bury her with this, but, given feelings she expressed to—to me about marriage, I believe she'd want you to have it. If we wait much longer, however, edema will necessitate cutting it off—or the compression procedure I used on Ruth."

She nodded, releasing him to work the ring down Hazel's finger and into Celia's waiting hand. She squinted at the engraving inside. "It's so worn. I can't read . . . m . . . ga . . . fr . . . your guy. '47. Hold on. I need better light."

At the window, she read the eroded words. "*To my gal from your guy. 1947.* Will you look at that, Burn. So awkward. And sweet. You don't sound so tough, Grandpa Joss." And there, in the middle of her heartbreak, her laugh filled him like music.

Celia slipped the ring onto her right hand and wiggled her finger.

"We even wore the same size *rings*." She pressed her lips to the band. "My gal, too. With me still."

In the driveway, doors slammed. Men's voices filled the foyer. Rocket leapt from the bed into the hall, barking at the heavy, approaching footfalls. Celia swiped tears, kissed her grandmother's cooling cheek and empty hand once more and made room for the men to work.

35

CELIA

RING

AT MIDNIGHT, HER MIND still reeling, Celia slipped from her narrow bed to the dresser and dug through clothes for the stray sock she'd tied with a shoelace. She pulled the bow and released a silver band. Its blue-green stone winked in her phone's light as she slipped it on the finger where Burnaby had placed it at Heyday, eleven years before.

She tiptoed across the hall. "You asleep?"

The mattress squeaked as he rolled. "No."

She felt her way to his bed. "Hold me?"

He lifted the quilt and took her in.

36

COBB

DIRT

I TOLD MOMMY THIS: "At the party I crashed into Miz Steffen and I yelled sorry, and she told me to hush and then she went to bed and she died."

Mommy said, "Yes, that's the order of the things that happened, Cobby" and then she told me I had her listening ear and that she felt the hurt in me even though she was wetting the comb in the faucet and smoothing bumps in my hair and then tucking my fancy shirt with plaid on it into my brown cord-a-roys.

So I said to Mommy, "Now me and Willie gots to wear our church clothes only it's not Sunday, and after church we will go to the semi-terry where the diggers will put Miz Steffen in a hole way down deep, only she's really going to heaven, right, Mommy? She won't stay in that dark dirt, will she, Mommy? How will she breathe down there?"

Mommy wet the comb again and spread water on my head where

the cow licked. And then she told me, "Oh, sweetie. You know how the shell of a snail isn't the snail? How it's only a house for a snail?"

I didn't say anything to that but I put my chin to my chest two times.

Then Mommy told me, "'Member how if the shell breaks then the snail can't live in it anymore?"

Then I told her, "Yes, 'cause when Willie steps on a snail it crunches and the snail can't slide around."

Mommy said, "'Zactly. The body that will go in that hole in the ground today is Miz Steffen's shell. It broke and now she's in heaven in her brand-new one. The diggers will only bury the shell today, not Miz Steffen."

I wanted to know so I asked Mommy, "Can I see her new shell?"

Mommy told me, "Someday, love. But not yet. When you do, it will be a happy surprise like a birthday."

I patted my knee and I said, "And this is my shell?"

Mommy said, "Yes, Cobby."

I said, "So Miz Steffen won't be down in the dirt and she can breathe."

Mommy petted my cheek and told me, "Yes, Cobby, breathing air sweet as flowers. Now run get your brother and you two wait outside for Daddy while I get my things."

At the church our preacher was talking and Daddy put his arm across the bench behind me so his fingers touched Willie's neck. There were paper squares and a little pencil in the wood holder on the bench in front of me, so I took a paper and the pencil and drawed the big box made of wood boards and the flowers on it. Then I runned out of room on the paper so Mommy gave me another one and I drawed the inside of the box and it had a long twisty shell in it with a face that I drawed to look like Miz Steffen's there on the paper the man gave me when we sat down.

Then people stood up to sing but I didn't because I had to draw Mommy and Daddy and Willie and Ruthie and me all on a long-back horse that Doc Hayes said was a prayer. It had a long neck and a tail like a flag and it was a question prayer. *Did I break Miz Steffen's shell when I bumped her? Was my voice a smashy rock?*

Then I thought about how I wouldn't see Miz Steffen for a long, long time, and I made big tears that wet my picture of the smiling shell that was Miz Steffen, and the wetness made me stop drawing. Then the lady played the organ and the helper man put his hand on the bench which meaned that we could go outside and I was glad.

I crawled in the car's back seat by Ruth and rolled down my window and counted nineteen telephone poles from the church to the semi-terry up the hill with stubbly fields all around it where wheat growed before they cut it.

The semi-terry had green trees like walls in an outdoor house with a blue-sky roof. I pretended it was a upside-down room with a blue floor and beds with puffy cloud pillows and a green grass ceiling with square rocks in it overhead like heaven was overhead, not under my shoes.

Mommy showed me one rock with my sister Candy's name and some flowers and little boots like babies wear. And then a hawk with a browny-red tail landed in a tree and the upside-down went away and I 'membered I was walking on people's shells and the air smelled like hot pine trees and straw.

On a blue tarp by a green wall the diggers put a big heap of dirt from a hole with straight-line edges and pointy corners like a rectangle even Willie could draw. Daddy and Hugh and Ivan and Mr. Zender and Doc Hayes and one other daddy from church pulled the box out of the long car and Pastor talked and the box went on straps and went down, down, down into the hole. Then everybody throwed in flowers and dirt with their hands and then the diggers scooped the big pile of dirt into the hole.

But it was only her shell and Miz Steffen wasn't there and she could breathe.

37

CELIA

SPROUTS

BECAUSE THERE WAS NOTHING more they could do, after Hazel's funeral, Satch and Hugh seeded the fields with winter wheat. In the ensuing weeks, Celia and Burnaby harvested and mulched their raised garden beds and rented the Pullman house to a visiting professor's family. Burnaby moved the last of his things to the farm, and they set their shoulders to the plow of preparing their new home for winter. While he hung storm windows and insulated pipes against the coming cold, Celia stowed Hazel's squash in the cellar, set tomatoes on window ledges, blanched and froze beets and kale.

Tenderly they set aside the weave of Hazel's presence and strung fresh thread on the loom of their daily life: New playlists and recipes. Math puns. Celia strummed the warp of their days with kindnesses she chose and perfected. Burnaby's touches came often and softened her, and true to their plan and her promise, she stowed them for later.

But *later*? Nights, when his hands invited her with texture and weft, an old rat of fear—all teeth and claws—backed her into her bedroom, and she closed her door, alone.

Aggie, roaming the Palouse from Steptoe to the Blue Mountains for every species of wild hooved mammal she could find, cheered them during her stay, and, on one rare lazy Saturday, planted a cover crop in the emptied garden and photographed the farm. When she hung the picture she'd taken of Celia and Hazel at the anniversary party, they looked at it often.

They heard Hazel everywhere. And they missed her.

Nonetheless, like a floating lantern on a slow river, the light that was Hazel too quickly shrank into the downstream of their days. While Burnaby commuted to Pullman, Celia relinquished the remaining reins of her hawk study to Tara—on the sole condition that Tara let her release Hawk Five, should they need to test him again.

"No problemo," Tara said. Within weeks of Celia's resignation, newly hooded PhD Tara Soto officially replaced her in the University of Idaho's faculty pond.

Good thing. Celia needed the time and headspace, and not just for healing. Though her grandmother had handed Celia a notarized copy of the will bequeathing her entire estate to Celia, Hazel had failed to divulge anything about the farm's financial condition before she died. Celia spent days poring through Hazel's files.

One Thursday afternoon, she assembled her list of questions and drove to the Colfax office of her grandparents' accountant. Middle-aged Karl Lydiard, whom she'd met once at the farm, shoved glasses up on his bulbous nose and laid spreadsheets on the conference table. "Three thousand five hundred farmed acres, usually debt-free by year's end," he said. An aroma of Corn Nuts crowded the room. The bag lay open at his elbow.

Like a chipmunk. Celia pinched back a smile. *Alvin the Chipmunk.*

Lydiard lowered his glasses and looked at her. "But don't let that pad your belly. Land rich and cash poor, those Steffens. Most years were financial cliffhangers. Joss was a frugal manager, but he operated on the edge. Neighbors thought—still think—he was a fool for holding back that wild land of his. Three hundred more farmable acres, tucked between those piney hills? Best soil he owned, right there in that unique little world. Perfect for lavender. Profitable, lavender. Could have given him and Hazel a nice boost."

Lavender? Someone had researched that meadow, and it wasn't her grandfather. "With all due respect, Mr. Lydiard, I need numbers, not judgments."

"Right." He shifted in his chair and shuffled papers. "Hazel signed for an operating loan last year that's still outstanding, but given yields this year, you should be fine. Here . . ."

An hour later, Celia checked the last question off her list.

Lydiard restacked the financials. "As you can see, your cash reserves don't give you much of a buffer for another really poor year—which is sure to come. They always do. All your assets are in that dirt, which is exactly what you've inherited. But if you were to sell it . . . now that's another story. A professor like you . . . I can't believe this place jibes with your plans."

Celia resisted the temptation to give him the boot. Unfortunately, she didn't have time or knowledge—yet—to bring a new accountant up to speed on their operation. How had her grandparents tolerated this pushy little man for over twenty years? And more vexingly, *why?*

"You gonna sell the place? If so, I can connect you with somebody who'd give eyeteeth for that land." He clicked the plunger on his pen like Morse code.

Too eager, this man. "So you broker property, too?"

Lydiard laughed. "I have a lot of connections, is all. Could help make this terrible time a little easier for you. Young woman like you with those holdings? Why don't you sell them, reinvest in some good mutual funds, and you'll be set for life."

And the man was a financial adviser. "My, my. I trust you're certified to dispense that recommendation?"

Lydiard squirmed. *Texas Hold'em would eat the man alive.*

"Actually, strike that last comment." When he grinned, a fleck of green showed between a canine and a premolar.

Salad for lunch. Celia bit her cheek. *Good for him.*

"Directing your assets is beyond my professional arena."

"Arena, huh? Fortunately, I won't need your rodeo, Mr. Lydiard. I have no intention of selling."

"Ah. A lease then. Those same investors—"

Celia glanced at his framed credentials. "No need. I'm going to grow myself a little wheat."

His receptionist would have heard him laugh through the thick oak door. "You're joking, right? Not much room for error if you hope to keep the bank off your back."

"I heard you the first time."

"Your learning curve will be steep."

"I'm a PhD, Mr. Lydiard. I'm pretty good at learning. In fact, I'm learning a lot right now." She pushed back from the table. "And regarding the wheat? Satchel will help me."

He took her bait. "From what I hear, Mr. Milk is as good a manager as they come. He has not, however, been privy to the farm's finances. Hazel made that fact clear."

"Sounds like you knew her pretty well. Did she ever talk about what she planned to do with the place before she met me?" Celia had awakened from a sound sleep two nights running, needing to know.

"No idea. You didn't find any earlier will—or trust documents?" He leaned closer. Celia imagined him salivating over her answer, fork and knife in his fists. A wannabe attorney, too—an evasive one. He knew more than he let on.

"No, but I'm still looking. If my grandparents had old friends they cared about and included in an earlier will, before I arrived, I'd like to know. I tried to reach their former attorney, but apparently he passed last year—ten months after Joss did. His junior partner only held the latest document. The one deeding the estate to me."

Lydiard swayed like a paid mourner, his face hangdog. "Yes. Randy Sheridan. A real good friend. Such a loss."

"So you knew him." *Of course he did.* "Are you sure you can't give me any more history about my grandparents' intentions? Five months ago, Hazel didn't know I existed. Obviously, she would have had a different succession plan."

"And five months ago, you didn't know she or Joss existed. Happy as a clam over at the university with your cushy salary. Now, suddenly, you want to farm, with margins as thin as piano wire, most years. I've seen this before. City kids inherit, move to the country planning to conquer agriculture, then pack their U-Hauls a year later."

Celia held her face expressionless, trying to drum up a visual of Hazel dealing with this obnoxious little man. Why had her grandmother shared so much with him? Or had she? Who else knew what he did?

"My salary, my background, and everything else about me is my business, not yours, Mr. Lydiard." She gathered her papers and stood. "And I'm not going anywhere. If you're right, you can enjoy a good gloat a year from now at my expense. Meanwhile, I would like digital copies of all the farm records, tax returns, and correspondence you have on file."

"Joss and Hazel had duplicates of everything. You may find their paper records a little friendlier."

"I like computers, Mr. Lydiard. An innovative accountant like you—I presume you do, too? You converted to electronic files years ago, am I correct?" *Presume.* She pinched a smile at Burnaby's word— and at her bluff. Lydiard could have kept records with a feather quill and inkwell for all she knew.

He adjusted his posture, straightened his open collar. "Certainly."

She handed him a thumb drive and checked her watch. "I have a few errands to run. I'll pick them up in an hour."

Rain had arrived quietly in late September, joining ideal temperatures for birthing winter wheat plants. After the Steffen no-till equipment drilled seeds into stubble, a green shadow spread over the first fields planted, exactly on cue. They were still waiting for the later fields to sprout.

On a mid-October Saturday, Aggie declined a lunch of split pea soup, blew kisses, and aimed her Volkswagen toward home. Burnaby and Celia waved from the porch, then sat to eat. They were dunking sourdough bread in their bowls when boots thumped on the porch.

Celia opened the door to Satchel, pacing. Words burst from him and condensed in the season's first, and late, freezing air.

"We have a problem."

"C'mon in." Celia opened the door as Satch removed a knitted cap and gloves. He crossed his arms when she reached for his jacket.

"A real problem."

"Here. Sit." She pulled out a chair for him and took a bowl from the cupboard. "Soup?"

He shook his head, his worry hanging between them like winter. Steady Satch fighting a storm—and losing?

"Two hundred acres at least. The time, fuel, seed, crop. I know I applied that fertilizer correctly."

"What are you talking about?" Celia scooted her chair perpendicular to him and copied his lean.

"Hot nitrogen, probably. Wrong ratio injected with two hundred acres of seed. All of it killed at emergence. Somebody's been doctoring our tanks, Celia. I took samples to the lab this afternoon. No results yet, of course, but there's no other explanation for those chemically burned plants."

Celia stood and looked out the window. Spoons rested in cooling soup as their little group sat with the news. "Our saboteur," she said. The others had nothing to add.

38

COBB

THROAT

MOMMY SAID, "You boys will be tied to us today." That meaned roped with no rope because the hunters wear orange and shoot deers for Venny's son and today they can.

So after goat chores Willie rided to town with Mommy and Ruthie, and I rided in the combine with Daddy while he cutted the dry corn between the big hills. He says the corn feeds cows at the college dairy and is good corn because we don't plow and the land holds water to make it grow good.

I like to ride with Daddy because he lets me push buttons and I can bring my sketchbook in the cab and draw even though we're working, and he tells me names of trees and birds and what letters to write for their names. Daddy said because I pay tension and because God gived me good eyes, I see things and then I draw them.

I know what cornstalks sound like when they fall because I heared them when I watched with Mommy, but when I'm in the cab I can't hear them because of the motor but I think of their swishy sound when the cutter knocks them down and grinds them up, and I pretend Daddy and I are riding a red elephant eating and eating and eating long stems with cobs on them. Daddy says only one *b* not two like my name.

We are riding the elephant while it is eating corn and I hear a *cling bang clink* like a bell hitting hard on a rock and Daddy says, "Buggers, Cobb." He pushes a button and raises the front that is like the elephant's tusk-es and says, "Wait here," and he goes down the ladder and looks and comes back up and says, "Broke a gath-ring chain." He raises his finger and smiles and says, "I can fix it." Then he gets his toolbox behind the seat and pulls out a metal thing and says, "The missing link," and he laughs. Daddy's laugh has happy in it that feels like my favorite colors and I want to draw it but I also have to pee.

"Daddy," I say.

I am holding my front and he looks at my hand and digs in a bag and gives me my orange vest and hat and says, "Okay, go, then come right back up here. You can't be wandering today, understand?"

I shake my head up and down and put on the vest and hat and while I climb down the ladder, he crawls under the tusk-es and lies on his back.

Because we are on the edge of the field almost at the top I walk to some trees so I can aim my pee at leaves when I go. But I don't pee because a porky-pine comes out from a tree and I have never seed a porky-pine for real but I know what it is because of my books and all the points on it and how they look like a sea urchin in another book and the points wiggle when it walks.

I look back and Daddy's legs are still poking out from the elephant and I just want to see the porky-pine more so I can draw it, so I follow it up the hill until it goes back in the trees. And I look and Daddy is still working on his back and now I'm at the top by a thorny bush and on a different hill I see Hugh!

Hugh is walking up the hill on the R side like the *R* Mommy writes on my hand and I know it's Hugh because of his fatness and his fluffy hair, and he's wearing orange and holding a gun that's long like Daddy's. And I watch Hugh until he's closer and then a big deer with horns that look like tree branches goes up the L side of the hill where Hugh can't see it. And the deer is almost at the top now and it doesn't see me and neither does Hugh who is almost at the top on the other side of the hill. I yell, "Hey, Hugh," and I point to the deer and Hugh sees me and puts his finger by his mouth in that "be quiet" way and he gets to the top and the deer jumps in front of him, and I hear a bang and Hugh falls down and his throat is all red.

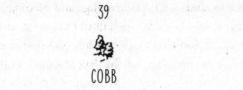

39

COBB

HORSE

I YELL "HUGH!" again but he doesn't answer me or get up off the ground, and I want to run to him but my legs don't work. Then Mr. Zender runs a white horse up the hill and he jumps off and bends over Hugh and I hear only him not Hugh talking so I know Hugh is too tired to get up or talk.

I seed that horse in Mr. Z's field before. Mommy calls it a gray only it's white like chalk. Now it waves its head and makes a snorty sound and digs dirt with its foot like a shovel and when it sees me it stops and its ears point at me.

I am listening with my eyes when it twirls and jumps and the foot holders on the saddle swing straight out and the chalk horse runs away over the hill and its mane and tail are straight out, too.

My feet still don't work and Daddy is yelling "Cobb! Cobb!" and running up the hill and his face says something I don't know, and I am crying and I fall down because of my shaking and Daddy picks me up and he doesn't care that my pants are wet. When Daddy holds me Mr. Z's face says what Daddy's does and Hugh's throat is still red. And I want the horse to tell me but the horse runned away.

I curl like a ball into Daddy and my head is at his neck and he covers my eyes with his hand and Mr. Z yells, "There was a buck," and I know that means the daddy deer with horns and Daddy yells to Mr. Z, "Stay. I'll get help."

Daddy helps me up the ladder because my shaking won't stop and he holds me and drives the combine home but Mommy and Ruthie and Willie are gone and so he holds me more and calls people and red trucks come with lights and he puts me in his pickup and my head is on his knee when he shows them where.

40

CELIA

BEER

TEXT SIGNALS CHIMED IN tandem from Celia's and Burnaby's pockets when they exited the farm store in Colfax. With a forty-pound bag of dog food in her arms, Celia ignored the tone, but Burnaby shifted a sack of grain onto his hip, pulled out his phone and glanced.

"Flory," he said.

"Probably reminding us to get that goat feed."

Burnaby hoisted his bag into the truck bed and relieved Celia of hers. She rounded the tailgate and stopped short. "Well, lookee here."

She tilted her head past the parking lot toward a commercial propane tank, where two young men leaned against a gray Ram pickup and talked to an animated trio of teen girls. One of them, a strong twentysomething man who towered over the others, popped a can lid, swigged, and belched. The swarthy second man set an empty can on the ground, stomped it flat, and caught a laughing, flashy blonde by the waist. A third man, his hat brim backwards and his profile familiar, leaned on a black Blazer, smiling at whatever the dark-haired girl at his ear was saying. Cold wind lifted her hair toward clouds scudding overhead.

"Think Ruth's invited to that little party? Maybe Ivan will save her some beer."

Burnaby closed the tailgate as more laughter carried across the lot. "Don't jump to conclusions, Celia."

"You have eyes too, Burnaby."

"I don't see anything incriminating Ivan over there. What if he simply pulled up to talk?"

Celia huffed. "Sometimes I think you'd give Pol Pot the benefit of the doubt."

In the cab, she clicked to the text. "Says it's urgent." She punched Flory's number. "Hey—" Receiver pressed to her ear, she went cold. "Oh no."

Burnaby touched her elbow.

"It's Hugh." Her hand found the handle and flung the truck door open. "Shot," she said, and sprinted across the lot toward the mechanic's lifelong friend.

"No, no, *NO!*" Celia wailed. She jumped from Burnaby's truck and ran toward the vehicles in the barnyard, where medics transferred a black body bag from the sheriff's SUV to a gurney and wheeled it toward the ambulance.

Ivan's Blazer skidded to a halt beside her. "Huuuugh!" he bellowed as he jumped from the rig and ran to the rolling cart. He gripped the rails and pressed his face into his friend's midsection, his sobs agonized. The medics looked away and waited.

At length, Burnaby gently pulled him upright. Ivan scanned his surroundings. His face contorted when he spotted his father standing between the sheriff and an older woman.

"It was an accident, Son." Grief hollowed Oren's face. Wind caught his orange cap and sent it scuttling across the gravel. Ivan tracked its path then noticed his dad's hunter-orange jacket. His eyes darkened.

"You? *You* shot him?" Ivan lunged at his father, but Burnaby caught his shoulders, turned him, enfolded him. Ivan ground his face into Burnaby's coat and cried like a child.

"Come with me," Burnaby said, and steered him toward the house. The EMTs secured the gurney, closed the doors, and drove away.

"Oh, Oren," Celia said. Her chest felt full of rocks she'd hurl at him, if she could.

The sheriff stepped between them, touched his hat. "Vance Petersburg," he said. "And Delores Young, coroner." An older woman raised her down jacket's hood and dropped her chin.

"Petersburg. As in Alaska," Celia mumbled absently, then raised her voice. "What happened?" She didn't care who answered. Bile rose in her throat, and she swallowed hard. Delores stood with her back to the wind.

Oren's tears seeped into his crow's feet. *Crying.* Whether from wind or grief, Celia couldn't tell. "I shot at a buck below the ridge," he said. "The boy can confirm. He saw it."

"Wait until I take your official statement, Oren, before you go talking," Petersburg said, then looked at Celia. "You're Hazel's grand-daughter, right?"

Celia nodded. "What boy?"

"Satchel's little guy. One of the twins." Petersburg rubbed his forehead. "They're in the house now. I tried to reach Hugh's parents, but they aren't answering."

"What happened?" Celia asked again.

Cold rain spattered Petersburg's hat. "I can't give you specifics yet." He removed a digital recorder from his pocket and waggled it at Celia. "We got our photos and took measurements, but Delores and I should go up there and walk through the whole thing with Oren one more time before this rain washes out tracks. Then we've got to have a psychologist find out what the boy saw. Terrible thing for a child to witness."

41

COBB

AGAIN

MOMMY PETTED MY HEAD and singed, and I took a nap but I waked up and I wanted to be by my daddy because he seed Hugh too. I finded him in the garage and he was on the ladder and pushing on the attic door. I shouted, "Daddy," but I shouted too loud and his feet made a little jump and he waved at his head and the ladder falled and he hitted the cement and didn't move.

42

CELIA

MUTE

CELIA AND FLORY WAITED for a graying, rail-thin nurse to wheel
Satchel from the recovery room into the wide hallway. Immobilized
by a cervical collar and suspended right arm, groggy Satch winked at
Flory with a swollen eye, and the women followed the bed into his
room. The nurse circled Satch like a beagle, adjusting traction lines
to his fractured elbow. Angry welts marked his face.

Satch lifted his good hand, and Flory held it to her cheek. "Looks
like you'll be right as rain, love," she said.

He squeezed her fingers. His words slurred. "They tell you about
all those pins and plates in there? And my wasp stings?"

"Who'd a guessed, eh?" Flory rubbed his hand. "Two hard frosts
already and those nasty bugs still alive in our warm attic. EMTs had
to wear nets."

"I wanted that box up there. That Little League team plaque for
Hugh's parents. Did—?"

Flory touched his lips. "I'll get it later, love. For now, you rest. Celia will sit with you. Kids are in the waiting room with Burnaby, but I don't want to leave Cobby."

"Howsh he doing?" He shifted. Tried to lean.

The nurse's lips cinched. *Like a lifeguard,* Celia thought, *blasting her whistle.* "Words are fine, Mr. Milk, but movement after a concussion like yours isn't. Your brain's swollen."

Flory squeezed her husband's toes through the blanket. "No wasp stings, but he's shadowing me everywhere. Cries if he can't touch me. I slept in the twins' room with him until about midnight, then moved him to our bed, but he woke up every couple of hours. He's not talking, Satch. Not a word."

"Bring him to me?"

The nurse scowled and left the room.

"In an hour or two. Let your head clear a little more. All this . . ." She swiped the flat of her hand at the traction wires and neck brace. "He doesn't need to see all this *and* hear you talking drunk."

Satch's eyelids drooped. Celia sat on the empty bed beside him, then pulled up a chair and waved her phone at Flory. "I'll text you when he wakes up."

Five days after he fell from the ladder, vertigo still relegated Satchel to a wheelchair, so Burnaby pushed him, nauseous and late, across the bumpy graveyard grass and into the tide of dispersing mourners. Alongside them, Cobb, his legs dangling beneath his mother's arms, buried his face in the collar of her heavy wool coat. Willie trailed somberly, dragging a stick. He peered into Hugh's open grave at the casket, laden with roses and a sprinkling of soil.

"A box like Miz Steffen's, Cobby. Where his shell is."

Cobb raised his head and peeked in the hole, then tracked the flight of a redtail from the wall of trees into the swept blue ceiling. A weighty look passed between his parents, and Celia's heart squeezed.

She pressed her forehead onto Burnaby's shoulder, then withdrew an inch, leaning on air.

Ivan waited in the parking lot as Ruth hurried to her brothers. She held their heads in turn and kissed them. Her mother dropped heavily into a chair, still holding Cobb. Willie sat, then lay, then sat again beside his mother and brother in the otherwise empty row.

Ruth turned away from them and crouched by Satch's wheelchair. Her whisper was furious. "You brought the boys! Why, Dad? Haven't they . . . hasn't Cobb seen enough?"

Satchel stretched toward Ruth's ear. "We planned . . ." He glanced at the boys, assessing earshot, Celia guessed. "Your mother had every intention of staying home with them, but when Burnaby came for me, Cobb grabbed his jacket and ran to the truck. Your mom tried to peel his fingers off the handle, but he fought like a wildcat, then flopped on the ground when she and Celia tried to get him in the house. He threw gravel at all of us until Willie got the truck door open and they jumped in."

He sighed and touched his lips—and blew a kiss toward Flory. She caught it from the wind. "Maybe being here will help him somehow."

Engine exhaust condensed behind the Blazer in the emptying lot. Ruth waved at Ivan and stood.

Satchel ticked his head toward the vehicle. "You go on ahead, honey. Ivan needs you right now. We won't be long."

Like one section in a jointed pull toy, Ivan's SUV fell in line with the cars winding down the hill. The gravedigger huddled against the chill on a backhoe. Burnaby knelt by Satch's chair at the grave's edge, praying aloud. "We don't understand, Lord, but we trust you. Hold Hugh, heal him. Heal us . . ."

Celia stood at Hazel's nearby headstone, listening to her husband's trust and love and surrender that, try as she might, she could not reconcile here in this third funeral, this fourth death in half a year's time. Pain like this? His hope bewildered her.

He would link his perspective to entanglement, of course, and would tell her that though death's vast span temporarily separated

Hugh's body, here at this graveside, from the God who loved him, their friend remained alive and present with the God he loved in return. Burn would say that no chasm of death could disentangle God from Hugh—just as atomic particles, once entangled, could never forget one another, even a universe apart. He'd explained it to her so many times.

But as much as she loved science, her mind simply wouldn't stretch through quantum anything to find a Creator who loved her like that. Instead, she considered the stub-tailed hawk and its stumbly hops to its healer. She held that visual, and it held her.

43

FLOOD

SLEET'S TEETH BIT INTO NOVEMBER, bringing precipitation farmers counted on to soak their fields deep. The sting was welcome, its absorption gradual. Ground crusted and froze, and when the temperature inched past freezing, the earth sipped.

But the week before Thanksgiving, a warm front boiled in from the south in a three-day downpour. Another storm blew in on its heels. "Gully-washers," Satch said. Though stubble held even the contaminated Steffen fields in place, mud flowed like lava off bare Zender fields across Old Hollow and stopped the school bus two days running.

After dark on November 26, Satchel hung his dripping hat and jacket by the farmhouse door and delivered the lab report on October's tank samples to Celia. She opened the rain-spattered page on the kitchen counter and leaned over it.

Satch pointed to a highlighted section of the report. "Nitrogen didn't kill our field," he said. "Atrazine did. Systemic herbicide, added to the spray buggy that feeds the seeder. Our crop didn't stand a chance. Whoever did this knew where we left the tractor at day's end. Easy to poison a tank when nobody's around." He rubbed the back of his neck. "Upside is that they only hit us the last three days of planting. Still a good near two hundred acres, though, killed outright, and now we've probably lost use of that ground for a year."

"At least we know what we're dealing with. If only we knew who." Celia pulled out the farm map and scribbled calculations. More hits. Insurance money had arrived for the burned crop and combine, but the prorated machine value meant they had to locate an affordable used replacement. Satch, practical but fussy, was coming up empty-handed. "You got any leads on a new mechanic?" she asked.

"Not yet. I planned to talk to a guy this morning, but Ivan brought me another problem. A more immediate one. I hoped we could deal with it without troubling you, but we can't even get to the tanks." He slumped onto a chair. Pinched the bridge of his nose, blinking.

"You okay?"

"Fine. Just a little dizzy now and then. Ivan called his dad to help so I could come here—and go home to rest for a while. I can't dig with this arm, anyway."

She pushed the report aside and eyed him with concern. "Smart of him. What tanks?"

"Clogged culverts by our three south storage bins. Silos full of grain and immersed in two feet of water. Good seals on those tanks, so the contents should stay dry, but there's no guarantee. If water penetrates and that wheat molds . . ."

"Really? The water's that deep?" The terrain around the elevators wasn't ideal, wrapped as it was by a steep horseshoe of land and the elevated roadbed, but Joss had included safeguards against storm water in the site's design. Thick concrete pads raised the galvanized bins above the bowl's floor. Celia recalled Hazel saying the county engineer had shaken his head at the hillside drains and *two* oversized culverts under the road. Joss overbuilt the whole thing, Hazel said, the infrastructure hardly worth the ease of access.

Considering its design, this storm's water should have poured to lower ground, nowhere near those tanks.

"Yes, and rising. And the road's washed out by the creek. A county crew's there now, but until they get through, we can't haul an excavator or an auger in there."

"What's the matter with those culverts?"

"Both pipes are plugged, with nothing visible at the intake. One, I understand, but two? Ivan thinks it's intentional."

"What's *your* assessment, Satch?" Celia tossed her pencil on the table. Was he having cognitive trouble, as well? Her throat tightened with worry. The Satchel she knew would have alerted her to this flooding *before* showing her a long-delayed lab report. "How could somebody stuff a drain in this weather?"

"Jammed in the dry season, Ivan figured. Nothing we'd notice walking by, unless the obstructions were close to the pipe mouths. The drains are clogged deep. Ivan ran a rod in one and said it was hard as concrete."

Maybe it is concrete. A chill pricked her neck. Ivan, reporting sabotage *again*. Celia's suspicions of *him* had faded, but Ivan's theory about the pipes suggested he held his own suspicions. What did he know? A preposterous possibility struck her: Did he suspect his *dad*? And if so, *why*? Why would Oren want to hurt them?

She threw up her hands. "I'm new to the farm's financials, Satch, but if this keeps up, I don't see how we can stay solvent. Lydiard evaluated the books again last week, and he says we're in trouble. While I question where his interests lie, facts are facts. If we can't find out who's doing this—and stop the bleeding—we'd be better off getting out while we can. Not worth the financial or emotional stress."

She shaped her fingers in a square and framed Satchel's injured arm, strapped in its sling. "Look at you. Those headaches you have now? And who knows how your elbow will heal? Not to mention your wordless little boy. You don't need all this."

"Whoever's doing this *wants* us to quit, Celia. Why else would they target this farm? I don't know about you, but I'm not one to cave to evil."

Satch's words rallied her. Gave her purpose. Cave to evil? Neither would she.

44

CELIA

THERAPY

"LOOKIT, LOOKIT, LOOKIT!"

Celia rose from her stool at Flory's kitchen counter and opened the sliding glass door to the source of the shout—a noisy, wind-chapped child in a puffy parka. Willie stomped snow from his boots on the outside doormat and held a brown, sweat-stained Cenex Farm Supply cap over his head.

"Lookit!" he said again. His breath steamed in the frigid air. "Hugh lefted it in the shop on the workbench only I never seed it because of his big toolbox but the new 'chanic moved the box and I seed it and it's Hugh's and I brung it for Cobby for a birthday present."

Toolbox. Hat. Soda can. All exactly where Hugh had left them an hour before the accident and—in the elixir of unspoken denial—where they had remained for nearly two months, as if Hugh would swing the shop door wide, settle the cap on his flyaway hair, swig a burpy gulp, and pull out a wrench.

The women's eyes locked on the cap, and Celia tensed with anger. *Move the toolbox? How dare he? And the cap?* When her irrational ire at the new mechanic flew toward Willie there in the snow with the hat in his hands, she banished it and wrapped her heart around the child.

Flory filled her lungs to their depths, pulled Willie inside, and lowered his hood. "Boots off, birthday boy."

"Okay, okay, okay. Soon's I give this to Cobby." He slipped her grasp and trailed clotty snow past the Christmas tree to the wood-stove, where his brother sat in a beanbag chair. Teeth pressed into Cobb's lower lip as he curled over a drawing, pinching his pencil.

"Cobby, I gotted this for you. Lookit. *Lookit!*" Ignored, Willie hid the hat behind his back and bent sideways, his cheek on Cobb's paper. He swatted at the pencil. "I gots something for you."

Cobb raised his chin, his expression flat. Willie waved the hat like a flag, planted it on his brother, then tipped his head, assessing. "Hugh lefted it for you."

Cobb touched the brim and resumed drawing as Willie, beaming, turned to the women, who watched quietly from the doorway. "He likes it!" He raced to the counter, swiped a fingerful of frosting from the birthday cake, and squeezed through the glass slider steamed by Rocket's breath.

"Willie!" Flory waved gloves at him through a crack in the door. Willie stuffed hands through the gap and she wrestled them on. Dog and boy bounded away before Cobb removed the hat, traced the logo with his pencil eraser, and patted it back onto his head. Celia and Flory slipped to the kitchen, watching sidelong as Cobb pulled his sweatshirt hood over the cap, found his parka and boots, and headed for the door.

Flory caught him, zipped his jacket, and fed fingers and thumbs into mittens. Then she kissed his hooded head and opened the door to his brother's path through the foot-deep snow. When Cobb caught up to Willie and Rocket, she turned from the window and retrieved the boy's drawing pad from the hearth.

"We found him a pediatric trauma therapist who tried engaging him through play therapy—clay, sand, figurines, puppets—but no go. Apart from stuffing a toy horse in his pocket, he wouldn't connect. Then she opened her cupboard and he beelined for the drawing supplies. No surprise, eh?"

She flipped to the first page and handed the sketchbook to Celia. "Here's what I was telling you about. I dated them in the corners, starting a week after the accident."

"Did Cobb section this off—or did she?" Pencil lines crosshatched the page, separating a series of graphite illustrations that bore little of the fine detail in those on the refrigerator and bulletin board and the twins' bedroom walls.

"He did, but only for the first couple of pages. He's careful with paper, so I'm guessing he worried about using too much of the therapist's supply. When she told him the book was his, the sketches got larger. You'll see. It's the entire story, Celia. And then some stuff none of us understand."

"But no spoken words?"

"None. He won't even write the ones he learned this summer or in those first six weeks of kindergarten. Satch disagrees, but I'm not letting him go back to school until he talks. You think that's wrong?"

"Does he want to go?"

"Nope. He used to race his brother to the road. Now he watches from my lap until Willie and Ruth climb on the bus. Then he dives back into that sketchbook."

Celia carried the drawings to the table. Flory sat beside her, where she could keep tabs on the boys rolling white torsos of snow people in the yard. "They're in order, only top to bottom, then left to right."

"This first one's plain as day." Celia pointed at a stick woman. "That's Hazel, right? And Cobby bumping into her at the party?"

"Sure looks like it to me."

Celia smoothed the page. "And this one, with the ladder and the man falling. Is that Cobby with his mouth open?"

"That's our guess. See those black lines? We think he's shouting at his dad."

When Celia moved to the next frame, she rotated the paper sideways, upside-down, upright again. "I don't get this one. It's all willy-nilly."

"Stay with it. Tell me what you see." Flory raised the page to direct sunlight—and closer to Celia's nose.

"Shrubs, maybe. Trees. Cornstalks? What's that thing . . . a *porcupine*?"

"Probably, though Cobby won't respond when we ask him. Won't react at all."

"At the bottom . . . Is that a shoe? Laces?"

"Yes. Cobb's. I'm sure on that one. See the chicken on the toe?" She dug in a basket by the door and handed Celia a faded navy canvas shoe. Sure enough, the outline of a chicken on its white rubber toe cap matched that in the sketch. "There's a coyote on the left shoe. Black Sharpie, his tool of choice."

"So he saw a porcupine."

"And followed it. Look at the next frame down."

This scene was clearer, with a tiny combine at the left edge of the frame. Flory tapped stick-like legs poking from beneath it. "Satch blames himself. Says he assumed Cobb had climbed back in the cab."

At the right of the frame, a stick figure in hat and vest followed a spiky little creature past cornstalks and trees. "From the looks of this, Satch crawled under the tractor and Cobb wandered off."

"Yep."

Detail increased in every sketch, riveting Celia as she crept down the page, then returned to the next column and a bird's-eye view of a tiny combine in a sea of corn. Then a sketch of a buck, bounding. Then Hugh, she figured, his head down, climbing a stubbled hill.

Then more, close-ups: Two finely drawn hands: one small, one large and fat, tilted from wrists as if waving. The deer's front quarters only, leaping toward the crest of a hill. A hunting cap and wispy hair, the body attached to them beyond the boundaries of the page. A hunter from the waist down, legs bent in an uphill creep, rifle at his waist. A mouth—Cobb's?—spitting heavy black lines . . . another shout? Hugh—full-faced, with a shushing finger to his lips.

A bullet, its speed marked with streaks, filled an entire frame. Below it, a buck's rump and flag-tail, airborne, legs tucked, retreating. Then the antlers above a hill's crest. Then Hugh tumbling sideways, his neck a petaled flower.

Tears streamed down the women's cheeks. Flory flipped to a drawing of Satch, running, his arms spread beyond the page, his face stretched in a wordless cry of fright. Then jeaned, fat legs, askew. A hunting cap on the ground, upended.

Frame after frame after frame.

Next came Oren, Celia guessed. A man anyway, his features a scribble, his outline a wavy blur as he flew from the back of a stocky horse. The images after that showed a horse's head sideways in a toss, loose reins like whips and a man hunched like a snail over Hugh.

"Like celluloid," Celia said. "A movie reel."

"He saw the whole thing."

"Poor little guy. A horror for anyone, but for a five—now six-year-old—and one as sensitive as Cobby?"

Flory looked through the window, to the twins leaning into a snowball as tall as their chests. "Imagine having that in your head. He can't find words big enough, I guess."

Celia touched a sketch of Cobb's head. "If only he'd talk."

"The counselor said he's processing through these drawings. Her goal is to keep the story in a flow that integrates with his ongoing lived experience, so that the trauma can gradually shrink on his timeline, rather than isolate in his memory where it can grow. She said if he walls out the accident—compartmentalizes—it'll stay hot in his brain. Apparently when tragedies like these go underground and remain unaddressed, they can freeze interpretation of the trauma, in this case in the perception of a five-year-old. That stuck spot can dog him for life. She wants us to bring the pain into the light and walk through it with him."

"For how long?" Celia said.

"As long as necessary. We're in a marathon, for sure, but healing will come if we stay the course. We've got the best help available, eh? With him, nothing's impossible."

"I thought Cobb's therapist was a woman."

"She is. But we're trusting the good Lord's counsel, too." Flory smiled and tapped the sketch pad. "Now for the mysterious drawings. See if you can make any sense of these. We can't tell if he's going deeper into his experience in a way that will help him, or if he's avoiding that awful image of Hugh burned into his mind. At least he's playing with his brother now, eh?"

Curious, Celia flipped to the next drawing. A new scene, this time filling a full page, showed a saddled, rearing, riderless horse with flared nostrils. Cobb had drawn one eye pale, one eye dark.

Flory fanned the page edges behind it. "Somewhere after his third or fourth of these bigger drawings is when he started interacting with Willie again. The therapist believes Cobb has mastered part of the trauma. He's not so afraid now, and he seems more purposeful."

Celia leaned over the sketch. "I've seen this horse in Zender's field. And Ivan rode it the day Hazel chewed him out for hunting coyotes in the meadow. One blue eye, right?"

"Yeah. Supposedly he's Oren's roping horse. Name's Drummer. Pricey, that one. And believe it or not, he's a gray, not a true white horse. Pure black when he was born, but by his seventh birthday, every hair on his body was snow white. Only that black muzzle—or a close-up of his skin—gives him away."

Flory looked out the window at the boys wrestling in the snow. "According to Oren's ex-wife, Ingrid, he bought the horse at auction with money they'd set aside for a kitchen remodel. She called it the last straw and moved out."

"What was he thinking?"

"Who knows, eh? Oren doesn't even like the animal. He says he can't trust him. Satch said the only reason he was riding him the day Hugh died was because that big bay of his went lame."

"Burn says horses pick their people sometimes."

"Ruth would agree with that." Flory touched the horse's nose in one of Cobb's drawings. "She says Drummer will do anything for Ivan. Dependable as gravity."

"I wonder what Drummer knows about Oren that we don't." Celia pulled the drawing closer. "Look at the detail in this one, Flory. As if Cobb were close enough to touch its coat. That other drawing . . . Did the horse dump Oren?"

"Oren claims Drummer frog-hopped when he fired the gun, then bucked *after* he dismounted and ran to Hugh. Either way, the horse took off. Ivan stayed with Hugh's parents that night, so Oren and the sheriff searched for Drummer all day in that terrible storm. They finally found him outside Oren's barn, the saddle off to one side and covered in mud, but that rifle was still in its scabbard, with the shell casing right there in the chamber."

"They ruled it an accident pretty fast." Though she couldn't peg why, the decision niggled at Celia.

"But everything lined up, eh? The deer and horse tracks in the field, those first drawings of Cobb's—they all supported Oren's story. He aimed at the buck a hundred fifty yards out with the hill as a backstop. The horse hopped, the shot went high, and the bullet hit Hugh just as he popped over the hill after that same deer. Stupid of Oren to shoot from the horse's back, but it's not illegal, and he and Ivan do it all the time hunting coyotes. Who'd guess he'd aim at a buck and kill his son's best friend instead, eh? Now he's got to live with that." Flory's shoulders sagged. "And so does Cobby."

Celia shook her head. "Oren shouldn't have been hunting on our land."

"Hazel and Joss always gave him access during hunting season—as long as he stayed away from that prairie. He didn't ask you?"

"No."

"Did you post the land? You know, with *No Hunting* signs?"

Celia stared at her.

"You still have a lot to learn, girl. Without clear red lights, everything's a green go for Oren."

More pages. The focus of the boy's drawings shifted, and his meticulous detail returned. Consumed entirely now with the horse, Cobb dedicated an entire page to a suspended hoof and the extensor and flexor muscles above it. Another illustration showed the animal's neck from poll to withers with the long floating mane tousled from agitation and flight.

Others: The horse's barrel, dark with sweat around the cinch. Velvety nostrils. A man's boot, the heel high in the stirrup. *Off-balance? Dismounting?* An empty saddle with stirrups flying.

Foam dripped from the bit in a carefully wrought muzzle on a page Celia nearly tore from its spiral wire binding, eager as she was to see the scene she glimpsed after it. Now the entire horse filled a page. Ears forward, neck low, tail and hooves dusted by the powder earth, the stock-still animal stared at the artist. Whether real or imagined, the encounter Cobb conveyed was intimate, intense.

But it paled to the one that followed. Lash-rimmed, Drummer's shiny, pale eye owned the page where, reflected in the ovoid pupil, Celia saw Cobb, his own eyes large, his mouth a startled O.

"Oh, wow, Flory. Wow."

"Right, eh? What do these drawings *mean*, Celia? Why the pre-occupation with a horse he encountered for only a minute or two, tops?"

Celia closed the sketchbook's cardboard cover slowly. "You need to show these to Burnaby. He and Cobb used to talk while they drew horses. He may have some ideas for you."

Snowballs flew as Satchel appeared at the corner of the house. He clamped Willie, kicking and giggling, under his good arm. Cobb followed, as quiet as the snow that was falling again.

"Look, Flory!" Celia said. Her friend plunked a tray by the door for snowy boots and followed Celia's sight line. "Cobby's smiling."

45

BURNABY

DRUMMER

THE BARE GROUND thumped hollow under Drummer's hooves
in the ringing cold of February. Outside for firewood, Burnaby heard
the horse descend the hill behind the house. He waited while Ivan
rode toward him, then lowered the wheelbarrow of downed locust
he'd split before winter.

Breath billowed in frosty clouds from horse and rider, silhouetted
beside him now in the frail sunrise. Burnaby blocked the rays with a
hand. "Twenty-eight degrees."

Ivan patted the horse's neck. "Yeah. Wore extra layers today.
Drummer needed a tune-up. Haven't saddled him for over three
months."

The door slammed at the Milks' house. Ruth waved and hurried
toward them.

"Hey, Burnaby." A grin spread to her eyes. "We're gonna watch the frost line run down the slopes. You know, when the sun hits it? How fast it moves?"

"I do." He'd climbed the ridge only yesterday to observe the phenomenon. A waning, half-button moon had snagged the morning sky like fabric.

The saddle creaked as Ivan shifted. Ruth grabbed his arm and the cantle and swung up behind him. Drummer spun and jumped ahead when Ivan nudged, and the pair loped uphill across the frozen ground.

Burnaby again hefted the wheelbarrow but lowered it at the sight of pajama-clad Cobb standing barefoot in the barnyard, his skinny arms extended toward his sister and Ivan and the retreating horse. He hurried to the boy, opened his coat and enfolded the quiet child, who continued to stare after Drummer. "It's cold out here, Cobb. Let's get you back inside."

Flory met them halfway. "I've got him," Burnaby said, though the boy's hands, clasped at his neck, zinged skin over his C-7, T-1 vertebrae.

Inside, Cobb wiggled free and dove onto the sofa beside a large, open sketch pad.

"So he's still at it?" Burnaby asked. They watched from the foyer as Cobb dug under cushions for his pencil.

"Yes, his second book. He filled the first." Flory stooped for a tossed hoodie and returned it to the coat tree. "He draws more every day. Always horses now, though. Well, always that gray of Ivan's. You want a cup of coffee?"

"Thank you, no. I'm out here for firewood. I like the house comfortable when Celia awakens." He'd seen his breath when he looked in on her, so had added a quilt to her narrow, solitary bed, wishing again that she would allow him to warm her.

Cobb tore a corner from a sketchbook page and ran over to stuff it in Burnaby's jacket pocket. In three bounds, the boy reached the couch and resumed drawing.

"Thank you, Cobb. I'll see you soon."

The child didn't look up.

Flory followed Burnaby onto the stoop. "Bet I can guess what that is," she said.

He fingered the paper in his pocket and extracted a scrap the size of a postage stamp. On it, a stylized horse he recognized.

Flory seemed confused. "I expected Drummer. I've seen this horse somewhere, though."

"It's a prehistoric geoglyph in England—Oxfordshire—composed of the hillside's chalk substrate. Some months ago, Cobb enlarged it from one of your books. He asked me to help him flesh it out, though once he realized its context, I don't believe he proceeded."

"So why on earth would he put a miniature in your pocket?"

"I'm considering his likely rationales."

Better to say nothing for now, he thought. Any theory he'd suggest could shape therapeutic direction with Cobb. Without more certainty, an untrue premise could mislead those trying to help him.

"If you come up with anything . . . anything at all that might help him . . ." Her forearms crossed her chest in an X as she rubbed biceps and triceps through her thin shirt. Her jaw chattered.

"You'll be the first to know, Flory. Here now, back inside with you."

On a Saturday afternoon in March, Burnaby watched Celia walk the lane to the mailbox, her beautiful hips and arms swinging, fluid. His ache to hold her beyond the gestures she would allow nearly overpowered him. *Patience,* he told himself and thought of Hazel. *And no gifts of dead mice.* So when Celia set mail on the counter, instead of swathing her in his arms and carrying her upstairs, he merely squeezed her shoulder. Practiced now at not responding in kind, she looked up at him and smiled.

And she handed him an envelope with a large, tidy *B* printed on its face. "You're the only B around here. Taped to the door, boy-high."

Inside, a full-page sketch of the Uffington White Horse.

"Another one," Celia said. "I can see your wheels turning, my mister. What's he saying? You must have some idea, or he wouldn't be addressing them all to you." Six more identical drawings of varying sizes adorned their refrigerator—and the front of the dishwasher.

He hesitated before he spoke. "When he first asked me about this animal, I told him I thought it was a prayer. I'm only guessing, however, so am reluctant to share my—my belief with his parents."

"A prayer."

"Yes. He may simply be informing me through the drawings, or he could be asking me to join him, though his specific petition remains a mystery. Regardless, I told him I would pray, too."

"How did he respond?"

"He didn't, but another sketch arrived shortly thereafter."

"You need to tell Flory, so she can tell his counselor."

"His Counselor already knows."

"She does?"

"Not that counselor."

Celia sighed—a frequent response to him in recent months. "For as much as you want to nail down diagnostic certainties, your trust in the unprovable absolutely confounds me. For eleven years I've tried, but I will never, never get it."

He knew a reply could interrupt their crawl back together, but denying truth would corrupt it. "I'm a quantum physicist. How can I demand certainty when quantum mechanics is *founded* on—on the unprovable?"

She turned away from him. He reached for her but thought better of it and let his hands fall. "Cobb's recovery is not solely dependent upon human intervention, Celia."

"If you have information that will help him, you can't keep it to yourself."

He was framing an answer when the sight of a small, bundled-up figure trudging across the yard interrupted him. "You're right. I should tell Flory, and I will, but—but not so she can inform a human in an office."

Celia's cheeks puffed, then flattened as she taped the new drawing to a cupboard door. "Flory said he brightens when he sees that we've hung these."

"I've noticed that, too." Burnaby grabbed his coat from the hook and opened the slider to the little boy. "Well, hello, Cobb. I was just heading out for more wood. If you're free to help, jump in the wheelbarrow. I'll give you a ride to the shed."

46

BURNABY

SPARKS

COBB STAYED FOR DINNER. When Satchel came for him, red
sauce painted the boy's chin and the front of his shirt. Burnaby bade
them good night as Celia, on hands and knees under the table, wiped
sticky noodles from the wooden legs and floor.

"Burnaby." Her neck craned toward a nearby baseboard. "Another
one."

He dropped to one knee between the table and wall. Touched the
penciled lines on the wooden trim board. "When did he draw this?"

"I don't know. While we were cooking? He's fast now. Makes one
in a few seconds."

Burnaby walked his gaze from the primitive horse to his wife. She
brushed a loose strand of black hair from her cheek; he felt the swipe,
electric. Through chair legs he stretched an arm, pressed a hand to
her thigh. They'd been connecting so well, rekindling their shared
life, and though his patience wobbled, he'd respected their sleeping

arrangements. Knew he'd do so forever, if necessary. But it was time to stop skirting the issue. Off guard and tender about the boy, maybe now she would talk to him.

"Only one night, when Hazel died, Celia, and that was about comfort."

Hunched beneath the table, Celia drew knees to her chest. He waited until she reached for the sauce-smeared cloth before his voice crept ahead in a low rumble, on uncertain ice.

"May to March. We've spent ten months in separate beds. I've done everything you've asked, and I was serious when I said I'd have that vasectomy, if that's really what you want. I miss you. I miss us as we used to be. Don't you?"

Tears pooled above her lower lids, but she blinked them away. "No snips, Burn. I couldn't take that away from you. You know reversals aren't guaranteed. What if you and someone else someday—"

"Someone *else*?" He tightened with shock she surely registered, but he didn't care. How could she, for a single second, envision him with any woman besides her? Even the *thought* of anyone else was profoundly impossible to him.

But he had to accept the fact that she *could* see them apart, and potentially with others. Had to acknowledge that for all his early trust that she would come to the same belief in their holy, entangled oneness, he couldn't make his faith hers any more than he could guarantee that she would love him like he loved her. He'd taken that risk when he married her. When he'd assigned his faith to her and presumed she would adopt it.

Regardless, he would never relinquish hope. His pledge of *for better or for worse* to her at Heyday included this season, too. He would see them through it, come what may.

"I can't ask you to wait forever," she said.

"I was only checking. I'll give you as long as you need."

"It's not fair of me. I haven't been fair to you for a long time."

"If you want me to tell you again how sorry I—I am for hurting you, I'll do so a thousand times more. I'll show you."

"You already have, Burn, in every way you know how. I forgave you a long time ago. I've been so . . . you name it. I'm the one who needs you to forgive me. I'm still so scared, though. And conflicted."

"About being with me?" Entirely possible he'd missed clues. "Or about getting pregnant?"

"The doctor said—"

"Don't you understand that you're more important to me than keeping my vasa deferentia intact?"

"But I want a *baby*."

"We can adopt, Celia. There are so many children we could love—and who need us."

"But I want *your* baby."

Her words arrived radiant, and they permeated him, the air under the table, her countenance. On the heels of his discouragement, a miracle.

He squeezed her knee, then extracted himself from the turned wooden legs. "There's something I'd like to show you. We'll have to—to wait for it, but we're adept at that, right?" He took the dishcloth from her, tossed it in the sink, and pulled her to her feet.

"Now?"

"Tonight, but not until nine at least. We can do these dishes, then I'll need to gather a few things." He peered through the window above the sink at the thermometer. "Thirty degrees, so dress for it. We'll be hiking."

Portable speaker, connecting cable, MP3 player, fleece blanket, picnic quilt. He checked the playlist for her favorite recording of the song and the six other versions she'd long ago insisted they add to their collection. *Good. Still there.* She'd deleted so much of their shared history. He'd found residue of her uprooting from Pullman for weeks after he returned from England.

By eight thirty he'd filled his pack and they were climbing the hill, this time to the north, across Old Hollow. The dying winter's earth shushed their steps, and they imitated the quiet, their voices soft. At the crest, Burnaby slid the flashlight into his pocket. Above them, an eternity of stars swam like minnows in the Milky Way and schooled in the deeper, moonless waters past its shore.

"There she is," he said, pointing two fingers into the sky. "My Alioth." He hoped she remembered.

Close behind him, she slapped his rump. "You," she said, laughing. "If you mean distant, then yes, but I haven't been much of a star."

He'd planned to stop at a farther rise, but her touch, the billion-coin skyscape, and his rousing heart arrested him. His long, forced torpor evaporated like his condensing breath.

Her arms horizontal, Celia spun in the crusty dirt like a ballerina—and laughed again. In the dimness he could make out her parted lips, a wisp of her breath in the still air.

"A surprise for you." Unloading the pack, he spread the old ground quilt they used for picnics, shook out the blanket, set up the speaker. Pachelbel's Canon in D spread like cream into the delicious dessert of sky.

She froze, then swiveled to him. "That's the very best version, Burn."

"Ha." He dropped his gloves on the quilt and walked toward her, extending his hand. "A dance?" *Ha.* He could scarcely keep time, but she'd dance for both of them.

She paused, considering, then giggled and reached, her fingertips poking from open-tipped mitts she'd found in Hazel's drawer.

Burnaby snapped his hand away. "Let's imagine," he said. His wiggling fingers coaxed hers upward.

"From the Book of Common Prayer," he said. "Our vows. At Heyday." Feet planted, he drew a loop over her head as if spinning her. With a cushion of air between their fingertips, she spun as if there were no gap at all. "To have and to hold," he said. She twirled again beneath his suspended fingers. "To love and to cherish."

The melody wove around them. As if dipping her, Burnaby leaned over one knee, an arm hovering beneath her shoulder blades until she tossed her head and arced her upper back across it and a layer of air. Her arms splayed, palms facing up. Her chin aimed at the stars.

He kissed the swipe of starlight at her throat, imagining photons. "With this ring I thee wed," he whispered. "And with my body I thee worship." She rolled upright then and danced around him, her arms still spread. She was everywhere at once. Dimensional. *A shimmery standing wave,* he thought.

Even in the cold, he was sweating, transfixed, drenched in a broth of galaxies and feet scuffing earth. And in Celia, an electron in her orbital dance. Elemental. Rapturous. He spoke the vow's conclusion quietly: "In the name of the Father and of the Son and of the Holy Ghost."

And while the music floated like fog down the hill and into the night sky, he closed the space between them and took her face in his hands and kissed her cheeks, her forehead, her mouth with all the months of love and longing and hope he had kept and held for her.

She stalled. He sensed her uncertainty and almost withdrew. Then, a decision: she took his fingers and slid them under her coat, onto her skin.

He braced. Searched her face. "Are you sure, Celia? If not, I . . ."

Wordless, she nodded and opened his coat, her fingers pinpricks on his skin.

"Only if you—" he said.

She pressed a finger to his mouth, then kissed him. With her *yes,* he felt his skin relax, awaken. Cross over. He received her touch, and his hands replied, traveling the landscape of the silken body he knew as well as his own. At her sharp inhale, the two of them sank onto their knees together, onto the quilt, under Alioth and her brothers, under the heavy fleece blanket.

And while Pachelbel's second rendition played, and the third, and the fourth, Burnaby loved his wife, and she loved him back until, inside of her, an explosion of zinc atoms matched the stars overhead with sparks of life that were older than, and the herald of, each human's story. Burnaby had seen such sparks under a microscope. But these, inside his Celia? Neither heard their holy shout of conception.

Afterward, she leaned into him, between his knees, both of them muffled in the blanket he'd torn from his bed. He kissed the crown of her head and checked his watch: 10:30. Bringing her here had been a long shot, he knew. The Milky Way, and their dance and union beneath it, were enough. More than enough.

But if the aurora he hoped for showed? What a gift that would be to her. They could wait for it awhile yet.

She was drowsing in his arms when the first tinges of green arose like leafy tendrils from the rolling horizon. Within minutes, pink bloomed on those stems and spread across the sky's black palette. He nudged her, stroked the side of her throat. "Look, Celia. Even in a deep solar minimum."

Northern lights. The scent of her hair. He inhaled the wonders and rocked her.

47

CELIA

SNAPPED

THAT HAMMERING. Logy with sleep, Celia tied the frantic thuds to her husband. Lit by the cod eye of the full April moon, Burnaby hopped one-legged across their bedroom floor, his foot tangled in denim. Another series of thumps rolled up the stairway before he wrestled both legs into his jeans. Celia slid into the warm spot he'd vacated and sat up. Burnaby zipped and buttoned and rushed to the hallway, shirtless.

The front door . . . who?

She called after him. "What time is it?"

"Two twelve," he said, before his feet pounded down the wooden stairs in time to another concussive round.

The milky light caught her own clothes, puddled on the floor. She pulled the T-shirt over her head and slipped on sweatpants as the deadbolt clicked and the entry door creaked open. Lights came on as she hurried downstairs and she squinted as Ivan burst inside, sweating, his unzipped jacket floured with dirt.

"We need you, Doc." His chest expanded as he caught his breath. Burnaby was already tying on boots, his jacket loose and open over his bare chest.

Fresh from her dreams, Celia struggled to make sense of these men and their urgency. Her tone was strident. "Who? Where?"

"Drummer," Ivan gasped. "Badger hole caught his front right. Went down hard. I thought you'd hear him screaming from here."

"Where?" she asked again, tracking Burn as he left the room and returned with the duffel of supplies he kept at the ready.

"At the windmill. With Ruth."

"Which windmill?"

"The one with no blades—and that underground cistern. You know, behind the old Hoke cabin. We harvested there during week two. A shortcut across the ravine from here."

"You crossed Hoke's ravine?" No wonder he was so filthy. That route was rugged, steep. And by moonlight? A wonder he didn't break his own leg. "You were with *Ruth*? Oh, Ivan, seriously? After everything? Satch won't let you near her again until she's thirty."

"I know, I know. I'm screwed for life, but that's the least of my concerns right now. Dad threatened to sell him. I was pissed. Needed to get the horse outta there. Needed to talk to Ruth."

Celia snagged his wrist. "Is she hurt?"

"Shook up. Has a few scratches is all. Don't know how we got off so easy. Horse fell and we went flying. Coulda been goners."

Burnaby pulled keys from a drawer. *In his surgeon mode*, Celia thought. Until this was over, they'd all be his assistants, extensions of his hands and feet. His mind would envelop the horse.

Her husband zipped his coat. Pulled a wool hat over his ears. "Is the animal down? Thrashing? On his feet?"

"We got him up and quiet. His foot's hanging there floppy, but he's guarding it. Sensible. He got caught in a fence wire once. Cut bad, but he just laid there and waited for me."

Burnaby nodded. "How high on the leg is the break?"

"Looks low to me. Cannon bone seems fine. Not sure though.

Didn't want to touch it." Ivan paced to the window and back. "That old stock trailer out back. Floor's still good, right?"

"Burn gave the whole thing a twice-over last month," Celia said. "Floor's solid."

"It'll hold Drummer, then," Ivan said. "I don't dare get our trailer. My dad'll follow us out there and shoot him the second he realizes he can't sell him. He hates that horse. I think he blames Drummer for the path of that bullet."

As if, Celia thought.

Ivan's back went ramrod straight, and he stared at Burnaby. "You won't shoot him, will you?"

"I don't shoot horses, Ivan."

"I'll pay you to fix him, Doc. I have money saved. I'll work however long it takes, do whatever it takes."

"I'll come. I'll do what I can." Burnaby pulled another set of keys from the drawer and tossed them to Ivan. "Hazel's car. We're selling it, so it's gassed up. You'd better get back out there, by—by the road this time. We'll follow shortly."

"You sure you know where to go?"

"We do." Celia pulled on boots and a beanie. "But I'm calling Ruth's parents first. They need to know."

A forlorn look crossed Ivan's face. "I figured," he said. "Do what you gotta do." The porch boards rang hollow as he jumped from them. She watched him sprint over moonlit gravel to the Crown Victoria beside the barn.

A light appeared in a downstairs window at the Milks' when Celia dialed their landline. A second one lit when she hung up. *Another hard night for Satch and Flory,* she thought.

Minutes later, Burnaby backed his truck to the old trailer. Celia shone the flashlight and signaled him into hitch alignment. Frost scraped and flew from the windshield under the flailing wipers as heavy ball settled into metal socket. Celia clipped and pinned attachment chains.

Satch jogged toward them as Burnaby connected the taillights.

"You're sure Ruth's not hurt?" Steam from his labored breathing caught in his flashlight beam. The light jumped from Burnaby to Celia, now inside the truck, retracting her window.

"Ivan said she was okay," Celia said. Satch's concern for his daughter entered the cab and pressed on her. "I can't believe Ivan would leave her if she were injured." Or would he? How else would he get help?

"Satch." Burnaby cranked the key. "Do you have any short strap iron or rebar?"

"Check that pile behind the barn. I hate to ditch you here, Burnaby, but my first concern is for my daughter, not that horse. I can't wait for you."

Burnaby shifted the rumbling truck into gear. "We'll be there as soon as we've loaded steel and bales."

Satchel slapped the car door and trotted toward the farm truck, his crooked arm a chicken wing in the moonlight. Burnaby backed the trailer to the century-old horse barn and heaved the sliding door open to a stack of eighty-pound bales.

Celia climbed the stack and shoved two bales off the top toward the open trailer. Burnaby hoisted one atop the other, lashing them to the inside of the trailer's metal wall to create a narrow, supportive stall for the injured horse. Then he disappeared behind the barn and returned with an armful of narrow metal scraps. He dropped them into the trailer, threw and latched the heavy door, and climbed into the truck beside Celia.

"Think there'll be fireworks out there?" Celia said. "She snuck out *again*."

"First things first, Celia. We'll all need to—to keep our heads."

The cab went quiet, both of them deep in their thoughts. Another curve uphill, and the horse, Ruth, and the dilapidated windmill showed against the hillside in Satch's high beams. Ruth held a lead rope clipped to Drummer's bobbing chin. A tangle of reins and girth lay atop the saddle ten feet away. Only the blanket remained on the horse's steaming back.

Ruth's forehead pressed into the animal's withers above front quarters anchored by a single sturdy leg. Opposite, a hoof hovered inches from the ground, useless. Ruth's lips moved nonstop. Was she singing?

Satchel, inches from Ivan's ear, gestured as he spoke. When truck and trailer pulled up, Satch approached Ruth, who jerked a shoulder from under her father's hand. He retreated to stand by Ivan, but didn't look at him. They stood like soldiers, their arms crossed, chins high.

Burnaby parked the rig near the injured horse. Ruth raised her head when he stepped from the cab. "He's shaking," she said. "Gotta be in so much pain."

"We'll take care of that as soon as we can." Burnaby checked the horse over, then ran a hand the length of the damaged leg. Celia knew his fingers read the limb like a second set of eyes, interpreting the condition of muscles and tendons and bones as if the skin were transparent. When they reached the unnatural jog in the longest pastern bone, his tender palpations slowed, exploring for fragments and the angle of fracture. The horse flinched and hoisted the leg higher.

"A fracture in P-1. The skin's intact, thankfully. No contamination from a compound break to contend with."

Ivan appeared at Burnaby's elbow. "Can you fix him, Doc? He'll be the best patient you've ever had."

"We'll stabilize him and get him to the clinic. I'll know more after I see X-rays. Ruth, give Ivan the lead."

"But—"

Ruth turned from them, and the lead went taut. Drummer's nostrils flared. He snorted, jerked his head.

"Ruth." Ivan and Satch, in unison.

Two steps and Ivan was at her side, whispering to her as he took the rope.

Burnaby attached needle to syringe and extracted liquid from a vial. He pressed the plunger until a drop appeared, then tapped the horse's jugular vein.

"Painkiller?" Ruth asked.

"Dormosedan—to calm him, but not enough to topple him in transport. No painkiller yet."

"Why not?" Ruth pleaded, squirming as if the pain were hers.

Burnaby slipped the fat needle beneath the skin, retracted the plunger until blood swam in the sedative, then injected the solution into the horse's neck. "Pain is the horse's friend right now, Ruth."

Her face screwed. "How can that be, Doc? Look at the poor guy." Muscles clenched and released along the animal's body in a succession of quivers.

"C'mon, Ruth." Ivan said. "You can see that jaggy bone through the skin. What do you suppose would happen if Doc blocked a nerve and Drummer stepped onto that foot?"

Ruth hung her head. "Smithereens."

The injection soothed everyone, though. Within two minutes, Drummer blinked and dropped his eyelids to half-mast. His ears flopped sideways.

"Thatta boy." Ruth rubbed the animal's forehead. "Not shaking anymore."

"I'll need your assistance now," Burnaby said.

Celia joined the others, at the ready. "Want two of us to hold him?" Ivan said. "Like crossties?"

Burnaby assessed the horse, who stood quietly, his eyes soft. "No, you hold him, Ivan. If he hops, turn his nose toward that good leg. We'll give him room. Often the least restraint is the best restraint."

Celia brought Burnaby's bag and removed rolls of casting cotton and scissors. From the open trailer, Burn retrieved a bucket, a jug of water, and a piece of flat-bar steel the height of a horse's knee.

Celia knelt beside her husband as he filled the bucket and cut lengths of the casting material, but scooted out of the way when Burnaby eased the fractured bone into alignment and padded the break. Drummer's sides heaved and he leaned onto his haunches as Burn worked, but he held steady. And when Burn laid a flat metal brace from hoof tip to knee and applied the cast, the horse grunted but stood, sturdied and calm.

Like he sturdies me, Celia thought. How had she ever lost sight of that?

"Let him rest a few minutes before we load him," Burnaby said.

"C'mon, Ruth. Let's go home," Satch said. "They can take it from here." Ruth didn't resist this time. Celia tracked the farm truck's lights until they disappeared behind a hill.

Ivan led Drummer to the trailer, and the horse followed like a three-legged puppy. Then Ivan climbed into Hazel's car and followed the trailer as Burnaby eased across the field and onto the county road.

Celia leaned into the truck's door, studying Burnaby as he drove toward Pullman, reviewing his handling of the previous two hours. He had given the horse room when the animal needed it most. *The best restraint,* he'd called it.

Room—like Burnaby gave her. His open-handed love had held her better than any tight rein ever could. Only Burnaby called it *grace.*

48

BURNABY

POST-OP

A NIGHT TECHNICIAN ROUSED to the sounds of a rolling exterior door and the echo of irregular hoofbeats when Burnaby and Celia delivered Drummer to WSU's Veterinary Teaching Hospital. Ivan parked Hazel's car and followed them inside.

"Four thirty. I figured it was you, Doc." The technician opened his laptop.

"Joe, bump my eight a.m. and insert this animal for a two-hour block." He noted the clock: 4:22. "Call Mac and the anesthesiologist at six and let them know. Cast removal, radiographs, a P-1 repair."

The tech tapped in the instructions, then gathered the horse's history from scraped, dirty Ivan. Burn settled Drummer in a stall.

Celia propped her head on her arms on the stall gate. Burnaby eyed her with concern.

"Thanks, Joe. I need to get my wife home. We've been up most of the night. Tell Mac I'll be back by seven. And when you and Ivan get to billing, redirect charges to me."

Joe raised a thumb. Ivan stared at Burnaby. "Wow, Doc. Thank you. This horse—he's important to me." He cleared his throat. "Care if I stay with him for a few minutes?"

The second Burnaby and Celia stepped outside, she protested. "Ivan's recklessness caused the accident, and now you're rewarding—"

"I'd prefer to—to support, not vilify him, Celia. I expect trouble when his father learns what happened. Ivan will need our encouragement." He pressed a hand into the small of her back and guided her toward the truck. "Too, I considered his motives. I'd ride a fast horse cross-country any night for you."

At nine forty-five the next morning, Mac shut off the anesthesia and pulled the endotracheal tube from Drummer's throat. Three hours later, Burnaby met Ivan at the horse's stall, where Drummer, his lower leg resin-casted, nibbled hay from a hanging net.

"A longitudinal break. Diagonal and clean, fortunately. No chips," Burnaby said. "The bones aligned without incident, and I secured them with lag screws. We're dosing him with Banamine for pain relief, and with penicillin and another antibiotic for the next week. He'll continue on phenylbutazone later."

"But he'll be okay?" At Ivan's voice, the horse raised his head and nickered.

"Impossible to give you a certain prognosis this early. Much depends on the crucial post-op period, and on your willingness to work with the horse as he heals. When he's stable enough for—for transport, I can bring him home to Hazel's, if you like. There are good stalls in that old barn. Celia and I can monitor him, and the goats will befriend him. I'll give you a rehabilitation plan that will last anywhere from four months to a year, depending on his progress."

Ivan faced the ground, nodding. "I'll do anything for that horse."

"Over my dead body."

Oren knocked a tablet from Burnaby's hand as he burst past him, his fist clenched at his son. "My name's on that animal's registration, not yours, and I'm not paying a nickel for all this." He glared ominously at Burnaby, his jaw set. "You send me a bill and I'll sue you, Hayes. Now get out of my way. That horse has already caused enough misery, jumping when I shot at that buck. No selling him now he's ruined, so what's the point in all this? He'll be coyote bait come tomorrow."

Oren yanked a lead rope from a hook and lunged toward the stall. Ivan stepped in his father's path like a shield. The medical staff froze as the two men squared off in the concrete alley.

Ivan's face burned red. "You touch him, Dad, and I swear, I'll take you down right here."

"I'd like to see you try," Oren muttered at his muscled son. He took a step back and eyed the gathering crowd.

"You'll get no bill, Oren." Burnaby moved calmly to the stall gate and stood like a towering, protective wall between his angry neighbor and the horse. "And since it sounds like you're finished with him, we'll take this damaged horse off your hands."

Oren glared at observers until they dispersed, then stared at the horse. "Good riddance." His index finger thudded into Ivan's chest. "I'll see *you* at home," he said, and walked out. Burnaby's brain conjured a charcoal trail of smoke in his wake.

Two routine equine surgeries later, Burnaby returned to Drummer's stall. He was bent over the horse's casted limb when a disheveled Flory appeared at the stall's solid, chest-high gate. Above it, at her side, he saw tousled, sandy hair.

"Hope it's okay we stopped by. Celia said she's meeting you for dinner in town, so I figured I could catch you." She gathered a handful of papers from her purse and waved them at Burnaby. "Sketches of Drummer, his leg broken, his leg healed. Cobby heard Ruth telling me what happened, and he dogged me all morning."

Burnaby unfolded the pages to more of Cobb's extraordinary, wordless storytelling.

Flory continued. "This afternoon, I lost track of him twice. First time, I went outside and found him drawing that geoglyph on the barn siding with chalk. Second time, there were more chalk drawings—on the house, the sidewalk. He was sitting in the car, with white chalk drawings of that horse on the *tires*. So . . . here we are." She raised her shoulders, her head at a cant—a combination of gestures Burnaby recognized as bewilderment. Or surrender. "How's the patient?"

"Have a look." Burnaby opened the gate and Cobb sidestepped along the wall toward Drummer. The horse stopped chewing and dropped his head to the boy, who peered up at his mother. When she nodded, he slid down the wall to the stall floor and watched the horse reverently.

"You two have a lot to talk about," Burnaby said to Cobb, then signaled Flory toward the gate. She followed him into the alley.

Burnaby spoke quietly. "Why don't you leave him here with me. I'll finish up shortly and take him to dinner with us. We'll have him home by seven."

"Oh, he'd like that, I bet. Cobby, you want to stay here with Dr. Hayes while I go to the store? Have supper with him and Celia?"

Cobb looked at her sidelong and nodded.

She blew him a kiss. "Okay then, sweetie. Meet you at home, eh?" She zipped her purse and smiled at Burnaby. "Thanks. See you two at seven."

Burnaby watched her leave and raised a laptop to Cobb. "Are you comfortable in there while I finish up a few things? I like to keep Drummer's gate closed, but I'll be sitting right here, outside. Is that okay?" *Good company for each other,* he thought.

Cobb's smile spread wide, and he nodded again. Burnaby closed the gate and sat beside it on a folding chair, completing the day's reports.

Until a small voice from inside the stall arrested him.

"I'm sorry you broked your leg, Drummer horse. Did it hurt a whole bunch?"

Burnaby held his breath. He dared not move. After a pause, the high little voice spoke again.

"I think about you lots and lots, you know. I sawed you look at me on Hugh's hill, and then you comed to me with Ivan and I thinked you heard me call when I drawed you. Did you? Did you hear my pictures?"

Another pause. Burnaby leaned toward the gate, listening intently. A vet student approached, and he waved her away, a finger to his lips. His heart raced.

"And now you broked your leg and I thinked you did it for me. Did you? Or did Ruth talk to you before you breaked it? Did she, did she, did she? Did her words make you break it? I need to know that so much. So much, so much, so much."

Burnaby craned toward the gap at the gate's hinges and scrambled to interpret the boy. So, Cobb was calling Drummer in those sketches? Did the child consider the injured animal another prayer horse, like the Uffington geoglyph?

Drummer tugged feed from the net again, blew, and resumed a rhythmic grind of teeth on hay. *What* was Cobb praying? And what did he mean about Ruth's words causing the horse's tumble?

The top of Cobb's head appeared above the stall. A small hand reached over the half wall to the latch, and the gate creaked open to a somber child.

Burnaby closed his computer. "You hungry, Cobb?"

The boy bobbed his head.

Did Cobb suspect anyone had heard him? Burnaby gathered the drawings and slipped them into his jacket. "Very well. Let's go find Celia."

49

CELIA

SORTING

"HEY, COBBY!" Celia scooted deeper into the restaurant booth and patted the seat beside her. Cobb bypassed her and scrambled onto the opposite bench next to Burnaby, who pulled off the boy's beanie and coat, smiled down at him, and slid him a paper place mat and pen.

Just like Harris, she thought. Burnaby's dad had *known* his children. He had heard them and anticipated their needs, fed them patience and kindness and wisdom. How easily Burn would imitate him. How naturally her husband would be a dad, with a parenting cupboard as full as his was.

She absorbed his tender attention toward Cobb as if he were loving her. *This is how it could be,* she thought. In caring for one, they'd care for the other, and be nourished themselves. She considered her own bare mothering shelves and the dawning fact that Burnaby would help her fill them, if what she suspected was true. If, against all odds, this life didn't end like the others. She'd be so careful this time.

Terrified. Overjoyed. She'd described herself as both to Burn the day her breasts began to ache. Had cried from an emotional slurry when she missed her period. She held her breath and peeked again at his text hours earlier. His photo of the familiar box, there in the pharmacy aisle. His **Got it. We'll know tonight.**

He glanced up at her and smiled. "Flory and Cobb visited Drummer this afternoon." He opened his jacket and reached inside for the drawings. "They brought me these."

Shortly after seven, Celia and Burnaby delivered Cobb, drowsy and chocolate-streaked, to his mother. "Bath time, Cobby," Willie shouted from behind Flory. "I lefted you the water."

"You're quiet," Celia said, when she and Burnaby reached home. She sat at the counter, reading the home test's instructions. Burnaby stood behind her and pressed his thumbs into her trapezius muscles. "Oof. That feels good." She smiled up at him. He was learning. So was she.

She closed her eyes, relaxing into the massage—until his deep bass rumbled. "Cobb talked, Celia. He spoke to Drummer, in the stall. I was typing notes in the alley, so he—he couldn't see me and didn't know I was listening."

"What?" She spun on the stool to face him. "Actual *words*? From his *mouth*?"

He sat beside her, his brows low. "Yes, and I'm still trying to grasp them. Do you recall the Uffington horse?"

"You called it a prayer."

"Yes. I believe Cobb has transferred that association to Drummer. All those drawings? He's been praying through them, I think, and somehow believes the horse will deliver his message, whatever that is. He asked Drummer questions."

"Like what?"

"Ones that clearly made sense to him, but that I've yet to figure out."

Celia knew from the familiar tightness of Burnaby's lips that he wouldn't spill details until he shaped a hypothesis.

"Please tell Satch and Flory, Burn. Right away." She didn't want to push him, but Flory and Satch were aching for a breakthrough. For direction.

"Not yet. Let me consider the boy's queries for a few days. Maybe I can be more helpful then. If they bombard him with questions, the boy may clam up completely."

"They need to know!"

"Nothing will change in another few days, Celia. I'll bring Drummer home first."

"No, Professor. You aren't required to have every answer. What they need most is hope. I'm calling Flory. Right now."

The test could wait for a few more hours.

By eight thirty p.m., Ruth was home with the sleeping twins, and Satch and Flory sat on Hazel's old couch. While Celia poured tea, Burnaby told the Milks about the Uffington Horse prayer and about Cobb talking to Drummer in the stall.

"But what did he *say*, Burnaby? Why isn't he talking to *us*?" Flory almost got to her knees, imploring him to answer.

Celia knew Burn could repeat the boy's words verbatim.

But he didn't.

Celia exhaled, releasing her grip on how she thought this conversation should go. Burnaby loved the boy too. She would respect his intent—and his timing.

He answered quietly. "I'll bring Drummer home this weekend. I expect Cobb will talk to him again, as long as you don't raise his suspicions. I strongly suggest that you don't mention this to—to him. Best if he doesn't know I was listening and feels free to continue his conversation with the horse."

Satch's tense fingers broke the brim of the cap in his hands. "He's right, Flory. We can't tell Cobb we know. No questions. No hint to him that we know anything."

Flory sipped her tea, pressed her lips, then exhaled through them. "Fair enough. We have a plan then. When Drummer comes home, we let Cobby spend time with him. And we figure out a way to listen without his knowing."

As if dodging rent, winter's lingering chill skipped town the following Saturday, and the scent of warming earth and new leaves and line-dried laundry moved in. Burnaby hitched his truck to the trailer and left by noon to retrieve Drummer.

In a stall first occupied a hundred years earlier by plow-pulling mules, Celia leaned her pitchfork against the wall, crouched in the fresh straw, and rubbed Rocket's ears. The dog flopped onto the clean bedding with a contented sigh.

Drummer will like it here. She pictured the horse's nose over the stall's half walls, passing his healing days surrounded by friendly goats, as Posie and her kids nibbled alfalfa on one side and Biff and Cliff reared and clacked horns on the other.

Ivan arrived, whistling. He filled the horse's water bucket and loaded a hay cage with timothy. He dumped more straw and grabbed Celia's pitchfork. "I've got this," he said.

Celia stepped toward him, frowning. A bruise purpled around his eye. "You have a run-in with a door? A gorilla?"

"If my dad's the gorilla, then yeah. We had another little discussion at home, after he hassled me in Pullman."

"Think he'll come by here? Give you any more trouble?"

"I doubt it, but you never know with him. He's made his bed. At least now he knows I won't be around to straighten the sheets."

"You're not going to explain that to me, are you?"

"I would if I knew how. Or if I knew what was going on and could prove it. After your husband helped me with Drummer, I knew I had to get out of there, though, before anything else happened."

He spread some straw in the stall, leaned on the fork, and spoke evenly. "You know how you can feel goodness in somebody? I feel goodness in Doc. When he took care of Drummer and helped me, I could feel it. Satch has that too. Just by being around them, I knew I could stand up for Drummer and get away from my dad, where I feel something else entirely."

"They do have that effect." Though Burn would credit entanglement with his good Maker. And to think she'd almost left him. "Your dad punch you?"

"Yeah. Tried to stop me from leaving. I'm living at my mom's now. Looking for an apartment."

Ingrid. They'd talked briefly at the anniversary party. "Hazel loved her."

"I'm glad to be there for now. The commute isn't so bad, either."

Burnaby texted when he left Pullman, and Celia alerted the boys. When he pulled off Old Hollow onto the driveway, the skipping twins flanked the trailer like ushers—or tugboats—while Rocket zigzagged between them, barking. Drummer, his nose at a gap in the slatted stock trailer, whinnied at the welcome party.

The boys orbited as Ivan led the horse to his new stall. Ruth met them with a carrot. Satch and Flory returned from town as Burnaby unhitched the trailer.

Celia met them in the barnyard. "This may be trickier than we thought," she said. "I opened the windows above the stalls so you can listen out back, but as long as Willie's around, I doubt Cobb will talk, even if the rest of us are scarce. Looks like your eavesdropping will be limited to school hours."

"Or I can take Willie with me," Satch said. "I have a feeling Cobb's going to want to live in that barn. If he's sitting there drawing, Willie'll get bored."

Flory laughed. "You two want to come for supper? Five thirty?"

At dinnertime, Burnaby took her hand in a firm grip as they walked the Milks' lane. Celia smiled up at him without squeezing back, then sniffed the warm air. "Barbecue. Wish I were hungry."

A festive picnic table greeted them, its red-checkered cloth set for eight. While Ivan tended teriyaki chicken thighs at the grill, Ruth and Flory loaded the table with rice and garden greens and fresh rolls, baked beans and Ventura strawberries. Ivan brought chicken and joined the others at the table. Satch said grace, scooped salad.

"About your horse, Ivan."

Something in Satchel's tone. Heads whipped toward him. The table went quiet.

"I'm glad he can heal here. Glad the outcome wasn't worse. You both know that things could have turned out differently with that animal out there. And with you."

Ruth busied herself with her brother. Ivan nodded.

Burnaby lowered his fork. "Ruth."

The girl looked up from Willie, manhandling a knife through a chunk of chicken.

"Before Drummer fell, did you say anything to the horse? Or to Ivan? Anything at all?"

Ruth scrunched her nose. "*Say* anything? Are you kidding? Drummer was loping in the dark. I was holding on to Ivan for dear life. I couldn't have talked if I wanted to. *Why?*"

"The—" Burnaby said.

A squeak from Cobb interrupted. The boy's plate clattered to the ground. He slid from his chair and sprinted around the house, out of sight.

"What's that all about?" Ruth said.

Flory and Satch exchanged sharp, knowing looks before her chair tumbled. Satchel's scraped pavement in his rush. Burnaby and Celia rose as one.

This is it. Celia's skin prickled hot, then cold, as she hurried after Burnaby.

50

BURNABY

DISCOVERY

"COBB! COBBY!" Voices surrounded him, and Burnaby's colors shifted. Flory, Satch, and Celia—all of them orange, and all running ahead of Burnaby on blue lawn and green gravel—called for the boy. Shouts left their mouths as clouds, red and gray and spreading, as they checked hiding places in the yard. Behind him, Burnaby heard Willie's husky voice, and Ruth and Ivan talking, loud.

Cacophony. He slowed to a walk and blinked. Collective panic wouldn't do, wouldn't help the boy, though the child's frantic exit inspired it. The flush of emotion on Cobb's face loomed in his mind, confused him.

Then Ruth, Ivan, and Willie passed him and sped with the others through the narrow man door beside one of Cobb's horses chalked on the barn's siding. *Like hornets,* he thought, *at the hole to their nest.*

He followed them inside, the doorknob hot in his hand. Ivan, already in Drummer's stall with Willie, shook his head. Ruth dug behind boxes and feed sacks in the alley. Satch circled the tower of straw. Celia checked goat stalls while Flory peered in unoccupied ones stashed with dusty equipment and furniture. Their calls and urgency set goats bleating. Drummer snorted and blew.

So noisy. They should be cats, not hounds. Burnaby eyed the hay-mow overhead, walked to the wooden ladder nailed to the far wall, and climbed. A barn owl—tawny, silent, heart-faced—flew from a rafter when he stepped into the loft. The bird looped once through the cavernous space, then winged past a pulley at the open gable door.

On the floor below it, the little boy lay on his side in a heap of broken bales, crying audibly.

"Cobb." Burnaby dropped to his knees in the dusty hay, sending motes into the sunlight streaming from the hay door above. "You're quick."

Cobb sat up. Mucus ran from his nose.

Satchel showed at floor level on the ladder. "He's here," he called and stepped into the mow.

Ruth appeared next. Cobb spotted her, wailed, then shouted. "You didn't *talk to Drummer?*"

"His voice, Dad! Cobby's talking!" Ruth darted to her brother and plopped beside him in the loose hay.

Cobb threw himself at her, his sobs wracking. "Say it again, Ruthie, that you didn't talk to the white horse before he breaked his leg."

"Oh, Cobby. I don't know why it matters, but no, I didn't say a word after I climbed on him." She hugged the boy, kissed his teary cheeks. "Why are you asking me that?"

Willie, braced against the height by his mother's arms, climbed into the loft ahead of her. Celia followed slowly. Ivan peeked over the edge but stayed on the ladder.

"I hurted Hugh when I yelled to him and Drummer looked at me and I didn't know what he was saying and then I hurted Daddy when I yelled to him like I hurted Miz Steffen when I yelled 'Sorry, Miz Steffen' at the party. But I knowed the horse would help me and the horse said *Stop talking* just like Hugh and Daddy and Miz Steffen had told me *Shhhh.*"

Words blurted from Cobb now. Burnaby's brain raced to make sense of them.

"And I thinked about how Doc Hayes said the chalk horse took the olden-days peoples' prayers to their Saver when they needed help and how Hugh said a white horse will bring a Saver and so I drawed and drawed horse prayers that Daddy wouldn't die and that I wouldn't be bad anymore and hurt people again and that I could talk."

Cobb took a juddering breath and wiped his cheeks. Listeners circled him on rumps and knees, mouths agape. Flory petted his back. Burnaby stood near Ivan at the ladder.

"And I knowed inside me that Drummer would tell me when the Saver said yes to my prayer and that the Saver would make it okay and that Hugh and Miz Steffen are with the Saver so they are okay and that if I couldn't talk for a long, long time that was okay, too. But when Drummer broked his leg I worried that Ruthie caught the talking poison from me and hurted Drummer because she talked." His words rode the rhythm of his sobs.

His eyes lit then, and tears dripped into the corner of a cheek-splitting smile. He flipped his hands flat, palms up to the barn's trusses. "But Ruthie *didn't* make Drummer break his leg because she didn't talk and now I know that Drummer broked his own leg so I could talk again. So people will be okay even if I talk."

Magical thinking, common in preschoolers. Burnaby remembered his own creative thinking at age five—his child's view that disconnected events were somehow related, and that he influenced them. Cobb seemed to believe he caused Hugh's accident, and Satch's fall, and Hazel's death in her sleep.

"My love, my love." Flory lifted Cobb from Ruth's lap and rocked him. "So you believe your words hurt your daddy and took Hugh and Mrs. Steffen away from us? And you stopped talking so you wouldn't harm anyone else? And then you asked God for help by sending him prayers in horse drawings?"

Cobb sniffed, his voice small. "Yes."

"But the horse was real and it was Drummer, right, Cobby?" Willie clapped his hands on Cobb's cheeks and pressed their noses together.

"You know Drummer is real, Willie." Cobb scowled at his brother.

Satchel was weeping. "And then Drummer sacrificed his leg so you could be set free from this talking sickness? Do I have that right, Son? You're saying Drummer saved you?"

Cobb squirmed free of his mother and hid his face in his father's shirt.

Willie pulled Cobb's hair. "Nuh-unh. That horse isn't your Saver, Cobby."

"Owww, Willie. Stop it."

Satchel laughed. "You've got the gist, though, Cobb. We've got plenty of time to clean up the details."

Only Burnaby noticed Celia hurry to the loft edge and vomit.

51

CELIA

SKID

"CAMELS, YOU SAY." Celia walked outside the farmhouse, searching for a better connection on the crackling line.

"More feral ungulates," Aggie said. "Hooved wild mammals, this time with humps. Hundreds of thousands of camels, roaming the Australian outback. More wild camels than anywhere on earth. Their ancestors got dumped out there when gas engines showed up. I get to shoot the whole spread. Front cover, *Nat Geo*."

"Well, that's exciting. You already there? You're sure cutting out."

"Nope. At a cabin outside of Aspen. Cloistered so I can organize a few thousand pics before I leave the country for eight weeks."

"In the mountains, then."

"Yeah, well, you need to know about this. Any more issues with vandalism out there?"

"Not so far this season, but it's only May. Satch is bringing equipment home every night, and Burnaby hung surveillance cameras. Yesterday the one trained on the house quit, but we'll check it out."

"Don't wait too long. Last night I found a couple of photos that may interest you. No, that *will* interest you."

"What kind of photos?"

"Long-lens images, taken on your farm. I cropped them from the background of some nice elk shots. You'll see. I'll send 'em right over. Show Burnaby and Satch, then let me know what you think. I'll be in Colorado until Monday."

"Will do, love. Talk soon."

Celia's inbox pinged minutes later. She opened Aggie's first attachment and texted Burnaby at work. **Sending email. Call when you get it.**

When she saw the second photo, she dialed Satch. No answer. **Call me ASAP**, she texted. Shaky, she stumbled to the paddock, where Drummer snoozed in the sun. She paced the length of his fence line, then continued uphill, surveying the house and farm buildings and land Hazel left her. *So much work. And now these photos.* Not good for her. Not good at all. Her body needed care, not all this stress.

And she still had to deal with this new offer on the farm. The second in as many months. Both from the same conglomerate, according to the agent, but they'd upped the terms on the second one. Maybe she should reconsider.

Satchel rang when she topped the ridge. "What's up?"

"Got something to show you. The sooner the better."

Burnaby drove in as Satch climbed the porch. Celia pulled up chairs for the men, settled her laptop on the table, and clicked a thumbnail on her desktop. A narrow man beside a spray buggy filled the screen. Dark gloves, beanie, jeans, navy puffer coat. His back was turned, and he held a two-gallon white container.

"Who took this?" Satch said, his nose inches from the image. "And where?"

"Who do you know who's built like that? Do you recognize the equipment? Time of year? Landmarks? And what's in that jug?"

"Sky, flat ridgeline, stubble. It could be anywhere in three counties," Burnaby said. "If it's even in Washington. Autumn, probably."

Satchel examined the man in the photo. "Without seeing his face, the guy's a mystery. If he is a guy. Looks more like a city boy or girl than a farmer." The front legs of his chair left the floor, then thumped down when he tapped the screen. "The rig is ours, though. I replaced that PTO pump. Hose is some green line we had left over. Who took this?"

"Aggie, when she was here last. There's another one, too." She scrolled to a second image—the partial profile of a beanied man from his large nose up. Edges of a five-o'clock shadow showed at his cheekbones. The sprayer tank blocked the rest of his body.

"I don't recognize him." Satchel stood, then sat again. "Pics like these, why didn't she show us earlier?"

"She just found them. What's in his hand?"

"Lots of products come in jugs like that." Satchel squinted at the first photo. "Can't see the label, but it sure could be atrazine."

"Pretty sure I know who he is," Celia said. She spread two fingers on her laptop touchpad, enlarging the image. "This guy jams a finger in every pie. It all makes sense now."

※

"Thirty years at this job, Dr. Burke-Hayes. I've sent a lot of cases to the prosecutor." Sheriff Vance Petersburg thumbed through Aggie's photos, then flicked them aside. "If I bring a count of felony malicious mischief to him based on a snapshot of a giant schnoz and green hose, he'll laugh me out of the office. You got any other proof that Lydiard's your man?"

"Yes, if you'll count four separate conversations in which he's tried either to scare me or discourage me from farming Steffen property."

"He's an *accountant*, for Pete's sake. It's his *job* to advise you."

Celia shook her head. "Lydiard goes way beyond financials. Stuff he shouldn't know, like particulars from both of my grandparents' wills. *And* about a recent offer from a corporation to buy me out, which, of course, he encourages me to take. The guy wants me to quit."

"I see. Do you know the principals behind the corporation?"

"I tried to find out, but owners are buried. Admin names only."

The sheriff rubbed his ample belly. "If you could tie Lydiard to the corp's originators, that could help. Still slim pickin's though. You're talking circumstantial evidence, and it's his word against yours on what went on in his office. Sorry, Doctor. Whether or not you find him unlikable, the man has no record and owns a stable, successful Colfax business. Where would you even find a motive?"

Before midnight, at a kildeer's piercing *dee* and trill, Celia rolled drowsily toward Burnaby and tuned her ears to the open bedroom window. The cry grew distant in the night air. "Did you see where I marked the nest in the gravel, Burn? Something scared her. I hope nothing raided it."

Burnaby closed his book, clicked off the small light clipped to its cover. "Yes. Six eggs. The nest's in camera view, so—so we can check for marauders."

"I thought that camera didn't work."

"I reconnected a wire after dinner."

She plumped her pillow, pulled the quilt to her chin. Her words slurred with sleepiness. "How'd it come loose?"

"I don't know."

Burnaby slipped from the bed and went to the window. Celia watched him scan the still grounds, lit by a gibbous moon.

Boys tumbled from the Milks' house the next morning when Celia parked at their front walk and opened the rear doors of her Jeep. Flory followed the twins to the vehicle, a child's booster seat in each hand. "Saturday field trip, ready or not."

"Oh, I'm ready. Going to be hotter than purple blazes down there, though." Celia stuffed a saltine in her mouth while Flory buckled the boys in their seats and stowed an insulated lunch bag. Migrating swallows had returned to the river, along with older ospreys, back to check on their overwintered juveniles. A nature lesson for the twins would keep her mind off the past.

"I brought you a sandwich." Flory watched Celia chew the cracker. "Or are you still urpy?"

Celia shrugged. Smiled feebly. "I'm okay. A little blue. Baby died a year ago today."

Flory's hand found Celia's on the shifter. "Anniversaries can kinda sideswipe you, eh? This time next year should be better. Lots to look forward to."

"I hope."

"Ahhhhhhhh." The boys made a game of their wobbling voices as the car bumped and shuddered down Old Hollow past turfy pillows of young wheat.

Celia panned the lush hills, then frowned at the road. "The county should grade this before long, right, Flory? Washboard's getting worse." She nudged the gas pedal, then eased off, but the Jeep vibrated, regardless. The shaking lessened when they reached the pavement, but persisted. "My alignment's messed up, too. Burn's been after me to get it fixed. Hang tight. We'll be down the hill in ten."

In a blink they wound into the Snake River breaks, along the crests of green velvet slopes that had replaced winter's sepia ones. Celia tensed at the drop-off, remembering the steepness that had dizzied her the previous year and the swing of Hugh's truck down the road's hairpins. Like a satin ribbon, a watery blue dressed the valley below.

"Beautiful, beautiful." Flory lowered her window and stretched an arm toward the river.

Celia's phone rang, then a text pinged. Not the place to answer.

Whomp, whomp, whomp. Racket from a front wheel poured through the open window. "Dogs, that's annoying. I should've taken the car in last week."

Suddenly, at a breathtaking curve to the left, the Jeep lurched and dropped to the right, connecting with the pavement in a metallic screech.

"A tire!" Flory gasped as a black, chrome-centered disk flew down the precipitous slope toward the river.

Instinct told Celia to steer toward the skid, though the decision took her around the end of a guardrail and onto the treacherous slope. The Jeep pivoted on its naked hub and careened downhill.

The boys screamed. Flory threw hands over her face. White-knuckled and powerless, Celia gripped the speeding car's wheel until the vehicle bounced twice and crashed head-on into a basalt outcrop.

52

BURNABY

CAMERA

AFTER HIS MORNING ASSESSMENT of Drummer, Burnaby strolled from barn to road for the *Spokesman-Review* stuffed in the tube under the mailbox. He glanced at the headlines and turned toward the house, alone until Celia returned from the river with Flory and the twins.

Inside, he prepared some oatmeal and opened his laptop to check the readout from the camera he'd repaired. The device had gone dead two nights previously, and the loose wire troubled him. If the malfunction was intentional, someone wanted a blackout, and the reason couldn't be good.

He thought of the nesting bird. Had she sensed an intruder? Why else would a sitting killdeer leave her gravel scrape, crying, after dark? Most likely an animal had disturbed her, but the bird would fly from a human, too. They'd heard her alarm about midnight, long after the house went dark. Burnaby's book light wouldn't have shown through the window.

He scrolled fast through photos time-stamped before eleven thirty. Twenty minutes apart, Rocket and the Milks' cat wandered through light from the porch. A good thirty feet away, on the far side of Celia's Jeep, the sitting bird showed as a dark blot in the driveway.

In an eleven fifty-five capture, he saw something else.

A figure, thin and dark, rounded the corner of the house in the shadows, and—*how foolish*—stared directly at the infrared camera. Burnaby had never met Lydiard, never seen him, but the photo of a man, his nose prominent, his eyes close-set, was clear. Celia wouldn't have to guess this time.

Three frames later, the camera caught the man in profile behind the nest. A bird, its wings high, showed near his hip. Frame six captured the man as he crouched with a lug wrench at Celia's right front tire.

Burnaby felt the blood drain from his face. He grabbed his phone and dialed his wife, but the call went to voicemail. He punched letters, frantic. **Stop driving. Pull over. Call me.** The text went through, so he waited a minute for her reply before he tried again. *On the hill already.* She wouldn't answer on that road.

He grabbed his keys, paused to press Satch's speed dial, and leapt off the porch, phone to his ear as he raced for his truck.

53

CELIA

AFTER

STEAM BOILED FROM the crumpled hood. Celia inhaled and pulled free of her airbag. Her quaking hands felt for her seatbelt and unbuckled it. "Flory! Boys! You okay?"

Already on her knees, Flory bent toward the back seat, her voice shaky but soothing. "There, there, Cobby. Any bumps, sweeties? Quite a ride, Willie, yes?"

Strapped in their seats, both boys sat shocked and crying, but uninjured. "A mercy from God," Flory said, her breath ragged. "Miraculous."

"How did we not flip?" Celia said. "Or roll the whole way down?" She reeled at the dangerous incline, thankful beyond words for the boulder. "A foot to the right or left, and we'd have been—"

"But it didn't. And we aren't." Flory leaned to view the unwalkable grade. "We'll be safest if we stay in the car." She found her phone. "No service. At least we're visible from the road. Better shut down that engine." She dabbed Celia's cheek, abraded by the airbag. "You hurt anywhere else? That seatbelt . . ."

"Low on my hips." Celia rubbed her belly. "Nothing squished." And no, they hadn't flipped or rolled. *Nothing squished,* she repeated silently, though worry skittered in her, already crawling her mind like an animal. The impact . . . Her baby . . .

A redtail, hunting the tilted land below, sailed past her at eye level. Wordlessly, she begged the bird for her child's life.

Flory eyed her with concern, rubbed her shaking shoulders. "Celia . . ." she said, then closed her eyes, went quiet, her hand at Celia's nape.

Praying, Celia figured. But not to a hawk. *To whom, then?* Farther downhill now, the bird soared like her stub-tail—small and carried. *But carried by whom?*

He is for us, Celia. Through her interior din she heard Burnaby as if he were part of her, holding her. All at once she simply knew that he *was* part of her. Burnaby, her husband, her love.

Who is he, Burn? I need to know.

The hawk crossed an outcrop and disappeared behind it.

And then, sure as that unseen hawk was flying, Celia sent a cry to someone bigger than the bird. A cry she would pound into this hillside if she could. A plea, a *prayer* for their baby to the One Burnaby loved.

A pickup appeared, traveling uphill. Flory stood through the sunroof and waved a sweatshirt. The driver slowed and blared his horn.

Half an hour later, an aid car pulled over at the spot where the Jeep had left the road. Then a tow truck and a team with ropes and evacuation sleds and harnesses. Then Burnaby. Right behind him, Oren.

Flory stroked the boys' legs. "We're going home, kids. Monday at school you'll have the best show-and-tell ever. We'll see the birds another day."

54

ACCUSED

"HOW ABOUT attempted murder?" Celia dropped a pile of photos from the security camera on the sheriff's desk.

"What's this?" Sheriff Petersburg spread the stack across a clutter of papers.

Burnaby lowered himself to a chair near the sheriff's desk, elbows on knees. "An explanation of why Celia's vehicle skidded off the Almota grade."

"And you are?"

"Celia's husband. Burnaby Hayes." No handshake.

"Take a look," Celia said. "Karl Lydiard, dead to rights. The night before my wreck, he loosened lug nuts on my Jeep. My wheel fell off on the Almota hill as I drove a car full of friends." Friends she wanted to keep forever. "We could've rolled to the river."

Petersburg looked somber. "He still has rights, Dr. Burke-Hayes."

"C'mon, Sheriff. These pics catch him red-handed. If they don't incriminate him, nothing will."

"Have a seat there by your husband, Doctor, and I'll take your statements. Then I'll pay Mr. Lydiard a visit."

Celia muttered under her breath. Continued pacing.

"What's that, Doctor?"

"I said I hope it's with handcuffs."

"We'll see." The sheriff opened his laptop and again pointed Celia to a chair. "You want to go first?"

An hour and a half later, Sheriff Petersburg stood. "I think I have all I need from the two of you. I'll let you know what's next. Given the severity of the accusations, I recommend that you retain an attorney."

Celia protested. "We aren't at fault."

"Just in case. This may get complicated. If—"

"I need to see Vance." A man, loud, in the reception area.

"He's—No, sir, you can't—"

"Vance!"

Celia gasped when Karl Lydiard burst into the room.

Lydiard sniffed at Celia and Burnaby, then aimed himself at the sheriff. "Good thing I stopped in before these two framed me."

"Whoa, whoa, Mr. Lydiard."

The man's face flamed. "Mr. Lydiard, Vance? *Mr. Lydiard?* We go to school together for twelve years, and now you're going formal on me?"

Petersburg smiled at the couple. "Excuse us, will you?" Lydiard's eyes locked on the sheriff.

"Not on your life," Celia said. "You couldn't drag me away from this little exchange."

Lydiard wheeled toward Celia. "Don't you dare try to stick me with this. I had nothing to do with it."

The sheriff interrupted. "I suggest you hold your thoughts, Mr. Lydiard, until I can take your report privately."

Burnaby's fingers twined loosely over the space between his jiggling knees. "May I ask how you learned about the accusations, Mr. Lydiard? Or why you presume we're discussing them?"

"'May I *ask*?'" Lydiard mocked, nasal and high-pitched, before he cut loose with a string of profanities. "You, fancy horse professor, *you* told Oren about some guy caught on your security camera hurting your wife's rig. *You*, yesterday, at the side of the road, while your wife there sat on the top of her car on a shortcut to the river, blamed *me*."

"You could have killed us all," Celia spat.

Burnaby laid his hand on her thigh, his face unreadable. "Interesting, Mr. Lydiard. Did I blame you, or did Oren? I don't believe I mentioned who was in those photos, only that they existed, and that the—the perpetrator had caused the accident. A four-way conversation, as I recall, with Oren and two medics, both of whom can corroborate my account."

Petersburg listened, slack-jawed, before he interrupted. "I'll say it again, Karl. Hold your tongue. Give me a private statement."

"A *statement*? As if I have something to state?"

Petersburg waved the stack of photos. "I'm afraid you may, Karl."

"I'm not listening to this." Lydiard flung the door open and stomped out of the office. Sheriff Petersburg hurried after him. In the foyer, the receptionist bent over a calendar as if she were deaf.

Celia leapt to the window, cranked open the casement, and leaned down. Burnaby stayed seated.

Outside, Lydiard's lips wagged. "He's cussing," Celia whispered. "Oh, that man's got a mouth on him." She cranked the window wider. "He tore Petersburg's shirt!" She had pegged the accountant at their first meeting. He'd absolutely lose at poker, every time.

Voices seeped through the open window. "We can talk about this later, Karl. Calm down. Go home." Petersburg grasped Lydiard's shoulder.

Karl shook him off. "Up yours, Vance!" He hurled himself into his car and slammed the door. Tires screeched.

From the sidewalk, the sheriff watched him drive off, then tucked his shirt. Fingered the rip in his sleeve.

Celia moved from the window to the door and held it open for him.

55

CELIA

EVICTED

KARL LYDIARD'S ARREST for arson, malicious mischief, and attempted murder made front-page news in every southeast Washington town for sixty miles. Though his Spokane attorney urged the prosecutor to link the crimes to Oren Zender as the mastermind of a coercive corporate scheme to acquire the farm, at this early stage in the investigation, Lydiard's whistle blew into thin air.

True, some members of the group had worked with the accountant's firm, and a branch of their conglomerate did offer to buy the Steffen farm, but legitimately. No thread of evidence yet connected them to any wrongdoing. If investigators didn't find Lydiard's name on corporate records, others' connections to the charges would likely fall flat.

But Karl Lydiard's indictment would stick. Presented with enlarged photos of himself at the spray tank and kneeling by Celia's Jeep, he blurted a detailed confession. *Folded early,* Celia thought, relieved. He wouldn't bother her, or the farm, again.

Mid-June, Oren rapped on the frame of Hazel's door and peered at Celia through the screen. "Horse looks good," he said.

"He has a ways to go. What do you want, Oren?"

"Buying a sprayer farther out Old Hollow. Saw your and Ingrid's cars, so thought I'd stop by, say hello."

Mild, gracious Ingrid appeared in the foyer behind Celia. "I may as well tell him now. Always good to have a witness."

"Come in then." Celia swung the door for Oren and ushered the pair to the kitchen table. Arms folded, she stood at the coffee pot, then reluctantly poured him a cup.

He sat across from Ingrid, settled an ankle on his knee, and smiled at his estranged wife. "Pretty as ever."

"That doesn't work anymore," Ingrid said. "Not with me, anyway."

He laughed and wrapped hands around the steaming cup. "What were you going to tell me?"

Ingrid glanced at Celia, who nodded, bracing herself.

"I may as well get right to the point, Oren. When your lease of my property expires after next harvest, I don't plan to renew it."

Oren spilled coffee on his shirt. "You can't do that, Ingrid."

"I can, and I will. Our settlement left me the discretion to renew or not renew. A sticking point in our separation. In case you forgot, I won." Ingrid's voice had dropped to a near whisper, but Celia heard the strength in it. "I want you to vacate the premises by December thirty-first of next year."

"How can I do that? The crops, the equipment. What am I supposed to do, sit in that house and twiddle my thumbs?"

"I want you out of the house, too. You have a solid year and a half to liquidate or remove any of your equipment and to move out of my house. I'll cancel any further obligations you may have with me. But after the end of next year, I never want you on my land again."

"You're divorcing me, then. Finishing what you started."

"No, I'm protecting our boys, and myself, and these good neighbors. If you want a divorce, you'll be the one to pursue it. Whether you file or not, it will be in your best interest to take good care of the place until you leave."

Oren planted his forearms on the table and leaned toward her, his fists tight. *A bull,* Celia thought. A charging bull, about to lose everything.

"You can't," he growled.

Ingrid sat quietly and held his glare. "Watch me."

"What'll you do with all that land?" He glowered at Celia. "Professor girl and her sidekicks can't handle that much ground."

Professor girl? Sidekicks? Celia frowned. Coughed.

Ingrid stirred sugar into her coffee. "I've already discussed it with the boys. Ivan wants nothing more than to farm. Mike said he'd love to come home from Arizona and partner with his brother, so long as you're gone. I'll move into the house with them until I can remodel the cabin."

Nostrils flared, neck bowed, Oren swept his cup aside. "We'll see about this, woman."

"I already have. You can leave voluntarily, or I'll have you served."

Celia watched in awe as Ingrid folded her hands and closed her eyes as if saying grace.

Dust from Oren's tires had settled when Ingrid retrieved her tote from the coatrack and rummaged for a file. "I'm still deciding whether or not to give these to Karl's attorney. Oren downright salivated over the sections I've marked. He always figured it was a sure thing. But when Ivan told me that you, Hazel's blood kin, had shown up out of the blue and moved in with her?" Sadness seeped through her laugh. "I figure Oren was in nothing short of a tailspin—and on a fast hunt for another way to . . ." She shrugged. "You'll see. The connection's a short leap."

She handed Celia the thick folder and kissed her cheek. "I'm so glad we'll be neighbors. I'd love to help with that new baby when she comes."

Ingrid's car shrank down Old Hollow before Celia settled into an armchair and opened the file of Joss and Hazel Steffen's last wills and testaments—multiple versions, signed over the preceding twenty years. She thumbed through the pages, stunned. Yellow highlights in each document outlined Oren's first right to purchase the Steffen real estate on insanely generous, prearranged terms. Sale proceeds would go to the church Hazel had loved.

Celia chilled. *The Steffen farm was as good as his—until I arrived. Lydiard must have been his plan B, to scare me off or get rid of me altogether.*

Running the farm for a group of investors would have been a distant second to owning it outright, but if Oren controlled the Steffen acres, plus all of Ingrid's? *Pretty big hat, Mr. Zender.* She thought of the hats Oren wore, and clicked her tongue at the irony.

But oh, his eyes and smile under their brims. She remembered her response to him, her vulnerability, and shivered. Had Oren's interest in her been a ruse, too? His plan C?

Her mind roved to other threats, both imaginary and real, that she'd spent her entire life denying or dodging or fending off. *No more hikes alone until she's born, okay?* Even Burnaby's quiet request on behalf of this child had sent Celia into a nosedive, flooding her with worry. *What if the worst happens? The very worst?*

Wheelhouse rats, Satch had called her fears. Now, she realized, an imped redtail was circling those rats, and they were fleeing.

A cloak of gratitude settled on her, calmed her, and she patted the small mound at her navel. Neither Oren nor anyone else hungry for her land could hurt the farm anymore. They couldn't harm her or those she loved, either.

I'm safe, she realized. *Protected. Freed,* no matter what the future held. And a most astonishing thought: She was all those things because she was *cherished*—by a love so beautiful, so wondrous and strong and *safe*, she suddenly wanted to *surrender* to it. To receive it, and pass it on.

Burnaby was teaching her how.

56

BURNABY

MIGRATION

"SOLSTICE TODAY," Burnaby said as Celia stumbled into the kitchen, her hair snarled from sleep. She bumped him *hello* with her hip and slid past his hand at her belly into the wooden chair where her grandmother had welcomed each day. He flipped a pancake, then raised the blind above the table to a brilliant sliver of light at the lip of the hill.

"You haven't changed your mind?" He set a stack of cakes on the table. Handed her a bowl of sliced strawberries.

"I can't think of a better place, can you? We can spread her ashes at sunset, then camp out there, like Hazel used to. Spend the night as she settles in."

She tagged along to the barn after breakfast, where Cobb, still in pajamas, fed carrots to Drummer from a half-empty bag. Beneath him, water pooled where he'd filled the horse's bucket to overflowing.

Burnaby smiled as he checked the horse's leg. "Your mother may want a—a few of those for your dinner."

"Drummer likes 'em better 'n me," he said. "A'sides, Ivan said I could ride Drummer when he's all better and Ivan will teach me and if I feed him he will know me and like me and not buck me off."

"Ivan will teach you well, Cobb." Burnaby spun the bag closed and handed it to the boy. "Why don't you run this back to—to the refrigerator. Then you can give him this, instead." Cobb took the apple and ran, carrot sack swinging.

Celia filled the feed net with hay. "What if we name her Aurora?"

A name. Each time he'd asked, Celia had resisted naming their deceased child. The week prior, he'd come across the Steffen family Bible among Hazel's books, where Hazel had added Celia's birth, and his and Celia's marriage. She'd also written *Baby* beside a blank, with birth and death dates the same.

"A good name," he said. "We'll write it in that Bible."

Celia grinned and brushed hay off her shirt. "And our new little girl's name below it. What if we call her Hazel?"

"I like that, too," he said.

"Let's pack the same kind of gear we stuffed into those Triumph saddlebags for Heyday. I have that dress somewhere." She laughed. "I know you still have that shirt. We'll sleep under those stars." She swept loose hay in the alley, humming before she stopped abruptly. "What do you think, Burn? Do you want to? If you don't—"

He took the broom from her and leaned on it, drinking her in. Sparks dropped from her hair into the hay, multicolored. "I think my Celia has come home."

Late afternoon, Celia awoke from a nap, then walked for the mail. Burnaby settled a backpack and a tote of food into the truck and leaned against it. The gold tinging her spread to the hills, the driveway, the grass, then faded when she approached him, head down, phone to her ear, wearing a look he didn't recognize and didn't like. His instinct to protect her and their baby, to make things right for them, was a mountain inside him. She shoved the phone in her pocket.

He closed the truck door. "You look pensive. Did that call trouble you?"

"Nothing to fret about today." She forced a smile. "Let's go."

Her silence sucked air from the cab, and as he drove it stuffed itself into his nostrils, his ears, the ducts of his eyes. He gave the intruder permission, lest it push back through her. There'd be time enough to ask.

But when they crossed the footboard hill and parked near the rutted old route into the prairie, her crushing mindset lifted like one of her hawks. She leapt from the truck, buoyant. "At last! I'd have been out here a month ago, if Satch hadn't talked me out of it." She slammed the door hard, then pirouetted right there on the trail.

"Satch said if I waited, it'd be better than Christmas." She ran to Burnaby as he reached for his pack. "C'mon, let's take a peek. We'll come back for all that stuff."

He followed her around the bend and past the confluence, where she stopped short at the bright explosion of life. "Oh, Burn." Everywhere they looked, balsamroot blanketed the meadow like a yellow choir. More flowers he couldn't name bloomed in a kaleidoscope of hues. His own colors rose as Celia's wonder gilded her, radiant with what he believed—what he *trusted*—was hope.

His wife, a mother again. A mother still. A mother *now*—of this new child they'd both learn from, and love, and raise on prayers that would know their destination.

By the time they returned with their gear, wind rose off the big river, its steep breaks hot below them. Clusters of monarchs rose from the carpet of nectar-rich wildflowers, then bivouacked and resettled on the milkweed and clover like witnesses, their torches lit.

They unpacked the mat and sleeping bags, the camp stove, their wedding clothes. He turned while she dressed. She pulled his Heyday shirt's flaps away from his skin and buttoned them, and they waded into the meadow to the bank of the creek. And when they had cried and laughed and christened her, Aurora's ashes—which in Burnaby's mind assumed shades as varied as the meadow flowers—flew onto ground where they'd nourish and last, and into the water, where they'd travel to the brawny Snake and beyond.

Afterward, soup boiled on the stove and they dunked their bread and ate it like a sacrament. When the sun sank low, they climbed the headboard hill and sat on an outcrop to watch. And when a redtail lifted from a pine and *screed*, Burnaby saw it as evidence of their love grafted and restored.

"Same one?" he asked.

"Could be." Celia shaded her eyes against the disappearing sun. Her voice felt lavender. "Did you know that all spring, huge flocks traveled that sky in the dark? Mostly the delicate ones, thousands and thousands, passing night after night, over the county, our farm, and right up there. Little water birds and passerines, fifteen to twenty miles an hour. Radar detected them more than half a mile high."

He didn't know.

"Sometimes I heard their wings."

He didn't know that either.

"Tonight, Burn, the sky will be quiet. You know why?"

He shook his head.

"They're home now. Nesting." Her brows arched high. She blinked back tears and pulled him to his feet. "Let's go." He thought he sensed fear in her, but how often had perception evaded him? Her gauzy dress brushed flowers as she hiked to camp wordless, beyond reach of his comfort. With him, but beyond him, this woman he loved.

He thought she was sleeping, but she shifted. Nudged him. She spoke toward the stars—all dressmaker sequins, stitched to velvet. "That call I got today?"

He rose on one elbow.

"Doctor's office. They want to schedule those other tests." Her inhales stuttered.

He listened until they eased, his mind running hills. A smile stretched his cheeks. "Ha." He tunneled into the sleeping bag and kissed her belly. "I had braced myself for difficult news."

She gripped his hair and tugged until his nose brushed her cheek. "I thought you would want—"

"Oh, Celia," he whispered. "Think of your stub-tailed hawk. No more tests. Tests won't change our minds." He flopped onto his side, reached for her braid, and coiled it around a finger. Searched her profile in the skimpy moonlight.

She sighed. An owl flew past, its silence like theirs. Burnaby watched it disappear over the dark meadow before he leaned to her ear. "He is *for* us, remember? For her. Life's breath—God's breath, Love's breath—is growing her, even now."

A mosquito hummed near her cheek, and she fanned it away. "Okay," she said, her smile rising. "Yes."

His heart surged. Tomorrow he would pick her some flowers.

A Note from the Author

NEWLY MARRIED, Blake and I loaded our meager belongings into two cars and moved to a tumbledown rental between the railroad tracks and the Palouse River in Colfax, Washington. For the next few years, my husband commuted to the WSU veterinary college in Pullman, I taught at the local high school, and we worshipped at a small country church near the breaks of the Snake River. After we moved away, many of my former students stayed or returned to the area, some to grow wheat like their parents and grandparents before them—and they became our lifelong friends. We've returned year after year for decades now, to visit, remember, and explore.

While the rolling croplands in the Palouse are magnificent both in their productivity and beauty, the land to which I find myself drawn lies between those fields—in the steep eyebrows and canyons, and in the ravines, riparian corridors, and small acreages untouched by large-scale agricultural equipment. These patches of native habitat comprise all that's left of the once expansive, biologically diverse Palouse prairie, now one of the most critically endangered ecosystems in the United States.

I inserted Joss's imaginary prairie around a Penawawa Creek tributary, in one of the steep, wild canyons that early inhabitants traveled between the highlands and the Snake River. While not intended as a comprehensive record of flora and fauna in native prairie, the virgin meadow's description and role in the story will, I hope, capture imaginations and hearts, fostering a desire to learn from our remaining unaltered landscapes and to care for them alongside, and in harmony with, the massive, necessary machinery of commercial agriculture.

Happily, there are a growing number of generous, helpful experts and community members working to revive and revitalize the Palouse prairie. Indigenous Pacific Northwest tribes with historical presence in the Palouse and local organizations deeply committed to the prairie have made important inroads in the preservation and restoration of native ecosystems. Several groups offer ongoing education and support for those interested in prairie plant propagation, preservation, and replenishing. For more information, visit any of the resources below to connect with them.

> Palouse Prairie Foundation, palouseprairie.org
> Palouse Land Trust, palouselandtrust.org
> Idaho Native Plant Society, White Pine Chapter, whitepineinps.org
> Palouse Conservation District, palousecd.org
> Latah Soil and Water Conservation District, latahswcd.org
> The Phoenix Conservancy, phoenixconservancy.org
> Joe and Mary Hein, rosecreekseed.com
> Nimiipuu Protecting the Environment (Nez Perce),
>   nimiipuuprotecting.org
> Whitman Conservation District, whitmancd.org
> Palouse-Clearwater Environmental Institute, pcei.org
> Coeur d'Alene Tribe: Wildlife, cdatribe-nsn.gov/nr/wildlife

Participating in land's regeneration is a joyous undertaking. Whether you engage with the natural world in the Palouse or elsewhere, may you hear the Creator speak love to you through every seed, and may you reply with loving care for his beautiful creation.

Thanks for reading.

Acknowledgments

SOMETIMES THE BEST PROPULSION is simply being heard—and encouraged to take the next step. Jan Soto, you did that for me. As I read to you day after day, your responses convinced me that the narrative would breathe and move. Thank you for all those hours and for your boundless love. Your observations and support were life-giving, and they spurred me on.

Others of you offered a wealth of knowledge and skill. Your help was priceless. Gary Largent, I'm grateful for that memorable combine ride through your bumper crop and for all those hours talking. Your experience, knowledge, and love of the land helped me translate wheat farming to the page. John and Cory Aeschliman, your innovative no-till methods healed your ground and showed others how to do likewise. Thank you for years of conversations and photos and pickup rides on precipitous hills to see results. I can't look at those fields now without treasuring the microbes and worms and the water held deep.

Don Beckman, our discussion of leg fractures and surgical repairs of horses is stamped into these pages. Sy Garte and Jerry Maurer, your clarifications about quantum mechanics, experimental physics, and mathematics helped the story ring true. Steve Groen and Cal Buys, from atrazine to gathering chains, your details fed believability. Greg Nolan, you introduced me to the Triumph Bonneville and those who rode that bike. Burnaby would have leaned into a swamp somewhere without you. Jim Heilsberg, your hospital info sent Celia to the right location.

Alexandra Shelley, our talk early on aimed the story's path. Ellen Notbohm, editor and expert on children with autism, your suggestions helped me add perceptive layers to Burnaby and the entire narrative. Artist Emma VandeVoort Nydam, you interpreted the lay of the landscape and summarized it beautifully in the frontispiece map. Thanks a million to each one of you.

Other early readers—you, too, added perspectives no one else could give. Ruth Sebring, Ellen Bouma, Lisa Largent, and Avery Ullman, thank you for interpretations that showed me what to keep, toss, or revise. The book's better because of you.

My amazing agent Cynthia Ruchti, thank you, start to finish. Not only did you find an ideal home for the novel at Tyndale House with your characteristic grace and excellence, but you've wisely navigated, advised, and encouraged me ever since. I love working with you. And Janet McHenry, thank you for connecting us—and for seeing possibilities I couldn't imagine. Our Santa Cruz beach walk lives on.

David Hall, Elizabeth Brackney, Shelley Chambers Fox, and Ronnie Hatley of the Palouse Prairie Foundation and Lovena Englund from the Palouse Land Trust, thank you for a bounty of information about the native Palouse prairie and its restoration—and for connecting me with others. Thanks, too, to Cameron Heusser and Peter Mahoney of the Schitsu'umsh (Coeur d'Alene), and Julian Matthews of the Nimiipuu (Nez Perce) tribes, for resources regarding both the history of indigenous peoples in the Palouse and the tribes' work to recover and restore their ancestral prairie.

Readers . . . I'm so glad to call you friends. Thank you for reading my books, for telling others about them, and for praying and cheering me on as I wrote this one. I treasure you.

Maggie Rowe and other Redbud Writers Guild Buds; Sisters Dar Elenbaas, Shelly Kok, Bev DenBleyker, Donna VanderGriend; Laura Buys, Bonnie and Bryan Korthuis, Jacquee and John Larsen, Cheryl and Mike Grambo, and Steven Kent—I thank every one of you for praying. You have blessed and encouraged me beyond measure.

Jan Stob and Karen Watson, you prayerfully championed the book at Tyndale, and Jan, you guided me through its birthing. I couldn't be more thankful. Sarah Rische, what a privilege and joy to work with you again. Your keen editorial observations lit my imagination and improved the story's sweep and depth. The skilled, artistic efforts of all of you at Tyndale create such a synergy of excellence. Thank you for applying your gifts to this work.

My Blake, you lived the Palouse with me, and then fed and loved me through the writing about it. Your patience and wisdom in our life together could only be Spirit-led and fortified. Thanks for spot-on input and veterinary particulars, too. Oh, how I love you, my mister.

And most of all, I praise and thank you, my precious, beautiful, triune God—for entangling me in your love. Every word I write is because of you and for you. May all glory be yours forever.

Discussion Questions

1. Burnaby has improved his social skills in the years since Celia first knew him, but many of his autistic traits remain. Discuss how Judah Kemp helps Burnaby adapt without disrespecting him. Do you agree with Judah's approach? Why or why not?

2. Most of the story takes place in Washington's remote Palouse region. What impact does the setting have on the story? How did you respond to it? How does Joss's prairie, in particular, come to illustrate hope?

3. What did you learn about Celia from her response to suffering? What did you learn about Burnaby? How do their worldviews affect their interactions and choices in the midst of pain?

4. When did you first realize that Burnaby and Celia have been living without close community or friendships? How does their isolation affect their marriage? Is their situation unique in today's world? Discuss.

5. What effect has Celia's mother had on Celia's relationships? In what ways do you agree or disagree with Burnaby when he tells her, "Neither of us are our mothers or our fathers, Celia. Though we certainly carry them with us, we—not they—will decide what parts of them we want to keep and what we'll discard"?

6. Burnaby's touch aversion and emotional detachment when he's concentrating alienate Celia. How is this situation different from many marriages? How is it similar?

7. When Hazel challenges Burnaby to show Celia more affection, she tells him to "ditch the rodents, young man." What does she mean? How can this concept apply to all relationships?

8. Do you believe Oren masterminded the sabotage? Did he intend to kill Hugh? How did you arrive at your conclusions?

9. How and why is Ivan's relationship with his father so complicated?

10. Hazel says that Celia has taken her losses "like bullets instead of surgeries." What does she mean? When and how does Celia change?

11. Chalk horses appear throughout the story. What do they represent to Judah? To Burnaby? To Cobb? To you?

12. In the closing scene, Burnaby reminds Celia that "He is *for* us." Do you think she finally agrees? Do you agree that God is for us? Why or why not?

About the Author

FOR MOST OF HER LIFE, Pacific Northwest naturalist and best-selling author Cheryl Grey Bostrom has roamed the rural and wild lands that infuse her fiction, poetry, and devotional writing. A Christy Award finalist, her debut novel *Sugar Birds* has won more than a dozen key honors, with a Carol Award, *Christianity Today*'s Fiction Award of Merit, and American Fiction, Nautilus, Reader's Favorite, and International Book Awards among them. An avid photographer, she lives with her veterinarian husband and a small pack of Gordon setters in Washington State. Connect with her at cherylbostrom.com.

CONNECT WITH CHERYL ONLINE AT

cherylbostrom.com